When Life Stood Still

Melek

This book is dedicated to EvaLina Milliner, 1890-1955

Any resemblance to names and persons in this book,
living or dead, is coincidental.

Cover image Copyright© 2016 Melek

ISBN: 978-1-62249-362-3

Published by
The Educational Publisher Inc.
Biblio Publishing
BiblioPublishing.com

Table of Contents

David O. Edwards

Angela M. Milliner

Melek

Chapter 1

He lived on the corner of John Street, in the small Welsh village called Porth. Most of the houses on the street had two rooms up, two rooms down with a tiny box room, not big enough to swing a cat and none had an inside bathroom. A couple of houses had three rooms up and two rooms down but no bathroom. Stone row terraced houses without garden or lawn, except for those on the railway track side, had a little garden. David's family lived in the two-story house with a basement, on the hill at the top of the street. There were ten siblings, eleven counting David. One can see their front door even now painted dark green with a bright shiny brass doorknob and a matching brass doorstep. They shone like the sun in the sky and David's mother liked the gleaming glow so much that she used to clean the brass every week and give it a shine every day.

John Street, Porth, was just below the mountain, Penrhiwgwynt in the Rhondda Valley. Porth was not just a dot on the map. It was considered the capital of the Rhondda, not that it had anything of grandeur like Cardiff city with its castle, university, and cathedrals but because it was positioned alongside the river Rhondda.

There were two Rhondda Valleys, Rhondda Fawr and Rhondda Fach, often called just, "The Rhondda." They were definitely the most well-known of the South Wales Valleys. In 1807, a poet looking across the mountaintop observed *'such scenes of untouched nature as the imagination would find it difficult to surpass'*. This is where Angel grew up; the majority of her best memories were made here where she lived with her grandmother, down the street from her best friend, David. Just the two of them; her father was an occasional visitor.

Often when David and Angel were children they would climb up the mountain and romp, play in the buttercup fields, and swing on the branches of an old oak tree. They never cared about the time because they had so much fun. David had two brothers still living at home, and being the youngest child had more freedom. David loved to climb the trees and look far and wide as if he was looking from a ship's mast to the sea beyond. At these times he would shout, "Ahoy!" His voice echoed in the wind, carrying through the vales. Then he added more words, sentences, and they too would repeat in the echo. Every weekend they went to their special place on the mountain, rain or shine. Angel sat on the top of the old fence near one particular tree and watched David with excitement. It was funny really; most of the fence had fallen down over time. But there stood a small part of the fence and gate just underneath the tree, almost as if it intended to be there just for Angel to sit on.

One particular weekend they had homework from their choir teacher. Everyone needed to practice the Welsh Anthem and some hymns ready for Church. As they were up the mountain and far away from everyone David started singing the first words and Angel sang the last. Their voices seemed to hit the mountain on the other side of the valley and return with some delay, like a choir in the distance. It was fun for them to sing the words although they weren't particularly interested in practicing the Welsh Anthem. It was supposed to be sung with reverence and very slow. As many times as they could they would sing it with a beat since no one from their town could hear them up there. With every song their "make-believe choir" echoed back as though it sang the chorus.

David loved to sing and quite often he would make up songs.

"I had a girl, Angel was her name, and she had long brown hair just like a horse's mane."

Of course, Angel believed she couldn't compete with his voice. She had a high-pitched tone that her singing teacher said was soprano. Angel tried to sing with David, who complained as soon as she opened her mouth.

"Oh, you make my ears hurt." He clapped his hands over his ears. Then he would go on with his made up songs.

"Why don't you fill your so picky ears up with dirt?" Angel would reply, hurt that he didn't like her voice.

He got a little offended by her response, but like most kids they continued trying to outdo each other.

"You can't sing any old thing." David was bossy but a great singer, opinionated and right in his youthful sensibility.

"Huh, we'll see about that David Edwards, teacher's pet," Angel told him. She was sure that's how he gained favor. "I can sing but I don't want to hear everyone say I crack the light bulbs."

"Let's hear you then, sing something," David demanded. But it was a constant tease between them.

"I'll sing when I want to." Angel would pretend to pout and rub her eyes as though she was about to cry. Then he would nudge her with his shoulder and charm her with his smile. He was so handsome, even at nine years old. His black hair sucked in the light that brightened the sky. It was a rich coal color, with red tinges, that blew up and down in a swirl around his head when he swung upside down on the tree limbs. He was Angel's best friend and she loved him as the big brother she never had.

Angel's mother left shortly after she was born. Her father had to work away from home so he took Angel to live with his mother. She only saw him every couple of months. Angel's grandmother was a good woman who taught her, even at a young age, to show love, even when people were unlovable; to forgive those who hurt her as best as she could; and ignore those hateful children at school who bullied her.

Life was lonely for Angel. She didn't have any brothers or sisters so she would pretend her stuffed bear was an imaginary sister. It was alright, but Angel couldn't have a conversation with her.

The bear originally had fine golden red fur and music in her tummy if Angel squeezed. Eventually her music box broke down so she didn't play music anymore, and her fur had worn away where she had been squeezed so much. She had a tiny cut off pencil in her ear to hold it up. The bear was very old and Angel was told it had been her mother's, and the only thing that was passed on when she was a baby and went to live with her grandmother.

Angel didn't really cherish the bear because it had been her mother's, but because of the sweet music it played. It was the only bear Angel had all those years. Maybe the pencil in her ear had some significance, but Angel didn't know the story.

David was her rescuer and her knight in shining armor. That's why she had so much fun when they were together. He was everything to her and she appreciated his company even when he was showing off. She knew David made life extra exciting for her, as she was very shy.

During the times they climbed the mountain, they hunted for treasures, like slate pieces that fell from roofs of old buildings. If they were lucky they would come across rams' horns that were shed by the males during their battle for dominance.

The roof slates could have various uses. They used them like chalk on the pavement stones, drawing pictures and lines for their hopscotch games. David's older brother, Ian, liked the bigger pieces of slate that they found. Ian used them like a canvas on which he would draw his beautiful artwork. Ian was good at drawing sheep and horses. His inspiration came after seeing Milkman Rhys coming early every morning, down their street as he made his daily deliveries with his horse and cart. The sheep trailed behind as if they were following their shepherd. Ian had plenty of experience watching them. The sheep always searched for food -- kitchen scraps that were in the rubbish bins along the street. It was funny to see some of them get stuck, head first, upside down in the bins with their back legs running in the air. The neighbors would find their rubbish bins all over the pavement and many times the lids would roll down the street.

Angel remembered Ian was so good at drawing on the slate, he sketched a picture of one of their neighbors, chasing the sheep down the street with her rolling pin in one hand, hands and arms covered in flour. That was Mrs. Probert and she lived at number 16 next to her grandmother's house. Of course, no one ever caught the sheep, as they were nimble of foot and quick. They would also poo little currents everywhere and people could easily slip and fall if they tried to run without looking where they were going.

Each weekend, the children wandered a little farther across the mountain. In the distance they saw what looked like the remains of an old barn or a house. They jumped for joy to find something new that they hadn't explored, even though they couldn't stay long.

On this particular day the children went up the mountain to bring back bits of treasures they had found at the ruins -- a broken cup, a pot, a knife with a pearl handle, and some old copper pennies. The last treasure Angel found was a couple of farthings and a half-crown, the currency a little weathered with time. Farthings were difficult to find, as they were very small and were only worth a quarter of a penny, the lowest denomination of British coins that would soon go out of circulation. But, the half-crown was worth a lot more. Many people kept them as souvenirs, some gave them to local museums, but others sold them to collectors.

"Hurry, Angel. We need to get down before the rain comes. Those clouds are going to wet us down to the bone."

"I'm hurrying, David. Your legs are longer than mine."

"We'll be in so much trouble, Angel." He slowed down to wait for her.

It was getting darker and darker as they made their way down the rugged cliff and it was even more difficult to see where they could safely place their feet than it had been in the daylight. When they arrived at the bottom they still had to pass over the milkman Rhys's field to Penrhiwgwyt Road, then York Street and Porth Street that led them to John Street. The children hurried down the streets, rushing in the darkness.

David's mother was on the doorstep with Angel's grandmother who looked very, very worried.

"Where have you been?" her grandmother cried. "Angel, I was so worried about you." She hugged Angel to her, holding her close.

"I'm sorry, Nene. We were having fun. And singing and we didn't know the time."

David's mother, Mary, scolded David through the door of the house. "Your dinner is already on the table, go and wash your hands, David."

David's mother turned to Angel's grandmother and said, politely, "Lina, we have plenty today, you and Angel are welcome to join us."

Lina glanced down at Angel, the wind picking up ahead of the storm. Angel's beautiful almond-shaped eyes filled with hope, they never ate anywhere but their home. A change might be good for both of them. Lina thought she could make it up to Mary somehow.

"We'd love to join you, Mary." She ushered Angel into the warmth of the home, already filled with boisterous voices and full of love.

Angel unbuttoned her coat and slipped it down her arms. "Wow," she whispered to herself, hanging her coat on the knob at the end of the staircase. "I'm having dinner with my knight in shining armor, in the big house on the corner of the street." David lived in the biggest house because of their large family.

At the table, David was delighted to show his treasures off, excitement raised his voice. "We also found parts of an old barn and a house up there on the mountain but it was getting dark so we couldn't stay and explore. Maybe tomorrow, after Sunday school, we could go back and see what's there. I bet there's some buried treasure." His voice lowered to a whisper, his eyes glistening with excitement.

"Oh yes, I want to go, David." Angel agreed with a big smile but a glance at her grandmother showed Lina's concern again. She lowered her head and kept eating, glancing from the side of her eyes as her Nene Lina spoke to Mary.

This woman was all she had in the world. Lina loved Angel, cared for her, and sometimes she got upset with Angel if she didn't listen and that was quite often, she had to admit.

It was easy to see her grandmother had already talked with David's mother and father about her concerns -- two young children up on the mountain by themselves. It was not surprising to hear her say this evening, "Maybe Ian could go with them. I would feel much more comfortable if Ian was there. After all, he is bigger and more responsible."

Ian was nearly sixteen and David and Angel were only eight and nine. Ian raised his dark bushy eyebrows and fidgeted in his chair, then he shuffled his feet heavily when it was mentioned. He would rather stay at home and sketch away the afternoon than climb the mountain. That would be exercise and Ian didn't like too much exercise.

Angel dropped her fork on the floor so she slipped off her chair and was kneeling under the table when she noticed David's legs moving too; he was soon down on his knees also. They giggled, giving away their places under the table.

"What are you two doing down there?" Mary asked, lifting the edge of the tablecloth.

"Nothing, Mam. Angel dropped her fork and I was helping her find it." David was always quicker with an answer than Angel was.

They were giggling at the thought of Ian climbing the mountain. He was slim and tall but didn't really like doing much except kicking the ball around his back yard into his make believe goals. The only other activity they caught him doing was lying on his bed dreaming and sketching.

Ian had a cat that hung about close to the house for Ian's attention. When he was out with the ball, his cat wasn't too amused when he kicked the ball toward it. One could hear it meowing every time the ball went the slightest bit close to her.

Ian finally answered, "Hmpf, I suppose so. Maybe, if I take some paper and pencils I could draw while these two run around like raving idiots," he agreed reluctantly.

"Alright then," David's father, Ethan, replied. "If you just watch them and make sure they don't break their necks, it will be alright with me if you all go up there together tomorrow." The man of the house spoke, giving his approval. That always ended the current topic of conversation.

The following day after Sunday school, they went home and changed into their old ragged playing clothes, ready for abuse because they couldn't be mended any more. David and Ian put on their Wellington boots.

David muttered with a low voice so Ian couldn't hear, "Angel, where are your wellygogs? There may be insects lurking in the long grass. And, I know you don't like insects."

Angel couldn't find them so she pulled up her socks as high as they would go and put on her holey shoes. They were warm, stuffed with plenty of newspaper over the holes, and sturdy enough to climb the mountain. She leaned close to David, hoping he'd follow her quiet answer.

"I can't find them," Angel whispered to him, afraid if she raised her voice and the adults heard, she wouldn't be allowed to go with them.

"Oh, never mind." David sighed.

David's mother found an old flask she had stored in the pantry, washed it out and filled it with milk and carefully put it in Ian's satchel. Lina added Welsh cakes and some Bara Brith cake bread she had made. They were ready to go on their treasure hunt and have a picnic too -- except for Ian.

"Ian, where are you? Come on! We're ready to go." David shouted up the stairs for Ian, but Ian was in no hurry. He had to comb his hair into a style that was popular in those days and adjust his neck scarf. Ian was one to show off his appearance wherever he went. Although his family wasn't much better off than Nene Lina and Angel, Ian had flair with used clothing that he adapted to keep up with the fashion styles.

"Ian, where are you? Come on!" David shouted, again, louder this time.

"I'm coming, what's the big rush anyway." Ian came down the stairs and carefully placed his comb in his back pocket, and adjusted his neck scarf again.

They were finally ready to go on their adventure. Off they walked, waving goodbye to their parents and to Nene Lina. It was a beautiful day after the storms of the night before. The air brittle and clear, it was easy to breathe. They walked up Penrhiwgwynt Road and on through the milkman's field carefully, as not to spook his sheep or his sheep dog that was always on the alert for trespassers.

Over the stile they climbed and ran to the next field as quickly as they could. Then climbed over the small rocks that lay about them as they approached the bottom of the mountain but they didn't pay any attention, as the smaller rocks rolled underfoot. They were going to have lots of fun.

They climbed; rocks fell around them and tumbled to the ground below as they hiked ever higher. Each step they took upwards more rocks loosened. It was getting harder to find solid rock or dirt to grab hold of and place their feet, one by one as they followed each other up. There was another way up the mountain, but this way was quicker. They didn't care. They were on a mission – a treasure hunt! Up the mountain they went ignoring all the signs that said, "*PERYGL – PEIDIWSCH A DRINGO – CREIGIAU GOSTWNG* (DANGER – DO NOT CLIMB – FALLING ROCKS)."

David sang a song, "We're on a hunt, a treasure hunt. Up the mountain we go to find treasure from long ago."

It didn't take so long this time. Excitement gave their feet wings. First they stopped at their usual place and David swung on the tree and sang his songs.

"Whau hoo, whau hoo! We're having fun on the mountaintop. Ian came with his drawing pot." Ian had an old glass jar filled with small pencils and bits of crayons.

David was funny and made Angel laugh. It was a good place to have their picnic. The Welsh cakes and Bara Brith bread were sweet and good and they washed them down with the milk from the flask. When they had finished all the goodies and milk they were refreshed and ready to continue exploring.

Ian found the landscape to his liking as he sketched pictures in his little notebook. He was so occupied he didn't notice they went on playing; David swung on the tree and sang joyfully. With each sway of the branches, leaves fell like soft snowflakes, not white, but green as the grass. A softly colored rainbow in the distance over the nearby hill to the valley below gave a warm comforting feeling. Ian, mystified by the separation of colors, hastily sketched his next page then went back to add detail.

An hour or so passed by and Ian finally realized they were there for a different reason, to find treasure. Coming back to reality, Ian announced they needed to get up and go. On they walked further up the mountain to the top. It wasn't so bad a trek from their tree, as there was plenty of long grass to walk through without rocks. Being at the mountaintop fascinated Ian. There was too much for his artistic passion to absorb and Angel and David noticed he enjoyed being with them.

In the distance they glimpsed some old ruins. They thought it could have once been a house, or better still it could have been a castle. That would be so exciting if it were a castle.

Melek

Chapter 2

The air was fresh and the sun lifted its head from behind the clouds, making the fields of buttercups glisten in its rays. It was so beautiful, just like Angel's favorite fairy tale. White fluffy clouds, blue sky, sun scorched buttercups and to top it all - a vibrant rainbow much more colorful than the one they noticed before.

The ruins didn't seem that far yesterday, but today they seemed miles away as they walked through thick fields. But the sky was glorious and the sun shone brightly, as if it was shining just for them and they were headed to the end of a galaxy. Every blade of grass glistened and the buttercups were thick and plentiful. Heather grew in rich purple color, alongside the hedgerows, and what a beautiful sight it was. The smell in the air was fresh.

Alongside the hedgerows, blackberry bushes grew thick with thorns, but between the dangerous limbs, fruit ripened in the sun. The bushes were heavily laden with blackberries. Oh, they tasted so good, a rich deep blue color, plump, juicy, and so sweet. They perfumed the air with an aromatic berry fragrance. It would have been a great harvest if they could have picked them and taken them back in a sack. Maybe next weekend they could pick them and take them home for Nene Lina and David's mother Mary.

"Can we come back and pick these next week? Think of the jams, all lined up on the shelf." Angel popped a couple into her mouth.

"Or the pies Mama could make." David rubbed his stomach, licking his lips with a grin. He pulled a couple and munched them as they continued walking, keeping up with Ian who was busy looking around.

Angel listened to the chirping of birds circling around them, flying up above. It was a perfect day for Ian to join them; this day picture perfect for his artist's soul. The sun warmed their backs as they walked on. Ian would not be able to complain to his parents about having to watch over the youngsters on this day. There were so many things he could draw, the colors so bright and beautiful.

As they trudged through one field to the next, they passed apple trees laden with fruit, and the apples that fell to the ground made a thick sludgy carpet. Ian reached up to pull a fresh apple from one of the trees.

"Get me one, Ian," David shouted.

"Me too, please," Angel added, pushing close to David.

It was no trouble for Ian to pull the apples from the branches above, as he was much taller.

In the distance they saw brown and white dots. As they got closer they could see the dots took the shape of cows grazing in the fields. In the next couple of fields were fat, dirty-white curly sheep with black faces and ears, some lying down and some eating grass. Others were upside down, twisting into the grass, as though they were scratching their backs.

Onward they plodded over stonewalls that looked as if they were about to fall down. Ian told them as they climbed over yet another one, that each farmer built the walls from old stones with their own hands adding one stone on top of the other to border their land. That way each land holder knew his boundaries. If the cows got mingled, all they had to do is look for the place where the rocks tumbled down. Older than Angel and David, Ian learned all this in school.

Into yet another field Ian led the way, constantly shouting, "Come on, come on." It seemed they walked forever. As soon as Ian saw the ruins, he took off running.

"Wait for us!" Angel screamed, racing to keep up.

"Come quickly, don't waste time dawdling." Ian was a boy of few words. He kept shouting to David and Angel, "Quick, come on, come on."

It took a couple of hours for them to reach the ruins.

Slate was scattered everywhere for quite a distance before they even came close to the remains of the old home. There were many small jagged pieces but also good-sized ones. Ian was so excited he was trying to dump as much of it as he could into his satchel. If he took all he wanted to gather, it would mean they would have no room for anything else. Slate was heavy to carry so they couldn't take too much.

"Leave us some room in the satchel, Ian. We want to take back some treasure, too," Angel reminded him, already looking on the ground.

"I'll save you room, but not too much." He quit gathering and chose one to work with, he settled and pulled out his colors, ready to draw more. Angel watched him a moment, but the pull of treasure soon had her scrambling behind David to search.

David found some rusty pots and pans and an old black clothes iron. As she walked inside what may have been the kitchen of a house at one time, Angel saw an old rocking chair that had lost one of its legs near the fireplace. It was amazing, the fireplace was intact, and it looked identical to her grandmother's back home.

There was a black cast iron oven on one side and rods across the other side that once held coal or logs, but they had rusted. The stove stood freely without the support of a wall and chimney behind it. Looking around more of the room, she even found an old gas lamp. Smudged with soot and covered with dirt, aged and beautiful, she knew the fragile glass wouldn't make it down the mountain in the satchel.

"Angel, look," David called from his place, turning over things to see what was underneath. Angel went out to see what he'd found, excitement making her features flush and her eyes brighter.

"Mama would love these." He held up some of the old rusty pots to give to his mother.

"I think she would. Maybe we can clean them first and give them to her." They kept searching in the immediate area. In the corner under many broken timbers they found spoons and some old copper and brass mugs with letters engraved on them.

"Look at these, David. What did they drink out of them?" Angel pretended to take a sip.

"Not dirt like you, Angel." David laughed, teasing her. "Let's see. Maybe this one was *E* for Edwards, like my last name. And this one," Angel nodded and brushed off more dirt.

Two had *C* and there were two more with letters *D* and *O*, but the letters were almost worn away and could barely be read. David was anxious to get them into the satchel quickly, their time was growing short, but Ian had already stuffed in a huge amount of the slate.

Angel reached for a couple of the spoons she thought her grandmother would like. Nene Lina collected spoons. Every time her father came to visit with them he would bring a spoon from some place he had visited on his travels. She had quite a collection. Mostly they were silver ones with flags, designs, and some different shapes.

Lost in the discovery, it took them a while to decide what they would take home.

"You need to leave some of the slate, Ian. There won't be any room for our things and you need to share," David told his brother, watching while Ian handled the slate pieces, trying to decide what to keep and what to leave.

"I want to take some of these home to Nene, too." Angel had the smallest pile of treasures.

While they scavenged the area, Ian heard thunder rumbling. He stopped choosing and got up to look. He saw fork lightening in the distance.

"We need to leave. The storm is close. We must get home before the rain starts." Gathering their things, they started walking away from the ruins, but the rumbling got louder and closer and they could feel the vibration under their feet. The satchel loaded and heavy, they would be slower heading back home. They simply couldn't leave their treasures behind. They were the reason for their journey.

Before they could turn and head for home, horses appeared from all directions. Spooked by the storm, they started a stampede toward the only little shelter in the area. The trio froze, unable to push past the big bodies as the horses rushed towards them through the foundation of the house.

"Oh my God, Ian, what do we do?" David stood fast behind Ian, who was trying to stand tall to appear bigger to the wild horses.

They huddled together in the hope that the horses wouldn't trample them to death. Angel was scared, leaning against David and Ian as they watched them get closer. It didn't seem they were going to stop, but the horses finally slowed down and milled all around them, stamping and breathing in snorts.

"David, I'm scared. They're so big and tough." Angel started crying. David puffed out his chest, now the rush slowed down. He straightened and shouted at the closest ones.

"Shu, go away, go away." He waved his arms looking even bigger.

Of course those horses wouldn't go anywhere. They just milled around the children as the storm brewed. Then they settled and began feeding on the long grass around the old building foundation. There was another old building too that appeared to be much bigger, what was left of it anyway. It looked like the remains of a barn in the field.

David was getting nervous. He liked horses, but not when they kicked up speed and were surrounding him. He started singing, making up lyrics again.

"Horses coming, horses wandering all around. Brown ones, black ones, and white ones too, slowing down and jumping on you!" Then he tickled Angel to make her laugh.

"What are you singing David? it sounds stupid," Ian said, not amused at all by their antics.

"Do something. How are we going to get back?" Angel gestured to the herd of horses blocking their way through the field and home.

"Angel, it's alright. They're quiet now. Actually, I think they liked David singing even if it was a stupid song." Big brother had come to the rescue, calming both of them in his own way.

"David, sing to me like you did on the tree, maybe they might go away." Angel held David's hand in both of hers, looking up at him, sure that he could sing the horses into leaving.

"Yeah little brother, sing to her. Let's hear what you got." Ian crossed his arms, waiting.

"Stop being mean, Ian," David told him, trying to come up with a set of lyrics.

"I'm not mean; I'm just as frightened as you. They're wild horses and I don't know what they'll do next, but obviously they like you singing. So sing to them." Ian unfolded his arms, gesturing to the horses around them. They were so close the children could hear their teeth grinding the grass down before they swallowed it.

"What do you mean they are wild? Where do they live?" Angel asked. "They have a home to go to, don't they?"

"On the mountain silly, where do you think?" Ian told her.

"Well, do they just roam around from place to place?" David asked. The more they talked, the horses calmed, and so did the children.

"Mostly," Ian said. "But some of these horses are captured and they are sent down the mines to work with the men, like some of the horses that worked with Dad." There was a cold wind and raindrops were falling. The storm caught up with them.

"Come on, it's time to go home before the big storm. Get your treasures and let's go quickly."

"What about the horses, Ian?" Angel shouted, still afraid of the large animals surrounding them.

"They have weather proof hides. They will be alright and they are calm now so come on quickly." Ian beckoned them to follow. He led the way through the horses, sometimes pushing against their sides or their rumps to make them move. They stepped aside as the children made their way clear, scared as those big bodies moved on hard hooves.

They had their stuff together but before they made their way down the mountainside, Angel called to David, "David look, that horse over there. He's on his own and he looks hurt."

"What are you talking about?" David looked around, trying to see the horse Angel pointed out.

"Look, David there's blood, he's hurt." She moved closer to the animal, her hand out to touch its side, as Ian had done to push the other horses aside.

"I don't see any blood, it looks like dirt to me." David moved closer, looking at the horse's leg.

"No David, look. His leg is hurt he's holding it up and it's bleeding." Insistent, Angel moved closer to the horse.

Ian was getting irritated. He knew they needed to go back down the mountain before the storm got really bad. He wasn't prepared to spend the night up here.

"Kids, it's time to go home." He reminded them, voice full of patience he wasn't feeling.

"No Ian, he's hurt. David help me please he's trying to walk but he's limping. David, please sing to him. Please. It will calm him." Angel ran to the horse, her hand so small against the side of the animal.

"Angel found a horse, with a limp. She wants to fix it but we didn't bring liniment." David sang softer than usual as he stepped up to Angel's side.

The horse didn't look like he was going anywhere, but just stood there. His nostrils opened up and he let out condensation in the chilly air. He opened his mouth and Angel could see his teeth, then he let out a squeal and dragged his hoof on the ground.

"David, he really likes your singing, he's trying to talk to us."

Ian now was more than irritated, as he wanted to go whether the horse was hurt or not.

"Ian, please let's help him, it's really cruel to go home and not help." Angel was so soft hearted and she was beginning to cry.

"Oh, girls are so soppy!" Ian rattled back.

He took off the scarf from around his neck and threw it towards David. David loved animals and couldn't bear to see them hurt either, but Ian was standing there watching their every move.

David folded the scarf and knelt down beneath the horse's head. The horse could have trampled on David but was motionless and looked helpless. He was definitely hurt; David showed Angel a great gash on his leg.

Ian stared at them.

"Oh, Ian look at him, he really is hurt and needs our help." David showed Ian the cut on the horse's leg.

"The horse is not a 'he' it's a 'she'," Ian snorted slowly at them.

"What are you talking about, Ian?" Angel asked, looking from him to the horse's face, as if that would give her a clue.

"Well this horse doesn't have the parts that a male horse would have." David looked puzzled at Ian, and Angel hadn't a clue what he was talking about.

"You'll learn about the birds and the bees when you get older," Ian shouted and looked up at the sky. "Come on, we have to go it's getting darker and we won't see our way back."

"So the horse is a girl?" David answered.

"Oh, that's so nice, a girl horse. We must give her a name. She is so beautiful. Can we call her, Buttercup? What do you think David?" Angel cooed to the horse, still petting her side, and moved up to her neck as the horse bent forward, and closer to David.

"Well, while you are deciding on a stupid name for this horse we are going to get drenched. It's going to pour down with rain shortly. Look at the clouds over there," Ian complained as he pointed.

"Yes, I think so, Angel. Buttercup would be a great name. After all, we found her in a buttercup field. Buttercup, Buttercup."

Angel was excited the name fit, she was the one to give it to Buttercup.

When David said Buttercup, she swished her tail as though she recognized that the name belonged to her.

"Oh David, she likes us. Look she's trying to rub her head over us."

"I wish we had a saddle and a rein, I could ride her," David replied, bravado back in place.

Ian hadn't finished with his comments. "You kids are going to drive me nuts. We came to get treasure but now you two are nursing a horse. What next?" He smiled when he said it. Of course, Ian liked horses. He was always sketching them.

David worked to clear the dirt off the cut on Buttercup's leg. It looked like the blood was dry and the cut clean.

This was a different kind of horse; she had white fur all over her body - not like the others. They were mostly brown-black or white with big brown and tan splotches. Buttercup was beautiful and her name fit her well. It saddened Angel to think they had to leave her up on the mountain with the others, even though she galloped with them.

Ian finally convinced them they had to leave and go home. David ran to Buttercup and knelt down by the side of her, not sure if he was praying or just talking to her. As for Angel, she had to give her a big kiss on her face even though she was taller than Angel was and wild, she didn't care. Angel stood up on her tip-e-toes as much as she could and put her arms on Buttercup to steady herself while Buttercup tilted her head forward. Angel kissed her on her face.

Buttercup snorted, shook her head, and swished her tail with approval.

"Now I have two soppy kids," Ian commented. "We are going now," he shouted, finally out of patience.

"Alright, Ian," David shouted back.

"Ian, but will we see Buttercup again?" Angel asked.

"Most likely. Now you kids have just about done everything you shouldn't do to a wild horse," Ian answered hurriedly.

Tears came to Angel's eyes as she left. Looking back at Buttercup, Angel said, "I think she feels sad, too." Buttercup stood motionless, looking their way. Angel turned and hurried back to her and hugged her, her arms up around Buttercup's chest as she looked up at the curious horse. Buttercup's head dropped to Angel's level and Angel could see her big shiny eyes looking at her as Angel's tears ran down her cheeks and wet the horse's fur. "I love you," Angel sobbed. Buttercup breathed heavily.

"Oh my God, what are you doing? She is wild! She doesn't understand your wailing. Come on now!" Ian called to her.

From there on Ian complained non-stop. "Do you realize what you did with that wild beast? It was so dangerous. She only had to move quickly or pick up her hoof and kick at you and you could have been crushed to death."

They had to listen to him as they followed him across the mountaintop. He never seemed to run out of breath, constantly reminding them about the dangers of wild animals, throwing in warnings of bears and mountain lions and other creatures.

Chapter 3

Down the mountainside they went, but a slightly different way that didn't seem to be as dangerous. They didn't encounter any falling rocks. It was so cold with the wind, and the rain made the grass became slippery under their feet. Ian continued his complaining all the way. When he ran out of animals and danger, he started on the weather and how changeable it was, they could have been trapped on the mountain for the night with no shelter, no coats, no food.

Angel and David tuned him out eventually, enjoying the hike back as much as the one up. They sang and danced a bit, teasing each other and having fun.

Finally, they could see what once could have been a path. They followed it, winding down, and eventually it led them to the milkman's farm. Angel and David waved as they passed by and he shouted back, "Where have you kids been? It's getting dark. You shouldn't be out here alone at this time."

"It's alright, I'm with them," Ian replied.

"Is that you, Ian, I hear?" The milkman, Mr. Rhys, was older and hard of hearing.

"Yes, it's Ian. If I wasn't with them they would still be up there kissing and hugging wild horses."

"Really? Horses! It's been a while since they came. There must be a storm coming. You better run home quickly."

They took off running through one of his fields as a short cut.

"Watch out kids, there's barbed wire," Ian shouted. He hadn't seen it until the last minute.

Too late; Angel caught her ankle on it. The wire tore her sock and cut into her skin.

"Ouch!" Angel screamed and fell on to her hands and knees, her ankle caught on the barb.

"Now what?" Ian yelled back. "I might have known. Soppy girl wasn't looking where she was going."

Angel cried over the torn skin and blood. As always, David came to her rescue. He helped her up and let her lean on him while she limped the rest of the journey.

"Think happy thoughts. Think about Buttercup."

He was right. As Angel thought about Buttercup it did make the pain ease. She remembered Buttercup had hurt her leg, too. So she could be as brave as the horse on the mountain. Before she knew it they were in town and at the street below the road that wound up the mountain, and soon they would be at David's house.

"Can you make it home, or should we carry you?" David asked her. She was leaning on him still, but barely limping.

"Carry her?" Ian grunted.

"I'm alright to get home." Angel eased back, taking her treasures from Ian. They waved at Nene Lina and watched as Angel hobbled down the street.

Angel could see her grandmother standing at the doorway waiting.

"Come on, get those wet dirty clothes off and sit by the fire, Angel. I'll warm up some soup for you." Lina rushed Angel into the house, setting her bag down beside the door. Straightening from her bent position, Lina noticed Angel's bloody sock.

"Angel, what happened? You have blood on your sock and on your ankle. Let me see." Nene looked and wiped the wound with a soft, warm, wet cloth then put some Vaseline on it and soon it stopped bleeding.

Warmed by the fire, Angel sighed, tired after her long day. So many things happened she didn't know where to start telling her grandmother.

While Nene was stirring the soup she said, "You were a long time, Angel. I know Ian was with you both but I was thinking you would be home before dark."

Lina made the best-ever soup Angel could remember. She would pick up meat bones from the butcher's shop and go to the market to get left over vegetables just as the market closed, as they were cheaper then. Sometimes she added Marmite if it wasn't to her liking. Wow, what a treat it was to taste the hot flavorful soup.

After Angel warmed herself with her Nene's soup and the heat from the coal fire, she showed Nene her treasures that she found. Lina looked in amazement at all the things Angel managed to bring back from the mountain.

"Where did you find these spoons?"

"Oh, Nene!" Angel barely kept from shouting with excitement in their small room. "They were at the ruins up on the mountain."

"What ruins?" Her beloved brow scrunched up as she tried to remember where Angel was talking about.

"The ruins David was telling his mum and dad about last night, you know up on the mountaintop? We saw this old house, well what was left of a house and part of a barn." Angel squirmed, unable to sit still. Just telling her Nene made the memory so clear it was as if she was back up the mountain.

"Nene you should have seen it – it had lots of things, a stove like ours, mugs, spoons, and chairs.

"Nene, it had horses. They came galloping across the mountaintop when the thunder started. They scared me at first but Ian told us the horses were useful in the mine where his dad worked."

"The old house on the mountain-top? Horses! Oh my goodness," she exclaimed. "You three walked all the way to Cradoc Edwards' farm. That is miles away and I didn't think there was anything left up there after all those years of bad storms."

"Cradoc Edwards' farm? Who is Cradoc Edwards?"

"Edwards' farm is where David's family grew up. Uncle Ethan's grandfather lived up there when Ethan's father was a baby. They had a beautiful farm – chickens, sheep, goats, and horses. They were very hard working people and loved animals."

"Show me what you found up there."

"Nene, I found these old spoons – look if I rub the dirt off and breathe on this one I can almost see myself. Wow! Look, Nene." Angel waited with little patience while her Nene went to get her spectacles.

Nene looked in amazement at the spoons that had passed the test of time. They were old antique type. She wondered whom they could have belonged to and be still up on the mountain.

"Have you finished your soup Angel? Put your shoes on and this warm coat. We must go and see David's mam and dad."

Angel was puzzled and thought Nene was angry with her. Angel did what her Nene had said and went with her to David's house.

Ethan was on the front porch, smoking his Woodbine cigarettes with a glass of cider in his hand. On the ground around him there were crumpled ends of cigarettes littering the floor. A packet of Woodbines contained 20 cigarettes and there were more than 20 ends on the ground. Mary was a clean woman and they weren't left from the day before. Woodbines were strong unfiltered, pure nicotine cigarettes and hard on the lungs if smoked excessively.

"Evening, Lina," David's dad said. "Welcome. What brings you here at this time? It's getting late for the kids."

"Yes, it's getting late but I must talk with you and Mary." She shooed Angel into the house. "Go and find

David. Maybe you two can play for a few minutes while I talk with David's mam and dad."

Off Angel ran. She didn't want to be around a bunch of old folk anyway.

"Angel and David brought down some treasures alright, have you seen them?"

"What treasures? David ran to his room as soon as they came back, I have no idea what you're talking about."

"You know how kids are, they either tell us or try to be sneaky and keep a secret." Lina smiled.

"Hmmm, I hadn't thought of that. But what can be troubling you, Lina, about the things they found? It's getting late."

"Angel showed me these." She handed the spoons to Ethan. He looked at them, jumbling them in his hands.

"Those, they're only a bunch of old spoons, what's so important about them?"

"Angel said she found them up on top of Penrhiwgwnt and told me about the brass and copper mugs that David found."

"Lina, they are probably a bunch of old rubbish someone didn't want and left them up on the mountain top."

"No Ethan, they are not a bunch of old rubbish. They might be to some other people but I believe these belonged to your family. Look closer, Ethan, see what Angel brought home."

"Well, they look like rubbish to me – old dirty spoons." By this time Mary came to the porch.

"No Ethan, they are tarnished, not dirty. Mary, do you have some Brasso or copper cleaner I can use and show Ethan what they really should look like?"

"Yes Lina, I'm sure I have some somewhere, let me look."

"Bring a cloth too, please."

Mary disappeared into the kitchen for a few minutes and reappeared with Brasso, copper cleaner and some old rags.

"Here, Lina." Mary handed the cleaning stuff to Lina.

"Alright then, let me see how clean I can get one of these spoons." Lina carefully put the rag on the top of the open tin and shook it gently. "Now let's see," and started rubbing the long handle of the spoon. The rag was black almost instantly, although the copper cleaner came out of the tin as a thick milky white fluid. The same thing happened with the patterned head of the spoon when she rubbed it with Brasso; the rag turned black while the beauty of the spoon emerged from years of harsh seasons.

Mary was shocked how beautiful and clean the spoon became, but Ethan had no interest in any spoons. "Oh my goodness, Lina. It looks beautiful."

Ethan was suffering a bad lapse of depression again. He had been unemployed for months and had lost interest in life. Life in the valleys had always been hard. A man looked for four basic things when he was going to work in the pits, a roof over his family's head, a chapel, a men's choir, and a rugby or football team.

Ethan was one of those men who worked as a miner in the dismal tunnels that lay underneath the ground in Rhondda's coal mines. In those days he worked twelve to fifteen-hour daytime shifts, digging out coal alongside the horses that were used to pull the carts full of coal throughout the mine. Even though he had daytime shifts then, it was dark when he went to work early in the morning and was dark down in the mine except for the light on his helmet. After his workday was done, it was evening and Ethan rode his bike home in the dark.

The helmets the miners wore had a light at the front to help them find their way in the mine. Other than that, there were no lights and definitely no lanterns to show the way through the tunnels.

A lot of the mines eventually closed down when all the coal was mined. There were terrible accidents where miners were trapped, dying in the tunnels from the gas explosions and there was no way to get to them. Many of the surviving workers had to find other careers elsewhere, and quickly, to support their families. Some went to the Welsh railways, some went to work in the Corona Pop factory in Porth, and others left for England over the Welsh border.

But Ethan didn't have the desire to go to England. After all, what was there? His family was here in the Rhondda.

Each day his heart became heavier and heavier and finally he took to cigarettes and an occasional drink or two. He could never smoke down in the mine and had no desire to put any fags in his mouth like his friends after work.

Ethan began working in the mine when he was 15 years of age. Some of his friends were younger. John Davies, he was only 12 years old. There were several coalmines in the local area to work at if they had transportation to reach them like Ethan, who rode his bike. The choices were Porth, Cymmer, Blaenllechau, Blaencwm, Cymparc, Gelli, Llwyncelyn, Maerdy, Pentre, Treherbert, Ynyshir, Llwynypia, Brithweunydd, Trealaw, and a few more nearby, Tonypandy, Tylorstown, and Wattstown.

Education was not a priority if one came from a poor family, and Ethan and his brothers did. They helped their Mam make enough money to support the family so further education was not possible for any one of them.

He had worked in the mine for over thirty years – he was still a young man really but he felt the burden of being unemployed and worried how was he going to support his own family now.

Ethan was heartbroken not to have a wage to bring home for his family, but it was important to him to find work that he looked forward to and enjoyed because he felt no joy all those years down the mine. It was dark, very damp, and unhealthy. Some of his friends developed tuberculosis or "dust" disease. These men remained confined to their homes. He was fortunate enough not to develop either but had colds frequently from the conditions in which he worked. He would have been worse if he had smoked cigarettes after work as his friends did in those days.

Those working days were very dismal. He was in charge of the horses as well as digging out the coal. The coal was the Rhondda's "black gold" and considered their bread and butter. There were no pneumatic drills or electrical equipment to dig coal; it was a man's strength, a pick, and a sledgehammer. It was heart breaking to Ethan to see the horses as they trudged through the mines every waking hour pulling heavy carts full of coal, day in and day out. The horses were there till their last breath. A horrific life they led under the ground, such beautiful animals that once roamed freely on the mountaintop.

The memories still lingered and many a night he laid restless thinking if he could have done more than just feed them and clean up after them.

He loved the fields up on the mountains before his family came along, and the mountains always appealed to him. Once again his mind wandered. It was his solitude, his awakening place, where he dreamed and played as a young boy. Maybe that was what he needed, to go back to his roots to clear and refresh his mind.

Ethan knew of an old shack on the mountaintop left vacant, but he wasn't sure if it was his grandparents' homestead or possibly some other relative his parents had. Years ago he played there but never had the chance or opportunity to revisit his childhood play areas. He was always too busy in the mines or finally falling asleep in his rocking chair at home with his family.

Maybe one day he would return, just to see where he played as a young lad. He really enjoyed the times listening to his Mam say they visited his grandparents old home. Ethan knew that the stories she told were made up, but still they captivated his mind. The sweet jellies and preserves his grandmother had made and stored for Christmas time, and the hot Christmas pudding with brandy sauce trickling down the sides were delights he'd heard about so many times but never gotten enough of.

He would dream at night, that he snuggled up with his brothers and sisters under the warm quilts his grandmother made beside the wood fire. In the morning they woke to see what Father Christmas had left in their Christmas stocking.

The stockings were lying on the floor, too heavy to hang on the mantle. They were laden with little hand-me-down metal toy cars, nuts, some chocolate, apples and occasionally an orange, if they had enough. Those were hard times but they really were the good old days. His Mam made the best of what she found.

When times were good, breakfast consisted of bacon and eggs, lavabread, fried tomatoes, and sometimes, baked beans and that would last until suppertime.

Now here was Lina, trying to rekindle those memories his Mam shared that Ethan had long forgotten. Times seemed even harder for him now, trying to support his growing family with hardly anything. He sold his toy metal car collection and comic book collection for another month's gas for their lamps. What else could he sell?

He spent most of his nights sitting on the front porch smoking his Woodbine cigarettes and watching the stars. Gazing up at the dark mountain wondering where the last 30 years had gone down the pit.

For more than a century, high quality, smokeless coal was extracted from the earth in the Rhondda Valleys, South Wales. Collieries dotted the valleys, where tens of thousands of men made their livelihood digging coal from the rich seams that ran from several feet to more than a quarter mile deep under the surface. The huge economic engine built the industrial port cities of Cardiff, fifteen miles south and Newport, and fueled the British navy from the later years of Victoria almost until the Second World War. Now the coalmines were silent, unprofitable in the modern economy.

The pits closed, and like Ethan, many remained in dying serpentine towns lining the vales.

"Ethan, are you listening to Lina?" Mary enquired. Ethan was miles away in his thoughts.

"Ethan, maybe a good night's sleep is what you need, we can talk again tomorrow."

She glanced from Ethan, lost in thought, to Mary with a shrug. "Mary, can you call Angel for me please, it's late and I should get her to bed."

"Yes, of course Lina." She stepped into the house. "Angel, your Nene's calling you. Come on sweetheart, it's getting late."

Nene held her hand and they walked home without a word spoken. Nene was in deep thought and Angel was very tired. The excitement of the day suddenly hit her.

Lina rocked in her chair by the fireplace, her favorite spot once Angel went to bed. She worried over Ethan and his depression.

How could she get Ethan interested in going up the mountain? David and Angel were always up there on weekends enjoying the fresh air and looking for their treasures. It was no good nagging Ethan into going, but perhaps she could encourage him with the positives – fresh air, away from the daily stresses, and this in turn might lift the depression that loomed over his mind.

The following day Nene was up bright and early. She raked out the fireplace and replaced it with wood logs from the neighbor. A tree fell onto the railway tracks; they cut it up and cleared the tracks. The neighbors shared their fresh bounty. The burning wood gave a pleasant aroma throughout the house.

"Angel, come and have breakfast then get washed and dressed ready for school. David will be here soon waiting for you."

They both walked to school together; their classrooms were next to each other even though David was one year older. They came to the top of the hill and the lollipop lady was ready with her stop sign to pause the traffic for them to safely cross the road.

"Good morning, David. Good morning, Angel."

"Good morning, Mrs. Jones," they both answered politely.

It was Monday. Monday was the day their classes shared music and singing together. As they already practiced their school song up the mountain it was easy for them to show off a little in front of their classmates.

The school bell rang for them to assemble in the hall. An announcement was made that a train that ran below Angel's back garden hit and killed one of their neighbors, Mr. Probert. He lived next door in the terraced houses that backed onto the railway line.

Mr. Probert worked in the signal box. He was the man that pulled the signal to allow a line to cross over to another and that would divert the train to another direction under the bridge. Also, he had control of the water tower. If the train engine needed water when it got to the station, it was easy to fill up the water pipes from the big rubber funnel that hung down from the water closet. So once again the train could puff out steam and go on to Pontypridd and then Cardiff and Tiger Bay.

Mr. Probert worked the night shift and each night he would remove some timbers from his fence and slide down the bank on to the train track and then run as fast as he could across the lines to get to the signal box before any trains would come.

When Angel saw Mr. Probert, she didn't hesitate to tell David. Together they would watch him, then say their prayers, and meet up for school the next morning.

At first, when the children were up late enough to see him, they thought it was funny. Soon, with no changes in his work schedule or the way he went to work, it was simply another part of their childhood

On this occasion, Mr. Probert was late for work. He had suffered a bad bout of flu and this was his first night back on duty. He wasn't a young man anymore so it took him a little time to get across the tracks. He ran but caught his shoelace on one of the ties across the track and fell. The train did not see him in the darkness and he wasn't found until the fog and rain lifted the following morning.

The other announcement was that a student found a five-pound note in a toilet. The toilets were outside and it was freezing cold out there. Word spread quickly throughout the school that some body used a five-pound note to wipe their bum and then drop it in our toilet. Five-pounds was a fortune. Angel had never seen a five-pound note anyway, but she knew it was a big white piece of paper with fancy writing and worth a lot of money.

What exciting news. Who would have that kind of money to use for such a purpose and throw the money away? Angel wondered afterwards if it was a story to take their minds off Mr. Probert's death.

The following morning after the children went to school, Lina was back again at Ethan and Mary's. This time with her homemade scones and jam she wanted to share. She was always so grateful to Ethan and Mary for having so little but always sharing with her. In her own way, she wanted to help them as well and pay back their hospitality.

"How are you this morning, Ethan? Did you get a good sleep last night?"

"I did get a little," he admitted, a bit grudgingly.

Mary intervened. "He walked to Taffs fish and chips late last night. That might have helped."

They both knew that walking to Taffs might have settled his mind, but offered up more problems than he could solve in a night. He would gaze up the dark mountain and to the twinkling stars above, and then come home.

"Well, that's good to get out in the stillness of the night and no one around to bother you." Lina spoke in a positive tone.

"I suppose so," Ethan answered quietly. He coughed, the cigarettes making his voice hoarse.

"If you haven't had breakfast yet, perhaps you might sit with me for a while and enjoy these hot scones with butter and jam. I've just made them."

"That sounds good to me, Lina," Mary replied. "Even though there's a little breeze this morning we can sit on the porch with the warm blankets you gave us for Christmas."

Off to the porch they went, sitting comfortably in the old rocking chairs and snuggled up with the blankets and Mary brought out some hot tea.

"What have you got planned for today, Mary?" Lina was inquisitive, to say the least.

"Oh, just the usual washing and cleaning."

"What about you Ethan?" Lina turned to Ethan, her bright eyes and manner much like a bird.

"Hmm, well, hmm…perhaps I could make a start on the basement. There's so much old rubbish down there and we could do with the extra area for the kids to play when it's wet outside." Both women could tell his heart wasn't in it; it was a chore that he had to accomplish.

"That's a wonderful idea, Ethan. You might come across some treasures of your own." Lina was trying to lay a path to treasures, not in the basement but up the mountain.

Mary knew what Lina was hinting at and smiled as she reflected on the possibility of Ethan finding something that would trigger memories of his happier childhood.

Lina was determined to mention something about his childhood. Perhaps that could spark the desire to go up the mountain. She knew Ethan was a very stubborn man. If he didn't want to do something he wouldn't, no matter who tried to encourage him. There was no more she could do, only leave him be and to his thinking about his basement.

Mary was listening and after Lina went home she said, "Ethan it can't hurt if you just go up and see. You never know. You might find something that will bring back a few happy memories of when you were a little lad."

"I'll think about it, Mary."

That evening after dinner, Ethan told Mary as he shrugged into his coat, "I just want to walk a little bit. I'll go as far as Taffs fish and chip shop. I'll be back in a few minutes."

"Alright, Ethan, you know he's shut for the night, don't you?" He nodded to show he'd listened to her. He closed the door on her next words, reaching for quiet and hoping to find it in the chill night walk.

"It's getting late, too, and the kids have to be up early for school." Mary spoke to the door, her heart following him.

Ethan often walked to Taffs – she didn't know if it cleared his head or he just wanted to gaze up at the shadowed mass of the mountain. Taffs was close to the milkman's farm. The path the children took to the mountaintop followed around the fenced boundaries of the farm; except, when they chose the quicker way, through Milkman Rhys's fields.

Ethan never crossed the farm boundaries, just walked past the edge of town, and stood gazing up at the edifice that blocked the stars. Hands in his pockets, face turned up, expression eclipsed by the darkness of night and the memories that haunted him.

Chapter 4

The following day, Lina again visited Ethan and Mary, taking something with her to offer them as she always did. Mary felt lonely for adult company all those years while Ethan was down the mine so it was not surprising Lina would stop by. Sometimes taking homemade bread for the children or helping mend their clothes. Most often if she were early they would offer her a cup of tea.

When they finished breakfast Lina said she needed to go down to the Town Hall to check on something.

"Ta ta. I'll be back this afternoon," Lina said as she closed the door behind her.

Lina was determined to go to the Town Hall and see if there was any record of Ethan's family living on the mountaintop. Records were often lost, or never recorded, on parcels of land that folks owned in those days. The local Parish Church would have records of christenings, births, and deaths but that was not what Lina was after. However, the Church records might document where the births took place. In those days, births usually took place in a person's home, not in a hospital unless there was some medical problem.

Lina was a little early for the Town Hall but she waited patiently on the doorstep until the front door opened. It was not long before she saw James, the clerk. She talked with him as he began his day and told him what she was looking for.

"Don't worry Lina, Mary visited a couple of days ago and we came across a rolled up parchment document. In fact, Edith found it in the bottom of one of the storage boxes. It stated that the Edwards family bought a parcel of land on Penrhiwgwynt mountaintop many years ago. Quite a few acres actually, and it had the plot marked out in sketched form."

"When I visited them with breakfast this morning Mary didn't say anything." Lina seemed surprised.

"I expect if Ethan was around she would keep it quiet until she had the opportunity to talk to you about it. She was very happy when she was here and saw the document herself. Don't worry, I think if you both work on Ethan he will eventually give up and go up, and perhaps go with the kids." James had been in town forever. He knew everyone and everything it seemed.

"I don't want him to give up, James. I want him to be enthusiastic about it all."

"I understand what you mean, Lina. That was a bad choice of words on my part. I am sorry."

"Don't worry, I know you mean well, James. I better go now, as I do have a number of things to do before Angel gets home from school."

"Alright, Lina. I hope to see you at Church on Sunday."

Walking back to the house she muttered quietly, "What a stroke of luck James found the document for Mary. Yes, it really is. I hope Ethan Edwards will go and claim his inheritance soon. But we have to get him up the mountain first."

Mary hastily cleared the dishes after lunch and Ethan escaped to the basement, away from any further chatter the ladies shared. She was certain he would find something somewhere in the basement that would trigger his memory, if he were that determined to clean up. A bit later Mary joined Ethan in the basement and said, "Ethan it can't hurt if you just go up and see." Once again almost as she said before, "You never know. You might find something that will bring back a few happy memories of when you were a little lad with your Mam."

"I'll think about it Mary. Let me see if I can get some cleaning done down here." After a few hours Ethan came up to the kitchen.

"I just want to walk a little bit. I'll go as far as Taffs fish and chip shop. I'll be back before the kids come home from school."

It was daylight still and that was unusual for Ethan to walk to Taffs in the daytime. Perhaps something down in the basement had triggered some thoughts. Mary watched his retreating back as he walked down the street. She dried her hands on a towel, wondering.

Ethan arrived at Taffs. Dylan Edwards was preparing for the evening customers. Ethan tapped the door gently, not to cause too much alarm for Dylan as he was getting up there in years.

Dylan was just finishing his preparations to open shop for the evening's dinner when he heard the tap at the door. "Hello Ethan, what brings you to see me at this time?"

"Well, I just wanted to talk with you. You knew my father and grandfather."

"*Ìe*, I did, that I did. What is on your mind, son?" Dylan replied.

"Yes well," Ethan was getting lost for words on how to put his question. "I don't want to be an inconvenience to you."

"Ethan, you should know you are welcome any time to come and talk with me. I am an old relative of yours so that gives you more reason to come and see me. In fact, I knew you had been here most evenings and I'm surprised you haven't tapped the door before now." He pulled the door open to admit Ethan. "Come in, son."

"You knew that I was here at night?"

"*Ìe*, of course son, I knew. I saw your fag ends on the ground in the morning and I got a quick peek of you one night when I looked out of the shop window. I noticed you walking up and down the ramp looking up at the old girl. What's troubling you, Ethan?"

Ethan sat on the old Church pew under the window. He sighed, gathering his questions. Then stooped forward with his elbows on his knees and his hands clasped under his chin.

Dylan watched him a moment, then began setting up the register. He straightened paper for wrapping up the fish and chips and made sure he had a good supply of pickled onions on the shelf.

There were no chairs or tables. It was a come in, buy your fish and chips and take them home kind of place. Most of the time, the young would have eaten them on the way before they even arrived home.

"Well, not troubling me exactly. I'm curious, but I know the fish and chip shop keeps you very busy."

"Ethan, come to the point. What is it, son?" Dylan propped his hand on the counter top, pinning Ethan with an encouraging gaze.

"Uncle Dylan, you won't believe this but I was down in our basement just trying to tidy up a bit and get rid of the rubbish down there. I came across my father's old wooden desk. I didn't spend too much time with it, but I found this horseshoe." He pulled the rusted shoe from his pocket.

"Do you remember anything about my father and grandfather? Did they like horses? I really can't figure out why he would have left a horseshoe in a drawer of the desk."

Horseshoes always hung on the wall or over a door to bring good luck.

"It's funny you should ask that because I was thinking the other day, 'I should have talked with Ethan, or talked with Mary when she came to buy some fish and chips and mentioned the kids had been going up and down the mountain to see the horses, and the treasures they brought down.'"

"Ethan, your father loved horses and so did your grandfather, and it seems young David does so I think it must be in your blood, too."

"Why do you say that Uncle, it must be in my blood?" Ethan turned quickly to look at Dylan.

"Well, let's go in the parlor a minute rather than us be in the shop. It's more comfortable in there." Both men walked into the parlor and sat down.

"It was really pitiful what happened." Dylan shook his head.

"Your father's father was out on the farm and his wife, Clarinda found him. Clarinda was really Klara, she came from Croatia. Clarinda's name meant 'a clear bright beauty'. Oh, she was a beauty and your grandfather fell in love with her the moment he set eyes on her. Oh, she was a beauty, yes she was that." Dylan repeated himself, making his point like other older folk.

"But, but what happened to my grandfather?" Ethan asked, trying to curb his impatience.

"As I was saying, he was out on the farm land. There had been a terrible storm. The horses broke out of the field, and were heading back to the wilderness. It took him a long time to catch some of them wild horses and he didn't want to lose any of them. It was the last ones he was pulling into the field."

"Wild horses, he caught?" Ethan interrupted but was more than curious.

"Yes, Ethan. Your grandfather caught the wild horses and trained some and let some go to the mines. Poor devils! Oh what a terrible life those poor beings had down them mines." Dylan was just not getting to the point quick enough for Ethan.

"You were telling me what happened." Ethan was bursting with more questions.

"Of course, son. Let me think what I wanted to tell you. *Ìe*, I remember now." Dylan lifted his finger, pointing up, nodding in agreement.

"Cradoc told me that the King of England tried to drive the wolves out of Wales. He imposed a heavy tax on the Prince of Wales and his people. He invented the tax as a way of eradicating the wolves and the taxation was to bring hundreds of wolf heads to his kingdom. The king thought that this would eradicate one of the natural wild resources in Wales and give him more power. He was unsuccessful because even hundreds of years later there is evidence of wolves in Wales, but they are almost extinct because of the powerful determination of this treacherous King." Dylan took a deep breath.

"Cradoc would never hurt them and treated them as family members.

"There were wolves on the mountain, but not many. *Ìe*, I was scared when I first went up. Then, Cradoc told me wolves were no problem. Leave them alone but just don't let them get to the sheep, that's why he had a sheep dog named Taff. 'Wolves are a reflection of us.' Cradoc used to say. And, so many people have a preconception of what wolves are like. You have to live with them to understand them, and when they get used to having you around they become your friends.

"They were his friends. I watched Cradoc many a morning from the window. He would lie in wait for them, because he knew they would come and lick his face, nuzzle close and then go away; just as they did with their own alpha wolf. He felt the sincerity of their emotions and was contented to share them. Often he would say, 'we need wolves and wolves need us to let them live, they are social characters and are devoted to their families and look after each other.'

"He considered them highly intelligent; in fact, he used to say they are a reflection of us in so many ways. Then your grandfather told me about the Welsh Prince, Llywelyn the Great, Prince of Gwynedd. He killed his faithful dog Gelert after finding him covered in blood. He thought it was his baby son's blood.

"Only later did he discover that the blood belonged to a wolf that Gelert killed in defense of the young Prince. The Prince was so saddened at the fact that he killed his dog that there was a monument for Gelert, called Beddgelert. It's there still today.

"Believe it or not in Welsh mythology, both St. Ciwg, "Wolf Girl", and Bairre, an ancestor of Amergin Gluingel, were said to have been suckled by wolves. So you see, we don't hurt wolves unless it is absolutely necessary. We just leave them roam." Dylan was well into the story by now and Ethan took a deep breath, grabbing for patience while he waited for his Uncle to remember what he wanted to pass along.

"In fact, up the valley there was a female Welsh collie that died giving birth to her nine puppies. A wolf was nearby and you know a wolf's sense of smell can cover a vast distance. This female wolf came and took the puppies into the bushes and cared for them as her own cubs until they could fend for themselves. Somewhere up the valley I am sure there are half wolf and half dog descendants from those 9 pups and the wolves that are lurking around on the old girl could very well be some of them."

"Cradoc was amazingly intelligent without much schooling. I think that was one of the reasons why Mam was so upset and frustrated when he left for mountain life. I was always amazed at the knowledge he imparted on anything and everything. He would have done so well in University if he had had the chance. But, in the Rhondda our people are poor and money is needed to go to University. We don't have the same advantages as the English." Water under an old bridge for Dylan, he took a deep breath. "Cradoc though, he was never angry, upset, or cruel. He was the kindest of my brothers and was amazingly funny at times.

"Enough about Cradoc for the time being." Dylan got out his rag and blew his nose as if he was blowing through a trumpet.

"I must get back to work, Ethan me lad. We can talk some more when I get the fish and chips cooking." He was obviously hurting from the good memories of his brother but with sorrow for his loss.

Ethan sighed.

"I'm getting to it, son. I just wanted to tell you about the wolf before I forget. Don't be too impatient with the old man, here."

Ethan felt bad, he was much younger in years; Dylan was old enough to be his grandfather, all but a couple of years. He mustered his patience and politely waited for Dylan to continue.

"As I was about to tell you, your grandfather was out trying to pull the horses back home into the field."

"What do you mean?" Ethan questioned.

"I was getting to it, son." Dylan waved his hands in a 'settle down' motion. "He was pulling three or four horses at the same time back to the paddock with ropes when one of the ropes broke. Oh God, God rest his soul." Dylan made the sign of the cross on his chest with his hand.

"What do you mean? Please tell me, what happened."

"He was pulling the ropes and one of the ropes broke, ohhhhhhh."

"Yes, one of the ropes broke." Ethan said impatiently trying to get Dylan back to the present.

"Oh God, the rope broke. The horses were already making haste together towards him but when the rope broke he lost his balance and fell under foot." Dylan shook his head and turned away sniffling.

"What?" Blurted Ethan.

"The rope broke, the horses galloped over him and he was still attached to the other ropes. The horses dragged him all over the field until they came to a stop. He was down on the ground, he was bloody, he was all cut up…he was dead, oh Ethan. Ethan, my brother was dead." At that Dylan pulled out his old rag from his pocket and wiped his eyes and blew his nose hard and wiped his eyes again.

"Oh God, Ethan, my brother, your grandfather was dead and your poor grandmother, Clarinda found him." Dylan sobbed as though it had just happened.

"Clarinda, was my grandmother?" Ethan questioned.

"*Ìe*, Ethan. Clarinda was your grandmother. She died not long afterwards. She died from a broken heart."

"From a broken heart, how can that be?" Ethan questioned again.

"Your grandfather was all she had in her life. When he saw her he fell in love with her as I said, but her Croatian parents were against any relationship with a Welshman. Those parents of hers hated the Welsh but they brought their horses here to sell. All they were interested in was money for their Lipizzaner horses. Most likely her parents had an arranged marriage with a Croatian for Clarinda," he mentioned with a disgusted tone to his voice.

"There were plenty of them in those days over here; they brought the horses. If your grandfather couldn't afford their horses they would just let them wander over the mountainside. Then they would turnaround and expect your grandfather and grandmother to feed them and let them stay before returning to Croatia. A fine how-do-you-do bunch of low life men, if you ask me!"

It was a lot for Ethan to take in but he was thinking and thinking.

When Dylan recovered from his sad memories he said, "I had better be getting on with my work, otherwise I won't be opening shop today. Come back again tomorrow we can talk more, alright?"

Of course Ethan wanted to know more. "I'll be back tomorrow then." Ethan walked back home with a million thoughts running through his mind. He had known very little about his grandfather or grandmother and least of all that his grandmother was Croatian. But, this didn't really answer any of the other questions he wanted Dylan to answer.

When Ethan arrived home he told Mary that he had talked with Dylan at Taffs chippie and shared the information Dylan had imparted. Ethan said he would go back and revisit him when Taffs was closed this time, so as not to interfere with the lunch and dinner openings. Mary was delighted he was going back to talk with Dylan but didn't say too much to Ethan. She could see he was in deep thought and maybe conversations with Dylan would be an answer to her prayers.

He went back down to the basement but Mary could tell something was troubling him. It wasn't too long before Ethan returned to Mary in the kitchen.

"Mary, put the kettle on me love, let's have a cuppa?"

Mary instantly filled the kettle and stood it on the black oven in the fire grate. Then she washed the teapot; laid two cups and saucers on the kitchen table. While the kettle was boiling, she brought in a cake tin from the pantry and proceeded to cut the cake that Lina made earlier and brought up to share with Mary and Ethan. Ethan was interested in what cake she had at hand. He leaned in and sniffed the cake, licking his lips.

For a while he had been off his food and hadn't really been eating much of anything, so she was pleased to see his interest in the cake.

It was rewarding to Mary to see that Ethan wanted a cup of tea with her. She didn't dare ask how many pieces of cake he wanted on his plate but left the cake tin on the table just in case he wanted a few more pieces. Lina made a delicious fruitcake from the fruit she bought at the Co-op and Ethan always enjoyed it.

The water was boiling. Carefully, Mary tucked a rag under the handle of the kettle and wrapped it around so not to burn her hand and brought it to the kitchen sink, then poured a few drops in the teapot and swished the water around to warm the pot then poured it out. She added three heaped teaspoons of tealeaves and poured the hot water into the pot and stirred it well before replacing the lid. She let it stand for a little while to brew.

Tea was ready. "Ethan come and sit here." She nodded at the chair. "We can share Lina's cake together." Mary waited patiently while Ethan decided to join her. He was obviously troubled about something.

Ethan watched as Mary poured the tea through the strainer into his cup. He enjoyed the cup of tea that Mary poured and ate the piece of cake she put on his plate. Suddenly, Ethan interrupted the silence, "Mary love, when I went to Taffs I talked with Dylan." Then Ethan went silent for a couple of minutes. He followed with, "Uncle Dylan started to tell me about my grandfather Cradoc and grandmother Clarinda. I didn't even know those were my grandparents' names, my father never mentioned them." He started drinking his second cup of tea.

"I didn't even know that my grandmother Clarinda was from Croatia."

Mary sat quietly waiting for Ethan to say more. She could see that Ethan was in deep thought.

"I'm going up to Taffs again tomorrow. Dylan suggested I visit again so we can talk more."

That evening, Ethan was happy to sit in the kitchen in front of the fire with Mary as she knitted. Watching Mary knit reminded him of his mother knitting for the family and that prompted Ethan to ask, "Mary, I've never seen you knit before. What are you knitting?"

"Lina is teaching me to knit. She is a real blessing to me and I appreciate her friendship very much. She taught me to sew patches on the kids' play clothes and now she is teaching me to knit. She is so kind." Mary dropped her hands to her lap, still holding her place in the row. "None of the other ladies at Church or our neighbors seem to bother with me." Mary was so happy to tell Ethan of her longtime friendship with Lina.

It was a good night sitting around the fire for both of them, watching the flames from the coal in their little kitchen fireplace. It had been a long time since they sat alone together, simply enjoying each other's company and sharing time. Normally, Ethan went out on the porch to smoke his Woodbines and Mary would get on with whatever other chore needed attention or sit happily by the fire repairing clothes, alone.

Mary smiled at Ethan and then felt her cheeks warm up.

Ethan made a joke, "I made you pink, I made you embarrassed." He reached for her hand, taking it in his and turning it over, opening her palm. He drew a heart in the softness marred by calluses. "It's been a long time since I've done that." A note of pride was in his voice.

Mary felt her cheeks with the palms of her hands. They were burning. He had touched a spark within her but she was still a little self-conscious even after all their years of marriage to let him know that, so she answered, her voice a little breathless, "Not really, we just haven't sat together for so long watching the coal burn in the fire grate; the heat feels good on my face." She jumped at the chance to change the subject, looking for anything. Then she smiled. "Do you see what I see?" She pointed to the fire. "The flames are making colors and patterns?" Mary was determined not to let Ethan think she was still nervous or embarrassed. She pulled her hand from his, taking up the knitting again.

Ethan quickly said, "No, but I see a beautiful lady that needs to go to bed with her husband now."

"Now?" Mary questioned, her voice coming out a nervous squeak.

"Of course, now." Ethan got up from his chair and put out his hand, catching hers as she stood up.

Ethan walked with Mary to the bottom of the stairs and lit the candle in the holder, while guiding Mary up the stairs he carried it to light their way.

All the way up the stairs Mary was thinking, thank God I am over the childbearing age. They could not afford another baby, even though some women have had babies late in life – she always passed the news off, as most likely they were accidents.

Mary remembered that couldn't happen to her because her womb was removed after David was born.

Chapter 5

Ethan was up as normal, early on Saturday morning and out on the porch smoking his Woodbines. He seemed rested. Mary was preparing breakfast for the children when Angel and Lina arrived just in time to nibble on the scones just out of the oven. Mary invited Lina up earlier to try her scones. She'd been practicing and hoped they were as delicious as Lina's.

Lina smiled, as she tasted one. "Mary, these are really good."

Mary was so happy. She had been waiting for Lina's approval when she tasted her scones. Mary followed the directions to the letter, hoping they were tender just as Lina had showed her. Even Ethan commented how good they were.

"Mary, these are delicious. The best ones you have made, not hard but really soft and tasty." He was a bit lost for the right words. "With Lina's jam they make a great breakfast for everyone, and I'd like another one please."

It was difficult for Mary to take the time to get anything cooked perfectly with a large family. It had been just a matter of cooking something edible for everyone with her budget and time. Every bit of her waking hours were consumed with cleaning, cooking, patching clothes, and trying to grow some vegetables in garden pots.

Lina encouraged Mary, as it would definitely help with her budget to grow fresh vegetables and not have to buy them at the Co-op. Lina brought Mary some seeds and some roots from her own garden. Perhaps seeing vegetables grow might help Mary relax and divert her attention from her mundane existence.

This particular morning it made Mary feel very good that she had made a great scone that met with Ethan's approval. Lina smiled wide at Mary.

Ethan announced that he needed to leave and go up to Taffs. He promised Dylan he would come up earlier in the day before his lunchtime rush to talk more about his grandfather and grandmother. Maybe Ethan could help Dylan carry in the spuds from the pantry to the shop. An old man, eighty-nine years of age and alone in life, needed some help.

Dylan was a widower. His wife, Olga passed away years before but he kept her picture hanging in his shop all those years. Olga not only was the mother of his children; she was his soul mate.

When Ethan arrived at Taffs, Dylan was ready to sit down and talk in his kitchen parlor. He made some tea and the milk and sugar was ready for Ethan if he wanted them.

Dylan started the conversation. "Son, what is it you need to know about your grandfather? I feel there is a lot you don't know and maybe I can help you understand what went on in our family."

"You have mentioned our family a few times now but I don't know too much. Where did you live before Taffs, Uncle?"

"Son, did you know I was your grandfather's middle brother and we lived up on the farm, too?"

Ethan shook his head in amazement but then it seemed sensible to him. After all, he was his grandfather's brother and he remembered someone saying they were close.

"Well, can I ask a question?" Ethan stirred his third cup of tea.

"Of course Ethan." Dylan leaned back in his chair.

"Where did you get the name 'Taffs' for your fish and chip shop?"

"It's a long story really, but for the time being I will tell you. Taff means Welshman so instead of putting Taffies, that would mean Welshmen. I chose the name "Taffs" it sounded better. I was including my sons in the name, just incase they wanted to join me in the business sometime. It is also from the Bible days, Hebrew to be exact, and more modern since then Taff is Welsh for Davydd or David. My real name is Davydd Dylan Edwards, but everyone calls me Dylan as we had an Uncle called Davydd."

Ethan kept the name in the family by naming his son Davydd, but pronounced it David.

Dylan continued to tell Ethan about the family. "Your grandfather was the oldest, then there was Matthew, then me – Davydd Dylan, then Thomas, then Owen, and Rhys was the youngest boy of us six boys. We also had two sisters, Megan and Gwyneth, in our family.

"Anyway, I was going to tell you, your Grandfather loved to go on expeditions; always wanting to find out what it was like to sleep under the stars. He used to climb up the mountain just like David and Angel except he'd be up there for days and days. No wonder our poor mother, Mam we called her, was always worried about him. She didn't know from one day to the next if he was dead or alive. I often wondered what he did for food and water but he told me he made a campfire and caught rabbits to eat." Dylan rubbed his hands together, a pleasant memory for him. "I made a joke one time and said, 'Be careful, you might grow long furry ears!' He wasn't too pleased but he laughed anyway."

Ethan interrupted, "What happened?" Before Ethan could finish his question Dylan was telling him about Clarenda, his grandmother.

"He had the horse farm with Clarenda. They had five children, three babies died at birth, only your father and his brother survived. When he met Clarenda, his world changed. He was happy and more interested in worldly things, rather than just the wilderness. Clarenda was so beautiful. So was her sister, and I married her sister, Olga. It was a hard life up there on the mountain then and it wasn't like it is now."

The penny didn't drop at first as Ethan was trying to figure everything out in his head, "You, Uncle Dylan married Olga?"

"Yes, of course I couldn't let her go back with those brothers of hers to Croatia, could I? They hated Welshmen so they might as well hate two of us Welshmen instead of one – safety in numbers, I would say, that I would! We two were inseparable anyway. I mean Cradoc and me."

"You said inseparable. Were you always at the farm, too?"

"*Ie* Ethan, I was." He nodded his head. "I used to help your grandfather catch the horses and train them. He was a young boy then, strong and full of energy and I thought I was, too." Dylan sighed, thinking of long ago.

"Well, what happened to my grandfather?" Ethan prompted Dylan, who shook himself free of that long ago life.

"I'm getting to that, son. Now where did I put my spectacles? I'll need them to put the gas on to fry the fish and chips."

"Here they are." Ethan picked up the spectacles off the sideboard and handed them to Dylan.

"Let me put on the gas first so the fat can heat up," he assured Ethan as he walked into the shop. He soon came back and sat down again.

"As I was saying our mother, Mam, had no idea what he was up to. So one day she got all of us boys out of bed early, even before it was light. She wanted us to climb Penrhiwgwynt. She had spirit alright, she tried herself to climb, but it was hard for a woman up the ragged cliff side by herself and with a skirt! Her inquisitiveness was so high at that point and her adrenaline was running wild; she would try anything she could to find out what he was doing up there. Oh yes, our Mam wanted to know what he was doing to look like a tramp when he came home.

"When Mam finally got to the top she shouted for him but it wasn't until after our mother cried and screamed and cried some more did he finally appear out of the bushes. He had made himself a shack out of branches and leaves. You couldn't see it at first; you had to really search for it as it was well hidden out of view in thick bushes. Dylan straightened on the chair, leaning as if he was still looking for the shack again.

"Cradoc couldn't see what all the fuss was about. He was up there enjoying life as he thought it should be lived, loving the earth and fresh air. He was definitely a lover of the wilderness." Dylan shook his head.

"When all the commotion died down he explained his thoughts. She didn't understand any of them but he still tried to convince her he was definitely alright and he enjoyed the outdoors. He wasn't totally alone as she thought; he had the wildlife to keep him amused. He could catch rabbits and cook them, he found wild onions and plenty of wild blackberries and he could drink rain water as it dripped down the leaves of the trees; all he had to do was hold a leaf in a funnel shape and position it beneath a leaf on the tree and he could drink the water as it fell down from the sky. It seemed to rain more often up on the mountain. He was happy as a lark.

"Cradoc helped our Mam back down the cliff when it was time to go. It seemed it was harder getting down than going up. That was something he mentioned too, that he might clear some area and make it easier to get up and get down, maybe a narrow path through the bushes on the down slope.

"When he did come home he shared dinner with us. Oh, he was overjoyed to tell us stories of where he roamed and what he did. Then he collected more things together and was ready to go back up again to his new home." Dylan shrugged his shoulders. "He would return in a couple of days, when he needed something else from the house.

"Seeing his eagerness for the outdoors Mam really didn't need to worry, as he wouldn't come to any harm up there, and she became less anxious about it all. In fact, she said, "There isn't a Pub with beer and wild women up on Penrhiwgwynt so maybe he will be alright up there." Dylan shook his head. "It was a different way of life. Mam thought that if he kept coming and going up and down she had better crochet him a jumper or two and make a couple of blankets to keep him warm. She was always saying, "It is very bleak up there on that mountain, just like the Moors."

Dylan fidgeted as he searched through his memories to tell Ethan more about the family. He rubbed at the stubble on his chin. The hair so grey it was nearly invisible.

"One of the blankets he took up to Penrhiwgwynt is now cut up and used for other things, Ethan. That roll over there by the door now keeps the draughts out." He pointed across the room. "And the rest I cut up for blankets, one on that sofa and the one on my bed." Dylan again got out his rag and wiped his face. It was hard for Dylan to express his memories of his mother.

Ethan found it easy to detect that he missed her and everything he could recall about her.

"As time went by, he finally revealed that he was going to stay up there and not keep coming down so often. Oh she was upset, our Mam that is." Dylan waved his hand, and nodded, as that was what Cradoc wanted. "To live on the top of a mountain was just plain stupid. Of course, our Mam hit the roof. She screamed and hollered. Was he insane, was he nuts or something?

"She even shouted, 'if your father was still alive he would have beaten you, Cradoc Edwards, black and blue, to knock some sense into that thick skull of yours.'

"He didn't care. He was determined that this was where he wanted to be and nothing would stop him.

"Days went into weeks and then months, when one day he reappeared and said he had built a house up there. Matthew and I decided to go up and see. He had to get supplies so he asked our Mam if he could take some old things she wasn't using anymore with him. She was almost afraid to think of what he really needed.

"He got his old school satchel from under the bed he vacated, and stuffed it with an enamel plate, forks, knives, a tin mug, and a couple of big spoons. And, oh yes." Dylan held up a finger to make a point. "A blanket or two that our Mam made for him, he carefully rolled up. He tied rope around them so he could hoist them on his back just like an old tramp! Then he tied an old saucepan on to the rope at one end." Dylan shook his head at the memories.

"He told us if we were going with him we would have to carry our own blankets and whatever else we needed. Then he suggested that we bring more pans and definitely knives as he could do with a few sharp ones. And maybe, if there was a saw around the place bring that too, matches as well if Mam had a few boxes she could spare. He announced it was getting a nuisance for him to rub two stones together to spark wood to make a fire; matches would definitely help him out.

"I had no idea what to expect, he was definitely different from us. He thought differently and looked different. By then he had grown a wild looking beard and his knotted hair was tied back with a piece of old rope. He looked a mess and needed a bath. Oh my God he stank to high heaven." Dylan smiled and waved his hand under his nose.

"He definitely needed to brush his hair. Mam made comments, you're *uchafee*, which meant dirty nasty, but she had no intention of offending him. She was just trying to bring him to his senses once again." He shrugged, lost in thought for a moment, and then continued.

"Mam carefully laid out some towels and soap for him to take a bath and boiled the water on the fire in an aluminum bucket. All he had to do was add cold water to his liking. She had taken the old zinc bathtub from the fence, where it was hung when not in use. She had already placed it in front of the fire grate for warmth.

"The next day he was up at the crack of dawn and was pacing the kitchen wanting to know when we were getting out of bed." Dylan smiled.

"*Cumbuyu,* I haven't got all day, where are you?" he shouted to us.

"He was definitely not patient. He was now independent to a certain extent, lived alone, needed very little from anyone and it was obvious he had become almost a recluse and a wilderness man.

"Cradoc saw the old axe rested against the door frame. As he was making his way out of the house, he asked our Mam if he could take it."

"Of course you can. It's getting rusty just hanging around here. You probably need it far more than we do.

"I remember she waved her hand at us as we walked out. But there were tears in her eyes and a catch in her voice." Dylan's eyes watered and he paused a moment to clear his throat.

"Uncle Dylan, I can smell hot fat coming from the shop." Ethan noticed it a few minutes before but he didn't interrupt his Uncle. It was over an hour since Dylan had put the fat on to heat in the two deep fry cookers – one for the fish and one for the chips.

"More to come another time, I must get about my business now. Customers will be coming for their fish and chips." Dylan got up quickly and hurried into the shop, concerned he was going to cause a fire. He called over his shoulder, "Come back tomorrow, Ethan, we can talk some more then."

Ethan followed him into the shop.

"Can I help you with anything, Uncle Dylan?" The old man was more than overjoyed at the offer.

"That would be wonderful for me to have your help. Thank you, Ethan. Will you cut up the newspapers over there so I can wrap up what they want?" A new vitality filled his Uncle and Ethan smiled to himself. Dylan was a headmaster, happy to have someone to boss around. "Also, could you slice up the spuds in about three-quarter inch wide slices for the penny daps?" He held up thumb and forefinger a width apart to show Ethan the size. "Don't peel them. They fry better with a bit of skin on." Since his wife had passed away, Dylan was completely alone taking care of his fish and chip shop by himself.

Ethan never realized that fact, as many times as he'd come to his shop. Dylan definitely needed help. He should have been more aware, and that thought made his heart ache. Now he was the one clearing his throat.

"You know, Angel's favorite is the daps." Ethan told Dylan, when he could talk.

"I know that, that I know. When Lina can afford it she buys a batter dipped deep fried slice of cod's roe when they come out of Church on Wednesday night." A silence fell between them. Ethan finally nodded with a lift of his lips, not quite a smile. He'd been given a lot of information.

"Go ahead, son. Go ahead and get those daps cut." Dylan told him.

Ethan nodded and straightened his shoulders. "I'll get them for you, Uncle. Yes, yes I will." He smiled at mimicking his Uncle's way of repeating his words, and then went to pull the sacks of potatoes up to start cutting them.

The men worked in silence for a time, getting the shop ready for business. When they found a place to stop, Dylan as prepared as possible for the lunch rush, Ethan stepped to the door.

"Come again tomorrow, Ethan. We'll talk some more." Dylan repeated.

"I'll be here, Uncle. Tatty bye."

"Tatty bye, Ethan." Dylan closed the door and took his place behind the counter.

Ethan walked home to Mary, still thinking about all that Dylan had told him. So, there was life up on Penrhiwgwynt after all.

When he got back to the house, Mary already had lunch on the table. She cooked a stew with drippings and vegetables. Whenever Lina could collect the drippings from the neighbors she always shared some with Mary. Drippings were the juices left in the pan after the meat cooked. It made a tasty base for the vegetable stew; a bowl of stew with a hunk of bread would definitely keep everyone going till evening.

Ethan was quiet the rest of the day, trying to absorb all that his Uncle Dylan had told him. He fell into a rhythm with the visits.

Chapter 6

Ethan visited Dylan every day before lunch and helped him with the heavy stuff from the cold room and pantry, and sliced the spuds as he was told. Dylan looked forward to his visits very much as he had company again, and of course Ethan helped him.

One day, Ethan needed to go to the doctor. He told Dylan he could come late after his evening dinner when the shop closed and he could smoke a Woodbine with Dylan. Of course Dylan was happy. He enjoyed Ethan visiting. It was just like old times when his children and Ethan's father and brother were around him.

Dylan lost two of his sons, one died in a mine accident that took hundreds of lives, and one other died from "dust" disease. Inhaling the dust as they dug for coal ruined the lining of his lungs. His grandson died in the mine when there was an explosion long before the slag flood. Slag was the very small pieces of poor quality coal that couldn't be used for anything other than dumping it and piling it up, making more grey hills in the valley.

Dylan had other children and grandchildren but they moved up north to Newcastle Emlyn where they started a hotel hoping to make a few bob more than in the valley. It was clean and fresh with plenty of green fields for the eye to observe. The River Emlyn was plentiful with wild salmon. People could float or paddle their coracles, small oval shaped wooden boats with frames covered with animal skin and thick layers of tar, quite an invention, and catch the salmon in their hands. It wasn't hard work, so they said. Dylan's sons didn't want to stay in a town that lacked industry, so he was basically alone in the Rhondda.

That evening, Dylan thought it was Ethan that came through the door. He shouted from the back, "I've been waiting for you to ask more questions. It would give me an idea what is troubling you, Ethan, but first let's have a cuppa, shall we? I'll put the kettle on."

There was no reply and Ethan didn't appear in his kitchen parlor, so Dylan went into the shop. Dylan was surprised it wasn't Ethan, as the shop was normally closed at that time. There were three young lads, one seemed polite and asked if he could have a piece of fish, he was hungry.

Dylan said, "Well, it so happens I have three pieces left over, so I will be happy to share them with you, one each, alright. I'll get some paper to wrap them in." As he turned around he was hit on his back and shoulders and fell to the floor. At first he was in shock, it hurt and he was scared they were going to kill him. He stayed there and pretended he was knocked out and waited. Dylan could hear them talking.

One leaned over him to see if he was moving while the other one was growing impatient trying to open his money till. Instead he picked the whole thing up and threw it down on the flagstones near where Dylan was lying. Dylan's injuries could have been worse from the impact down on the flagstones. Fortunately, the robber threw his till a little distance away from him.

When Ethan finally arrived, he saw Dylan on the floor, blood coming from his face where he had fallen. "Uncle. Oh my God, are you alright? Did you fall?" Dylan didn't answer.

Ethan quickly lifted Dylan up off the floor and carried him carefully to the sofa in the parlor; he hardly weighed anything, he was nothing but skin and bones even though he was tall. "Thank God he's still breathing," Ethan thought to himself.

He wiped the blood from around Dylan's face and got some water for Dylan to sip. Ethan thought, poor Uncle

Dylan, he was eighty-nine years old. He had macular degeneration and couldn't see more than a couple of pinholes out of one eye. The decrease in his eyesight started about ten years ago.

Dylan must have passed out on the floor from the pain while he was waiting for Ethan.

Ethan watched as Dylan come to.

"They hit me from behind, three of them, and I fell. It hurt. I couldn't get up. I pretended I was out so they wouldn't do anything else to me."

"Did you get a glimpse of what they looked like, Uncle?"

"The one that leaned down over me reeked. Probably hadn't had a bath for months. I could smell the Brylcream in his hair; it stank to high heaven. As they moved around getting what they wanted and emptying my till on the floor, I could smell some kind of perfume with the mothballs."

How could someone do that to him, he was old and almost blind? If anyone needed anything they only had to ask and Ethan knew Dylan would have given it to them, no matter what it was. Ethan was furious as he listened to Dylan. Not knowing how injured his Uncle was, he needed to get help.

"Stay here Uncle, it would be better not to move until I come back. Try and relax. I'll be back in a minute. I just want to get some help." Ethan thought to himself, "I must get help quickly."

Ethan rushed outside into the street shouting, "Help! Somebody help, my Uncle Dylan's hurt." He saw a police constable running around the corner. He must have heard Ethan calling for help. "Bobbie, come quickly. Uncle Dylan has been hurt." The Bobbie ran through the door like greased lightning. Everyone loved Dylan and they would drop what they were doing to help him.

"Uncle Dylan, the Bobbie is here."

Dylan was coming around and started talking again.

"Take your time, it's Bobbie Matthews. I'm here to help you." The Bobbie was a frequent visitor to the chip shop. He knew Dylan well and was angry when he saw the injuries on the old man.

"I went to get paper to wrap up their fish and when I came back one of them walloped me. When I dropped to the floor I thought it was better to pretend I was out cold." He touched his lip. "They could have killed me." Dylan paused, his lip swelling where he hit the floor. The blood slowed but hadn't stopped and the Bobbie took the towel Ethan handed him to pass to Dylan.

Bobbie Matthews replied, "That was a good idea. God knows what they would have done next if they thought you were alright. Do you know what they looked like, what did they say?"

Dylan took a breath, as if it pained him. "I would recognize the people who robbed me if I ever encounter them again."

Bobbie Matthews questioned that in his mind. Dylan was almost blind; whatever did he mean he would recognize the thief?

Dylan was anxious to get off his sofa and told him, "Everyone has a scent of their own, no matter whom they are or what they do. I can tell you next time if he comes again; I will recognize him."

"What do you mean?" Bobbie Matthews asked, taking notes.

"Well, he had a peculiar odor." Dylan finally struggled to sit up. Bobbie helped him, adding a cushion against his back.

"What, like body odor? Like he hadn't taken a bath in a long time?" Bobbie Matthews asked again.

"No. Not really like that. It was more of a sweet odor. Perhaps cologne or something like that, but it was a distinct smell and it was mixed up with something else. If I didn't know any better, I would say he smelt like moth balls. He also had a different accent to us Taffies."

"What accent? Where do you think he came from?"

"If I had to guess, I would say over the border; perhaps the Midlands, maybe Birmingham."

"Why would you say that, Dylan?" The Bobbie sat back on his heels, busily scribbling in his notebook.

"The accent wasn't quite as harsh and nasal as some Londoners sound."

"Is that right?" The Bobbie was definitely interested in his observation. "How old do you think he was?" Bobbie questioned Uncle Dylan closely.

"A whippersnapper of a lad, maybe nineteen or twenty-ish."

"You're sure about that moth ball smell, are you?"

"*Ìe,* I am sure, very sure I am moth balls."

Bobbie wrote all this down, "Body odor, like cologne and moth balls, nineteen or twenty-ish, accent like the Midlands." When Dylan nodded his agreement, the Bobbie turned a page in his book.

"What about the others? You said there were three of them."

"That's right, three of them but one was too polite, he didn't fit with the others." Dylan shook his head, wincing in pain and stopped with a hand to his face. "The other one just reeked dirty, and the Brylcream in his hair stank to high heaven."

"Alright Mr. Taff. I'll go back to the station and share the information with the Chief."

Bobbie immediately went back to the station and spoke with Chief Tom, the Chief of Police, and they documented the information Dylan had given Bobbie.

Chief Tom was quite interested. He said he would go and see Dylan in the morning. Maybe Dylan might remember a few more details.

Ethan stayed with Dylan until he was able to move comfortably and get into his pajamas with his cup of milk and go to bed. He didn't really want to leave, but Dylan insisted and Ethan could come back tomorrow. Dylan didn't want Ethan to be overly concerned.

It was early morning when Dylan was up and moving around as normal, trying to get into his usual routine, although he was still hurting from the blow and fall.

"Dylan, how are you feeling today? You must be still in pain after what you went through last night and ending up on the floor?" Chief Tom asked. He'd come to see Dylan after breakfast. He'd gone over the information from Bobbie Matthews' report to refresh the details before he spoke to the victim.

"I am so glad Ethan came, otherwise you could still be unconscious on the floor and who knows what would have happened to you."

"*Ìe*, everything is well as can be now. Perhaps the rest helped." He brushed a shaking hand over his face. The old man had been shaken by the attack. Chief Tom took in every movement. "The bruises are coming out now so I look like I've been down the pit." Dylan tried to laugh a bit but disgust and anger laced his words. "It would have been better if the lads asked me for some money, I would have given it to them and all the fish and chips they wanted if they were hungry."

"I know you would have Dylan, but obviously they wanted something else." Chief Tom said.

"I think they wanted the thrill of stealing, maybe their lives had become boring or they just didn't have the right direction. Some lads take longer than others to know what's right and what's wrong. The life of working hard, caring for family and friends, doesn't seem to appeal to some of these youngsters. It must be the thrill of committing a crime instead."

Chief Tom went over the facts again, no new information from Dylan to help them. He walked back to the station, wondering how the old man still had such a sharp memory. Even this morning he'd recalled exactly what he'd reported to Bobbie Matthews. Dylan was a remarkable man, beaten black and blue, he was on his feet today and tending to his business like any other day.

It wasn't more than a week or so that the clerk of the reports office found out that Mr. Evans reported a robbery the week before. Apparently, only clothing was stolen but the funny thing was that they identified the clothing as being in boxes in a storage room. The Evans' family didn't use the clothing anymore so stored them in moth balls to keep the moths out and from eating everything.

In the meantime, when Bobbie Matthews went back on duty he heard about the robbery at Mr. Evans home. He was asked by Chief Tom to visit Mr. Evans and ask for a sample of clothing. The Bobbie was very interested, excited actually; maybe he could solve both robberies himself.

Bobbie rode his bicycle, flicking the bell as he went to get everyone out of the way. He was in a hurry on his mission. When he arrived at Evans' home he told Mr. and Mrs. Evans that they might have a clue back at the station as to who had stolen their clothing and explained the circumstances of Taffs robbery.

The Evans' knew Taffs Fish and Chip shop well. It was where they first met each other one night after Church and shared a penny dap together. They were much younger then, Mrs. Evans recalled. "Poor Dylan, he's a good man, how could anyone do that to an old blind man?" she exclaimed.

Bobbie interrupted, "Pardon me, but I'm in rather a hurry to get to Taffs' before a lot of people get there for their lunch, but I need your help. Could I have a small sample of the clothing you have in storage, to take to Dylan? I want to see if he can make an association with the clothing you have with the odors he had smelt on one of the robbers." The Evans' were only too pleased to go to the storage and get a jumper.

Bobbie returned to Dylan with the sample item. "Dylan,

can you tell if the lad smelt like this?" Bobbie was waving the jumper in the air near Dylan.

Dylan shouted, "Come closer instead of waving your arms around like a fussy old woman." He watched the Bobbie waving something in the air, like a matador in a bullring. His head hurt, his back hurt, and the Bobbie was acting ridiculous.

Bobbie stopped his waving and carefully balled the jumper up and put it near Dylan's nose.

Dylan inhaled carefully. He thought a moment, taking another sniff. "It does smell like him but there was another odor with it, maybe some of that expensive stuff men put on their faces after they shave, what-you-ma call it?"

"Do you mean cologne?" Bobbie interrupted.

"I remember that now you mention it, that after cologne stuff, but I couldn't tell you if he had shaved or not. I didn't dare open my eyes."

"Things are piecing together, Dylan. I think we might be on the right track to catch these buggers," Bobbie Matthews assured him.

Back at the station, the Bobbie and Chief Tom documented the information of the moth ball clothing in his ledger but they were puzzled about the other scent.

Later that same evening, down at the local pub, the radio was announcing the future football games coming up, Aston Villa and Cardiff City were playing at Cardiff.

One of the customers slammed his empty pint glass on the bar and shouted, "Another pint. So I can celebrate Villa slaughtering Cardiff."

"Arrogant bugger," the bartender said to the customer that he was talking with, tipping his head to indicate the loud mouth.

"What was it you were drinking?" bartender Di asked.
"Pint of bitter."
Bartender Di put the glass sideways under the tap and slowly pulled the arm down until it was about an inch and a

half from the top of the glass, then stood the glass upright to add the froth.

Carefully standing the glass on the bar, he waited for payment.

The young lad picked up the glass and down the hatch it went all in one go. He slammed the glass on the counter and shouted, "Another."

Bartender Di was already suspicious with this lad. He didn't think he would be paying for his drinks like his other customers at the end of the night. Everyone paid his or her tab on time. Just as he expected, this lad didn't, he just rushed through the door pushing everyone out of the way. The customers and Di himself went outside to see where he had gone, but the street was deserted and he was nowhere in sight. It was very unusual. No one ever did that in this town.

It wasn't long afterwards that the Bobbie on duty came in on his way home after his night shift. "What on earth has happened here, everyone looks a little puzzled?"

"Shocked, more like it, Bobbie. Some lad was in here shouting his mouth off about Villa slaughtering Cardiff, and then he robbed me of three pints of hard bitter," Bartender Di sounded disgusted.

"Really?" said Bobbie. "What did you notice about him, was he with anyone else?"

"There were two of them, three really, but one didn't say anything and he looked nervous, sat at that table near the dart board." He pointed toward the table in question. "The one in the wool plaid suit was playing darts and the other one had his hair glued and sticking up on top like a cockatoo, he also smelled dirty, stinking bugger. Why?" He lowered his hands; he'd pantomimed the spiked hair.

"It's my job to know all the details. By the way, did you know that Dylan was hurt and robbed?"

"Dylan? No! Is he alright? What happened?"

"It seems he was attacked from behind and fell on his face on those flagstones. It's a wonder he didn't smash his face or die down on those cold stones."

"Who found him? Bobbie?"

"Ethan found him. Dylan is much improved and recovering now." He waved his hands to assure Di Dylan was better. "In fact, Dylan gave me a description of the thieves. He even told me what they smelt like. Amazing really, for an old man to be so descriptive."

"You know what they say Bobbie, don't you?" the Bartender interrupted, "When one sense goes, the others heighten until you kick the bucket. I mean Dylan's senses kicked in, I don't mean he's going to kick the bucket," he added quickly with a smile.

Bobbie replied, "Ethan always goes in to see Dylan every day. Thank God he went in that time, too."

"Now, if we can find these dirty buggers we can charge them with three counts of theft. They took clothes, money, and your beer. Then assault with the intent to injure a reputable elderly shopkeeper, Dylan."

"Better find those dirty buggers quickly before they do any more harm. Thank God they weren't here last month with all the coronation celebrations going on," the bartender added.

"I'd forgotten that - the Queen's coronation. I wonder if they came here to catch us off guard. We are a small town in the Rhondda; usually not much goes on here and we don't have all them organizing committees they have in England to keep everything going. They are still celebrating everywhere. Interesting, it is, very interesting, very interesting indeed," Bobbie repeated with growing excitement before he left.

The next day, the Bobbie saw Chief Tom again and logged in what he had learned the night before from Dylan. The details matched perfectly. The robbers were around nineteen or twenty - one wearing items of clothing with a mothball pong, one with his hair glued up with Brylcream, and they all had an accent possibly from the midlands in

England, and with a damn attitude.

"Now Bobbie, let's settle down here and examine the details carefully. Maybe those three are making their way up the Rhondda rather than down to Cardiff. If they just came here over the border they would have to go into Cardiff first, then up here. Most likely by train if they were trying to get here in a hurry, or by bus through Pontypridd. I'll get in touch with Cardiff Station and see if there's been any activity there that they can tie this case to."

When Ethan arrived the following day, Dylan was a little embarrassed to announce to him that he felt vulnerable and old because he couldn't defend himself.

"Is there anyone close to you who can help?" Ethan asked about relatives.

Dylan hung his head, shaking it side to side. "No, Ethan. My son died down the mine from dust. My grandsons went north. They don't come back to the valley." He sighed, sadness filling the gust of breath. "It's as if they have forgotten me here."

What a shame. Dylan was still a loving gentleman. He placed a hand on Dylan's bent shoulder, feeling the fragility under the loose fitting shirt.

"I want you to know that I care a great deal about you and I'm worried this might happen again if not with you, with someone else," Ethan declared, his voice rough with emotion he wanted to hide.

"*Ie,* I know son; you make a world of difference to my life. You know, you also mean the world to little Angel. Have you heard that little girl sing, Ethan?" He quickly found another topic to turn off the feelings flooding them both.

"No, I didn't know she could sing. No one has ever

mentioned anything about Angel other than that David goes up the mountain with her. I think they are best friends." Ethan stepped back, taking a breath and nodding.

"Oh Ethan, she sounds like an angel – her voice is so beautiful and so sweet. I hear her at night when she goes with Lina to Church." He turned to pick up his apron from the counter. In a few moves, he had it tied around his waist. "Lina has a good voice, too. One night, I thought it was Lina but then they sang a duet together a capella and her voice, I could have sworn it was an angel from above." Dylan was so happy about the information he gave Ethan.

"Really, I never knew. David says that Angel tries to sing but makes his ears hurt when they are up the mountain, and then he laughs like he enjoys teasing her."

"She is a little soprano, Ethan; Lina is too, but she is older now." He stepped behind the counter, picking up a towel to wipe the surface already clean enough to eat off. "She has such a beautiful voice for someone so young in these parts of the Rhondda. She comes here with Lina after Church. Her eyes twinkle when she asks for her daps with her pennies in her fist. Her smile brightens her face up. Never leaves without thanking me and giving me a little hug. Even though I am going blind those little eyes are just like the stars in the sky twinkling."

"I never noticed," Ethan felt guilty when he replied. Ethan went on to ask a few more questions. "I know she has lived with Lina a long time, but where did she come from?"

"We knew Angel's mother left her when she was a few weeks old. Her father was devastated. What was he going to do with a two-week old baby anyway? His solution was to bring her to his mother, Lina. Gilberto had no choice."

Ethan looked sad, "How awful for her father. I don't know what I would have done if my Mary had left. I can't imagine."

"I can't imagine if that had happened to me, either," Dylan replied.

"How could a woman leave her baby? Where is this woman now, where did she go?" Ethan sounded angry now.

"All I remember is that someone said her mother left the Rhondda but never turned back to see her little girl. Lina has looked after her all these years. Gilberto comes when he can, but that's only every couple of months. He can't look after her all alone. He needs a woman's help." Dylan needed to get it off his chest.

"Gilberto, that sounds familiar. Wasn't he Ernesto's son? Ernesto died, didn't he?"

"*Ie,* he did, he did that, he died lifting his pig. It was sick, you know and he couldn't leave it out in that terrible weather." Ethan wanted to laugh as he hadn't heard this story before but as Ernesto had died he didn't think he should.

Dylan continued, "Lina had another son, Haro. He contracted polio from swimming in the reservoir. The sheep used to drown in it, falling off the mountain. He was a brilliant mathematician. So was Gilberto."

Ethan was trying to listen carefully to understand what Dylan was saying.

"Oh, Gilberto could sing, too. He was a tenor in the Male Voice Choir for a little while. Then Gilberto left and went to Birmingham, chasing after another dream of his.

"Then tragedy struck again, when he met Angel's mother, God knows where she came from. He was swept off his feet with her beauty and she was only sixteen."

"Well, how old was Gilberto then?"

"Oh Gilberto was about nine years older than she was. Lina was a bit concerned to hear of the age gap. Anyway, Gilberto had to get a decent job that paid a bit more than singing. He was a good mathematician you know but he was distracted by his singing career." He folded the towel and put it down on the shining surface. "What there was of that. Fortunately, he got a good job working in finance in the council house. Then they went away." Dylan shook his head, lost for a time in his memory, but really immersed in Lina's tragic life.

"Lina has had hard times in her life. When Haro wanted to go to University, and by Jove he was intelligent, Lina carried him to the University in Cardiff. I mean really carried him, when she got off the train. There was only one bus a day, and that ran in the morning, she missed it. She knew he was better than the valleys so she got off the train and walked from the station with Haro on her shoulders. But the University wouldn't accept him because he was a cripple."

Dylan was so upset he almost cried, his memories were great but he wanted to tell Ethan so he understood the hardship of life in the town.

"Then Lina married *that* Edwin. That's why they lived in the railway house down the hill from you. Edwin was a very abusive man but he did provide a house through his job on the railway. Can you imagine the life Lina had when he was alive and her looking after her boys as well as putting up with *that* Edwin? I often wondered where he came from but no one knew. Then Angel came along when she was a couple of weeks old. Life wasn't too good for Lina or Angel then." He moved away from the counter, bringing Ethan along with him. "Angel is growing up just like Lina, sweet and innocent."

Ethan followed his Uncle, wanting to share a bit that he knew with Dylan.

"Lina helps Mary, you know. She comes every day to see her and has encouraged her with sewing, cooking, and now she is growing some vegetables in pots, truly amazing woman."

"Lina is very kind hearted and will definitely help if she can, long before anyone could notice you needed help," Dylan added, his gaze still looking into the past, remembering all the times Lina was there.

"I remember when Angel had chickenpox. It was time for Gilberto to visit and *that* Edwin muttered something in the street about that but the neighbors didn't hear exactly what he said. Lina put Angel to bed in the back room downstairs and Lina slept at the foot of Angel's bed so that Gilberto would have Angel's room, clear of any sickness. That meant Lina was with Angel not Edwin.

"I remember once she told us when Gilberto came home, Edwin claimed that Angel was scratching because she was too hot with such long hair. Oh my God, Angel screamed as Gilberto cut her hair short." Dylan clasped his hands and rocked in his chair.

"*That* Edwin was not happy. He thought Lina spent too much time caring for Angel. Lina tried to stop Gilberto, as Angel looked so pretty with long hair." He paused and shrugged, the time past and today was another day. "'Course Edwin didn't like a fuss disturbing his life, but he seemed to be enjoying it this time. I expect it was because Angel was so upset. I think Gilberto was trying in his way to help his mother, with shorter hair Lina wouldn't have so much trouble brushing tangles from Angel's hair. Oh that satisfied *that* Edwin alright." Dylan showed his anger.

"Lina is a good woman, what talents she has she will pass on to Mary and I hope that Angel will have a chance to learn all her talents before her father takes her away."

"What do you mean, her father takes her away?" Ethan was concerned.

"Lina has that look like my Olga had before she got really sick. I don't think she is well but she would never tell anyone. She keeps things to herself and never says anything. She never told us how Edwin treated her. It was Mrs. Probert that told us." Dylan leaned closer, lowering his voice. "She could hear through the walls." He straightened. "Thank God, *that* man finally died after his heart attack. You know, Gilberto didn't like him either. I am sure he had good reason not to." Dylan shook his grey head, sorrow painted shadows on his features.

"What do you mean Lina has that look?" Ethan raised his voice to get Dylan's attention.

"She's looking washed out, tired, and she's getting thinner," Dylan answered.

"So you think because Lina might be sick, Gilberto will come and take Angel away. Where to?" Ethan was more than curious.

"No, I don't think he will just take Angel. He loves his mother. He has always tried to provide for her, even being away. I am sure he will want to provide a better home for Lina near her sister, Mari. Mari lives in Birmingham. Angel would have to go with Lina. That's what I meant about Gilberto taking Angel from here."

Conversation for the rest of the evening between Ethan and Dylan was limited then, both were thinking deeply.

Ethan helped Dylan with the spuds and said to Dylan it was late and he needed to go back home.

"Nos da, Ethan."

"Nos da," Ethan replied and went back home. His heart was heavy and he found it very difficult that night to tell Mary about Lina. Also, he was thinking if Lina left that meant Angel would have to leave, too. He knew that Mary would be saddened to think she would lose her friend and the only woman in the world that cared about her and all her family. Also, David would lose his best friend, Angel.

Thoughts of his grandfather didn't fill his mind that night but Ethan tossed and turned thinking about Lina, and he could have sworn he heard singing.

Mary told Lina in the morning that Ethan was dreaming out loud about an Angel singing.

Lina laughed and said, "I don't think so Mary, Ethan may have heard about Angel singing in Church." They had things to make, so stopped talking about Ethan's dream and got to work.

Chapter 7

It was Wednesday. Lina said she needed to leave a little earlier from Mary's house and go home to get supper ready before Angel got home from school. It was Church night and she didn't want to be late. They attended St. Paul's Church up the street from Taffs.

That evening, Ethan stayed at Taffs a little longer than normal, cutting spuds and making the batter, helping Dylan. They chatted while they were working. It was going to be busy with everyone coming for their dinner after Church. As time passed, they heard the singing start. Dylan shouted to Ethan.

"Stop that banging and come here, son." He shifted his weight from foot to foot, waiting on Ethan. He pulled him closer to the door holding it open.

"Listen Ethan, listen to her singing." Ethan stepped out to hear the sweet sounds of Lina and Angel. It was very heartwarming to him. He shook out a Woodbine and lit it. He stood on the doorstep looking up at the dark mountain, his mind wandered and wandered. Dylan shouted, "Ethan, are you still there?"

"Yes, Uncle just having a fag and listening to the singing." When he finished his cigarette he went in to Dylan. "Oh my God, if I didn't know any better I would have said yes, Angels are singing up there."

"What did I tell you, Ethan? Lina and Angel will be down soon, coming to pick up a dap or two and maybe a cod's roe for Angel.

"I believe Lina is hurting from old wounds as well. It must be so difficult for her to forget the past even though she married *that* Edwin with all his faults and anger. There is something strong, and fragile at the same time, about Lina. I am sure Lina is grateful to have Mary's friendship too, you know. She connects with Mary and that is good."

The basic connection to someone who smiled when they met, and hugged when they left and that someone made her happy once again. Ethan got busy with the many tasks Dylan needed done. They spoke on and off while time passed. Both of them stood by the register, counting coins and borrowing change from their pockets to fill the till.

"Her heart is still broken even after all these years. *That* Edwin did nothing to help Lina heal, only added more heartache to her already troubled life. She didn't look for love after Ernesto passed away; she was trying to survive. Edwin finally got his claws into her and she relented to marry the bugger." Dylan was not only upset, he was angry at the very thought of Edwin.

Ethan listened carefully to what Dylan was saying and asked more questions about Lina. "What do you mean get his claws into her?"

"He was not a nice man – I could see through him after Olga told me to observe him when he came into the chippie. He broke her down to marry him by providing that house on John Street. None of us ever found out if he had a family somewhere, but he was a mean man. Now she is alone again but *that* Edwin can't bother her anymore."

"I'll wait and perhaps walk home with them, as I live on the corner; no point in them walking alone in the dark, especially as there are some culprits around."

"Good idea, Ethan." Dylan smiled at him, nodding and satisfied of their safety.

Ethan looked up and sure enough there stood Angel and Lina.

Angel asked for her penny dap. "Mr. Dylan, may I please have a penny dap? Here's my penny." Her eyes twinkled as she handed the penny to Dylan.

Lina quickly added, "And, a cod's roe, please?" She handed Dylan a sixpence.

Ethan watched as Angel stood at the side of the counter waiting for Dylan. She held out her arms and hugged his hips with a loving smile.

"Goodnight Mr. Dylan, God Bless," and out the door she went waiting for Lina to say goodnight.

"Uncle, I'll see you tomorrow, lock the door behind me and I will walk home with Lina and Angel." He'd made sure the chippie was clean and swept for the evening.

"Alright then Ethan, *Nos da*," Dylan replied. He locked the door behind them, taking no chances with his safety. He turned off the light, checking to make sure the fat was cooling. He fixed a cuppa and carried it to his favorite chair. The fire was warm and the night busy, he began nodding off. A chill woke him with a shiver and he pulled down a blanket to cover his shoulders. Lina made it in his favorite colors, dark green with specks of white. It made him think of the sheep on the mountain. The black mixed in reminded him of the black coal that sustained the town in better days. He sighed and gave in to sleep.

Ethan and Lina walked together. It was quiet and very dark, almost as though the stars had hidden themselves behind the chimney pots. The hour was later than usual for their walk home. Lina had stayed behind at the Church a little longer than normal. She and Angel rushed down to Dylan's before he closed.

"Oh Ethan, that's very kind of you to walk us home," Lina said. Angel was skipping ahead, but even her normal joyfulness dimmed in the dark. She'd sang her heart out after a full day at school. Lina was proud of Angel.

"I'm happy to walk with you Lina. In fact, it's not far from my own house." He pointed to his door then passed it with his charges. Ethan walked them to their door and waited for Lina to open it and light the candle sitting on the table before saying anything.

"Goodnight Lina, see you tomorrow. Don't forget to lock the door."

"Goodnight Ethan, God Bless you for walking us home. We enjoyed your company and I feel safer with a big man close by." She closed the door with a smile and nod to him.

He listened as she locked the door. Turning to walk up the street, he thought how things changed so quickly.

No one used to lock their doors, but since the robbery and Dylan's attack it was better to be safe than sorry. People did as a precaution now. Just never knowing if something else like this could happen again, and people feared they might be lurking around waiting for another opportunity to strike. If they were lucky those three had gone up the Valley.

A few days later word got around that one of the three turned himself in up the valley at Ferndale police station. *The South Wales Echo* heard the news and a reporter interviewed the Chief of Police to find out more about the culprit.

Everyone was talking about it in town. The news traveled fast as more people heard about it. Bobbie Matthews couldn't make his rounds for being stopped so many times.

"Is it true what the paper said?"

"Have the police found the other two robbers?"

"What will happen to the one who confessed?"

Bobbie Matthews answered all the questions he could. He was exhausted when he reported back to the station. He sat down on the bench with a deep sigh.

"Matthews, what is troubling you now?"

"Chief, you wouldn't believe it. Everyone wants to know what happens next with these buggers."

Chief Tom smiled. "Hopefully the others will cross our path again and we'll get them." He was ready to head home himself. "Until then, keep trying to answer the curiosity of the public. You've done a good job so far." He walked to the door, patting the exhausted Bobbie's shoulder. "Keep it up and get some rest."

Matthews nodded. He'd be walking home on sore legs. That was for sure.

The story didn't change even as more people talked about it. The details remained the same.

Apparently, the burglar that turned himself in was the youngest boy out of the three and lived with his grandfather. It hurt him so deeply to think that someone could actually do that to a man his grandfather's age that he gave himself up.

He obviously wasn't like the other two. He had principles by which he lived, to some extent. He explained that he met them in a Pub in Birmingham, after an Aston Villa game.

As for the other two – making them feel guilty didn't happen because they were too involved taking what didn't belong to them.

The next day when Ethan visited Dylan he expected to learn more about his grandfather but he was surprised that Dylan didn't mention anything about Cradoc. As soon as Ethan arrived Dylan was anxious, "Let me tell you about Lina, Ethan, so you understand."

"She was one of eight children. Her family lived in Ynyshir you know, just up the Valley." He pointed as if they could see the distance. "They had a two up and two down house like those down John Street but the houses looked a bit taller and each had a basement under the pavement. They were fortunate to have a toilet, not many houses had one back then." He shook his head with a shiver.

"The toilet was outside and quite often when it was so cold it would freeze and even the door would stick, and you had a hard time trying to open it. Once it was open you couldn't shut it so if you wanted to use the toilet you would be exposed to everyone who went out back! I expect after a while it didn't matter. But it would be so cold if you couldn't close the door in winter.

"Right from the beginning Lina was different. She was sweet, kind, a little on the shy side, slim and so beautiful with her dark olive skin. In fact, I see where Angel gets her looks from, and that would be her grandmother, Lina. Oh my God, all the time people would say to Lina's parents, "You'll have to hang on to that girl. She is too pretty for these parts."

Her mother would just smile but her father was never pleased that people would make a comment about her and he always said, "Uh, they think I don't know how to bring up a girl!" He always had a negative assumption about things, especially Lina. It didn't matter really because she was so much like her mother and nothing like him, so patient and with a good spirit.

"Lina had two sisters, Mari and Ivy, and five brothers, William, Thomas, Arthur, Samuel, and Trevour who ended up dying in Africa. He was a missionary, Trevour was." Dylan nodded.

"Lina lived with her parents until she was twenty-two years old, very unusual in these parts. Girls married quite young, before they were twenty anyway. Lina learned everything she could from her Mam on how to be a good wife and a wonderful mother because she wanted to be a mother one day. In fact, she wanted to practice her talents on her relatives and close neighbors. Of course, some of them took advantage as if she was "a cook and bottle washer" cleaning up their messes. She never complained. She did what she had to do to give a little money to her Mam for her keep.

"She loved to cook. It didn't matter what it was, she would find a way of cooking it with flare. That was never seen in these parts before; she cooked little or plenty, whatever she could get." He paused for a breath, remembering in silence for a moment. "She learned how to sew, too and she made her own clothes and a few things for her Mam when she wasn't working." He fell silent for a moment, not long enough to strain Ethan's patience.

"Something interesting, her father was a tailor and had his work in the front room of his house. Along with learning to sew, Lina learned to make hats, millinery. It seems she fell into the trade that matched her name when she married Ernesto. Ernesto Cappellaio. Cappellaio, it means hat maker, you know. That's why they changed it to Milliner so there wouldn't be any comments about the name Cappellaio." He nodded and smiled at the coincidence.

"When Lina was at Church, and that was every Sunday and sometimes during the week, whenever her Mam went, she would be right there at her side. Lina observed every woman's hat and their girls' if they wore any hats. It was unbelievable. She got her bits and pieces and sewed them together by hand creating very flattering hats out of almost nothing for her Mam and herself. I remember well, when she stopped by the co-operative store I saw one of her hats.

"I was in there buying a packet of papers to roll some fags. We rolled our own in those days and the way was easy, so easy. I could never understand why people would want to buy them ready made at twice the cost." He lifted his hands, showing Ethan how it was done.

"I dipped my thumb and first finger in the bag of 'bacco' and just pulled out about two teaspoons to roll the fag. I used to rub the strands and smell the rose, then placed it along the long side edge of the paper, rolled it up and then licked down the other side of the paper to seal it over." He dropped his hands, smiling at Ethan. "I got good at it too 'cause I had plenty of practice – I think that's how I started smoking in the first place, making fags for my brothers and friends." He waved his hand at Ethan, dismissively. "You don't make them, Ethan, you buy them already made, those Woodbines you smoke, I mean." He pointed at Ethan's pocket where his current pack rested.

"What were you going to tell me about Lina, Uncle?" Ethan wanted to know more about Lina, not about making fags.

"Oh yes, Lina. Bless her. She stayed with her Mam and Dad until she got pregnant."

"You mean Lina wasn't married when she got pregnant!"

"No Ethan, let me finish. Lina got married secretly a year before. No one knew except for Mari and Ivy her sisters, and they definitely wouldn't tell their parents so Lina's secret was safe with them. I think her Mam would have accepted it but her Dad, oh no! He definitely wouldn't be too happy. It was as though he waited for something he could criticize about Lina. He couldn't find anything else and this would have been it. She was the model child of the family. She lived by the Word of God in all things and that frustrated him to no end 'cause he was not a Godly man but swore and complained all the time. He claimed he was so devout and expressed this outwardly to anyone that would listen. Others knew the truth. Lina was a sweet girl just like her Mam."

"Well, what happened to her when they found out she was pregnant?" Ethan was in a hurry to learn more.

"Oh yes. Her Mam said thank God you can get out of here now!" Lina's Mam said it as she meant it. It was hard for Lina to live in that house with that man, even though he was supposed to be her father.

"I always had my doubts whether he was really Lina's father or not but I couldn't say anything. Lina had olive skin and chestnut colored eyes like no one else in the family. Maybe her father also thought that." Dylan paused, lost to his memories for a while. "I am not saying that her Mam did anything wrong at all but she cared and looked after someone else's baby as her own. When Lina's Mam was near the end of her pregnancy there were complications with the baby and she was admitted into hospital but the baby died at birth. Another lady in the same hospital ward was dying from malnutrition and had no relatives to take care of her baby. Lina's Mam agreed to be her sole next of kin and take care of her baby as her own. The lady died not long after giving birth to Lina. Thank God Lina's father never knew. He definitely wouldn't have wanted some other woman's baby in his home, but he always suspected there was something different about Lina." Dylan took a deep breath before continuing his memories.

"Lina married Ernesto in secret, not to upset that father of hers. Ernesto was a real nice hard working young lad about the same age as Lina. They were so much in love." He clasped his hands to his chest, shaking his head as he remembered.

"Ernesto lived with his parents on a little farm not far from Lina's parents, on the green land at the other side of the mountain. Ernesto's parents were very old. They had him late in life when they thought they would never have another child. Ernesto did all he could to help on their farm. He definitely was a good-hearted lad and loved his parents very much. I think he felt some sense of obligation for them bringing him up but the love was definitely in his heart for them.

"When Lina left her parents' house she went to live with Ernesto's family on the farm. Sweet Lina cared for his parents till the day they died. She cooked, cleaned, and took care of all their needs as well as she could. Lina was so much in love with Ernesto, so she would have done anything for him and you bet Ernesto loved Lina, too." Dylan nodded his grey head in emphasis, and pointed his finger at Ethan.

"They had two children, Gilberto and Haro. I think I told you; Haro contracted polio later on when he was about 7 or 8 years old from swimming in the reservoir.

"Lina worked hard at her pastime making hats. Funny really, she used old sacks as the backing to make the skull cap and then cut up old clothing to cover the skull cap."

"What's a skull cap?" Ethan enquired.

"Oh yes, you probably don't know. A skull cap is the part of the cap that fits snug on the skull, much like the woolly hats that Mary made for you when you went down the mine, except these were made from old sack cloth that had been starched in flour water," Dylan answered and then got back to his story about Lina.

"When Lina could, and Ernesto needed supplies, she would go down the town and sell her hats while Jones filled up their cart with supplies. Jones kept the hardware store. She could get groceries there.

"She also took a shovel with her to scoop up the horse's manure and bring it back so she could use it for her roses and vegetables. Why waste it, if she could use it? She was a wonderful housewife and mother, very frugal and so very kind and loving." He walked into the kitchen, leaving Ethan by the fireplace. "I need a cuppa before we start today." He bustled about, clanging the pot and clattering the cups before joining Ethan.

"No one ever saw anything like Lina's hats. They were so different and definitely attracted attention." Lost in thought for a time, Dylan searched his mind for more to pass along.

"*The South Wales Echo*" was in town one time she was down there and a newspaper photographer took a picture of Lina and her hat and sent it to the famous London Milliners, a big hat company in London. A few months later there was a letter sent to Lina." He smiled widely, remembering. "Everyone in the town knew about the letter. It had the seal of the Crown."

"What crown?" Ethan chimed in.

"The Crown, you know the King or a Queen's crown?" Dylan repeated himself, as if Ethan were six years old.

"Where was the crown?"

"On the envelope, it had some sealing wax on the back."

"What's sealing wax?"

Dylan shook his head and smiled. Oh the things these youngsters don't know.

"It's wax that dignitaries like the Mayor or Prime Minister uses to seal a document, but in this case it had the crown pressed into it so it had to be a King or a Queen's seal, don't you think?"

Ethan shrugged his shoulders to indicate he didn't know.

"Well, anyway, the letter was hand written in a very flourishing style. I think schools call it 'old Elizabethan handwriting'.

Her Royal Highness, Queen Elizabeth, the Queen's Mother requests the pleasure of your company at Buckingham Palace. The note at the bottom stated. *Letter will follow this announcement.*

"Everyone in town was talking about Lina, even as far as Pontypridd and Cardiff. Every time they saw Lina or Ernesto, questions would be asked about the letter she received. Poor Lina, she was so embarrassed and definitely didn't like any limelight of that nature. She would rather go home and cook and clean than answer any more questions." He paused to pour the tea, bringing Ethan a cup and settling down with his in hand.

"Finally, after many months of arranging, Lina got to go to Buckingham Palace. Ernesto took her by horse and cart to the station and she took a train from Porth to Victoria, changing trains in Bristol. It's a very long journey." He nodded, adding the extra explanation.

"When she arrived she had no idea where to go. There she was, left on the platform at the station by herself dressed up as well as she could. She even borrowed her Mam's old shoes because they had a fashionable heel and laces. Ernesto polished them enough he could see his face in them!

"Lina was terrified. She was already tired from the journey. She had a couple of the hats she made in her portmanteau. She was standing under the huge clock as instructed in one of the letters, when the hands struck twelve o'clock. It scared her even more and she remembered dropping her portmanteau and crouching down. A man in a black uniform with a cap and a lady dressed in a very, very expensive coat with a fur collar, gloves, and a hat with a feather on one side, like a partridge feather, walked towards her. The man in uniform gave her his hand and gently pulled her up from the ground and then retrieved her portmanteau.

"Ernesto was telling me all this at the Co-op one day when I went to get some Gorgonzola cheese. There was so much he wanted to tell me. We were there for hours. He was full of the news of her travels and was so proud of her.

"He said Lina was very frightened until they introduced themselves and said they were sent by the Queen to meet her and showed her identification.

"When Lina recovered, as she was obviously in shock, they assisted her through the station and into the back seat of a huge black car that was waiting. Lina told Ernesto later they offered her a cup of tea. They handed her a bone china cup on a scalloped saucer with two sugar cubes on the saucer." Dylan turned up two fingers showing Ethan. "She was asked if she wanted some milk to go into the teacup." He nodded, obviously happy with the memories. "It was so good to hear that Lina was treated with such respect coming from the Rhondda.

"Anyway, as they drove away from the Station, Lina felt herself slipping on the seat and the cup fell over; fortunately, she had already drunk the tea. The seat was a deep Oxford brown colored leather and highly polished. As they turned a corner Lina told us she slid from one side of the back seat to the other. She remembered letting out a little giggle after a while, as she had never sat in a car, or on a slippery seat.

"Off to the Palace in a big black car was so exciting to Lina. As if she imagined she was Cinderella going to meet her prince! She said she stopped breathing as they drove through the gates of the Palace. The gates were tall and wide black iron with a big gold crest. There were guards dressed in red jackets and black trousers with tall fluffy hats. She said they acted like toy soldiers marching with guns. They walked in rhythm, clicking their feet on the ground, and then turning to meet each other clicking their feet again.

"As Lina looked up at the Palace it was so huge and majestic she gasped for breath. None of us would ever see anything like that in our Rhondda Valleys. She said she had to pinch herself again and again to make sure she wasn't dreaming it all. She said they drove into a courtyard and…" Then Dylan stopped to take a breath glancing up at Ethan.

"Of course, Ethan I wouldn't be telling you all this if Ernesto wasn't so excited about it all."

Dylan was fidgeting and looked as if he had something to do in a hurry.

"I need to finish before I forget the details, son."

Ethan nodded, seeing how caught up Dylan was in his memories of the time. He kept trying to see Lina as a young woman, on her first big adventure.

"Lina said the car stopped in the courtyard of the Palace. There were people standing on a huge doorstep in front of a large entranceway just beneath a huge archway, all dressed in black, some with white aprons and small white hats and the others in uniforms. One of them came to the side of the car, opened the door, rolled down the step, and offered Lina a hand to help her out of the car."

"She had an audience with the queen's mother. They spoke about many things, but she wanted to hire Lina to make hats for the royal family. She came back with bundles of left over fabrics from the suits already sewn by their tailors.

"Ernesto was always there to greet her and take her home after these trips to London. Every time she came home with these fabrics, beautiful taffetas, brocades, and satins. So beautiful for her to work with." Dylan sighed at the memories. "I know it's a lot to hear, but bear with me. This is important."

"The last time Lina went back to Buckingham Palace there was a terrible storm up the Rhondda. Ernesto's little farm suffered terribly with other bad storms but this one almost took his livestock. Ernesto rushed out before the worst of the storm and made sure his cows were in the barn with his chickens, but he went back out to get his pig. His pig had been sick and didn't have energy to feed itself or stand. Ernesto, being the man he was, picked up the pig, and carried her into his little house and to the kitchen.

"Ernesto was not a strong man but he had a heart of gold. He loved his animals and couldn't let any one of them be in harm. To Ernesto's detriment he died from a heart attack carrying his sow.

"When Lina returned from London, Ernesto was not at the station. Ernesto was always waiting for Lina after every visit she made. That he was not there for her after this trip was not typical. The porter at the station shut up shop and noticed that Lina was still there, waiting.

"This was so unusual he offered Lina a ride back to their farm. The Porter had a bike on which Lina sat on the crossbar. Wynn the Porter rode her to the lane to their farm, but did not want to leave Lina at the bottom. He rode her up to the little home and shouted for Ernesto. Wynn helped Lina off the bike and entered the house first, followed by Lina.

"Wynn saw Ernesto lying beside his pig and he knew both of them were dead. Lina was right behind him and saw both sprawled in front of the kitchen fire. She knew at a glance that they were dead. She screamed, ran to Ernesto's body, and laid on top of him trying her hardest to bring him to life. In that moment she realized she had lost the love of her life and her life would completely change forever without him. She vowed she would never go back. But it was too late, you see. Too late for them." Sadness filled Dylan's voice and he wiped a tear for the pure love story he recited. Dylan sniffed.

Ethan knew he was done for a while. They sat in silence, finishing their tea until time forced them to begin preparations.

With Ethan busy in the chippie, Dylan wiped the counter. He did that when he had a lot of thinking to do. Cleaning was mindless and his thoughts could wander. He was certain Ethan needed to go up Penrhiwgwynt, but how was he going to convince Ethan that the journey up would be rewarding beyond measure? Ethan needed to start now, not wait any longer. He straightened the already straight stack of papers, still working out the problem of how to influence Ethan.

What he told Ethan of Lina was to show him that life in the valley was not only hard work, but was miserable and lonely for some. Time was passing, all he was doing was giving an old man company, not that Dylan was ungrateful; but he also wanted to impart his history and give Ethan the life he so much deserved. Just like Lina. She had the opportunity to make a better life for herself when she married Ernesto but life took a bad turn when Ernesto passed away. Who would imagine that Ernesto would die so young? That changed the course of Lina's life. Maybe not the best life then, but now she had her granddaughter Angel and that couldn't be all bad.

Ethan reflected on everything Dylan told him while he caught up the work. The fat was hot, the batter mixed, and he did it without consciously thinking about it. Instead, Lina's early life and Ernesto's tragic end were on his mind. Things were good for her now, she seemed happy. But what was the point of Dylan's long story? It had to have something to do with Ethan's life.

Little by little, Dylan had been giving him hints about his family and the life they lived on the mountain. Ethan remembered little, but what he did remember was mostly happy. Mary and Lina both believed he should head up to explore. Maybe before his time ran out, thinking of Lina, he should make the trip.

Chapter 8

Lina was back to Mary and Ethan's in the morning with Angel. It was Saturday and it was a big day for the men with the Rugby game. Who was going to win was the topic of conversation.

David and Angel wanted to go up the mountain earlier than normal; maybe they would have more time to find Buttercup. Lina looked a little concerned, as a lot of people would be in the town because of the game. Ethan suggested to Ian that he join David and Angel.

"What, again?" Ian questioned in disbelief. Did they seriously expect him to babysit the kids again?

Ethan gave Ian a sharp look, his eyebrows meeting in the middle of his brow, and curled up his mouth. Ian immediately got his coat and satchel without a word and was at the door waiting on the younger ones to get ready.

Ethan said that he would go to Dylan's just to check on things. Mary knew it wasn't just to check on things but was hoping he was searching for information on his grandfather.

"I'll see you later, ladies." Ethan left them and headed to Taff's. He knocked on the door and thumbed the handle, pushing it open.

"Uncle Dylan, I came early to talk with you," he called out.

"That's good, son. What's on your mind?" Dylan stepped out of the parlor to greet him. He waited while Ethan hung up his jacket.

"I know these last couple of weeks you have been recovering from the attack and got carried away with Lina and Angel." He lifted his hands and shook his head. "Not that they aren't important, but I need to know more about my grandfather."

"I'm glad you're asking about my brother. Yes, we did get a bit off the subject, but that's alright. Lina and Angel are important, too. Where were we?"

"Well, you were telling me about being married to Olga, Clarenda's sister. My great aunt, I mean."

"That's right, I remember now. You see, when Cradoc was killed, Clarinda couldn't manage the farm even with Olga and me up there to help. It was really too much for her and having the babies to take care of, too. We did what we could but she was broken hearted all the time. She wanted to provide for your father and his brother but every day was lonely for her. She would go into her room and cry herself to sleep. We often heard her but there was no solace for her pain."

"What? With you and Olga up there, too?"

"It was lonely for her. She would go to bed alone after saying goodnight to the babies and us. In the morning, she would get up alone. Life was harder than ever for Clarinda. She hadn't long given birth and she was already a widow. She was worn out. When Cradoc died she was heavily pregnant with your father's brother and suddenly being alone, a mother and a farm owner with horses too, that would have been too much for any good man alone."

"Did you say that Clarinda was heavily pregnant with my father's brother when Cradoc died?" Ethan asked.

"Yes Ethan. The death of Cradoc brought her into early labor but the baby died. I was about twenty-seven then. Cradoc was three years older than I was, so that would make Cradoc about thirty. He might have been a bit older but I would say about thirty or thirty-one."

"I found Clarenda one day in the paddock, sobbing. I often saw her kneeling down, shouting at God for such a life he had given her. When she was alone, and I mean alone, she would cry out, "Where are you, I need you? You took

Cradoc; why didn't you take me instead? Why don't you give me an answer? How am I going to carry on?" He shook his head, seeing her in his mind's eye as she pounded her fist into the earth, her voice a hoarse cry to the heavens that never gave her an answer.

"Clarinda had stopped eating. She wasn't interested in anything except going to the paddock and talking to God or going to her room and crying herself to sleep.

"One day she just gave up." Dylan shook his head.

"What do you mean gave up? What happened; what did she do?" Ethan moved to the edge of his seat. Dylan's tone warned him in advance.

"She didn't do anything, really. She just kissed the babies when she put them in bed and said goodnight. Then she went to bed herself and never woke up."

"Oh my God. She died?" Ethan asked in surprise.

"Yes Ethan, your grandmother died from a broken heart. She loved your grandfather so much. Life wasn't worth living without him, even with two babies."

"What happened to the babies, the horses, and the farm?" Ethan held up his hands, encompassing the entirety of the question.

"We buried Clarenda next to Cradoc. Olga was heartbroken, too. She had lost her only sister. Clarenda was like a mother as well as a sister to Olga.

"Olga and I took your father and his brother and came down here, moving into Porth. We have not been up the mountain back to the farm. We looked after your father and his brother like our own."

"What happened to the horses and the farm?" Ethan questioned, his voice softer now and as sad as Dylan's. He had an epiphany. Dylan had been steadily telling Ethan the history of his heritage on the mountain. *This* was where Dylan wanted Ethan to go. He rejoined Dylan's conversation. He had more to think of and less time to consider what he wanted to do.

"We gave the horses back to the mountain, and the sheep. They returned to Penrhiwgwynt. They came from her so we gave them back to her – they ran free again. Free as the birds up in the sky, Ethan."

Ethan covered his face. Dylan patted his hand on Ethan's shoulder.

"Ethan, it's going to be alright, son." He patted the air between them with a smile. "Your granddad, Cradoc and your grandmother, Clarinda are with God. He created them as he created you and me. They lived by the Word of God. Times were extremely hard in those days. Maybe God took them early for a reason, son. Now they are resting with Him and waiting for someone to take their fertile land and make it useful once more."

It was hard for Ethan not to break down; he had to make himself aware he was a man talking with Dylan and not a boy alone at home in his bedroom, where he did a lot of soul searching when he was younger. Evidently a habit he carried into manhood if the last few weeks were any indication.

"So all those things David and Angel brought down time and time again…" Ethan swallowed hard, his throat clicking with the effort. "I've been thinking they were a load of old rubbish and all this time, in actual fact they were my grandfather's and grandmother's possessions."

"Yes, Ethan. They belonged to Cradoc and Clarinda."

Ethan and Dylan were silent for a while then Dylan started the next chapter.

"Ethan, find it in your heart to go up Penrhiwgwynt soon and see where you're really from. You used to play up there when you were young and went with your Mam and your cousins. Your family is buried up there, side by side on their farmland."

Ethan's mind raced with so many more questions but he just couldn't get the words out. Huffing a hard breath, he cried out, "Why didn't my father mention anything about my grandparents, their land or the mountain, when he was alive?

Even my Mam never said anything when she took me up to play. My Mam wouldn't even talk about my father, she just kept crying all those years if anyone mentioned his name or tried to ask about him. Most of my friends knew about their fathers but I could only assume there was a terrible secret."

"The only thing I can think of why your father never mentioned it was because his parents died up there, and he was taken as a young lad from the mountain to live in the valley." Dylan continued to explain that it didn't matter how much they showed him love. It must have hurt him very much to think he lost both parents and the sad circumstances under which they died.

Ethan's father, Thomas, just couldn't visit Penrhiwgwynt. He couldn't face the past or even think of a future up the mountain. Dylan and Olga tried to interest Thomas, without any results.

His mind focused on mining deep underground, not the green mountains high above the Rhondda. Dylan explained that Ethan's father chose to go down the pit, although they tried to stop him. He was under the impression that coal would be worth as much as gold one day with all the mines in the Rhondda, and that was why like so many he called it 'black gold.'

The Rhondda was rich with a natural resource to heat homes, cook food, and create industry. An additional incentive was that if someone worked down the pit for 20 years plus, then they would be rewarded with coal for the rest of their life as long as the coalmine didn't run out. There was no pension or retirement from the collieries in those days.

Thomas was one of those who died down the pit like so many other young men; he never had a chance. The accident that took his life was unavoidable because safety precautions weren't considered too important back then. It was estimated that the pit took a life every six hours and so it did, sometimes more.

"Ethan, you decided to go down the pit with your brothers. I know it was difficult, but all you lads did help your Mam. Thank God they closed the mine so now you are here, alive, with a family of your own and an opportunity to make a future. A better future than your father ever had."

Dylan continued that Thomas could well have overcome much of his sadness if only he had taken those first steps and retrieved a future that he so well deserved; he loved animals and he loved the outdoors.

When Thomas was a lad, Dylan and Olga tried to encourage him to see the outdoors; Sundays was Church, and then the rest of the day was family time. After Church and weather permitting, lunch would be a picnic. They spent time walking through the milkman's farm pointing out all the animals and playing in the hayloft. But, as soon as they got to the bottom of Penrhiwgwynt, Thomas froze. He'd look up and then run away. Dylan and Olga never found out what it was that scared him so much about the mountain.

"Sometimes," Dylan explained, "we kicked a football in the school playground to encourage Thomas or go to rugby games, and other times the family would visit Cardiff castle. We thought at one time, he might want to play rugby himself. Growing up in the Rhondda there weren't many opportunities so when there was a call for hiring in the mines, everyone rushed to grab the jobs in the pits. He would not accept the idea that there could be a very good reason for him visiting Penrhiwgwynt.

"You were very fortunate. All your memories as a lad of the mountain and playing in the fields were with your mother and your brothers. Your father would never go with us. Now it is your chance to make a better life for yourself. Consider it, Ethan. It's waiting for you."

Ethan got up and paced off the overwhelming emotions of everything he'd been told this morning. He needed a physical outlet. After a few minutes, he turned to Dylan.

"The problem is I know nothing about outdoors, the wilderness, horses or even flowers. It's good to see Mary wanting to grow vegetables and some flowers in pots but that would be a big life changing decision to start a farm. I don't know if I could do it." He shook his head, eyes down with his difficult admission.

"Of course you can, Ethan. Just map it out in your head, it will all work out. Go up with David and Angel. Just see for yourself what makes them so happy. You went up once. It will all come back to you."

"How do you know that? It's been so long. I've been down the pit for two decades. I had a family to take care of."

"Ethan you are doing nothing now other than keeping an old man happy with your visits. You must find a life for yourself. Mine is almost over."

"Don't say that, Uncle, please don't. I enjoy visiting you and I enjoy helping you when you let me. Peeling a few spuds is nothing. I need more to do to help you."

"Now, now Ethan; it's alright."

"Uncle Dylan, I will come again tomorrow."

"Alright, Son. I'll look forward to your visit." He walked Ethan to the door and leaned against it after Ethan walked out. It was a lot to tell the boy, but he needed to know. Dylan understood he wasn't going to be here much longer. He wanted to see Ethan settled and happy for the first time in his life.

During the day, Chief Tom visited Taff's. "*Bora da*, Davydd Dylan."

"*Bora da*, Thomas. What are you doing over this part of Porth? A bit of a walk from your station in that rain, isn't it?" Dylan was just giving a polite comment as he sensed something might be wrong.

"This morning I came on my bike. I can move a little faster on my bike."

"*Ìe,* you can that, that you can, that you can." Dylan often repeated his words if he found the conversation a little on the challenging side.

"Well, Mr. Taff, I thought I'd visit you and let you know we have some more information on that robbery of yours. The Bobbie, that was Bobbie Matthews that came to get the details from you on your robbery, is not on duty today. It's Bobby Terence today and he doesn't have all the information." He stopped talking for a moment. He got his notebook from his pocket.

"Well now, let's see. The one lad who gave himself up was sent back to Birmingham; their station can deal with his crime. We could only slap his hand in Porth and send him packing. They'd either have to assign Judge Llewelyn Jones to come in for one session or wait for our scheduled judge to come and that could be another three weeks.

"Cardiff station doesn't want the responsibility; his crime wasn't serious enough. And right at the moment they have other crimes to deal with. They had a jewelry robbery from that big gem store in Cardiff. Did you hear about that on the news last night?"

"No, the gossip hasn't made it to the chippie today." Dylan smiled. "So you're telling me the lad was sent back to Birmingham for them to prosecute?" Dylan shook his head. "That lad didn't seem to be offensive in any way, just got with the wrong bunch. I really hope they won't be too hard on him in Birmingham. It shows his character if he gave himself up," Dylan replied.

"Yes, I realize all that Mr. Taff. They have to concentrate on finding more details on the other two now. I heard that the robberies in Ferndale and the bar were the responsibility of those other two."

"Is that so? Chief Tom, how can I help you?"

"I was hoping you could remember something else about them. Anything that you think might help us. Ethan found you on the floor when he came that night. Could you see anything else from your position that might be a clue?"

"*Ìe*, I have, been thinking about that night a lot. I told you that they threw my till on the ground and took the money, didn't I?"

"Yes you did," Chief Tom replied. "But, is there anything else?"

Dylan could sense he was getting a little impatient. "Not that I can remember at the moment but I will give it some thought, some thought I will. I need to start my fryer and get a bit done around here before I open up."

"Well, yes. I do have many things to catch up, myself. I will go on to the Jones'. I have a bit to talk to them about. I'll be back then, Mr. Taff."

"*Ìe*, Chief Thomas, *cumbuyu* after lunchtime." Dylan invited him back.

"*Lawn*, Mr. Taff." Chief Thomas rode his bike down the road.

Dylan shook his head. The police chief held the language close. *Lawn*, Dylan thought he could just say alright, like other people.

The Jones' lived not far from Taffs. Chief Thomas rang his bike bell all the way, as if he was in pursuit of a criminal; everything and everyone either stopped or moved out of his way so he could go.

Dylan was in deep thought when Ethan arrived and Ethan was a little worried. To get Dylan's attention Ethan thought a few Welsh words would be helpful.

"*Bora da, sut mae?*" Good morning, how are you? These few words not only got Dylan's attention, they startled him to the point of saying, "*Dewdew.*" Good God. "You startled me, Ethan, everything alright?"

"Oh yes, you looked as if you were far away."

"*Ìe* was that, Ethan that I was, that I was." He nodded his head.

"I came to see if I could help you, Uncle Dylan. And, maybe talk a bit."

"*Ìe,* that would be very nice. I could do with some company." As Dylan handed the flour sack to Ethan he said, "You haven't forgotten your Welsh then?"

"No, of course not, Uncle Dylan. I grew up speaking Welsh. Mam spoke to me all the time in Welsh. I wasn't sure if she knew any English other than 'NO' and she didn't say that too often. You know in school they teach Welsh, and I've heard that they teach English now too." Ethan was pleased that he could still remember his birth language.

"Did you know that Welsh is the oldest living European language, but we are the only country that speaks it, shame that, that it is," Dylan replied. "I am able to talk in Welsh when some of the old folk come in. But, these youngsters today, it seems they don't know much Welsh and it is obvious they don't know much of English either, the way they speak!"

Ethan interrupted, "I'll go and get the eggs and milk, shall I?"

"Oh *Ìe*, Ethan. You know where they are. I was a bit late this morning to get the aluminum churn outside so the milkman could fill it up, so he left me four pints in them glass bottles." He pointed with his thumb to the pantry. Ethan was already in the pantry and Dylan called to him, "I don't like the bottles, they can break too easy." He heard the shatter of glass. Uh oh! *CRASH.* "I must have three bottles left now." He shrugged making another mental note to himself to put it out before he went to bed. Ethan must have dropped one of the bottles trying to carry too many at the same time.

"Oh God!" Ethan shouted.

"I expect you put some under your arm did you?" Dylan asked him, coming from the front.

"Well, yes I did. How did you know that?"

"I know! Most people do that. I used to when I was young until Milkman Rhys showed me. Never mind, son. Come here an' I'll show you how to carry them. Between your fingers, let me see your hands."

Ethan put out his hands in front of him after setting the remaining bottles on the shelf.

"Turn them over so the palms are up."

"Alright." Ethan followed his instructions.

"Now then, open up the first two fingers wide. Hold this bottle between them tight." He demonstrated. "No, not to make them white, relax a bit. All right then, now the next two fingers." He waited while Ethan fixed his fingers. "How do you feel?"

"A little daft at the moment, 'cause you have to show me how to carry two bottles of milk!" He fought the smile trying to take over his face. Dylan was serious and he didn't want to laugh at him.

"Don't feel daft, just 'cause an old mun shows you how you can carry six bottles of milk. As we don't have six bottles, so it has to be three. Open up those last two fingers and hold this bottle. Careful! Hold them tight." Dylan fought the smile. "Not that the blood stops flowing, Ethan."

Ethan and Dylan laughed together.

"Look I can hold three bottles in one hand." Ethan was so proud.

"*Ìe,* that you can. And, with two hands you can hold six bottles."

Ethan laughed some more. This was a fun time to be with Dylan.

"Now then, you can carry more milk bottles that way without breaking 'em!"

"I never thought at my age you would have to show me how to carry milk bottles."

Ethan and Dylan laughed more - a good laugh, though.

"Alright son, let's get the batter made."

"But, we haven't got enough milk now that I dropped a pint."

"Oh don't worry about that Ethan we can add more water."

Ethan emptied the bag of flour into the bucket. Then added the 3 pints of milk slowly and refilled a bottle with water 5 times to make 8 pints in total (a gallon). If the batter is too thick we can add more water just before we use it.

"Stir well Ethan, me lad, so we don't have lumps."

"How long do I stir it for?" Ethan asked, just like a child.

"Oh until you don't see any lumps, bubbles are alright. Now add one tablespoon of bicarbonate of soda two tablespoons of salt and one tablespoon of sugar."

"Sugar!" Ethan yelled in shock.

"Son, that's what gives the batter its good flavor."

"I wonder if my Mam added sugar."

"All good Welsh cooks add sugar and your Mam was an excellent cook."

"Uncle Dylan, I miss Mam. She knew what I was thinking before I even opened my mouth and she was a good woman."

"Yes she was, Ethan. I remember you used to daydream and she had a saying but I can't quite remember it."

"I remember. She would say, 'Dreaming again, Ethan? Nothing good will come out of dreaming unless your dreams come true.'"

"That's right she did, and you know what she meant by that?"

"Not really, Uncle Dylan."

"It makes sense to me. I think she meant dream, Ethan and make your dreams come true. Work for what you want."

"Hmm, I never thought of that."

"Your Mam was a good woman and wanted the best for you. It was her way of telling you what you should do, without exactly telling you."

"Now put the lid on the bucket to let the batter stand a bit and doesn't get dried out."

"It doesn't seem a lot of batter, only half a bucket full."

"It's alright, I don't get too many customers on Saturday morning; it's usually later, then I get a long queue that goes out the door just before the match."

"How long do we leave it stand in the bucket?"

"Let me see, what's the time now?"

"I don't know, Uncle, I don't have a watch."

Dylan pulled out his pocket watch and brought it up to his eye, blinked and stared at the watch. "It's already half past ten. I must get a move on. My first customers will be in at 11:30. Oh yes, and Mrs. Williams will come in for her mushy peas as well. Get that tin of peas down. It's up on the top shelf, will you?"

Ethan was surprised that Dylan knew exactly where everything was even with bad eyesight. "Do you have a tin opener?"

"*Ìe,* it's in the top drawer of that dresser in the hallway, it looks pretty rusty, but with a bit of fat it works good." Ethan looked into two drawers and lifted it from its spot.

"Got it. The handle is a bit tight to turn."

"Put a bit of fat on that screw, and work the handle a bit until it moves smoothly." Dylan handed Ethan a blob of fat he had on the end of his finger. "Works wonders, that fat."

Ethan did exactly as Dylan instructed and turned the handle a few times, each time easing the fat around the mechanism until it moved easily.

"Open that tin of peas, will you? And, pour the peas into the saucepan." When Ethan poured the peas into the saucepan Dylan instructed him to pour a bit of water in the tin and swish it around, then pour the contents into the peas so as not to waste the last bit of juice in the tin.

"Put the saucepan on the gas, stir well, on low heat. Add a couple of spoons of sugar as well."

Ethan was surprised to add sugar to the peas but it obviously did well, as they tasted so good.

This was Ethan's first time to help Dylan with some of the cooking. He felt good but also inquisitive enough to ask a lot of questions, some on the way he prepared the food, "Why do you add sugar?"

Dylan explained, "Oh it helps with the taste, it brings out the flavor. My Mam always did it and her mushy peas tasted so good. Now I must concentrate on getting the fish cooked. Drop some of those pieces of fish in the batter for me. Make sure they are covered completely with the batter." He paused and watched as Ethan followed his instructions.

"Now drop one or two individually in the hot fat. Careful now, don't let it splash out at you, you'll get burned." Dylan was anxious to give all the details. "You're doing it right, add some more; one at a time so they don't stick to each other. Good, that's it. That's enough for now. Shake the basket like this frequently so they get cooked all over and they don't stick to each other." He stepped up beside Ethan, showing him how to drain off the excess fat.

"What else can I do to help you, Uncle?"

"Well now, let me think." He put his hands on his hips and looked around. "We have the fish and the chips on, and the peas in the saucepan. Oh yes, get me a pack of those bags, will you? They're in the hallway, on the shelf, next to the dresser."

Ethan got the bags as instructed and opened the box carefully.

"Put the box next to the basket I drain the fish into. Just tear off the top of the box and then we can take out the bags one at a time, as we need them. Take those papers you cut last night for me, and place them just below the box, there. We are ready now."

Dylan pulled out his pocket watch again to check the time. "*Ie,* Mrs. Williams will be here any minute."

Ethan stood awkwardly beside Dylan waiting for his next instruction.

"Good morning, Mr. Dylan. I see you have a helper today." Mrs. Williams smiled at Ethan. "Oh my goodness, it's Ethan. I didn't recognize you. It's been a long time since I've seen you, Ethan. What are you up to these days since the pit closed?" Mrs. Williams was very direct and to the point with her enquiry.

"Actually, nothing yet," Ethan replied.

Dylan quickly intervened, "I got a little bit behind so Ethan is helping me this morning. I'm glad he is here." Perhaps that would delay her inquisitive questions. "Is it your usual, Mrs. Williams?"

"Yes, please Dylan, add an extra piece of fish today, will you please? My Tom is home and he likes a little bit of fish." Tom was Mrs. Williams' husband, he worked on the railway, and this must have been his day off.

"So how is Tom these days? I don't get to see him like I used to," Dylan enquired.

"Tom, he's very well, has the day off. You don't go to the pub anymore then, Dylan?"

"No, it's too cold to be out late at night at the moment. And since we had those good for nothing thieves here, I think it's safer to stay at home with all my doors locked. I never had to lock my doors before they got up to their mischief."

"They haven't found them yet then?" She pulled her purse out of her shopping bag.

"Not exactly. The young lad gave himself up but the other two are still at large."

"I hope they catch them soon."

Dylan gave Ethan the fish in one bag, the chips in another bag, and the mushy peas in a separate bag to wrap. "The vinegar is on the counter top if you want Ethan to shake some on your chips. That's three shillings this time, with the extra fish," Dylan announced.

Ethan wrapped the items up and gave them to Mrs. Williams with a big smile.

"Ethan, you haven't lost that lovely smile of yours, then. Must be off now before my fish and chips get cold." Mrs. Williams rushed through the door. Ethan stared as she left. He felt a little awkward. He wasn't used to getting compliments since he was a boy. Mrs. Williams was an older woman, about Dylan's age.

"Can you stay a bit Ethan, looks like I might have a queue out there?"

"Of course, glad to oblige."

"Good morning, Mrs. Evans. How are you today?"

"Good morning, Dylan. While you get my usual together let me tell you, the Bobbie came yesterday. He said they have been tracking those lads, you know, the thieves. They have had reports they were up in North Wales now."

"They've gone through the valleys already and moving up through North Wales then? I hope they lock them up soon. We don't want them back this way."

"I'm not sure why they haven't arrested them yet. There must be a reason. The Bobbie didn't say anymore. We'll just have to see."

"Yes, the Bobbies have their own way of dealing with robberies."

"I'll wrap them up for you, Uncle." Ethan carefully wrapped up the order for Mrs. Evans.

"Is that Ethan helping you, Dylan?" She dropped her glasses a little and peered over them stuttering out, "Oh my goodness! You look so handsome without all that coal dust all over you, Ethan. I'm glad they closed the mine, now Mary has her Ethan back in one piece."

"I'm glad to be home, too." Ethan forced a smile to his stiff lips. This was too much attention at one time.

"Helping your Uncle out are you?"

Ethan nodded his head in acknowledgement.

Next, in came Jones the barber. "Hello Dylan, I'm so busy today I need some fish and chips to keep me going. Have you got any cod's roe ready?"

"Plenty of fish and cod's roe, how much would you like?"

"Just two pieces of fish and one cod's roe, and double chips today. Then I can give Edward some. He's helping me out today, as the town market is open. There will be a lot of folk wanting their hair cut while their Mrs.' are shopping."

"That's three shillings and six pence."

"Have you got change for two half-crowns, Dylan? I don't have any change."

"You are in luck I do have change, that's one shilling and six pence change."

In the meantime, Ethan interjected, "Do you want vinegar on the chips?"

"Yes, and I'd like vinegar on the fish."

Ethan wrapped up the order carefully and sat it on the ledge just above the counter.

"Thank you, Dylan. Thank you, Ethan. You're a great help to your Uncle Dylan. Better be off now. Tatty bye."

Things quieted down and Dylan was able to breathe again at a steady pace. Ethan took the batter bucket and the baskets from the fryer to the sink behind Dylan.

"You have been a great help to me, Ethan."

Ethan spent the week working on the basement a bit more and helping Dylan in the chippie. The work kept him busy and his depression started to ease. Even Lina noticed he seemed different and more light hearted. He was still worrying about things, but not so much.

Chapter 9

It would be Saturday tomorrow and sometimes Ethan accompanied Mary down the town to the market. Mary was able to buy the leftover vegetables at half price late morning just before their cleanup for the weekend. This weekend Dylan, Ethan's oldest son was going with her. Ethan finished washing the batter bucket and dried his hands as Dylan came to his side.

"Are you doing anything tomorrow with Mary?"

"No, nothing in the morning. She's going shopping with young Dylan. Do you need some help, Uncle?"

"That I could do with. A spot of help tomorrow would be really good. Saturday early evenings are busy and I could do with help to be prepared. If you wouldn't mind helping your old Uncle one more day?" At Ethan's smile and nod, Dylan gave a silent thank you to God above to have such a grand nephew. "Thank you, Ethan."

"I'll be here by eight. Is that alright?"

"That will be a good time for me, and we can have a cuppa together before getting started. I'll see you then, *Nos da*, Ethan."

"*Nos da*, Uncle."

Ethan left and Dylan locked the door. He warmed up some milk on the gas and carried it with his candle upstairs to his bedroom above the shop and placed them both on the bedside table.

Dylan washed his hands and face and changed into his pajamas and slipped into his bed with his spectacles and Bible. It wasn't too long afterwards that Dylan fell asleep and the candle burned out.

In the morning, Dylan woke up by the birds singing. It must be about 6:30, he thought. As he stirred in his bed he realized he still had his reading glasses on and caught sight of his milk cup. He must have been really tired to forget to drink his milk before dropping off to sleep.

As Ethan wasn't coming 'till eight he quickly got out of bed and went down stairs. The extra hour would give him enough time to have a quick bath and be ready for Ethan's arrival. Dylan heated water on the fire and poured it into the cold water he had already poured into his bathtub; undressed quickly and sat in the bathtub in front of the fire.

The colors coming from the burning coal brought to mind his boyhood memories with Cradoc. The flames rose up and up as though they were jumping through hoops, curling as they disappeared and then joyously joining again to make a larger flame above.

When he was a boy with Cradoc, they would toss up a penny to see who had heads and be the first in the bathtub. Of course, whoever didn't get heads ended up in the colder, not so clean water to take a bath. The flames would have gone to just glowing lumps of coal. But, they were fun times.

Of course, when they were younger they could both fit into the bathtub. Some of those memories were of who would spread out their legs and tickle the other person in the bathtub. Splashes of bathwater would be on the floor and Mam would be irritable, but only for a few minutes.

He spoke to himself, maybe just to hear his voice or to bring life to the memories. "She would have to laugh when we both farted in the bathtub – what a noise! It seemed to echo through the whole house! And Mam would have to leave the room in fits of laughter that made her sides hurt, and her face reddened as bright as tomatoes."

Dylan was far away with his memories when he heard a knock on the door. A quick jump out of the bath, towel around his midriff and Dylan slipped his wet feet into his old slippers then opened the door to a very puzzled Ethan.

"Did I come too early, Uncle? I can come back a little later if you like."

"No, no, now is good. I must have been sitting in the bathtub for over an hour and forgot the time. I was remembering Cradoc when we were boys. We had so much fun. You know, I've been remembering a lot about Cradoc lately. It must be having you here helping me, that's what done it, company to pass the time away! You've given me time to think and thinking I've been doing.

"Thank you for that, Ethan I thought all my memories had vanished behind me; they were happy times and I'm very glad that I can think about them again."

"I have really enjoyed helping you out Uncle, but you are going to catch cold if you don't get some clothes on you quickly." He pointed at the short towel and slippers.

"That's right, son. Let me get dressed and empty the bathtub and I'll be right there."

"Don't worry. I think I know the ropes now. Make the batter in the bucket and set it aside. Open a tin of processed peas and pour them into the saucepan on low heat. Add a little water to the tin, swish it around, and pour the liquid into the peas. Add one teaspoonful of sugar and stir well. As they sit on the heat they will in time be mushy!" Ethan managed a smile as he recited the instructions. He ticked off each one on his fingers.

"Wash off about four spuds, do not peel them, dig out the eyes if there are any, and cut the spuds into slices about three quarters of an inch thick for the penny daps. Slice the rest of the spuds after washing them and peeling them, into long slices and then cut them through into long strips – not too thick and not too thin for the chips." He took an exaggerated deep breath before finishing the list.

"Before turning on the fryers, look at the fat if it's from the day before, skim the top a bit to get out all the little pieces of spuds that floated to the top. Now turn the fryers on low heat for thirty minutes and then turn up to medium.

After an hour, test the fat to see if it's ready by dripping a teaspoon of batter into the fat, if it sizzles, then it's time to cook the fish and the chips; if not, turn up the gas to high but be careful - watch it so it doesn't smoke or get too hot. When it's about right then I turn the heat back down to medium after about fifteen minutes, otherwise everything will get burned."

Dylan waved his hand and left Ethan reciting the list, nodding with each step until he couldn't see Ethan. He dropped the towel and dressed before draining the bathwater. He carried buckets full to the back and let the water flow down the drain, and then rejoined Ethan.

"Ethan, you remember well. I was thinking of writing the instructions down for you just in case but I feel I don't need to do that anymore. You've got it!

"This is good we can get started earlier today. I'll make a quick cuppa for us and then we can get on with it." Dylan hurried to his kitchen parlor.

"While you get the kettle on I'll start the batter, it shouldn't take long - then it can stand for a while. I'll turn the gas on low under the fryers while we have our tea."

"Good idea, Ethan, thank you."

Dylan felt good. If he could he would have skipped into his kitchen parlor. He filled the kettle with water and stood it on the black iron oven by the side of the fire. He got two cups down from the cabinet. He ran his finger around the top of the rims to make sure they weren't the chipped ones. He had kept all Olga's beautiful willow patterned cups and saucers and the plates, what was left of them; even the tureens she so carefully used for her vegetables. He felt his clumsiness had caused him to drop a cup or two, but he cherished what was left.

He got the sugar bowl and milk jug out of the pantry and filled the milk jug with some milk, being careful not to over fill. The water was ready, the kettle whistled through his little home and out into the shop.

Ethan shouted, "I'll be there in just a minute, Uncle."

Dylan remembered he had some current buns left in his biscuit tin Lina brought them when she last visited. He carefully placed the tin on the table.

"Alright son, sit down and enjoy a fresh cuppa made by your old Uncle and some current buns Lina brought last week. She is so good to me. I kept them in the tin so they should still be good. If not, we can toast them in front of the fire – I have a toasting rod over there on the hearth."

"That's very kind of you. I hadn't expected tea, and look, in a willow patterned cup, too. I remember my Mam had some willow patterned things but I don't know where they are now, probably broken over the years, or maybe Mary has saved them and put them somewhere safe from my calloused hands."

"*Ie,* your Mam had a set too, probably handed down from your grandfather. When we came down the mountain we brought what we could, a lot of things, actually. We just couldn't leave it all up there, that wouldn't make sense. We still needed some things down in the valley to live.

"When your mam and dad got married, Olga gave them a set of the willow patterned we had. It was a big set of a dozen cups and saucers, different sized plates, pudding dishes and tureens to match. We had so many of those sets. People didn't think we had anything special living up the mountain and we certainly accumulated two of everything. We were two families rolled into one really." Dylan found himself wandering back in time in his mind to those good old days he experienced.

"I expect if I tried to sell anything with the willow pattern at an antique market I probably would only get a few bob for them. So I'll hang on to them. If you don't find the set you were talking about, let me know. I am sure I can find a complete set for you." Dylan was back in thought again thinking of where all those willow-patterned things had been stored, maybe in the coalhouse. No one would think of looking there.

"They are scoundrels, those men that work in the Antique market. Always want something valuable for nothing. Better to keep them, I say. I have such good memories of Olga using them so I wouldn't get rid of any of them. They are yours for the taking now.

"Uncle, I had no idea you and my grandfather had all those things up the mountain. I'm beginning to think that your lives were far more interesting than it could ever be here, down in Porth.

"*Ìe,* that is true, son; life was different. In fact, it was like another world up there; fresh air, green grass everywhere, fresh fruit and vegetables, eggs, and the animals. We men looked after the animals and the women grew fresh fruit and vegetables and took care of the chickens. Olga and Clarenda made fresh bread almost every day and sometimes scones for breakfast with the jams they made. Breakfast was good and definitely filled us up for the day." He shook his head, licking his lips as if tasting the goodies he remembered. He glanced at the cuckoo clock. "Oh look at the time, Ethan!"

Ethan excused himself from the table and was in the shop in no time. When Dylan made his appearance he was shocked to see how Ethan had everything ready.

"Oh, Ethan. You are definitely organized and such a good help to me. Be careful, you are not working and I could take advantage of all your spare time to come and help. The only problem would be paying you - I wouldn't be able to give you a good wage that you so deserve; but I could help out a bit. Would fish and chips on the house whenever you want them, and a couple of quid here and there and my stored china be of interest to you, Ethan?"

"I would do it for free, you are family. If you need help I will be here. I don't have anything else worthwhile doing."

"No, no son I will pay you what I can. It would be an honor for me to pay you. You work hard. Your Mam would definitely be proud of you." Dylan swallowed hard, his eyes tearing at the thought of how proud she would have been. "Talk to Mary when you get home and see what she says about it. But, now I must get cooking." He turned away to change the subject.

"I will, Uncle." Ethan was happy thinking he could tell Mary he was helping Dylan on a regular basis but he certainly didn't want to take his money. Dylan's company was payment enough.

"Mrs. Jones, how are you today? You're usual, is it?"

"That's right, Dylan. Oh Ethan, here again are you?"

"That's right, Ethan is helping me. I am so grateful for young blood around me again. It brings back memories."

"That's good. Ethan, how is Mary?" Mrs. Jones was enquiring.

"Here you are, Mrs. Jones, your usual, that will be two shillings and six pence." She handed the half-crown to Ethan.

Ethan stared at it. "It's new. Did you get it today? Look, its dated 1953 and shiny bright. It must have been minted this year to commemorate Queen Elizabeth's wedding."

"I was lucky to be in the bank early this morning to cash my pension cheque. The cashiers had just brought out their tills with new coins. It's the first I've seen for a very long time. I was tempted to keep it but as I got two this morning I kept one at home. No point in keeping two of them when it will buy lunch."

Mrs. Jones left the shop shouting, "See you at Church, then?"

Ethan kept looking at the shiny coin in amazement. He hadn't seen a half-crown for a long time, especially a new one. He was thinking Mrs. Jones must be well off to bring in a shiny new half-crown to pay for her fish and chips.

Dylan was smiling the whole time. He was actually thinking what Ethan was thinking.

"Yes son. She has a bit. Her family was working for the post office years ago and got her a job there, too. Since she met her husband who also had a good job with the railway she's worth a few bob, you know. She's a good woman and worked hard.

"Ethan, would you mind when we shut up shop, getting me a few shovels of coal from the coal house out back? I'm likely to forget until evening time and then my fire will have burned out by then. Your help will save me going back there in the cold. I have a coal shovel in the coal house and the bucket is by the fireplace." Dylan was comfortable in asking Ethan to do a bit extra for him now.

Ethan would of course do anything for his Uncle Dylan and was only too happy to help him.

As soon as the shop closed, Ethan washed the fryer baskets, buckets, and saucepans.

"Why don't I get enough coal in for a couple of days? The weather forecast says it's going to be cold tonight and tomorrow. You will have enough coal and won't have to worry about refilling the coal bucket. I can get some more for you tomorrow."

"That's a good idea. I actually have a couple of buckets out there. You'll see them when you open the door."

The coalhouse was a lean-to, like an outhouse on the back of his little shop, next to his loo. The walls were painted white inside just like the loo and the roof was grey corrugated asbestos. It had a little window just enough for a little daylight to appear through. Dylan had painted the walls white on Olga's suggestion, as there was no electricity anywhere inside or outside of the house other than the shop. So it made sense to paint the walls white in his coalhouse, they reflected the light from the window.

It was time for Ethan to go back home.

"Ethan, take this fish and chips back with you, will you? There should be enough there for your family. I kept it back for you to take home. This will save Mary worrying too much about mouths to feed today. You have helped me a lot and I really appreciate it."

"I'll come back again in the morning and help you in the shop again. I am sure Mary will be glad to get me out of the house for a while. She's been saying that all I do is mope around the place. I'm not quite sure if she means I'm sulking or just plain miserable."

"No mun, I would say she means you are depressed. *Ie*, come back will you? It will be good for you to get out of the house and definitely good for me to have some company again."

"Alright then, I'll see you tomorrow." He waited until Dylan locked the door then walked away.

Dylan felt he was on the right track getting Ethan there with him, not just to help him out but he could talk a little more about life up the mountain, given the opportunity. Dylan had to tread carefully so as not to give away his real intention.

It was Saturday afternoon, most men would be at the football game or just talking amongst themselves about who would score what, but afterwards they would come back to Dylan's for their fish and chips.

It was only an hour later and there was a knock on the door. It was Lina.

"Hello Lina, what brings you here at this time? I usually see you and Angel after choir practice."

"Well, Dylan, I need help and I don't know who else to ask."

"Come in, come in, Lina. Sit down and we can have a cuppa. I'll put the kettle on, shall I? Alright then, kettle is on, cups, saucers, and-"

Lina interrupted. "Let me help you Dylan, we can talk while we make tea together."

"*Ìe,* we can." Dylan handed her the cups off the shelf. "Kettle is boiled, how many teaspoons of tea shall I put in the pot?"

"Not as much as I used to have," Lina told him. Truth be told, she was getting tired of tea. "Three teaspoons will be plenty and almost fill the pot please."

Dylan poured a little water in the pot and swished it around, then poured it out into the sink. Lina was right there handing him the tea tin from the cupboard and a spoon.

"Thank you Dylan, it's just like old times having tea with you."

"Yes, it's been long time since my Olga was alive, and we all had tea together."

"I'm so sorry, Dylan. I didn't mean to make you sad. Please forgive me?"

"No, no; I'm not sad. I was just remembering a good time we had together with my dear Olga."

"They were good times. Really good times, Dylan." She covered the hand resting beside hers on the counter.

"Lina, you have something on your mind. What is it?"

"It's nothing serious, but important to me and the children, Angel and David I mean."

"Go on, what is it Lina?" Dylan was concerned now.

"I have a favor to ask you; but please be discreet about the information."

"Of course Lina, what is it? What can I do to help you?"

"Oh Dylan, thank you so much, as it's very important. You know David has a good voice and you have heard Angel." Lina hesitated and drew a deep breath, it seemed like she was pulling invisible thread from her feet.

"Go on, go on, Lina?"

"This morning at our Women's Union meeting, Mrs. Jones announced that a school in Pontypridd was having a choir rehearsal for a special event at one of the Churches in about a month."

"*Ie, ie.* Go on." Dylan was more than interested as he enjoyed music, all kinds of music.

"She confirmed that at one of the school meetings they stated they might consider taking some of our best singers from Porth junior school to the concert." She twisted her hands, taking another breath.

"They had another meeting to discuss which children should go and to be fair they decided one girl and one boy. They decided on David and Angel."

"I don't see a problem with that, Lina. In fact, it sounds lovely."

Lina took another deep breath as though she didn't know how to say what was on her mind. You could tell Lina was not one for asking favors or announcing her wants. She was always a very generous person and would do anything to help a friend, but ask for something for herself? That would never happen.

"Well, Mrs. Smith said that they would like to ask the parents of David and Angel to go to the concert."

"That's a really nice gesture and that would be very good for our David and Angel. Have you told Mary about this?"

"No, not yet. In fact, I am a little concerned. I don't want Mary to become anxious and worried about everything. She has a lot to take care of as it is. The biggest problem would be Ethan. You know Ethan better than anyone and he has been very depressed since the mine shut down. It would take a lot of manipulation to get Ethan to agree to let David go with Angel. He might think it was a waste of time as he isn't much on music, or the Arts for that matter."

"Hmmm. I see what you are saying, Lina."

"I really care about Mary and I think this might help her. Give her extra faith that good things can happen to those who work hard and are still in need. She loves her children and this might help with a little excitement for them, too. But, Mary and Ethan are concerned about day-to-day living. This might feel like a financial burden and a little too much for Ethan to cope with at the moment."

"*Ìe, Ìe,* I understand that but that is not going to put you off mentioning it to Mary, is it?"

"Dylan, could you mention it to Ethan the next time he comes to help? I am sure they won't expect David and Angel to go this week. I am sure there will be more information coming soon. And, we are not exactly sure that they will not ask another school, too. I just want Ethan and Mary to be prepared that David and Angel will go with the school teachers so it won't be such a shock."

"I know Ethan will be concerned about the costs. Do you have any idea about how much will be needed?"

"Oh, that slipped my mind. There is no cost to either of our families. In fact, they will pay our bus fare to go with them. Mrs. Evans didn't mention anything about money at first, so I asked her if we would need to pay the bus fare for the children and that is when she said the transportation cost would be provided for the children and one parent from each family."

"What about clothing?" Dylan chimed in.

"All they need at the moment will be clean clothes, I don't think anything new needs to be bought and…" Lina paused and took another deep breath, giving a little cough at the end. "It would be such a shame to say no to this opportunity, as the opportunity may never come again."

Dylan answered, "*Ìe,* I see, yes I see. The opportunity is now and we cannot delay. Ethan said he'll be back this afternoon to help me. That will be in about an hour and a half. I must get my thoughts together by then."

"Oh goodness, I've been talking so much I forgot to give you this tart I made. It's apple with cheese. I made one for Mary as well. Let's have a piece of tart together before I go, shall we? I know you won't cut it just for yourself so we will cut it for both of us."

"That's very nice of you, Lina."

"It's alright, I enjoy cooking while I can."

"I'll put the kettle on, so we can have another nice cuppa while you're here."

Dylan reached up to get the plates and handed them to Lina while she got the knife, spoons, and forks.

"I'll go when Ethan gets here, so I won't be in the way." Lina didn't really want Ethan to see her there.

"Lina, you are never in the way. It's always a pleasure to have you around and Angel, too. You have done well in rearing Angel from a baby. I know that took a lot of hard work, besides loss of sleep, but God has blessed you with that love you share with her. She needs a good woman in her life. "

"Oh, Dylan! Don't get me crying. Angel needs a real mother, a woman that will be there as she grows up and encourages her when she has her own children. Someone with spirit, but she's stuck with me instead."

"Lina, don't talk like that! If God wanted Angel to have a younger woman don't you think that He would have kept the woman that gave birth to her right here? But, that wasn't in His plan. You are the best mother and grandmother Angel could ever have."

Lina turned away and wiped her eyes with the lacy handkerchief she rescued from the little pocket in her handbag.

"Now, now Lina. It's not time to cry, it's time to rejoice. God knew what He was doing, alright. Like my Olga used to say, God always provides for those in need and Angel needed you. He gives us the choice to take the right road or the wrong road in life. Some take the wrong road and never swerve to the right or look back, just like Angel's mother. And others take the right road and find that it is too long and twisted, that they don't want to wait to see what God has in store for them, they are not patient enough.

"It is always wise to tread carefully and prayerfully and God will help us on the way. Angel's mother left on the wrong road and never looked back. Your heart was in the right place when Angel was put into your arms. Gilberto knew what was right for his daughter. He couldn't provide himself, but he knew she would need you."

Now tears were filling Lina's eyes, to the point she had to gulp for breath. "It's alright Lina. I am only saying what is true, so do not feel embarrassed or ashamed." Lina reached in her little handbag for another buried handkerchief.

"What's the time now Dylan, I should go before Ethan gets here so you can talk?"

"Before you go I must say this tart is really good, it seems different this time."

"I'm glad you enjoyed it. I made some extra so I could share. Angel is still not eating. I believe it's because Gilberto didn't come at Christmas. You know she loves him so much and jumps for joy when she sees him. Since then she has been off her food. The only thing she will eat is sugar-sandwiches. She has to eat something more nutritious like cheese, eggs, and fruit so I combined them in the tarts. Maybe because it's sweet she will at least try it. I am getting worried about her."

"It's almost five o'clock. Lina, I'd better be getting things ready."

"Oh, I must go now. Ethan will be here any moment." She got up and took the dirty dishes to the sink and rinsed them off quickly, then wiped her hands on the tea towel that she placed over the door underneath the sink.

"Thank you, Lina, for the tart. It is much appreciated for you to think about me." Dylan placed one hand gently on Lina's shoulder before she walked to the door.

"Bye for now, Dylan. Please let me know what Ethan says. I'll stop at Mary's to give her the other tart and take Angel home. If I can talk with Mary discreetly without the children overhearing I will mention what I have told you."

"That will be good, Lina."

"Bye." The door opened and shut quietly behind Lina.

Dylan was in deep thought. How was he going to tell Ethan about the children going to Ponty when really he wanted to encourage him about Cradoc's farm? Maybe he could encourage Ethan in a different way by saying that David loved to sing up old Penrhiwgwynt because of the peacefulness and the scenery.

Chapter 10

Ethan arrived as Dylan was coming out of his kitchen parlor.

"Hello Uncle, as promised here I am and happy to help you."

"That's good Ethan, thank you. While we get everything ready I'd like to talk with you about something."

Ethan was all ears.

"I have some good news to give you and I know you will be surprised. It is about David."

"David! What has he been up to? Is something wrong?"

"No, no Ethan nothing is wrong. I said *good* news. It's school."

"School!" Ethan yelled.

"Yes, Ethan. He has been chosen to represent their Porth junior school and go to Pontypridd and sing with one of the schools there."

"David, sing? For school? What for?"

"Ethan, your son has been selected, do you understand? They want David and Angel to sing at the Treforest School together."

"How do you know this?"

"Lina brought me an apple tart and told me the good news. She is so excited."

"I don't think David can sing that well. He plays around making up songs about Angel and her hair and sings to horses; what good is that?"

"Ethan, that's a way he can sing; it's obvious he loves to sing. Otherwise he would just shout words at Angel and definitely wouldn't bother about soothing a hurt horse. Di

Jones, the milkman's brother, said he heard David the last time they came down from the mountain. At first, Di said he wasn't sure what he was hearing. You know he is a bit deaf. But, he said it was David and Angel. They were singing the Welsh Anthem but with a different beat."

"Oh yes, I have heard him sing the Welsh Anthem. It's not like it's supposed to be sung, with reverence. He sings it fast and with too much of that modern way of singing stuff."

"Ethan, that's kids these days. We used to do things our parents didn't approve of, I'm sure you remember?"

"How is singing going to help him later on in life? He needs to concentrate on his schoolwork and get a good education. Especially not wasting time going up the mountain singing to horses!" Ethan started working on things to get the chippie ready for business. Dylan followed him around, helping turn on the fryers but keeping up a steady stream of conversation.

"Oh, Ethan. He enjoys singing and he enjoys animals, what a great balance. I am sure you are thinking about what happened to you going down the mine and not being able to finish your school. Those days have gone, long gone. You had to go down the mine instead of pursuing further school for yourself. Otherwise you couldn't have helped your Mam. But times are different now."

"There are hardly any working mines left around here and David has two parents, you and Mary. David can do his schoolwork and sing at the same time and visit the place he loves. He is a very bright lad, haven't you noticed?"

"I'm not sure." Ethan paced the floor of the chippie, his hands on his hips. He wasn't good with surprises and this one was a shocker. "I'll have to think about it and talk with Mary. I can't believe our son has any potential at singing. I heard him sing, '*Ma hen wlad fy nha-dau yn an-nwyl i – mi*'

"I thought it was one of those kids from over the border. The anthem is sung by the Treaorchy Male voice choir, slow, a cappella and with so much reverence that you could almost cry listening to it. Just like I said, David did not sing with reverence."

"Ethan, that might be and it could be the key. Anything different catches attention these days. Let him go, give him a chance. Lina said that one parent could go with their child, and it's free! You won't even have to pay for the bus fare."

"Oh my God, my Mam would curl up in her grave if she knew about this."

"No Ethan, I think she is up there rejoicing with the Angels as we speak, playing the trumpet your father had."

"My Mam! Played the trumpet?" He stacked the paper and brought in bags. Dylan calling out when he walked out of sight.

"Yes, Ethan, she did. It was your grandmother Clarenda's. She brought it from Croatia but she didn't play - she sang. It was your grandfather Cradoc that played. At first it was to draw the horses towards the field when they heard the trumpet – it worked. We used to sing and dance up on Penrhiwgwynt while Cradoc played the trumpet.

"At first I must admit it was a terrible racket but Cradoc taught himself over time – he was good at it, too. When Clarenda died, we saved it for your father but he went to the mine early. He did sing though, but with his fellow miners.

"The trumpet wasn't used for a long time and then your Mam found it. It wasn't easy for her at first but she didn't give up, she practiced and practiced the same song over and over, probably driving the neighbors batty, but she kept at it and she was good in the end. That started her interest in playing!"

"My dad sang, you said? This is a shock."

"All Welsh men sing." Dylan sounded insulted.

"What do you mean?"

"We are a musical culture. There is a saying, 'To be born Welsh is to be born privileged. Not with a silver spoon in your mouth, but music in your blood and poetry in your soul'. Haven't you heard that, Ethan? Pass me the batter, so I can get the fish started, will you?"

"Uncle, are you telling me that we had musicians in our family?"

"Of course, Ethan. Every generation of our culture has musicians. It's in our blood. We are involved at a very young age at school and Church. It's how we grow up. It's what we do with the talent that makes a difference, not just for ourselves, but also for our culture. Your grandfather Cradoc played the trumpet, your grandmother Clarenda sang with my Olga and me. Your father sang in the mines and got a group of men together to start a men's choir at the local pub. Your Mam played the trumpet. Do you know that Mary can sing, too?"

"What? I didn't know that!"

"Oh, goodness Ethan where have you been and not noticed these things? Mary sang at school, and don't you remember she had her choir at your wedding? She joined them to sing the song you both loved. When you were down the mine she took the children to Church and sang there with Lina.

"Even Lina has a history of musicians in her family. Now then, that brings me to you. Can you sing, Ethan?" Dylan stared at him, the question hanging between them.

"When I was at school I suppose. I had to." He remembered working in the pit. "I sang with the men down the mine. You know, we sang to give life to the darkness and our toils. It helped us in case of gas pockets. We sang to make sure everyone was alive." The thought of it dragged his memories back into the darkness he'd started climbing out of in his mind. Dylan's bright voice brought him back to the present.

"Well then, that means you can sing. Some people think you have to be taught to sing with all that fancy teaching. But, that's not always true; you could have an aptitude for singing. I suspect David has that, definitely."

"So you think that my David can sing well enough to go to Ponty?"

"Of course, Ethan. The school wouldn't ask unless he could sing well."

"So this isn't a joke?"

"No mun. I'm telling you, it's not a joke! And it's not because David has a family background of musicians either, it's because he loves to sing and he sings well. And the fact that he enjoys the open air of the mountaintop, which is where he chooses to sing. Up there on Penrhiwgwynt without being criticized or laughed at. Don't be so hard on your lad, he has great potential."

"I need to talk with Mary about all this. And, you said Mary can sing, too!" Ethan shook his head in amusement and then laughed.

"Now, we must get on with cooking the fish and chips, we'll be having customers very soon. We can talk more, later. Alright, Ethan? Open a tin of peas will you son and pour them out into that saucepan quickly. Everyone will be here soon."

"It's almost time to unlock the door. What else can I do to help you? I should know by now but I was a little carried away there for a moment when we were talking about David and our musical families." Ethan snapped his fingers.

"I remember, of course, the paper. I didn't cut up the newspapers. Let me get the papers off the shelf and cut them up for you." Ethan carried a pile of newspapers into the shop and placed them carefully on the counter next to the bags. He took a few pages and began to fold them and then tear them up.

"Oh my God, Uncle. Look at this, there's a picture of David and Angel. It says they have been chosen to visit Treforest Secondary Modern School in Pontypridd for a concert. They're at Porth Junior school. How can they compete with anyone at Teforest school? They're all older." Ethan read the article in amazement.

"Ethan, let me look." Dylan picked up the paper to his eye and stared at it. "It's not a competition. Really! Lina didn't say anything about a competition; it's a concert. Maybe she didn't know that when we talked earlier or maybe I wasn't listening!" He moved to stand beside Ethan to see the grainy picture.

"I wonder if Mary knew anything about it. I'll take this page home so I can show her."

"Lina didn't say anything about photographs either."

That afternoon time flew by. The shop never lost its charm with neighbors meeting neighbors and family members. Even Tomas the butcher stepped in and bought fish and chips. Before he went out the door he started eating his chips. There was a game today; the shop always did well after the game. It's almost as though everyone that lived in the town came out to watch the game.

Dylan was pleased he finished off the crate of fish and the sack of spuds. Of course that would mean he could order more for next week. He folded the sack and set it aside as he talked to Ethan.

"I'll save the sack for Lina. She wants to make some new rag rugs." Dylan told him. "I asked her if she could make me a couple of cushion covers if she has any sack left. She's so talented, you know. She weaves in bright colors with any leftover sewing scraps. That would surely brighten my kitchen parlor."

Ethan listened with half an ear. He finished wiping the counters. He'd been thinking about the kids, and singing. He turned to look at Dylan.

"Uncle, you mentioned Lina's family had musicians. Did you mean her parents?" He leaned against the counter he'd just cleaned, crossing his arms, unable to contain his curiosity any longer.

"No, not really, her Mam sang but her father didn't as far as I remember. He used to refer to singing as 'a bloody noise', not as an art. Lina was so different from her father and still loves to sing, and I know Angel loves to sing with her at Church. Gilberto loved to sing, too; he was a tenor with the Maerdy Male Voice Choir and played classical guitar. Sometimes he would croon like Bing Crosby when he wanted to show off. He even looked like Bing at times when he dressed up. Gilberto was very handsome, you know."

"Well, what happened to Gilberto?"

"Oh, he went over the border to Birmingham to find work. He liked his finance officer job with the council but you know Wales is poor. The wages were not as good as England and he wanted to provide more for his mother. He always said Lina deserved her own home. She was too young to get a pension so had to make do with what work she could get, doing washing or sewing and cooking for neighbors. The rent was going up every year on the house she shared with Edwin. Edwin didn't leave even a penny to Lina when he passed away."

"What did he die from?"

"Lina would only say that he passed away. He was an aggressive man. The neighbors said they often heard him shouting at Lina. The morning he died, he was shouting and threatening Lina and she was crying. Mrs. Probert said her son was at home. He pushed the door open and he saw Edwin had his fists ready to beat Lina. Angel was there, kneeling on the floor in the corner. Poor baby was scared to death.

"Mrs. Probert's son took Lina and Angel to their house. As they were leaving through the door *that* Edwin yelled and threatened Lina again and then dropped to the floor with a heart attack. It must have been a terrible thing for Lina and Angel to see him die like that." Dylan shook his head at the memory, the tragedy.

A hush fell as the men thought over the past events. Ethan sighed.

"As soon as I clean up, I'll get the coal for you and I'll go home and talk with Mary about David and Angel in this concert."

"You do that, son. You need to talk this over." Dylan pulled the curtains over the window.

"I think we can lock the door now, all the customers have gone," he reminded Ethan, who nodded.

"Son, come back in the parlor with me a minute?"

Ethan followed Dylan into his kitchen parlor, he stirred the fire and added another lump of coal as Dylan pulled the curtains across the window. Dylan still had the blackout curtains from World War II over the window in his parlor, just like Lina had in her window. It seemed so strange that the blackout curtains were still used. A lot of the older generation used them to keep the heat in.

"Oh dear me, where did I put that bottle of vinegar now?" Dylan stood looking around.

"Uncle, I think I saw it in the pantry on the floor."

"Oh yes, I remember now.." Dylan nodded and waved his hand at Ethan. "Fish and chips are really good with vinegar. It cuts the grease and adds flavor."

"I better go now, Uncle. See you tomorrow." Ethan stood at the door, putting on his jacket. "Uncle Dylan, lock the door behind me."

Dylan commented, "We never had to lock anything before those scoundrels came over the border." He sounded so disgusted, but crossed to lock the door behind Ethan. As usual, Ethan waited until the lock turned before walking home.

Dylan then turned the light off and went into his kitchen parlor and closed the door that separated the house from the shop.

While Ethan walked home he thought about the photo he found in the newspaper and how he would approach the subject of David singing at Treforest school in Pontypridd.

Most likely Mary had some knowledge but hadn't shared any of it with him. Dylan said he thought that David had a good voice and that he only sang up the mountain to avoid criticism. But David had been chosen by the school, so he must be comfortable with his classmates.

He was almost home. He hadn't had any cigarettes for some time but he needed the time to figure out how to talk with Mary about David. He had no idea that David had any talent and he had always told David to stop making all that noise when he did start to sing around the house. The youngster was his flesh and blood and he wondered how he could have missed David's talent.

He exhaled the last of the smoke, dropping the lit end of his fag and stomping it out. Time to go home.

Mary was at the door to greet him. She gently said, "I'm glad you're home, dinner is ready, I made a stew with dumplings. The children have already eaten theirs and are getting ready for bed. I waited for you and thought we could eat together."

"That's a good idea, Mary. I'll just wash my hands and be there in a minute."

Mary was dishing up the stew as Ethan walked into the kitchen. There was something he noticed different about Mary. It wasn't the way she dressed or combed her hair; it was something else, something deeper. She was always kind and soft-spoken and this time was no different; yet there was something else.

Ethan sat at the table and Mary handed him some hot apple cider she made and the bowl of stew; hunks of piping hot bread were already in the center of the table. Mary didn't have to utter a word; she had a twinkle in her eye, a twinkle that was always displayed when there was good news. Mary blessed the food and both ate in silence. Ethan was too curious to finish his dinner so he asked Mary about her afternoon. That was something he had never done before.

Mary replied, "Lina helped me with the planting and brought some cake for us, Ethan. It does feel good for you to come home and have dinner with me, but I know you want to say something. What is it Ethan? What is it that is bothering you?"

"Nothing bothering me, really, but I wanted to ask you something, Mary."

"Alright Ethan, what is it?" Mary put down her spoon, gathering her hands in her lap.

"I was helping Dylan with the dinner and as I was cutting up the newspapers for him, I came across this." He pulled out the crumpled page from his pocket.

Mary wasn't sure whether to smile or jump up and down with excitement. She kept her seat and read the article. She waited patiently for Ethan to say more.

"Look Mary – that is David and Angel." Ethan pointed at the paper in her hand.

"Yes. It's David and Angel. Angel looks nervous but David is smiling." Mary sounded proud.

"Mary, did you know that David had this photograph taken at school and they want him to go to Ponty with Angel to sing?"

"I only found out when Lina came earlier and told me. I didn't know how to tell you." She shrugged her shoulder. "Up until now I have taken care of the children but I would like to share their achievements at school with you."

"I have missed so much of their lives. Thomas is now 25, no wonder he is a little distant towards me." Ethan regretted his time away. Now the past was catching up with him.

"No, Ethan. He has a wife and family of his own. That's why he seems distant; he's the same with me. He's maturing and trying to raise a family."

"What about Anne?" Ethan pushed away his meal, leaning forward, his elbows on the table.

"Ethan, Anne got a job in Maerdy. It was easier for her and less time spent on the bus if she just moved there. Don't you remember she's staying with your cousin?"

"I thought at the time I was providing for our family by working down the mine all those hours. But, in fact, I missed time with you and the children. I left you to take care of everything."

Mary watched as tears clouded her beloved's eyes. She got to her feet and walked around the table to his side.

"Oh Mary, I hope one day you will forgive me before it's too late." Ethan's head hung low as he took deep breaths to avoid crying. It wasn't manly to show emotion.

"There's nothing to forgive." Mary put her hand on Ethan's shoulder. Ethan clasped her hand in his. "You did what you felt you had to do and I am very grateful. And so are the children. I am just sorry time has passed by so quickly." She hugged him closer. "And, now I am so grateful that you are here with us. I won't have to worry every single day about whether or not you will come out of the pit alive and come home to us. Now it's your time to live again, Ethan." Mary kissed him on the neck. Ethan turned and caught a kiss on the lips. Ethan rose up and took Mary in his arms.

"Mary, you are the most beautiful and loving wife I could ever want. I am so glad you didn't give up on me all those years."

"Ethan, there's one person I wouldn't give up on and that's you. You took care of us all those years. I love you now more than the day we were married, and I thought I was crazy in love with you then." She went up on her tiptoes and kissed him. They came together slowly, no rushing, because they were alone. There was no place they had to be and this was one perfect moment both of them wanted to hold onto.

"Come on Mary, it's your bedtime." Ethan pulled back, glancing around the room.

"I thought our bed time was an hour later than this."

"Not tonight, your husband needs you."

"He does?" She followed his gaze around the room.

"I'll build the fire up and close the flue."

"Don't forget the fire guard, Ethan."

"Lock the door will you, love?" Ethan gathered their bowls and piled them on the drainer.

Mary locked the knob. Then pulled the metal sash across the door and dropped it into the metal groove the other side. She picked up the hallway candle and went up the stairs.

Ethan built up the fire and hooked the guard in place then carried the candle to the hallway and blew it out. The landing had a golden glow that shone down the stairs from where Mary had left the candle on the plant stand, while she checked on the children.

Ethan reached the top of the stairs and waited for Mary to come out of the children's room, he picked her up and carried her to their room.

"I need to get the candle before it catches fire." He set her on her feet beside the bed. Turning, he retrieved the candle and put it on the bedside table, then closed the bedroom door.

"Ethan, you didn't tell me if it was alright for David to go with Angel."

"Of course it is. I'm not a mean monster." He pulled his shirttail from his trousers, looking across the bed from her with an unfamiliar stretch of his lips. "But I'd like you to go with him."

"I wish you could come with us but they said only one parent. Would you like to go with David instead of me?"

"No, Mary. I think you should go and I think David would be upset if you didn't go with him."

He hung up his trousers, finishing undressing before Mary. He settled in bed, watching her. As she blushed, he blew out the candle. The bed creaked as she climbed in beside him.

Chapter 11

Mary turned over as she woke and saw Ethan's face. He was still asleep. She lay there for a little while observing his soft breathing. She studied his dark-skinned, peaceful face. His dark hair dropped around his face in ringlets that met his shoulders. He had not lost his good looks even after all those years down the pit.

Ethan opened his eyes and noticed that Mary was watching him.

"It's morning already," she whispered. "It seems only a few hours ago we went to bed."

"It was only a few hours ago we went to sleep." He told her with a smile. "How long have you been lying there watching me?" He stretched, wrapping his arm around her and pulling her close.

"Only long enough to see you are still so very handsome."

She moved towards him and kissed him on the cheek.

"What was that for?"

"Oh, just because."

"Because what?"

"You agreed to let David go to the school in Ponty."

"I get a kiss just because I let David go to the school. Hmm! I'll have to think about that for a while." He teased her.

"Well, while you think, I'll put the kettle on and maybe we can have a cuppa together before breakfast and the children move around. I still have just over an hour before Lina comes, and the children will need to be ready for Church very soon."

"That wasn't difficult to agree. If you say it's good for the children to do something or other, then that's alright with me. I'll get dressed and check on the fire. Hopefully, it hasn't gone out."

They rolled out of bed together, dressing and heading downstairs. He pulled her to a stop at the bottom of the stairs, holding her just long enough to steal another kiss. She smiled, her beautiful eyes glowing. She turned to the kitchen. Ethan followed.

"Kettle's on, I'll start the scones. The oven is already hot so they shouldn't take too long."

Ethan built up the fire with more coal and looked at Mary as she placed the scones in the little oven his Mam used. It brought back cherished memories of when he helped his Mam with the fire and she cooked.

Oh, oh! I hear a lot of fairy elephants coming down the stairs." Mary turned towards the hallway. "The scones are ready. Everyone sit down while I get the plates."

"I'll get the jam, Mam," David chimed in.

Ethan leaned over Mary's shoulder and whispered in her ear, "David seems so happy this morning," and then kissed her neck.

"So am I," she whispered back. "Maybe he heard your answer or maybe he is just happy it's Sunday. You know he likes to sing in Church with Angel. Why not come this morning with us?"

"I could do that. I'll get changed while you all finish your breakfast." Ethan grabbed a scone with his tea. He balanced the hot cup and the warm scone as he made his way back up to the bedroom.

Mary was just finishing up the dishes when Ethan appeared, tie, and all.

"This suit still fits me even after all this time."

Mary adjusted his tie and stood back to take a better look. He looked so handsome in his black suit with white shirt and striped tie. He had not worn it since his Mam's funeral but he had carefully put it away in the wardrobe.

"You're making me think I'm going to auction!"

"No, I'm not auctioning you off for anything. I'm just admiring my handsome husband." Mary blushed as she said it.

"I think the moth's got it. I see a little hole here." He pulled up the edge of his jacket, showing it to her.

Mary looked, "No, it's alright. It's where the extra button was sewn on. I need to hurry before Lina gets here. I must get ready." She turned to look at the children. "Are you kids ready for Church? Ian, where are your Church shoes?"

"Mam, David is wearing them, they're too tight for me." His tone suggested he'd told her this more than once.

"David, come here let me see. They need a quick shine. The brush is under the sink. Well, Ian what are you going to wear to Church?" She put her hands on her hips, at a loss.

"Maybe dad's old shoes." Ian shrugged. "They should fit me by now. Anyway, he's wearing those spanking brand new ones." The teen pointed at his father.

"Son, they are not spanking new. I take care of my shoes by cleaning them and brushing them well. That's why they look like new. When you're older you'll understand if you take care of things they will last longer and still be useful even if you have had them a long time." An echo of the spoons came to him as a fleeting memory.

"Hmm! Ethan, could you get those other shoes of yours? The ones with laces." Mary pointed to the hall.

"Oh no, not with laces. They keep undoing." Ian rolled his eyes. Thank God Ethan didn't see Ian's eyes; he would have been upset with his attitude.

"Ian, come with me and you can try them on then we'll see about the laces."

Ethan and Ian went to the cubbyhole under the stairs and pulled out his oldest black shoes with laces. "They only need a quick shine and put some newspaper in them and they should fit well." Ethan handed the pair to Ian.

Ian went into the kitchen and found David shining his shoes with the brush. "David you are going to brush off all the color if you keep doing that. Let me have the brush?"

"I just want them nice and clean. Can I keep them?"

"Of course, they're no use to me now I've outgrown them."

Mary shouted from the bottom of the stairs, "Come on will you, we are going to be late. If you haven't eaten breakfast, you'll just have to go without."

"Not on your nelly," young Dylan said in a low voice running down the stairs. He quickly grabbed a scone and stuffed it in his pocket.

Edward and William came down the stairs arguing about their shirts. "Mam, he took my shirt and won't give it back to me."

"Edward took my shirt, Mam."

William chimed in, "Mam, my shirt is too tight now and the buttons are starting to pop."

"No they're not, you're getting fat, that's what it is," shouted Edward.

"Alright, alright, that's enough, let's go upstairs and see what shirts you all have. Maybe you could change with each other." Ethan interjected.

In the meantime, Ian and David were sitting on the couch, trying to stay patient. Ian was drawing, as usual, and David was humming a tune.

Mary ran upstairs quickly and changed into her Sunday dress and Church shoes.

"Everyone ready? I think I hear Lina," Mary announced, coming down the stairs.

Lina knocked the door and David ran to the door to open it. "Good morning, Nene Lina."

"Good morning, David. You look so handsome all dressed up."

Everyone was in the hallway ready to go.

"Ethan, I'm so pleased you are able to join us this morning." Lina bent forward and whispered, "You will hear David singing this morning. Oh, he has such a lovely voice."

Angel skipped ahead with David, their heads together. The rest of the families followed them to the Church. The Church was already filling up with people.

Some of the ladies stood at the door huddling together as they looked at Ethan and spoke in Welsh, hoping he didn't understand. But he knew what they said.

"Oh my goodness, is that Ethan coming to Church?" Mrs. Probert stood in amazement, after she crossed herself.

"It is, and he looks so clean. I haven't seen him that clean for so long," added Mrs. Jones.

"Good morning, Mrs. Probert." He turned to the next gossiper. "Good morning, Mrs. Jones. Yes, it is I." Ethan spoke in perfectly accented Welsh. They were a little embarrassed when they realized Ethan understood what they said. Of course he would, he was brought up in a Welsh home and went to a Welsh school and spoke only in Welsh during his childhood.

The Vicar, Llewelyn was already on the steps welcoming everyone into the Church. As Ethan approached he shook his hand, "I am so pleased you came this morning with the family. Mary looks so happy." Then he turned to Lina as if Ethan attended every Sunday.

"Good morning, Lina. I am really happy you and Angel are here." He winked at the little girl with a smile. "Angel looks lovely in that dress. Did you make it?"

"Yes, I did. I thought it would be something special for Angel to wear as she is singing with David this morning." Lina beamed at his compliment.

Ethan didn't hear that David was singing too, but followed Mary to the pew.

When everyone was seated, Vicar Llewelyn walked behind the altar boys down the aisle from the door as Mrs.

Evans thumped on the organ. It was a very old organ and much energy was needed for the keys to work.

One time, Mrs. Evans thumped on the keys and one of the organ pipes fell down, narrowly missing her. On that occasion, the children at the service roared with laughter, but Mrs. Evans found it rather scary.

As the Vicar passed by each pew, the congregation stood up and made the sign of the cross on their chests in reverence and respect. When he arrived at the altar he gave his opening remarks and blessed the congregation as they stood. Then he announced the number of the hymn from the hymnal.

Mrs. Evans thumped the organ again and missed a couple of notes. All the children laughed, then there was a silence where you could hear a pin drop. After the congregation sang the hymn, the Vicar raised his hands slightly to advise everyone to sit down.

David and Angel walked from their pew up towards the altar and stood on the upper step before they turned to face the congregation. David inched backwards a little and turned and faced the left wall. At the Vicar's gesture, David began to sing, "Ein Tad," the Lord's Prayer, in Welsh.

His jubilant young voice was a joy to everyone. Angel came in on the second line as they agreed and they sang together a capella, continuing through to the end.

Ethan sat in amazement. When Mary looked at him, his eyes were filled with tears. The Vicar asked the duo if they would like to sing something else, they both nodded and Angel ran towards the Vicar and asked in a quiet voice if they could sing the Welsh Anthem, as David's father had come to Church.

At first, David was so concerned that Ethan would criticize his voice that he did not turn to look at him, but as soon as Angel returned to his side with a comforting smile and held his hand, he gradually turned towards the congregation.

David sang with such reverence that Ethan was filled with pride, and tears fell from his eyes. He sniffed and wiped his face, clearing the moisture - even as it returned while he listened to his youngest son sing for the first time.

Mary sat closer and put her arm through his arm and held Ethan's hand. It was truly a blessing to hear two young children sing without music, and hit the high notes as well as the low. The range of singing was incredible. The congregation was so moved that they applauded in the church. It was not normal that people would applaud any singing in the Church in those days, but it was indeed deserved.

The Vicar said a prayer and started his sermon. He spoke about, "Being Grateful for Small Mercies."

That morning's Church service brought joy to Ethan. He was encouraged, not only because his son was singing but also he realized how blessed he was even without a job. He was alive, with a loving family and a home left to him by his Mam. And, now a great friendship he never had before with his Uncle Dylan.

On the way home, Ethan stopped by Dylan's shop. Dylan had already started preparing for Monday's lunch. "I will be back in a little while to help you."

"Ethan, is that really you? You look very handsome in that suit, mun. Been to Church have you?" Dylan couldn't hold back his smile.

"Yes, Uncle and I got some looks from our local 'busy bodies.' I'll just pop home and get changed. I'll be back to help you and tell you all about it."

"Alright son, take your time. No need to hurry. You know I don't open till tomorrow."

"I know, but we can do the preparation together this afternoon then you can rest a bit this evening."

Dylan was pleased to have Ethan's help and Ethan was grateful for Dylan's love and companionship.

As Ethan walked out of Dylan's shop he caught a glimpse of his reflection in the window. He was quite shocked but felt good at his appearance. He stopped and rubbed his fingers through his hair then quickly turned and walked home. His cheeks flushed.

Mary had already changed out of her Church clothes and busied herself in the kitchen, preparing lunch for the family.

As Ethan came through the door he heard the children bounding around upstairs. Ethan shouted, "Could you fairy elephants take a nap for a little while," and then laughed.

Mary noticed that Ethan's attitude had changed towards the noise the children made. Perhaps it was not only because he came to Church and heard David sing, it was most likely his visiting Dylan. Ethan had another man he could share his concerns with and hear stories about his relatives, and where they came from.

Ethan went up the stairs and changed out of his suit and hung it back up in the wardrobe, put on his casual clothes, and walked down the stairs carrying his best shoes and put them away in the cupboard under the stairs.

"David, come here. I want to talk with you a minute." Ethan stood.

David thought he was in trouble and self-consciously came into the kitchen.

"Son, I want to say thank you."

David hadn't got a clue what his father was talking about but sat still on the stool until Ethan had finished what he was saying. "You made me very proud of you, I had no idea that you could sing like that. Where did you learn to sing?"

"Up the mountain, Dad."

"Up the mountain? Who is up the mountain?"

David chuckled, now he knew he wasn't in trouble. "The horses, Dad. Angel says they like my singing so I sing to them even when they are not close by. I think they can hear me in the wind."

Ethan was unsure what he meant but continued to say he enjoyed hearing him sing at the Church. "I'm sure you'll do well at the school in Ponty."

"I can go then? I can really go, Dad?" David's face lit up at the surprising news.

"Of course, son. I wish I could come too to hear you but Mam will be there and Nene Lina with Angel."

"Mam did you hear that? Dad said I can go; I can sing with the school." David was so happy. He skipped over to hug Mary quickly, then stepped back. "Can I go and tell Angel?"

"Of course you can, but be back soon for lunch. Dad is going up to help Uncle Dylan so he needs to eat before he goes."

"Yes Mam. I will be as fast as I can." He stopped suddenly, and then lunged at Ethan, giving him a quick hug before heading out the door. David ran to Angel's house and banged on the door excitedly.

Angel heard him running and shouting down the hill and opened the door when she heard David banging. "Dad said I can go with you to Ponty to sing."

Nene Lina shouted from the parlor, "Come in, David. Come in. I am so pleased. I knew everything would work out. Now you and Angel need to practice your songs when Mrs. Jones tells you what you will be singing. Perhaps Vicar Llewelyn will let you come with Angel and sing on Wednesday nights for our Mother's Union. I think the ladies would like that, too. When I find out I'll let your Mam know."

"Thank you, Nene Lina. I got to go now; Mam said we are to have lunch soon. My dad is going to help Uncle Dylan."

"Alright then, see you in a bit." He left with a wave and a wide smile.

Angel smiled at David as he left and said to Lina, "Nene, goodie! David can sing with me."

"I am really happy. I think David's dad is coming round," Lina smiled as she muttered the words.

"David's dad is coming down?"

"No Angel. It's what they say when someone is changing their mind and attitude towards something." Lina smiled at Angel.

Angel didn't quite understand but was happy that Nene was pleased.

"Go and change Angel, and let's have some lunch. Then we can go for a walk."

"Alright, Nene." Angel ran up the stairs and changed into her old play clothes and hung up her dress on the hanger, then laid it on the bed. She wasn't quite tall enough to reach the rail in the wardrobe. Angel looked and realized she had three dresses now for Church. It would soon be Easter again and maybe Nene could make another dress for her.

"Angel, are you ready? Soup is on the table."

"Yes Nene. I'm coming." Down the stairs Angel ran, almost tripping on the old rag rug in the little hallway.

"Careful now, slow down when you come down those stairs. Some of the carpet rails are loose and you might fall on that rug."

"I almost did, Nene."

"What did you almost do?" Lina returned to the sink in their tiny kitchen and couldn't hear Angel clearly.

"Fall, Nene, on the rug. There's a piece sticking out," Angel explained to her when she joined her at the table.

"Oh dear. I will need to look at it more thoroughly when we get back from our walk. Eat your soup so we can go before it starts raining. I can see some dark clouds."

Angel finished her soup and Nene took her dish and rinsed it out in the sink.

"Let's put on our cardigans and we'll take the umbrella just in case." On the way up the hill Nene asked, "Shall we see if David can come, too?"

"Oh yes please, Nene." Angel's delighted smile warmed her heart.

As they approached the top of the hill they saw David was outside talking with Ian. Ian was sketching as usual.

"What are you sketching, Ian?"

"Oh, just what I remember up the mountain." He had already drawn trees and horses on his paper.

"My, oh my, you are good at drawing, Ian. It will soon be warm enough to go up again and you'll have lots more to draw. The spring flowers will be in blossom soon; they are probably budding right now," Nene Lina told him as she waited on the youngsters.

"We're going for a walk. You can come, too," Angel told him.

"I'll have to ask." David held the door for Angel. They were in the house asking Mary. Mary came to the door smiling.

"Yes, David can go with you. What time do you think you will be back?" She was drying her hands on her pinny, her favorite apron.

"Oh, we won't be too long. It looks like it might rain soon." Ethan followed Mary to the door, changed from his church suit. He was shrugging into his jacket as they spoke.

"Ethan, I see you are ready to go somewhere, too." Nene Lina commented as Ethan appeared behind Mary in the doorway.

"Yes, I'm going to help Uncle Dylan for a couple of hours and tell him about the children singing in Church this morning."

"That's good, Ethan. I think your Uncle would like that. We can go that way." Lina looked around at the gathering. "Shall we walk together to the shop, we'll carry on a little further, and then we'll have to turn back before it rains."

"Alright then." David and Angel ran ahead of them, giving Lina a chance to talk with Ethan a bit.

"What did you think about David's singing this morning, Ethan?"

"I had never heard David sing with such reverence." Ethan shook his head and looked down at the ground for a few moments, "I know it's not manly to do, but I was in tears. He brought so much joy to me."

"Don't worry about not being manly, Ethan. Welsh men can cry, just as anyone else can. I am so pleased you enjoyed his singing. David and Angel will need to practice their songs. In fact, I thought of asking Vicar Llewelyn if they can come to our Mothers' Union meeting on Wednesday night. That's if Mary can come, too. Would that be alright with you, Ethan, for David to come with us?"

Ethan noticed Lina was breathing heavier and her steps were slowing down. He offered her his elbow and she took it. Their steps slowed more.

"Of course, Lina. Mary looks forward to coming with you. Now that I am at home at night, I can take care of the children." A wealth of emotion colored his correction. Indeed, Mary was happier that Ethan was involved with something he enjoyed. Lina's heart warmed.

"I understand what you mean. It's good for Mary to be able to mix with some of the ladies."

Lina was trying to help Mary get out of the house and feel comfortable around other ladies. Not that all of the ladies were friendly. Some were downright mean and gossipers. It seemed even in Church groups there were people like that. He'd experienced that this morning.

Mary always felt nervous and embarrassed because she imagined what they were thinking when they looked at her – that her husband didn't have a job, they had a large family and didn't have much money.

Lina was determined that Mary could hold her head high and not be ashamed about anything as she was a good person and took care of her family. They made it to the chippie, he patted her hand as he stopped at the door.

Lina smiled at him. "You're a good soul, Ethan. I'll see you in a bit."

"Well, Nene Lina, I'll say goodbye for now. Have a good walk." Ethan entered Dylan's shop.

Lina and the children walked as far as Milkman Rhys' farm. David shouted, "Look Angel, there's a rabbit. Shall we catch it and take it home?" Off they ran to the fence but the rabbit was too fast for them. In two jumps it was through the fence and hidden in the long weeds.

"That's a wild rabbit, almost looks like a hare. They can be fast, even though they can only hop around. They can hear well and can tell if there is danger approaching." Lina caught up with them with a smile.

"Is that why they have long ears, Nene? To hear with?"

"Actually, long ears are better to hear with and they can hear for a very long distance. Doesn't that sound like the story, Little Red Riding Hood, where the wolf had long ears?" David and Angel laughed together and walked ahead looking down at the wild flowers growing up against the fence.

"Look Nene, daffodils! Can I pick some and take them home with us?"

"That would be nice. They don't belong to anyone as they are outside the fence but you have to take care of them and put them in water as soon as we get home, alright?" Angel nodded and bent to her task.

Before Lina could suggest it, David said, "Can I pick some for my Mam, too?"

"Do you remember when we were preparing for St David's Day we talked about Wales having two emblems, the daffodil and the leek? At Church we had daffodils and you wore a daffodil on your cardigan to school?" Lina waited on them, always connecting simple things to lessons learned.

"Yes, I remember and we had leek soup when we came home from school. It was good, so good. Some of the boys wore a leek on their jackets to school. You did, didn't you David?" Angel questioned her best friend.

"Yes, my Mam didn't have any daffodils ready, so she cut up a leek to make it look narrower and pinned it to my jacket. It stank! Everyone in my class came up to me shouting, phu-weeee, and then held their nose! So I ate it!" David laughed.

"You ate it? I bet it tasted strong, as it wasn't cooked." Lina covered her chest with her hand as she questioned him.

"Yes it did, it was nasty, but in your soup it's delicious," he hastened to add. He loved Lina like his own grandmother. "I don't think I want to do that again!"

Lina gave another example. "That's alright, David. I expect some of the boys didn't have an emblem to wear. I had to wear a leek when my Mam didn't have any daffodils, and I used to eat it after our morning assembly. I didn't like it at first because it tasted a bit like an onion," Lina told them.

Off they ran picking up more daffodils and some dandelions as they went. To the children, dandelions looked pretty, too. They didn't care that they were weeds, they were having fun. Their laughter cheered Lina. She kept a weather eye out, the clouds were dropping closer, and the wind was picking up.

"Angel and David, we need to go back home now, the weather is changing. Come on quickly, there is a strong wind and it will soon start raining." She'd paused long enough to regain her strength and breath.

They ran back and turned to go home. As soon as they approached Dylan's Fish and Chips shop it started raining. Dylan was standing at the doorway and waved them inside the door quickly.

"Good thing I was standing at the door looking at the sky, you could have gone by. Come in for a bit and see if the rain blows over. I'll wait for Nene Lina to come." He saw she was lagging a bit behind the children. Her face pale in the wind.

"Thank you, great Uncle Dylan." David went past him with Angel in tow.

"No trouble at all, you can all sit in my parlor if you want until it blows over. I have some dominoes in that little cabinet near the fireplace if you two want to play while you're waiting." He pointed to the hearth.

"Hello Lina, come on in. I saw you earlier going up the street and I thought then it might rain. How are you feeling today?" He ushered Lina into the shop, waiting as she took a seat in the parlor.

"I am well, thank you, Dylan."

"You do look a little tired Lina, are you sure you are alright?"

"Well, I must admit I am a little more tired today for some reason. Maybe it's because I was trying to hurry to avoid the rain. A good walk with children should be done leisurely, not hurriedly, and then they can find joy in the surroundings and learn more about nature. Don't you think, Dylan?"

"Of course, you know I agree with you. Now, come and sit down for a bit, but first please tell me if you are alright. I worry about you. Gilberto is so far away and you only have Angel at home."

Lina nodded everything was alright, "I know Dylan, don't worry." She smiled to assure him of the truth of her words, waving her hand in dismissal of his concern.

"Make yourself a cup of tea, Lina, and sit for a while. Ethan and I are still preparing food for tomorrow. You know where everything is, right?"

"That will be nice, thank you. I can make you and Ethan a cup, too."

"Thank you, Lina. Make yourself at home and try and rest a bit?"

Dylan walked back to Ethan who was stocking up the shelves with jars of pickled onions and peas.

"Thank you, I do appreciate it, Ethan."

"You know I'm happy to help you. I've almost finished doing the shelves, what else can I help you with while I'm here?"

"Can you get some more vinegar and salt from the pantry, but before you go come a little closer, will you?" He motioned Ethan with one hand, and then lowered his voice. "I want to tell you something without shouting."

"What is it, Uncle? You look worried about something." Ethan stepped closer to the older man, lowering his head to be close. He automatically dropped his voice to a murmur.

"I am, a bit." He sighed, glancing over his shoulder. "Lina looks kind of grey and very tired, Ethan. I'm worried about her." He shook his head. "Before you get the salt and vinegar, can you fill the coal bucket? When you get the coal, will you talk to Lina and see if you can find out what she may be hiding?"

"Yes, of course, Uncle." Ethan nodded as he straightened up. He put a hand on his Uncle's shoulder then went through the parlor towards the coalhouse.

"Hello, Nene Lina. Dylan said you were here. I'm sorry I was a bit busy with the pickled onions when you came in. I see daffodils, who picked these pretty flowers?" The children looked up from their dominos at the hearth at his entry.

"We did Dad, I picked some for Mam." David told him respectfully.

"Your Mam will be so pleased you thought about her on your walk. What do you think, Nene Lina?" He looked closely at the older woman while she smiled at the children, her thoughts miles away. He noticed her pale cheeks, the flush made her look feverish. Her eyes looked tired.

"She will indeed," Lina replied quietly.

"I'll fill up the coal bucket for Uncle Dylan. I'll come back in a minute."

As he walked back through the parlor David shouted, "Look Dad, I'm beating Angel at dominoes." Then David laughed his little sheepish laugh.

"I can see that, David. But it's nice to let the girl win sometimes."

"Why's that, Dad? I'm winning fair." It was right in David's world that he beat Angel. He frowned over the game.

"I know. I don't hear Angel complaining. It's just polite to let them win. Maybe when you grow up a bit you'll understand a little better."

"It's alright, Ethan. Angel needs to toughen up a bit." Lina smiled at them. She was at the table pouring the tea and gave the children theirs in enamel cups so they wouldn't break if they dropped them by accident.

"How are you Nene Lina?"

"I'm alright, just a little tired. This rain makes the air heavy. It started just as we got to the front door. I'm hoping it will blow over soon. I'm really looking forward to the warmer dry weather, aren't you, Ethan?"

"Most definitely. I like the sunshine, myself. I never saw any down the mine!" He smiled at her as he set the bucket down and crossed the room.

Lina handed him a cup. "Here's a cup of tea for you, Ethan. I'll take one to Dylan." Ethan took the steaming cup and nodded his thanks. Lina picked up Dylan's cup and made her way into the shop area. "Dylan, where shall I put your tea?"

"Over here, Lina. You can rest it up on the top of the glass counter. Then I won't knock it over. Thank you." Dylan smiled at her, but his eyes worried over her.

"Alright then. I think the rain is blowing over, so I better take the children home before it starts again. Mary might get worried wondering where we are." She turned, her shoulders hunched in her jumper. "It's been a good afternoon. The wild flowers are in bloom already and it will soon be Easter." She looked out the window at the dripping afternoon. "That reminds me, the children will soon be performing so I had better start sewing their new clothes pretty soon."

"Easter, so soon. It makes me think that time is flying by so quickly. Maybe then the children can go up the mountain and get some good fresh air again," Dylan replied and winked at Lina. Lina knew what he was alluding to. She gave him a wane smile and nod. Going up the mountain might eventually get Ethan interested.

Lina walked back into the parlor and told the children to put the dominoes away tidily, so they could get home before the rain started again.

"We're ready, Nene."

"Alright then, let me swill your cups out before we leave." She wiped her hands on the kitchen towel quickly and said, "Ready now. Let's go." Stepping out into the shop she said goodbye and Angel ran to Dylan to hug him, as she always did before leaving.

Ethan said, "David, tell Mam I'll be home in a little while. Another hour and I should finish."

"Alright, Dad."

David and Angel were in the street and skipping ahead of Lina. "Wait, let's cross the road together. We don't have a lollipop lady on weekends. Look left, look right, and look left again."

David and Angel chimed in, "If all clear, quick march!" They both giggled as they crossed the road. Lina walked behind them to David's house. Mary was waiting patiently on the steps.

"Here we are, Mary."

"Mam, I have a present for you." David handed the daffodils and dandelions to Mary. "We found lots of daffodils up by the milkman's farm."

"Thank you David, I'll put them in a vase." She looked over his head at Lina. The woman looked exhausted.

"We saw a rabbit, too," Angel added excitedly.

"It had big ears. Do you have big ears, Angel?" David tugged on Angel's ears, teasing her.

"Ouch, that hurt." She slapped at his hand.

"Sorry, Angel. I didn't mean to hurt you." David gave Angel a little hug.

"I don't have big ears." She pouted.

"I know; I'm only teasing you," David replied.

"Alright then, we better get home. Bye for now, Mary. Oh, before I forget, I asked Ethan if David could come with us on Wednesday night to Mothers' Union. If Vicar Llewelyn says yes, then the children can come and practice."

"Thank you so much, Lina. It'll be lovely for David to come with us. He'll be out of Ethan's hair for a couple of hours. I'm still concerned that it's a lot of work for him when I leave all the children with him, even though he's been home a good few months."

"That's alright, Mary. I'm glad to help out." She hunched her shoulders as a drop of rain fell on her head. "Ooops! It's going to start raining again." She beckoned Angel to come along. "Come on, Angel we must hurry. Bye, Mary, see you tomorrow." Lina waved as she moved to the street.

David ran inside, Mary waved and shouted goodbye then closed the door.

Soon, Lina and Angel were home and inside. Lina slipped off her shoes and put on her slippers and added some extra coal to the fire. Angel took off her shoes and put her daffodils in a glass jar she found on the shelf.

"Nene, can you pour some water in the jar, please? I remember what you said. Don't pick any flowers unless I look after them."

"Yes, that's right. Do you remember why?"

"Yes. If I pick them and don't put them in water straight away they will die."

"That's right, Angel. If you don't want to care for them, you should leave them on the plant to make the birds and bees happy with their beauty. Oh Angel, your feet are going to get cold and you'll get sick if you don't put on your slippers." She filled the vase and set it on the table, she saw her granddaughter's bare feet.

"Nene, they have holes in them." Angel gently reminded her grandmother.

"Oh dear, can you bring them here? I can darn them so you won't be without them too long. In the meantime, get one of your thick pairs of socks out of your drawer and put them on while I take care of your slippers."

Angel brought the slippers to Lina and hurried off to get the socks. She put the extra pair of socks over the others.

"Angel, did you forget to take your other pair of socks off?"

"No not really, my feet were cold so I put my socks on again."

"I've finished darning your slippers. Now your feet will get warm in no time with two pairs of socks and slippers," she laughed.

"It will soon be supper time." She rose to her feet. "Angel, what about practicing your songs while I get the supper ready?"

"Yes, Nene. Shall I sing your favorite?" Angel smiled at her, the words to the hymn coming quickly to her lips.

"That will be so nice. Do you remember the words?"

Angel nodded and pulled out the little stool and stood up on it. She counted 1-2-3 and started singing, "The Old Rugged Cross."

Lina stopped what she was doing to watch. Angel knew all the words. Lina clapped her hands and said, "Angel that was so beautiful, thank you for singing my favorite hymn."

Angel jumped down off the stool and pushed it back into the corner and ran to Lina. "Nene, did I really remember all the words?"

"Perfectly, my little Angel." Lina was so happy and gave Angel a big hug with a loving smile.

Chapter 12

Ethan was busy in the shop when Dylan caught up with him after Lina and the children left. "Hello, Ethan. When you talked with Lina earlier did you notice anything?"

"Like what, Uncle?" Ethan stopped what he was doing and wiped his hands.

"When Lina was here after their walk. I tried to take a good look at her but it was almost as if she couldn't sit for too long and had to get up to do something. She looks very tired today. I'm worried about her, Ethan. Can you talk with Mary and ask her if she has noticed anything wrong with Lina?"

"Of course I will, but what do you think is wrong?"

"I'm not sure, but she looked grey and very tired when they diagnosed her with cancer about five years ago."

"Cancer, oh my God."

"Yes, Ethan. She was told she had breast cancer and had to go into hospital. She had one breast removed then. Angel was sent to live with Lina's sister over the border." Dylan often talked with his hands, motioning away to the remembered border.

"So that's where Angel went! I never knew and Mary said Angel wouldn't talk about it."

"Angel was so upset. Lina was her Mam as well as her Nene. Angel didn't want to leave and be with Lina's sister, she missed Lina. Also, Angel had to go to an English school and couldn't speak a word of English. We all speak Welsh at home, as well as at school. It's only in recent years that they are teaching both languages. Not only that, Angel looked different. We are poor in these parts. It isn't unusual to see darned socks or patched clothing, but over there it's so different.

"Lina's sister, Mari, lives in Erdington, Birmingham. She admitted that the English children teased her so badly about her clothing she cried every day and didn't want to go to school. Here we don't ridicule people if they have darned or patched clothes; it's what's inside that matters, but over there it was different."

"That's so cruel." It disgusted Ethan how cruel kids could act.

"I hope she doesn't have to go back. If Gilberto takes her, I don't think she will ever be back." Dylan shook his head.

"What do you mean…? I must talk with Mary. I know Mary will agree that Angel can live with us."

"Son, I doubt if Gilberto will let Angel stay here without his mother. He brought Angel here because of Lina."

"If it's cancer, Lina will get better, won't she?"

"You never know with that cancer, and Lina has had it once already."

"She was cured wasn't she?"

"Not exactly, it went into remission. They cut everything away that they suspected was cancer, but can it grow back again?" He shrugged. "No one knows. They are studying cancer at all the medical universities and Cardiff University is trying to do something similar."

"What will happen to Angel if something happens to Lina?" Ethan asked with a knot in his stomach.

"I'm afraid to think, really. I know Gilberto couldn't look after her; he travels all the time with his job. He would have to find someone that would take care of her. It would be extremely difficult for him to find someone that would really care about her. They'd say they were looking after Angel, but you just never know. I honestly think that Gilberto will have to put her into foster homes or the orphanage."

"What about Lina's sister?"

"Who, Mari? Her children got married and have children of their own. Mari has enough of her own problems."

"Oh my God!"

"Let's wait and see. Ask Mary if she knows anything, will you Ethan?"

"Of course I will. As soon as I get home and the children are in bed."

"Let's finish up then, Ethan. So you can get home in good time and I can do the rest tomorrow. You have really helped me. Thank you, Ethan."

"It was good for me to come and help. I don't have a job so I am very pleased to help you."

"That reminds me, Ethan. Did I mention to you already, if you are not busy, maybe you would like to help me on a regular basis? I will pay you of course. That will help with your family, too."

"We started talking about it one day and I think we got on to another subject." Ethan was humbled and proud he'd been such a good helper.

"Well, anyway Ethan. Do you think you could spare a couple of hours a day to help me out?"

"Of course I can, Uncle. I am sure Mary would love me to be out from under her feet every hour of the day."

"That's settled now then!" Dylan smiled and clapped his hands, another task crossed off his list.

"Go on home, now, Ethan. Come back in the morning and we can talk about it a bit more."

"Right then, I'll go now."

"See you in the morning son, about 9:00. Will that be good for you?"

"Alright, Uncle. See you then and I won't forget to ask Mary about Lina."

"Alright, son."

Dylan locked the door and turned off the light and retired to his kitchen parlor.

Ethan again had a heavy heart. This time he thought about Lina and Angel. What would happen to Angel if she went back to England? How would David take all this? Angel is the best friend he's ever had, more like a very caring sister. They enjoyed singing together, doing their homework, playing together, and finding treasure up the mountain. It would break his heart.

Oh, and Mary, what would she do without Lina? Lina has been a mother and sister to Mary. Lina has been the most loving person Mary and Ethan had met. She has never looked down on them like a lot of people in Porth. She has always been there to lend a helping hand. "It's our turn now; to repay all the love and kindness Lina has given all of us all these years," he thought as he walked home.

Ethan was almost home when he saw Lina's house down the hill. There were no signs of any light. Ethan opened the door to his house quietly, not to wake up the children. Mary was still in the kitchen and darning his socks.

"Oh Ethan, you came in so quietly you scared me when I looked up. I didn't hear the door close. Is everything alright?" Mary showed concern.

"Not really, Mary. Where are the children? Are they all in bed?" He paused to take off his coat, wondering how to start the difficult conversation.

"Yes, Ethan. What's the matter?" Mary dropped the darning into her lap, staring up at him.

"Let me take my coat and shoes off and I'll tell you." Ethan turned and hung his coat up on the hook behind the door and put his shoes in the cubby under the stairs.

"I'll make a fresh cuppa then." Mary always had water on the stove ready for tea at any time.

"Yes, that will be good, love. Thank you."

A few minutes later Mary came to the table with two cups of tea and cake. "Ethan, what is it? I haven't seen you like this for a very long time."

"I just don't know where to begin." Ethan was definitely disturbed.

"Sit down by the fire."

"Alright, love." Ethan took a deep breath, almost gagged, and blurted out. "Is Lina dying?"

"Oh my God, what did you say?"

"Lina, is she very sick? Is she dying?"

"Oh my God," she repeated. "Why would you ask that, Ethan?"

"Dylan seems to think there is something very wrong with Lina. He said she is looking very tired and grey again like she did a few years ago."

"Lina, oh my God, No!" Mary blurted out and covered her cheeks with her hands…then there was silence for a little while.

"Well, she did say today that she was tired and could she sit for a while before we started on the sewing. We are making a new dress for Angel and a shirt to match for David."

Ethan looked totally puzzled.

"You know about the singing at the school in Ponty, don't you?" Again Ethan looked as though he had no idea what Mary was saying.

"Ethan, what is it you're asking me?"

"It's Lina, have you noticed any signs of sickness or has she mentioned anything to you? Dylan said he feels there is something very wrong with Lina." Of course he remembered the children singing, but the conversation with Dylan earlier eclipsed all other thoughts.

"Honestly, I never thought something was wrong, I didn't. Really, I didn't. I thought Lina was just tired. Oh, my God, maybe she is doing too much and too much to help me. She helps me all the time. I had no idea, I didn't ask any questions. Shall I go down there now and see Lina?"

"When I arrived home, I looked down the hill and I saw her house in darkness. It would be awfully rude to go now, don't you think? She'll be in bed. Are you seeing Lina tomorrow morning like you do most days?"

"Oh yes, she said she's coming up in the morning after the children go to school. She's bringing up a sheet she thought we could use for David's shirt and Angel's dress. It's cream color. It will be perfect for the concert and for Easter."

"Can you ask her if she is alright? Dylan seems to think she won't tell us if she's sick."

"Oh yes, I will. In fact, I will make some scones for her. She always helps me make scones but this time I'll make them ready for her. What do you think?"

"Yes, that would be very nice. I think she'll appreciate that."

"I think I have some jam left too. Let me go in the pantry and take a look now, while I remember." Mary disappeared into the pantry with the candle. "Yes I have one jar left. It is the good, blackberry jam that she made last autumn, David and Angel's favorite jam."

"Mine, too!" Ethan chanted.

"Yes, we know! But, you like all the jams, so it doesn't matter which one it is. You just like sweet things, right?"

Ethan got up and took Mary in his arms. "That's right my beautiful sweet Mary, anything you and Lina make, I like. In fact, I like you more right now!"

"You do, hmmmm?" Mary humorously asked, looking up at his softened expression.

"You can wash the cups tomorrow. Come on now, let's go to bed."

"Well yes, I am a bit tired."

"I'll add some coal to the fire and close the flue." Ethan was already getting the coal.

"I can swill the cups out while you're doing that then."

Both were soon ready for bed. Ethan took the candle in one hand, locked the front door, and then grasped Mary's hand gently in the other and went upstairs. They didn't say anything more about Lina, letting the subject die down. They worked at reconnecting as a couple. While the family was important, they were finally finding time for each other.

Morning broke open with a bird singing on the window ledge.

"Look, Ethan. The first robin I've seen this year." Mary watched his bright breast as it sang. She sighed, loving the warmer wake up. "The weather is changing."

Mary lay back down for just a moment and said, "Spring is here!"

Ethan rolled over to look at Mary, his soft, long, dark curly hair touched Mary's cheek. Mary looked into his slumberous eyes that were focused on her chest as it moved gently up and down. She smiled at him.

"It will soon be time for the children to get up and visit Penrhiwgwynt again. Maybe they can find Buttercup." Mary tried to distract him and cover her emotions as his appealing look relaxed her morning get up and go feeling.

"Buttercup! There'll be plenty of buttercups everywhere."

"I know buttercups will be everywhere, I'm talking about Buttercup the white horse that David and Angel loved so much."

"Oh that horse, it's probably roamed off somewhere else by now."

"Oh don't say that, Ethan. That would break their hearts. Lina says Angel asks everyday if Buttercup is alright, or when can she go back up there to see her."

"That horse must have made a big impression on those two." He stretched in bed, the covers moving down his chest.

"They are children, they look forward to the beauty in life, and there's definitely beauty up there. Don't you remember?" She rose to her elbow, stroking the expanse of his chest. They wouldn't have time for anything this morning; the children were already making noise.

"Sounds like the fairy elephants are stirring." Ethan quickly changed the subject.

"Well, it was a nice thought of staying in bed a bit. I'd better get up and get breakfast ready for our little fairy elephants." Mary gave Ethan a kiss on the cheek.

"Come here, that's not enough." Ethan put his arms around Mary and squeezed her close then he puckered up and left a big kiss on her forehead.

"Alright then, I'm getting up." Ethan released her from his embrace.

Mary was up, dressed, and down the stairs in no time. "Come on children, it will be time to go to school soon. Eat up your breakfast and get ready." She cut the scones before putting them on the baking pan.

"Don't forget your scarves and gloves. It's still a little cold."

"Yes, Mam." David ran through the door leaving one of his gloves.

"Oh, I'll take it to him, Mam," Ian replied.

"David, wait. I've got your glove." Soon Ian caught up with David, "What is wrong with you? You left one of your gloves in the hallway." Ian slapped David on the shoulder with the glove.

"I was in a hurry to meet Angel so we could walk across together with the lollypop lady."

"Oh my God, David. When Mam tells you something, listen to her, will you?"

"I do, Ian I do."

"Well, this morning you didn't. You don't want to get sick do you?"

"Alright, here comes Angel. Bye, Ian." David turned and met Angel without answering his older brother.

"Bye!" Ian shook his head, wondering if David listened to a word he'd said.

Ian went back home to get his pencils that fell out of his satchel, then on to school.

"Mary, did you say Lina was coming up today?" Ethan joined the family as they rushed out the door. He closed it behind them, smiling, then went into the kitchen.

"Yes, as soon as the children go to school."

"I want to ask you something very important before she gets here."

"Ethan, what is it?" Concern was in Mary's voice.

"Well, Dylan shared his concern about Angel, also. What will happen to Angel?"

"What do you mean? Something will happen to Angel?"

"If Lina gets very sick, she will not be able to look after Angel." Ethan took her hands in his and straightened his shoulders. "Mary, will you let Angel live with us as family?"

"You know she can, Ethan. You don't have to ask. She is already like family to me and definitely to David. He thinks of her as his sister already." She smiled at him, love in her eyes. She loved this man. With so many children of his own, he was still willing to take in another to love and raise.

"Find out if there is something wrong with Lina. Is she sick? Tell her we will take care of Angel so she won't worry about her. She can live with us."

"I think I hear Lina now." Someone knocked on the door. "Come in, Lina."

"I'll get my things together and go." Ethan kissed Mary quickly and moved away to get his coat.

"Good morning Ethan, are you off to Dylan's now?" Lina smiled as she walked inside.

He helped her off with her heavy coat and hung it by the door. He thought she looked better this morning. "Good morning Lina. I am just off to help Uncle Dylan. Mary said you were both sewing this morning. It's good I'll be out of the way for you both."

"You have a good day, Ethan. It's a beautiful morning." Lina smiled at him.

"Yes, Lina, it is that!"

"Hello, Lina. I have the kettle on and made some scones already," Mary called from the kitchen.

"What a lovely surprise, I feel I need a cuppa this morning."

"Sit down. Sit here in the rocker by the fire while I get the tea."

"Thank you, Mary." The kettle whistled almost as soon as Lina sat down.

"I've warmed the pot ready for the water." She poured the steaming water over the leaves. "There, I'll let it sit for a while." Mary sat at the other rocker opposite Lina. "I want to ask you something. I feel something is wrong." She clasped her hands and took a deep breath. "Are you sick, Lina?"

"No, not really, just tired."

"Oh Lina, please tell me? You have helped me so much over the years. Now it is my turn to help you." She reached out to take Lina's hand. "I want to, Lina."

Lina's face was pale with tears in her eyes; she sat silently, rocking. It took her a moment to gather her thoughts.

Mary put her arms around Lina. "Please tell me. What can I do to help you?"

Lina blurted out, "I'm not worried about myself. I'm worried about Angel. If something happens to me what is going to happen to her?"

"Lina, Angel can live with our family. I already feel she is a daughter and I know David loves her as a sister."

"Gilberto wouldn't let her stay here." She shook her head, knowing he wouldn't see it that way. "He thinks he

could look after her but he travels and she can't be alone
while he is gone."

"Lina, you haven't told me what is wrong."

"I think it's come back." Lina cried silently in her hands.

"What! Oh my God. Lina are you sure?"

"I feel the same as I did before, I am so tired. All the
time."

"Have you seen the doctor? You must see the doctor."

"No, not yet. I just want to feel a little more energetic
before I go and I want to get our sewing done. They will
soon be singing in Ponty."

"Lina, the sewing is not as important as your health.
Let's go to the doctor together tomorrow."

"I don't want to trouble you. You have the family to
take care of."

"I insist, Lina. Let's go after the children go to school in
the morning."

"Alright. That will be alright." Having a plan, she wiped
her cheeks and settled back in the rocker. Mary rose from her
knees where she'd gone to hug the older woman.

"Have you told Gilberto? He needs to know."

"No. I haven't. Actually, I don't know how to tell him."

"He needs to know, Lina. When is he coming to see you
and Angel?"

"Next month, but I want to be certain before worrying
him."

"Let me get you a hot cuppa and scone."

Mary turned to look at Lina as she went to the sink. Lina
sat quietly, her face grey with no color and her hands
shaking. Still a young lady, but looking worried had aged
her. Mary fretted over her as she poured the tea and put some
scones on a plate.

"Here you are, a nice cuppa for you."

"Thank you, Mary." Lina took the cup and a scone, but
she didn't taste either of them. With a shake of her head,
dispelling the sadness in the air, she gestured to the folded

sheet she'd carried up. "Can you open the sheet and then fold it in half and lay it out on the table? I would like to cut out the dress and shirt for the children."

"Lina, it's not that important, it can wait. We still have three or four weeks to go."

"Time passes very quickly, before we know it, it will be Easter and they are singing just before Easter." She sipped the tea she didn't want, and lifted the cup a bit as Mary moved to follow her instructions. "Thank you, Mary. I have brought my tailor's chalk to outline the pattern. Do you have an old shirt of David's that I could cut up and use as a pattern? It doesn't matter if it's torn and has holes and rips, in fact that would be even better. Then I would know you wouldn't want it other than for rags."

"Yes, I do. The torn one that fits now, yes?"

"Yes, that will be good and I can trace around it a little bigger so he will have time to grow and enough for the seams."

"I was going to bring newspaper for the pattern but I didn't want to blemish the fabric with newspaper print. The ink sometimes stains and that wouldn't look good." Lina put down her tea and scone as Mary came down with the shirt.

Lina started on cutting it up close as possible to the seams so she wouldn't lose any of the size. Soon it was cut into pieces and the sleeves cut off and opened up, two front pieces, and the back and the collar and cuffs separately. She showed Mary what she was doing every step. "On the fold, we can cut the back of David's shirt. Let's lay half the shirt back on the fold. Can you pin it in place for me, please?"

Mary took the pins and did as Lina told her. Then Lina drew around the shirt back. She carefully took out the pins and placed one of the shirt front panels on the selvedges. Mary pinned it in place and Lina drew around the front panel. She carefully took the pins out and removed the shirt.

"Let's do the sleeves now." Mary watched with enthusiasm.

Mary watched with enthusiasm as Lina folded a shirtsleeve and laid it down on the table.

Lina explained, "Sometimes the sleeve cannot be cut out folded as one side is slightly different to the other over the shoulder. Let's see if this one is different." She placed it on the fold. Then Mary pinned it in place and Lina drew around it. It was the same size and Lina explained that sometimes it is not different for a child's shirt. She carefully unpinned the sleeve and cut around her markings allowing again for the one inch extra.

"Pull the sheet up a little, please Mary. We still have lots more fabric to use." Mary did as Lina asked and Lina placed the cut out sleeve on the fold again to make the second sleeve. Mary pinned it in place and Lina cut it exactly as the other all around.

"We haven't quite finished yet, I must cut out Angel's dress next, and with all the bits we can make the collar and cuffs for David's shirt and the sleeves and collar for Angel's dress. Oh, and if there is enough left over for two little pockets." She stepped back and stretched her back. Leaning over the table was difficult for her.

Mary pulled up the sheet again as Lina had asked. Lina carefully placed half the bodice front of Angel's dress on the fold and Mary pinned it in place. Then Lina placed the bodice back on the selvedges, allowing for one inch all around and marking with here tailor's chalk before cutting.

"Now for the skirt. We'll have to pull up the sheet again, make sure it is still folded in half please. I'm going to fold the sheet again so it is 4 layers and I can cut the skirt into two panels by placing half of the skirt on the fold."

"Shall I pin it in place?"

"Oh, yes please. I will draw around it as I did David's shirt and add one inch all around where the seams will be."

"Now I understand. The four layers are really the front and back of the skirt."

"We only have the collars, cuffs and sleeves left to do. The collar needs two layers and each cuff needs two layers. Angel's sleeves I will do just like David's sleeves but they will be much shorter."

Mary pinned as Lina instructed, and Lina drew the marks and cut around as before with one inch extra allowance.

"Oh my goodness, we are doing very well. Look, Mary, we still have lots of fabric left. I didn't realize this sheet was that big. I can make a belt for Angel's dress and a little collar, too. I nearly forgot, the pocket for David's shirt."

Mary and Lina pinned, drew the seams, and cut the fabric.

"There's still a lot of fabric left. We can keep that and make some more shirts for the other boys later on."

"That is a good idea." Mary noticed how the time had flown. "Let's have another cuppa, Lina. I know you must be tired standing over the table like that."

"I am a bit, but the excitement of making something with you for the children really helped me this morning. Is Ethan coming back for lunch?"

"Oh dear, I forgot to ask him and he didn't say." She propped her hands on her hips. She snapped her fingers. "I have a thought. Lina, let me run up to Dylan's and bring back some fish and chips for lunch. Why don't you sit here and have a rest till I come back?"

Lina settled back into the rocker and in no time fell asleep while Mary left and went up to Uncle Dylan's. As Mary was approaching the shop she saw Ethan come out of the front door.

"Ethan, I thought I'd come and get some fish and chips for Lina. Let's go back to Dylan's a minute."

Ethan was curious as to why Mary came up to the shop. She normally made something for lunch.

"I wanted to give Lina a break. She looks so tired, Ethan. Something is definitely wrong."

"Did she say what it was?"

"Not exactly. She said she thinks it's back." She leaned close to him, keeping the topic of conversation between them for now. "We talked about it a little and I said I would go to the doctor with her in the morning."

"Yes, you must be with her. I hope it's not serious. How can we contact Gilberto?"

"Lina said he is coming next month. I didn't think of asking if he might be here for the children's performance. I will go with Lina tomorrow and see what the doctor says."

"Where is Lina now?"

"I left her in the rocker; she is so tired I think she needs some rest. Have you finished helping Dylan?"

"No, I was coming back this afternoon but what I'll do is stay and help him for the lunch time and you go back to Lina with lunch."

"Yes, I will, but I must talk with Dylan before I go." Ethan held the door for her to enter first. Mary went to Dylan's side.

"Hello, Uncle Dylan." She hugged him and stepped back.

"Hello, Mary. How are you this morning?" Before Mary could answer Dylan said, "You look worried, Mary."

"Yes, I am. I am worried about Lina. I will go to the doctor with her in the morning. Maybe he can tell Lina what is wrong."

When Mary returned to the house Lina was fast asleep, but startled awake when the door opened.

"I'm sorry for waking you. Are you alright?"

"Yes, I think so." Lina said with a yawn and stretch.

"Let's do the rest of the sewing tomorrow. We can come back here after the doctor if you are up to it, Lina. Let's have lunch then." Mary placed the fish and chips on plates and brought the salt and vinegar.

"I don't know why, but food always tastes so much better when someone else has prepared it." Then Lina and Mary broke out in laughter as neither had cooked it

Chapter 13

The following morning both Lina and Mary went to see the doctor, but the appointment didn't go well. The doctor suspected that cancer had returned and Lina would have to go to Cardiff Hospital to see the cancer specialist for a definite diagnosis.

Mary did not know how to comfort Lina, but for her to be by herself she didn't think was wise.

"Let's go to the coffee shop in Hannah Street and have a cup of coffee. I know you like coffee, we both haven't had one for some time."

"Yes, that sounds really good right now." Lina didn't have the enthusiasm but going through Hannah Street would break up the walk a little. They entered the coffee shop and chose a seat.

Lina sat in silence while they waited for the waitress to take their order.

"Lina, I am so sorry. How can I help you?"

"I really don't have anything to do that I need help with, but I am worried about her. Angel, I mean. She is too young to understand."

"I know Lina, but if Angel knows that you are not well she will be less demanding and help in her little ways."

"Angel is a special little girl, she doesn't demand anything, and she is so caring. What will happen to her if something happens to me?" Tears dampened her cheeks.

"Please, Lina don't worry about such things right now." She patted Lina's hand to comfort her. "You are not certain yet, so please, let's wait. Most of all, please understand that I am your friend and I will do whatever it is to help you. If you need a rest, we can take care of Angel for you."

"I know you will do your best but if it is terminal this time, what will happen to Angel?"

"Oh please don't think that until you are certain. We will have Angel as part of our family. We already feel she is our little daughter already."

Tears were in Lina's eyes.

"There, there now. Please don't worry." Mary reached over and put her arms around Lina.

"Thank you, Mary." And she wiped her eyes.

"Ah, here's the coffee. Oh look, they remembered hot cross buns." Mary handed the money to the waitress and the waitress left the whole plate of hot cross buns.

"Mrs. Edwards, we can wrap up the rest you don't eat and you can take them home."

"Well, thank you. Wrap them up in two bags will you so Nene Lina can have some, too."

"Oh Mary, you didn't have to do that. I know you don't have the money," Lina whispered to her.

"Hush now Lina, I did exactly as you told me and kept a few pennies in a jar every time Ethan gave me the housekeeping money. So see, I do have the money!" Mary grinned at her, lightening the mood and proud she'd saved money.

"Thank you so much Mary, this is so kind of you. I really do appreciate this and what a surprise for Angel to have a hot cross bun, that I didn't make." They both found it funny, their humor returning after the tears, chuckling at the thought the coffee shop had cooked them. They finished the coffee and walked the rest of the way home. Their walk carried them past Lina's house and Mary paused with her at the step.

"Lina, do you want to rest now for a little while and come up a bit later, we can sew then."

"Yes, I think I'll do that. I'll come up after lunch, shall I?"

"Of course, whenever you feel a bit better." Mary left Lina at her house and walked up the hill. It wasn't too long before Ethan arrived.

"What did the doctor say?" Ethan asked with a worried look, hanging up his jacket.

"Lina said he thinks the cancer is back and she must see the specialist in Cardiff. Lina is very upset and she is so worried about Angel."

"I hope you told her that Angel can live with us and we will take good care of her. What about Gilberto? Did she say anything about letting him know?"

"No, and I didn't think about asking her. I should have but I was concerned that the walk was a bit much for Lina. We stopped in Hannah Street for a cup of coffee and a bit of a rest."

"Coffee! Lina likes coffee, too? Where is she now?" He looked around the entry.

"She's at home for a rest and will come up later." Mary touched his arm, needing the contact for reassurance and strength.

"Hmm. I hope she will tell Gilberto. Do you know when he is coming next?" Ethan put his arms around her, holding her close as he digested all she'd told him.

"It should be sometime next month that he will be here. Maybe, if she is seeing the specialist before he comes, she can tell Gilberto what he says, too."

"I'm going down to see Lina if she doesn't come up this afternoon. I am worried about her. When are you going to see Uncle Dylan again?"

"This afternoon, I said I would go and help for the evening crowd."

"Will you tell him?" She pulled away from him. "Yes, I think it will be good if you tell him but I am worried everyone will find out so tell him when no one is around.

Maybe he knows how to get in touch with Gilberto if there is an emergency."

"Yes, when I go up I will ask him that, too."

"This is the last night Angel and David will be practicing at our Mother's Union meeting and tomorrow is their big day. They sang so beautifully I was almost in tears," the Vicar said with pride. The whole room of ladies clapped with joy. "You will do well tomorrow little ones, bless you both," Vicar Llewelyn said as they were leaving to go home.

Thursday came and both Angel and David were ready to go to school. Lina and Mary walked with them to the lollypop lady and waited for her to stop the traffic before going on down the road to the school. They looked so dressed up, David in his new shirt and bow tie with his brother's jacket and trousers. David even shined his shoes!

Angel wore her new dress. It had a little collar with a pink bow in the front and two little pockets on the skirt front with pink bows to match. She wore the black patent shoes Amanda gave her. Amanda lived down the street and she had grown out of them and gave the shoes to Angel last year. It was the custom to pass on clothes and shoes to another family if they were outgrown.

Angel's hair was pinned up in a ponytail with a pink bow and streamers dangling down to her shoulders, matching the bows on her dress.

"Lina, thank you so much for making David's shirt. It is perfect and Angel's dress is so beautiful. I like the little pink bows."

"No, no! I didn't do it! You did a lot of the work, Mary. If it hadn't have been for you we wouldn't have finished them in time." She waved her hand in the air. "Mary, you are a fast learner, now you know how to make a pattern out of old clothing and to cut the pieces a bigger size, and you're also quick sewing them together. You were a great assistant. And, to think they were all made by hand! I must admit I do wish I still had my Mam's sewing machine. She had a beautiful treadle sewing machine." Lina shook her head in memory.

"Lina, what happened to your Mam's sewing machine?"

"My Mam would roll over in her grave if she knew." Lina shook her head, the thought saddening her. "I had to sell it with everything else when my Ernesto died to pay for the undertaker. Poor Ernesto, he worked so hard and died without even a decent burial. I will never forgive myself for that. He was such a kind and caring husband and father. He didn't deserve to die like that." Lina was so sad that she looked like she was going to cry.

"Oh Lina, please don't be upset." Mary linked arms with her, patting her hand. "Be happy today, Angel is going to sing. Let her see how proud you are of her." She locked arms with the older woman.

"I am, Mary. I am so proud of my Angel. She is a blessing to me. I thank God every day that Gilberto brought her into my life to take care of. I still wish her mother hadn't left like that. The poor child needs a decent mother."

"She has a decent mother, you Lina, you." Mary shook their locked elbows, insistent. "You have always said to me that things happen for a reason. I do believe God allowed her mother to leave for a reason. The reason as I see it is that you were able to take care of her."

They walked in silence for a bit, Mary busy thinking quietly, Lina enjoying the morning, trying to put the sad memories to rest again.

"Lina, I think there might be something in my basement. When Ethan's Mam died, we moved a lot of her things into the basement, as he was so upset he didn't want to part with any of them. If there is a treadle there maybe we could get it to work. I think Ethan would be very happy if we made use of his Mam's things instead of letting them rot in the basement." They walked a little farther.

"In fact, Ethan's Mam said she found some things that belonged to Ethan's grandmother, Clarinda. We never had time to really clean the basement out when Ethan was down the mine." Mary fell silent, remembering those days. "I didn't feel comfortable going through his Mam's things without Ethan being there."

"Perhaps you could ask Ethan first if it is alright with him if I help you look. I wouldn't want him to think we were rummaging through his Mam's possessions."

"Look there's Mrs. Hopkins, the headmistress and Mr. Trottman, Angel." Mary pointed ahead, stopping the conversation.

Angel looked happy when she saw Mr. Trottman. All the children loved Mr. Trottman and had the greatest respect for him. He believed that every child was worth spending time with to achieve the best they could at whatever it was they were given to do at school. He was definitely a great teacher and encouraged all the children to do their best. Many children who had excelled because of him once attended Porth Junior School.

It was time and everyone boarded the coach and sat looking out the windows. The children's faces were a picture – they beamed with excitement. This was their first time going on a coach and going to another school in Pontypridd. It was a miracle and a dream come true.

They arrived at Treforest School about 15 miles from Porth, just before 9:30am, the journey took only 30 minutes with all the traffic. The Alderman of Cardiff, Sir Herbert Hiles, MBE, JP and the headmaster were waiting in the entrance hall.

The Treforest choir was already waiting to go into the main hall. There were so many people in the hall that it was quite overwhelming to both the kids and their family members. David and Angel slipped off their coats and were led to the stage. As they walked up the steps they turned towards Lina and Mary as if they were saying goodbye forever, waving as they went.

"It's alright," said one of the teachers. "Your mams can watch you from behind the curtain so they will be close by, don't worry." She welcomed them with an encouraging smile. "Now walk on to those two big chalked X's on the boxes – do you see them? Alright then, just step up and turn to the audience." They both nodded very nervously.

As they entered the stage everyone cheered. Angel looked at Lina, suddenly very nervous.

"It's alright, I'm here. Just step up, and you David." David didn't seem to bother too much. He was wondering which X he was supposed to be on, not that it mattered. The school choir came in and stood at both sides and behind on the stage. It was a beautiful sight with all the pots of daffodils at the front of the stage.

One of the teachers thumped on their old piano and the choir began to sing. Then, their conductor spread out his hands and the choir was silent, instantly indicating to David to sing.

David started to sing a cappella, "Our Father Who Art in Heaven", accompanied quickly by Angel. It was so beautiful and the words echoed in the morning air. When they sang the first two lines, the choir sang a chorus in the background. It was truly a wonderful occasion. When they finished they got down off the boxes and stepped aside.

A young boy by the name of Thomas Woodward, later to become known worldwide as Tom Jones, came forward and sang. He had a different kind of voice, and one of the teachers told the children he was a baritone, and hopefully his voice wouldn't change, as he got older. The choir started to sing again and David and Angel were encouraged to walk back on the stage, this time in front of everyone, almost near the flowers to participate in the Welsh Anthem, "Mae Hen

Wald Fy Nhadau". It was a grand performance indeed, and the school and dignitaries applauded, giving the children a standing ovation.

Lina was delighted to hear Angel and David singing and to hear such compliments from those around. She was lost in the excitement and it was so good for Mary to see her saddened face relax and have a look of peace and joy.

After the performance, everyone was escorted to eat school lunch with the group in the lunch room. The lunch consisted of fish, peas, and mashed spuds, followed by a jelly. It tasted very good. Just as they were getting up from the table, another parent said to Lina, "Must have cost you a few bob for that dress Angel is wearing."

"Actually no, Mary helped me make it."

"Well now, I didn't know you could sew, Mary." She turned her head to look at Mary with disdain.

"Oh, Mary can sew beautifully. Did you see the shirt David is wearing? Mary made that. I know Ethan is very proud of her."

"Hhhmmm!" The woman left.

"Who was that Lina, do you know her?" Mary asked.

"Oh, you didn't recognize her? That's Mrs. Barrett from the Mothers' Union. She can be sarcastic when she wants to be, don't let her bother you. She is still very bitter her husband ran off with someone."

"Oh dear, I didn't know that." Shocked, Mary covered her mouth with her hand.

"Well, don't worry about it. I'm sure he is much happier. She almost nagged him to death." Lina waved her hand as she told Mary the tale.

"I always thought the ladies at Mothers' Union were very Christian and very kind." Mary's voice was shocked.

"Most of them are, but occasionally, like Mrs. Barrett, they spoil the atmosphere. The more you attend the more you will recognize them. I used to try and avoid them so I wouldn't be involved in any conversation, but the Vicar's wife told me to simply accept them for whom they are - busy bodies. Since then I have felt much better about going."

"Oh, will it get better for me, Lina?" Mary shook her head, never believing they'd ever accept her.

"Of course it will, Mary. Don't worry about those ladies. Be who you are, that sweet loving friend of mine. They will soon lose interest in trying to upset you. It will get boring for them eventually."

"Oh dear, Lina I don't think I fit in that group."

"Of course you do. It's really just one lady that is too vocal sometimes. The more you attend the better it will be."

"Look at my clothes, Lina. I don't have much; this is really the only dress I have that looks fairly decent."

"Mary, you look good. You are clean and your dress is well pressed."

"But, if I wear the same dress every time they will know I don't have any other clothes to wear." Mary fretted.

"If you were dirty then they could complain." Lina paused in thought, and then she smiled, snapping her fingers. "Don't worry, I have an idea. Let's talk about it when there's no one around. Maybe when we get home."

"I really can't afford to buy any material for a dress."

"I know Mary, don't worry about that. I have an idea and I think it will be perfect." This time Lina locked elbows with her friend, lending her a smile.

The afternoon went by very well with an escorted visit around the school, then back to the coach. All the way home David and Angel sang. It was a good day and they were excited about the whole of it.

When the coach stopped at their bus stop everyone was in a hurry to get off except for David and Angel, they were having fun singing all the songs and hymns they could recall.

"Come along now, we don't want to go to the bus station. It's time to get off the coach and go home," Lina reminded the children. "Don't run off, let's walk together."

Up the street and over the railway bridge they walked towards Mary's house, the kids scampering ahead of them. "What did you have in mind, Lina?"

"Oh yes." She paused for a few steps. "I have a new lacy tablecloth, it's almost cream, but it has a yellow tone to it. We can use that for a beautiful dress for you for Easter Sunday."

"That's in two days! And, I don't want you to cut up your new tablecloth for me." Mary took her arm in hand, insistent.

"Mary, it's alright. My sister, who lives in Birmingham, sent it to me but I don't need it. It's been in the dresser drawer for over a year."

"She would be very upset if she knew you were going to cut it up for my dress." They resumed walking.

"Don't be silly. It will be perfect. In fact, the only other thing I could use it for would be to make some curtains for the window. I have the blackout curtains up and they keep my room warm."

"Oh Lina, it would make a lovely curtain instead of those black outs. The war has been over for over 10 years." Mary scolded her smiling.

"I know; they have been up for a long time, but they are clean. I do wash them."

"Lina, I'm sorry I didn't mean they were dirty."

"I know you didn't. Don't worry about that. To be honest I'd rather have the black outs, then no-one can look in through the windows when Angel and I are there by ourselves."

"I didn't think of that."

"Now, then, I know it's Good Friday tomorrow. The children will be off school and Dylan will be cooking an abundance of fish and chips. Do you fancy fish and chips for lunch or dinner tomorrow?" Lina patted her arm as they started walking again.

"I could eat fish and cod's roe and chips anytime, every day if I could." Mary licked her lips.

"You sound just like Angel. She loves fish and cod's roe. Ask Ethan when he goes to help Dylan tomorrow, could he bring some home with him, and I'll give him the money. In the morning, I will come up after breakfast. I'll have to bring Angel so she won't be alone, if that's alright?

"Maybe Angel and David could play with Plastercine modeling clay. Angel has some packets she hasn't opened; Gilberto sent them for Christmas." She sighed, thinking of the holiday. "She was so upset he didn't visit she wasn't interested in the presents he sent."

"I remember you telling me about that. I think it will be a good idea. Ian might want to play, too. He is always interested in creating things and he can watch over them for us. Thank you, Lina."

"I almost forgot, do you have a petticoat?" Lina pulled them to a stop.

"A petticoat? Do you mean one to wear under a dress?"

"Yes. If we make a dress out of the lace you will need a petticoat underneath."

"Now I know what you mean." Mary smiled and nodded. "I have a cream one and a black one."

"The cream will be perfect. Can you get it out in the morning?" They started walking again.

"Yes, of course. See you in the morning then. Have a good night, Lina. Thank you so much for being with me and for David's beautiful shirt. He looked so good in it." Mary leaned in and kissed Lina's cheek.

"Yes, David and Angel looked really smart today. It was good to see the children enjoy themselves, too. Good night, Mary. Good night, David."

"Good night, Nene Lina and Angel."

Chapter 14

Lina and Angel arrived bright and early on Friday morning at Mary's house. David opened the door and shouted, "Mam's made hot crossed buns! Come and have some."

The aroma was very inviting as they walked through the hallway to the kitchen.

"What a lovely surprise you have made, thank you," Lina told Mary with a smile.

"Do you remember the blackberry jam you made last year? I kept a jar especially for today, to have at Easter with the hot cross buns." Mary set the jar on the table with a smile.

"That is so sweet of you."

"Ethan, are you coming downstairs to have some buns with the children? Nene Lina and Angel are here," Mary shouted excitedly.

"I'm coming!" He stamped his heels into the stairs trying to impress the children.

"Watch out, the king of the elephants is coming." They all laughed as he slid on the rug at the bottom of the stairs and hit his feet on the front door.

"Well, now you definitely arrived, alright!" Mary said with some humor as he got to his feet. "Are you alright, Ethan? You are moving very slowly."

"I just hit my back on the bottom step, that's all. No need to worry." He made his way into the kitchen, rubbing what was sure to be a bruise.

"Mary, do you have any Vicks left? I don't think Angel is feeling too good this morning; she didn't sleep well at all last night. I could hear her breathe, she sounded so congested."

"I do, actually. Let me get it while you all sit at the table. The kettle is on and everything is ready."

"Oh, thank you Mary."

"Ethan, what a shame you couldn't be with us to see the children yesterday. It was a splendid sight. Everyone applauded, even Alderman Sir Hines, MBE was there, too."

"I wish I could have gone. I missed seeing David sing, but I promised him I would come to Church on Sunday again."

"That will be really nice for the children to have you there, too."

"Well, I better go now. I promised to help Uncle Dylan this morning."

"Could you bring home some fish and chips for all of us when you have finished? We are going to sew this morning." Mary walked Ethan to the door and whispered to him where the others couldn't overhear.

"I really don't think Lina is doing too well but she keeps thinking of things to do and all of them are things to help us. I don't understand why."

"Don't let her do too much, Mary, let her rest. Maybe you could put the sewing off for another time."

"Alright Ethan, I'll do my best," she fretted.

Ethan leaned forward and kissed Mary on the cheek. She blushed as he reached for her hand. "See you in a bit, love." He smiled at her and tugged on his coat.

Ethan left, and Mary closed the door behind him.

Mary walked back into the kitchen. "Do you really want to sew this morning, because you look awfully tired? What if we sewed later, or even tomorrow? Have a little rest, Lina."

"I'd like us to make your dress for Sunday first. I'll be alright. Just a little tired."

"If you feel you need to rest we'll stop." Mary turned to the hallway and shouted, "Angel come here, Nene wants to put Vicks on you."

"I'm coming." Angel hated the smell and feel of the Vicks. She'd rather feel bad than have to suffer the stink.

"I'll put Vicks on your chest and your forehead. If that doesn't help, we'll do the Vicks tent." Nene carefully rubbed the Vicks on Angel's chest and did up her cardigan to keep the heat in, and then put just a little bit on Angel's forehead.

"Whoo eee! Yuck-a-fee! I'm not coming near you," David yelled.

"Hhmm, I have an idea," Mary dipped her finger in the Vicks and walked over to David while he wasn't looking and put her arms around him, tickled him with one hand and plonked the Vicks on his chest, down his shirt.

"Mam, why did you do that? Oh no, now I stink just like Angel." He wrinkled up his expressive face.

"Yes you do, but now it doesn't matter, because you both stink the same." Mary and Nene laughed.

"Mam, I was going to play with Angel. You know that, I was just teasing." He tried wiping the smell off on his shirt, but only succeeded in smearing it over more fabric, spreading the strong scent.

"I know, but Angel is so congested she can hardly breathe and it's not right to tease her when she doesn't feel well," Mary scolded him gently.

"Oh, Mam that's not fair."

"Do you remember what Vicar Llewelyn said last week in Church? 'Don't do to others what you wouldn't like done to yourself.' That means don't hurt your friend by teasing her because you wouldn't like Angel to tease you back. Would you, now, David? Please say you're sorry to Angel."

"I'm sorry, Angel. You know I didn't mean to hurt you."

Angel didn't say anything. David hugged Angel to reassure her he did not mean any harm and definitely didn't want to hurt his best friend.

"Why don't you two go to the front room and play with the Plastercine modeling clay that Nene Lina brought up. Take this tray with you so it doesn't get stuck to the linoleum or the rug. Your Dad lit the fire this morning to warm up the room so it should feel just right."

Angel and David smiled at each other, "Come on Angel, let's go." David grabbed the Plastercine and hurried into the front room and Angel followed. Ian was already in there, drawing horses and things on his paper.

"I am sorry, Lina, that David teased Angel." Mary joined her friend at the table.

"I know he didn't mean any harm. Don't worry. She really has to toughen up. What if I wasn't here anymore?" Lina waved her hand in dismissal, but a worried frown filled her expression.

"Oh, Lina, please don't say things like that."

"Well, I have been thinking a lot lately. I am worried, I'll be honest. I worry about Angel and Gilberto. Gilberto wouldn't be able to take care of Angel and she has a lot to learn."

"Please, Lina, stop worrying until you know what the Cardiff doctor says. Have you talked with Gilberto?"

"No, I haven't had a chance. He hasn't visited yet. He said he will come next week but I don't want to worry him."

"You must tell him; he needs to know what is going on." She covered Lina's hand with her own.

"Gilberto has a lot on his plate, I don't want to burden him with anymore." Angel came into the kitchen.

"Can you breathe better now?" Lina asked, and gently touched Angel on the shoulder.

"Not really, Nene."

"We'll make a Vicks tent for you." Mary went to get a bowl of hot water and set it on the end of the table and added a little Vicks to the water. "Come and lean over the bowl, Angel. I'm going to put this towel over your head so you will be in a tent. Just breathe gently and let the steam get up your nose. Don't touch the bowl if you can help it. It will be very hot."

"How long do I have to be in the tent?" She eyed the bowl and towel as if it were a spider headed for her. Angel hated spiders, scared stiff of the eight-legged beasts.

"Only about five minutes, that should loosen everything up."

After five minutes, Mary said to Angel, "Have you fallen asleep in there, Angel? It's time to come out of your tent."

"My nose is running." Angel was a little anxious about having a runny nose.

"That's alright. The Vicks has loosened up your sinuses so your nose will run. I'm taking off the towel. Sit up and you can wipe your nose." Lina handed Angel a beautiful lacy handkerchief she had in her pocket, with the initial A.

Angel took the handkerchief and wiped her nose. "Nene, whose hanky is this, it has an A on it?"

"It's yours," Nene said gently.

"Mine! It's a grown up party hanky, Nene. I don't have any like this!"

"I thought you would like it. I made one especially for you with an embroidered A for Angel. You don't remember? I slipped it in your pocket yesterday just in case you needed it."

"It's beautiful, Nene, thank you." Angel moved to hug Lina.

"I love you Angel, I'm glad you like it." Lina put her arm around Angel and hugged her.

Angel ran off to the front room to play with the Plastercine.

Mary cleared the table, wiped it, and washed the dishes while Lina unfolded the lacy fabric and spread it out over the table. She came prepared with her tailor's chalk and scissors again.

"Mary, I forgot to show you this dress yesterday. Mrs. Probert gave it to me, along with a pair of shoes that her daughter had outgrown. She brought them from Ponty. The style is too young for me, I wondered if you would like to try it on? I think it will fit, as you are slim just like Mrs. Probert's daughter. The shoes are pretty, too. I hope they fit you."

"For me!" Mary looked at the dress as Lina pulled it out of the bag she'd carried with her other sewing supplies.

"Yes, I think the style would be very flattering for you, and if you like it we can cut the same style for your new Easter dress. The shoes would go well, too. That is, if you like them?"

"I'll slip on the dress now." Mary ran upstairs to her room and within no time she came down in the light blue dress - it was a perfect fit.

"It looks so nice on you. Try on the shoes?"

Mary tried on the shoes but they were a little loose.

"That's alright Mary. Do you remember when we were younger and wore our Mam's shoes to play in? We stuffed them with newspapers; I think we could do that."

"Ian, can you bring me the newspapers from the front room please? The ones your dad left on the armchair." Ian appeared with a stack of newspapers.

"I didn't realize Ethan had collected all those for his Uncle Dylan. I know he won't need all of them. Perhaps we could use a few. How many do you need Lina?"

"Just one. It will go a long way. Let's see, shall we?" Lina cut the page off along the middle fold and then folded it into four, and then tore it into pieces. She crumpled up one piece and stuffed it down the toe in both shoes. "Try these on now, Mary. Do they feel tighter? But not too tight, as they may stub your toes."

"They're much better, but still a little loose. "

"Well, we must get them to fit properly so you won't lose them when you walk."

"I'm sorry. This is a lot of trouble for you, Lina."

"No, it's not at all. I think they will fit perfectly as soon as we've adjusted the paper socks."

Lina took the remaining two pieces of paper and stood one of the shoes on to it and drew around the shoe onto the paper. Then cut the two pieces together just a little bit inside her lines and then placed them both down into one shoe.

"Try this one on now and let me know what it feels like."

Mary slipped her foot into the shoe, standing first then taking a few steps. She turned her foot from side to side. Looking up at Lina, she smiled.

"It feels perfect."

"That's good. Now I need just another piece of paper, about half a sheet."

Lina folded the paper in half and did the same with the other shoe, stood it on top of the double paper and drew around it then cut it just a fraction smaller and placed the two pieces together into the other shoe.

"That looks really good, can I try them both on?"

"Of course, here they are. I'm hoping they'll feel comfortable now."

"They are so beautiful, Lina. Thank you."

"I only made them smaller, that's all." Lina waved her hand, dismissing the praise.

"Does it matter if they are cream? I usually wear my black Church shoes."

"They will be a nice change." She clapped her hands together, a smile on her face. "Alright then, I must get to work. You look so good in that dress I hate to ask you to take it off and let me make a pattern for your new dress."

"It's so comfortable I forgot I had it on."

Mary ran upstairs and changed back into her housedress and pinny and brought the dress to Lina.

"I have brought some wallpaper liner for a pattern – it's a bit thick but I'm sure it will be alright."

"Lina, you think of everything."

"Not really, I had to keep a list of what I needed when I made hats. Especially when I had to travel to London. I couldn't tell the future queen's mother that I left something at home. I had to be prepared. I'm not as young as I used to be, I've learned I can't always rely on my memory, especially when I am busy."

"To think you met the Queen when she was young, that must have been so exciting."

"You know, I really never thought about it as she was just a young girl then, when I made hats for her mother."

"Were you nervous, Lina, going to Buckingham Palace like that?"

"I'll be honest, Mary. I was so scared to death, the journey was long and so far away from Porth, and I was alone not knowing anyone. I really think that took over more than thinking about getting there. When I did arrive at the Palace, I was so nervous and then when I met her, the queen's mother I mean, I was worse. I wanted to make something she really liked especially, as my Ernesto used to say, I was in competition with the famous hat makers of London. I just wanted to please her and do a good job."

"But, you did Lina. She liked your hats. That's why she wanted you to go back time and time again."

"I know, but I couldn't, Mary. Not after what happened to my Ernesto. I left him that day to see the queen's mother. I should have stayed at home. He might be still alive now."

"Oh Lina, that wasn't your fault. No one could have known Ernesto was going to have a heart attack. It could have happened anywhere." Mary leaned down and gave Lina a quick hug.

"I still think about it and it has been many years now. He didn't have the chance to see his boys grow up and he never met Angel. He would have loved Angel. She is very much like him, soft hearted and loves animals. She keeps talking about Buttercup."

"Buttercup! You mean the horse up on Penrhiwgwynt?"

"Yes. She wants to go up and see her."

"David has been asking if he can go up with Angel as well, but it has been so cold and so wet lately. The grass will be slippery on that mountain."

"Maybe after Easter the weather will be better and we could all go for a walk up there. I think the children will be very excited. Maybe if we time it right, Ethan will come, too."

"Oh, that would be nice if Ethan came with us."

"Let's get your dress finished and we can talk about it some more later. What do you say?"

"Shall I put the kettle on, Lina?"

"That would be so nice. We could have a cuppa while we sew. Alright then, I must get on with making the pattern."

Lina spread out the liner on the other side of the table and laid the dress on the top carefully pinning it to the paper. "Come and see Mary, I'm going to draw around it with the tailor's chalk and then I'll cut it just a little bigger for the seams. We don't have to worry about sleeves it has the new style, cap sleeves and everything is in one piece. This one will be for the back of the dress and it is really easy to make."

"Will it be alright? The front bodice looked puffy when it was laid down."

"I'm glad you noticed that. Yes, it is slightly different because of our bust. I'll show you a secret how I will make the front. Alright then, I am going to cut around it allowing for the seams, just like I said." Lina allowed half an inch all around the pattern and cut the pattern about two and half inches longer. "I'm making the length longer for the hem like the back piece."

"Now for the front piece." Lina took the pattern and folded it and cut just about six inches above the waistline and cut in a diagonal direction towards the middle fold about four and a half inches. "This is for the dart that goes up the side of the dress. See, it will then be the same as the one you tried on." She opened up the pattern and laid it flat on the wallpaper liner, but this time she spread out the dart cut and pinned it in place making sure that the cut opening was about one and half inches separated.

"This is the most difficult part, just making sure there's enough space for a dart on the front pattern that I'm going to draw. It would be much more difficult if I had to make a larger dart for a fuller bust line."

"Well, you haven't got that problem with me." Mary and Lina laughed.

David interrupted, "Mam, can we have a drink and a biscuit in the front room please?"

"Of course, I'm making tea would you like a cup of tea or would you like some Ribena instead? Ask Angel and Ian, what they would like, too."

"I want some Ribena please, but I'll ask Angel and Ian what they want."

"That's a good idea. Let me know."

David came rushing out of the front room, "Mam, Angel and Ian want Ribena too."

"Well that mean's three glasses of Ribena, then. I'll bring them to you on a tray so there won't be any accidents."

"Alright, Mam. I mean, thank you, Mam." He quickly disappeared back into the front room where the laughter continued.

Mary made the tea and let it stand. Then poured enough Ribena to make the drinks and filled the glasses with water. Placing the glasses on a tray she added a small plate of current biscuits. "I'll take the children their drinks and biscuits. I'll be back in a minute, Lina."

"Everyone, here's your drinks and biscuits. Please try not to spill the drinks, so keep them on the tray, will you please. That Ribena will stain anything it touches."

"Our tongues too?" David shouted, eyes wide.

"Hmm, let me see." Mary tapped her chin, gazing at the ceiling and teasing her youngest. "Yes if you are not listening, but no it won't stain if you are listening to me."

"Woo hoo, look Mam's special current biscuits!" Ian pushed David out of the way to get to the biscuits.

"Why did you push me?"

"I wanted some biscuits."

Mary looked around the doorway listening to the children. "There's plenty for everyone. Just pick up the plate, Ian, and offer them to Angel and David first. There's enough for two each. I don't want you to spoil eating your lunch."

"I've got a surprise for you all on Sunday, so behave yourselves, will you?"

"What is it Mam?" David asked quickly.

"Well, if I tell you it won't be a surprise! Will it?"

"If it's a surprise, why do you ask every time, David?" Ian chirped in.

"She might tell me." He shrugged his shoulder, taking a bite of the biscuit.

"Silly, it wouldn't be a surprise if she told you."

Angel and David were discussing between themselves what the surprise could be on Easter Sunday while Ian continued with his modeling and Mary returned to the kitchen.

"They seem very excited in there."

"I told them I had a surprise for them on Easter, I expect I shouldn't have said that."

"It's alright, it gives them something to look forward to. I say things like that to Angel and she gets so excited. It's good to see her eyes sparkle."

"I got a few Easter eggs at the Co-op last week. They had a sale on a lot of things and I filled my book of stamps. They were actually free by the time Thomas took off all the discounts." She leaned in closer to Lina to explain.

"They will be excited. Don't forget, we have the Street Easter Party, too."

"Oh yes, but that's on Monday isn't it? Bank Holiday Monday."

"Yes, I will make a big trifle again this year for the adults and some biscuits for the children. Amanda's mam said she would make a sponge cake. And Mrs. Bailey said she had some tinned peaches in this week. I can use a tin in the trifle."

The little shop in John Street was owned by Mrs. Bailey and was opposite Lina's house. Mrs. Bailey sold mostly fresh vegetables from the farm up the valley and sometimes had tinned fruits and general things the neighbors needed.

"It's convenient, John Street shop. I can buy my spuds there so I don't have to carry them all the way up from Hannah Street. When they have some cabbage leaves left off the cabbages they give them to me, so I cut them up and fry them with mashed spuds and onions. Angel likes that. She doesn't eat much but at least she has started eating proper food again."

"Does she know that Gilberto will be coming soon?"

"Yes, I told her. I think that's why she started eating a little again. I got a letter from him so I read the part that he was coming, I thought that would excite her a bit." Lina's mind wandered what if Gilberto changed his mind or he couldn't visit. That would be devastating for Angel.

"I'm glad. She needs to see her father."

"I wish it was more often than once every couple of months though. He only stays one night. That's not really enough for a little girl."

Mary agreed with Lina.

"Alright then. Shall I show you how I make the pattern for the front again, because it is a bit tricky?"

"Yes please." Mary was already excited about having a new dress and seemed more excited to learn what Lina did to make such a dress.

"I spread the back pattern out onto the extra wallpaper liner, pushed out the darts, and I pinned it in place. I'm going to draw around it just a fraction bigger because we are not straight up and down at the front. We have a shape. See, on the top and sides I need to make just a little bit bigger."

"I never knew you could use the same pattern for the front as well as the back."

"Yes, but don't forget you must spread it out a bit for the darts. Would you like to pin it in place while I hold the pattern?" Mary carefully pinned it in place and Lina cut around the paper pattern, allowing extra for the seam.

When Lina finished she took out the pins and separated the two parts.

"Oh, I forgot to tell you as it is a shift style dress and really hasn't got a tight waistline we don't need any buttons. You can put it right over your head and tighten it up with a belt if you would like a belt. Now to cut out the dress in the lacey fabric."

Lina rolled up the remaining wallpaper lining and pulled the fabric into the center of the table, laid the pattern pieces down, and Mary offered to pin them in place.

"Would you like to cut out the pieces of lace now?"

"I can do that," Mary answered. "But I'd like to get you another cuppa first."

"No, no I can pour it while you do that and I'll pour you another, too."

"There is plenty of milk in the bottle and biscuits if you would like some." Mary answered.

"I think I'll sit in your rocking chair for a bit if that's alright."

Mary wasn't really paying any attention, she was so anxious cutting out all the pieces. By this time Lina had fallen asleep in the rocker. Not to disturb her, Mary took the pieces of pattern off the lace and folded up both carefully and laid the table. It was almost lunchtime. David came running out of the front room.

"Shhhhh, what is it David? Nene Lina has fallen asleep. I'll come in the front room with you."

David turned around and walked back to the front room. "Look Mam, what we've made." He pointed at the tray on the floor.

"Oh my goodness, a farm. Who made the horses? They look so real."

"Ian did, Auntie Mary," Angel replied in a hurry.

"I am impressed with the horses. The barn, house, and all those trees, it looks so real."

"Angel and David made those and also the fence." Ian said proudly about his brother and Angel.

"I am so surprised they are all still standing up. How did you do that?" Mary was trying to compliment the trio as much as she could.

"We used those old lollypop sticks to hold the Plastercine together and make the parts stay up straight so they wouldn't fall over."

"Well, that's quite an invention there. You will have to show your dad when he comes home. He will be home soon."

"Are we going to the chippie then?" asked David in a hurry.

"Dad is going to bring us fish and chips instead and a jar of pickle onions, as we finished the other jar. So, that will give you more time to play and make some more animals. What about sheep?"

"We did see some sheep and we saw rams up the mountain, Auntie Mary. We could make some of those."

"That would be really nice. Let me go back and see if Nene Lina has woken up."

"I must have dropped off to sleep. Sorry Mary. Where were we?"

"Don't worry, I've been talking to the children, and I think you should come and see what they made out of that Plastercine modeling clay."

Both Lina and Mary walked into the front room as Ethan came in the door. "Ethan come and see what the children have made."

"I have fish and chips in the bag." He held up the sack.

"I'll take them while you look at their masterpiece." Mary smiled and took the bag.

Ethan was surprised. "This is unbelievable. Horses, sheep, rams, and a dog! Look at that house and trees even a barn and a mountain. It reminds me of Rhys' farm at the bottom of Penrhiwgwynt."

Ethan stepped into the kitchen. "I am so impressed. The children have made such a scene. It was a good idea to use the Plastercine."

"It kept them busy while we were cutting out a dress." Lina joined them in the kitchen.

"Let's have lunch then." She unpacked the bag of food calling into the hallway. "Come on, everyone it's lunchtime. Wash your hands and come and say grace."

Soon they were all at the table and eating when there was a knock on the door. Ethan opened the front door surprised to see Thomas, the manager of the Co-op, standing on the doorstep with a box.

Chapter 15

"You won, Ethan."

"Won what, Thomas?"

"A television."

"A television? Come in! Come in!" Ethan looked at Mary who was in total shock walking up the hallway. It was raining and Thomas' coat was dripping. The box was soaking wet.

Thomas set down the box for a moment. "Let me get these wet things off. Don't want to mess up the Mrs.'s clean floor." He hung up his coat and pulled off his shoes. He didn't mind the holes in the socks. Picking up the box he followed Ethan into the kitchen. Mary preceding them.

"You said we won a television? I've only seen them in the shops, and the Jenkins have one. How did we win?" Mary questioned.

"You don't remember, Mary? I asked you to fill in your name and address on one of those pieces of paper and put it into the box on the glass counter top in the shop."

"Yes, but, but that was months ago, before Christmas wasn't it?"

"Yes it was, and now look. You are the winner of the big prize! You look totally shocked, Mary." He chuckled.

"Say something Mary," Ethan asked.

"Well, it's like this, my brother in Birmingham suggested having prizes. They are doing it all over Birmingham to increase sales. It works there and he said it would work here, too. It's a way of helping the community. We doubled our sales over December."

"Oh my goodness, and I won the big prize." Mary was in total shock. She could hardly stand up by herself so rested on Ethan's chest.

"Sit down, sit down," Ethan said to Mary.

"Whatever has happened?" Lina asked all the children.

"It's Mary. She is in shock. She won the television prize," Thomas explained to the entire family.

"That's a shocker, for sure," stated Ethan. "Mary, love, it's alright, you won, you won. Say something. Are you alright? Mary love?" Ethan put his arms around Mary and kissed her on her forehead. "It's alright love. You won us a television."

"I, I, oh … I won! I really won?" Mary could hardly say anything other than mumble a few words.

Lina brought a glass of water to Mary's side. After Mary took a few sips she struggled to say, "I thought if I didn't hear anything by Christmas I didn't win anything and that was alright with me."

Thomas thought it better to say something about the delay. "We staggered the winnings. The first winner would get the big prize, the television. The next five would get the turkey dinners and the other four would get a selection of cheeses." He explained to everyone.

"To be honest, we didn't have the television at that time so we couldn't give it to you at Christmas. That's why we never announced the winner's name. We posted a note saying the television had been ordered and we were waiting for its delivery."

Thomas was fumbling for excuses. "I had to order the television from my brother-in-law – he lives in Birmingham. It took so long to deliver; I started to think he was pulling my leg about getting one."

"Oh my goodness, everyone will know, and want to come and see it. Look at my house. I will have to get new covers for the sofa and chairs and make new rugs and oh, my goodness, get new curtains." Mary seemed in a panic and showed concern.

"Mary. Mary, stop worrying. It's alright, stop thinking about the unnecessary things!" Ethan was still trying to reassure Mary lightly, that just because she had won a television set they weren't going to change their lifestyle by investing in new things. He knew only too well their financial situation.

"You have a brand new television. Gerald will come later to get it tuned into the transmitter. If it doesn't get the signals strong enough he'll want to go up on your roof if that's alright? The transmitter is so far away and you may not get good reception with all the mountains and hills around here. He'll explain when he gets here," Thomas said as he was heading to the front door.

Mary seemed a little better when Lina started talking to her. Lina always initiated an atmosphere of calmness. "My sister lives in Birmingham and has something on her roof for her television, she told me last year when they bought their television."

Thomas was holding the doorknob but turned to confirm what Lina had said, "In Birmingham the land is flatter and no mountains so it is better for them and yes, I do believe they have started screwing a rod on the roof to help with the television reception. They have a lot of industry there, so that might have interfered with their reception."

"If Gerald has to go up on the roof it will be so dangerous for him, our roof is Welsh slate and will be so slippery. Will Gerald have some help?"

"Yes he will, Mary. Don't worry so much, he's done this before and we all know too well Welsh slate is slick. Let's see now, you will be the second household that will have a television in the street. You know Mrs. Jenkins has had one since last year."

"Yes, that's right, Amanda invites David and Angel to go down sometimes when there's a good children's program on BBC 1."

"Thomas, we only have electric in the front room, will Gerald know that?" Ethan commented.

"Don't worry. He will come and ask you where you want the television, so you can tell him yourself, alright? I must go now. They'll wonder what has happened to me at the shop."

"Everyone, when you have finished eating and drinking let's go and see how this works." Ethan picked up the box off the chair where Thomas had laid it.

Thomas said, "It probably won't work until Gerald comes." He was dressed for the weather again. He nodded and walked out the door, closing it behind him, leaving them with a wave and a smile.

The children ran into the front room before Ethan had anything else to say, and sat cross-legged on the floor waiting. Ethan took the television out of the box, stood it on the table near the front window, and plugged it into the wall then turned the knob. There was only a lot of crackling noises.

"Oh dear, nothing is happening," Mary announced.

Ethan assured Mary, "Mr. Thomas did say that Gerald will be coming soon to tune it. We will know when that is done. I'm sure he will explain everything to us."

The children were too excited for words; they weren't listening. "We can't watch anything yet then?" Ian asked, looking between the crackling set and his father.

"Not until Gerald has finished with whatever he has to do, then you can. Alright everyone?" Ethan paused a moment, looking around at every excited face. "Did you all listen to Mr. Thomas?" Ethan asked them. There were nods all round.

"Alright, dad." The children sat there for a while just staring at the television box that had a rectangular glass screen and knobs underneath the screen. David touched a knob when Ian shouted, "Didn't you hear what dad said? It won't work until Gerald gets here."

"I just wanted to touch the knob, and feel it."

"Well, don't touch it, don't touch anything." Ian sounded bossy and irritated.

Lunch forgotten, the children went back to playing with the Plastercine. Mary, Ethan and Lina went back to the kitchen to finish.

"Mary, I'll go back up and help Uncle Dylan for a couple of hours. If you need me to come home when Gerald gets here send Ian up, will you?" Ethan was standing by the door; Ian easily heard every word he'd told Mary.

"Oh, Dad, do I have to? I want to watch Gerald."

"If I tell you to do something, just listen will you. If your Mam needs me, I want you to come and tell me. Alright?" Ethan stared down his irritated son.

"Yes, Dad." Ian looked down in embarrassment because he was told off.

Ethan had never disciplined the children, as he was never there. This was a new thing for him, too. He had to adjust to his parenting for the first time in his life and give instructions. It felt different, somehow good, but somehow strange.

"I'll be back in a while. Nene Lina, will you be here when Gerald comes?"

"Yes, we are sewing so I'll be here for a couple more hours."

Mary was so distracted with the delivery of the television that she had forgotten about the dress they were making.

Ethan turned to the children and said, "Don't touch the television, are you listening?"

"Yes, Dad," Ian and David said together. Angel looked frightened.

"It's alright, Angel, you haven't done anything wrong. I just don't want the boys fiddling around with the knobs. I know you won't." He smiled at the youngster and Angel nodded in agreement.

Mary interrupted, "Nene Lina is showing me how to make a dress out of lace for Sunday."

"Hhhhmmm! A new dress! I will be able to show off my beautiful wife again!" Mary blushed.

Lina was placing pieces together and she did not hear all what was going on. When Mary returned to help, Lina had finished tacking them together. "Will you try this on for me and let's see if we need to make any adjustments. We don't need any openings or buttons. It has a nice boat shaped neckline so you can get it on over your head easy. Let's see, shall we?"

Mary stood in amazement. It certainly was very pretty and not even finished. "Oh my goodness, it looks so elegant. And this is for me?"

"Yes, Mary it's yours. Try it on with your petticoat and let's see what we might have to do before we sew it securely."

Mary ran upstairs and changed. She came down the stairs with her old working shoes on.

"Well, we can't have you wear those shoes, can we? Not with this dress!" They both laughed.

"Hhmm. Let me think. Yes, I remember Mrs. Probert gave me some other shoes too. Her daughter lost interest in them. She thought they would be good for me but to be honest they are a little too young a style for me."

"What about Angel?"

"It will take years for Angel to grow into them." She chuckled at Mary's expression.

"Tell me, what are they like?"

"They have a bit of a heel and there's a strap that comes over the foot. They are much like the style you wear to Church, but beige suede. Just perfect for you."

"Do you think they will fit me?"

"If they don't we can stuff them with newspapers like the other pair. I forgot to tell you. They are brand new!"

"New shoes! I hope they will go with the dress."

"I think so. I'll remember to bring them up next time I come. Now then, let's look at the dress. It looks good. I don't think we need to do too much to it. What do you think, Mary, is it comfortable?"

"It's a little loose around the waist. I think."

"Yes it is but we can add a belt to draw it in around the waist. What do you think, would you like that?"

"Yes, if you think it will look nice."

"I have some satin brocade at home. I've had it a long time; since the time I made hats. I think it will be enough."

"Oh that will be so nice. Thank you, Lina. You have such good ideas."

"Now, let's sew the seams. Can you sew this side with the backstitch I showed you? I'll sew the other side. Would you thread some needles with this cotton I brought up?"

Mary threaded the needles, one for Lina and one for herself and they proceeded to sew. "Lina you are so kind to me. No one else bothers with me. Why is that?" Mary wanted to know why people rejected her, particularly the women in the Church and the immediate neighbors.

"Mary, sweetheart. You are a good person and I want to help you. Then you will be able to do all this by yourself later on." Lina looked down, trying not to let Mary notice the tears in her eyes.

"I can't wait to see it all finished."

"When we have sewed the seams and the shoulders, I will show you how to curl over the neckline and the end of the cap sleeves. All we have to do then is the hem, and if that's alright with you let's get Angel to do that."

"Angel can sew, too?"

"Oh yes, she has sewed for a few years now. I started to show her early. Mainly because she is so lonely and it was a distraction for her then but it will help her later on in life if she can sew."

"I forgot all about the hem. It looked so nice as it is just frayed on the ends."

"We can't have frayed edges. People are not ready for that here yet. We need to sew it properly and then it will look chic."

"What do you mean people are not ready for that here?"

"It's a modern way of sewing clothes or rather not sewing. Up in London they have just introduced that way of leaving things frayed."

"Hmmm, how long do you think for that look to come here?"

"I don't know, love. It could take years and years."

"Does it look pretty when it's frayed?" Mary had a thousand questions. It was almost as if she was wishing for more knowledge on fashion.

"The man I saw at the train station was a tramp. Bless him, he was dirty, and all his clothes were frayed. He had a blanket that had holes in it. To me that new style looks unfinished and since seeing that poor tramp I really hope it doesn't come here."

"Those people who met you at the station, what did they say about him?"

"They didn't even look down at him lying there on the ground. But I was tempted to give him a shilling, poor man. He looked so dirty and I'm sure he was hungry."

"I hope we don't have any tramps here," Mary said quickly.

"We do actually, but usually they are at the stations. Not many in this part of the Rhondda. We all help each other so no-one gets to be in that state in life." She tied off her sewing thread, snipping the needle free. "If I go to Cardiff and have a few shillings or pennies in my purse I will give it to the tramps when I see them. They need food, clothes, and obviously somewhere to live."

"Oh dear. Don't they have anywhere to live?" Mary showed concern at the very thought someone could be homeless.

"No, that's why they are on the street. There is always someone worse off than us and these poor people usually don't have anyone in the world to help them."

"No family either?" Mary was shocked.

"Usually they have no family left, or maybe they have had something really tragic happen to them. I am sure they wouldn't be there out on the street in the cold and wet weather if they had a better life somewhere else."

"I didn't know that. I haven't been to Cardiff for so long." Mary sounded disappointed.

"We will go, I hope soon. Not to see the tramps but to just look around. Maybe take the children to see the peacocks in the castle grounds." Lina replied

"That will be really nice." The conversation ended and the ladies went back to sewing.

"You sew really well." Lina felt she needed to give Mary a compliment. She tried everything Lina showed her and she did a good job, too.

"If I do it's because of you. You taught me. I have the best teacher in the world and I didn't have to go to school to meet her." They both laughed again. Lina and Mary bumped shoulders in their laughter.

"Now then, we have finished the seams, let's press the seams open. Is your iron still hot?" Lina looked towards the fire grate where Mary kept her iron.

Mary had stood the old iron back on the stove next to the fire, hours ago. "It will probably be too hot right now; it's been sitting there since I pressed David's shirt earlier. I wanted to press it ready for Church on Sunday."

Lina moved closer to Mary, "That's alright. Stand it on the hearth if you can pick it up with this rag." Lina handed the rag to Mary. "We need to cool the iron off just a bit. We'll take out the tacking stitches and then you can try the dress on again while we're waiting for the iron to cool. Isn't that funny Mary, we normally wait for the iron to heat up not cool down." Both Lina and Mary laughed. What a lovely afternoon the ladies spent together sewing and laughing.

Mary enquired why she had to try it on so many times and Lina explained that it was easier to see if any adjustments needed to be done. Mary raced up the stairs after she put the iron down.

"Lina, look," she shouted down the stairs. "Look."

"Yes, it is really beautiful."

Lina picked up the pins and placed them where she thought it would be good to have a rolled neckline. She did the same with the cap.

"You can take it off now. Be careful with the pins around the neckline."

Mary raced up the stairs again and took off the dress, changing into her everyday dress and came back down.

"Let's sew the sleeves then. You do one and I'll do the other. I hope we won't pull it out of each other's hands." Lina turned to Mary again and asked, "Can you thread the needles again please? If there is a spare needle do that one too please. I think we might need it."

"What stitch should I use?"

"The herringbone stitch I showed you would be good, I think. Let's try it."

"Hmm, am I doing it right?" Mary proceeded to show Lina how she was doing her sewing.

Lina watched Mary closely, "You've got it. You have remembered well. Let's see what it looks like if you try just a little smaller stitch. I think they will look good even if they do show through the fabric."

"Is this better?"

"Let's see," Lina turned it over. "Much better. I know it will take a little longer but it will look really pretty."

"Alright then." Mary took out the thread and repeated all the stitches but smaller.

Lina smiled and laughed a bit. Mary was a quick learner and enjoyed sitting with Lina. Then Mary laughed too. It was a good experience for Mary to learn the correct size stitch for certain fabrics. They were busy sewing when Gerald came. Ian opened the door and allowed him in.

"Mam, Gerald is here," Ian shouted down the hallway.

Mary turned and shouted, "Come in, come in, we have been expecting you."

"Thank you." Gerald wiped his feet on the doormat, as it was still raining outside.

"Have you put the television where you want to watch it?" Gerald enquired, nodding at Mary as he hung up his coat.

Mary replied quickly, "Well we only have electric in the front room. Will that be alright; can it go in there?"

"Yes, that will be alright. It can't work without electric!" Gerald answered jovially.

"Hello kids. Oh my goodness haven't you grown since the last time I saw you? David you're getting to be a handsome young man just like your brother Ian." Gerald noticed that Ian was paying attention to everything he was saying, so why not give them both a compliment. And then there was Angel, sitting so very quiet watching with a curious look on her face.

"Angel, you are the sweetest little girl I have seen. I hear you sang beautifully yesterday at Treforest School. I expect you and David stole the show. Your Nene is so proud of you." Angel smiled and looked down a little shy.

Mary took his dripping jacket. "I'll put it in the kitchen on the back of the rocker near the fire so it will dry quickly for you."

"Thank you, Mary." He rubbed his hands together to warm and dry them. "Well, I must start my work! It feels good in here. That heat from your fire really does warm the front of your house, it does that." Gerald felt a little bit embarrassed and really didn't know how to distract attention from what he was about to do. "You know the transmitter is quite a distance on the other side of Cymmer, and behind that mountain. That's a long way off. Miles and miles away so it could take me a little time."

"What if you can't tune it, Gerald?" Mary spoke up anxiously.

"Oh Mary, my Mam always used to say to me, 'There's no such word as can't – it's not in the dictionary.' Then she would say to me, 'you can do absolutely anything if you just try.' She was an encourager that's for sure, my Mam I mean. So don't worry about it. If there is any difficulty, I know there's something else I can do. That is, if I can't get good reception."

Gerald would have to get up on the roof and attach a rod. Then drop a line as close as possible to the drainpipe to secure it. Still in an experimental stage in Wales, the rod worked well in the Midlands like Birmingham. Using a rod would give better television reception.

Mary was so happy that she had won something for the family - a television of all things! What luxury, Mary thought. Now the children wouldn't have to wait to be invited down to the Jenkins' house to watch a program.

The Jenkins lived at the bottom of the street at 7 John Street. They were a good family and invited all the children who lived on the street to watch pictures on their big wheel as well as their television.

They were the family who arranged the street parties, like the upcoming Easter one. Most households that could participate made up the party food. Usually there was a great selection of sandwiches with spam, ham and cheese, Branston pickle and pickled onions, and of course lots of cakes and trifles.

At every street party there were long tables down the middle of the street and everyone sat together. Sometimes, Mr. Jenkins would dress up as a clown or a jester and entertain the children.

Mr. Jenkins was also the street's Santa Claus. He wore his Santa suit and visited every child in the street in the middle of the night with his sack full of gifts. Of course, there were always stories from the children for days afterwards how they saw Santa leaving their gifts.

Gerald gave a sigh of relief as soon as he'd tuned in the television. "Now then, it's done. You can watch television. Mary, come and see. I don't have to get up on the roof. We're lucky."

Mary came rushing from the kitchen, "Oh that's wonderful, thank you Gerald. How much do I pay?"

"Nothing, Mary. You just have to get a television license and then that will be it. Tell Ethan, will you?"

"Are you sure Gerald? I don't pay anything."

"That's right Mary, you don't pay anything. It's all taken care of as part of the prize."

"Thank you so much, Gerald. Ethan will be so pleased, a television of our own. I'll tell him what you said about the television license when he gets home."

Mary ran to the kitchen and got Gerald's coat. "Here you are, Gerald. Your coat is dry now. Thank you again. I know Ethan will be so very pleased."

"Tatty bye, Mary. Tatty bye, kids!" Off went Gerald closing the door behind him.

"Ian, you are in charge of the television. Please don't play with the knobs. Just turn it off when you are finished watching, alright?"

There was another knock at the door and the door slowly opened. "It's Gerald again. I just want to remind you. Don't forget it's your street party on Monday; the Co-op will help and let you have a platter of cheeses free. We will try and deliver it by 3pm. If it rains, I expect you'll be in the Church hall at Birchgrove. See you then. Tatty bye, everyone."

Lina and Mary peeped through the crack of the door to observe the children with the new television.

Chapter 16

A ration book fell down as Dylan reached for more tins. "I needed that." He looked at the book open on the floor. "I wondered what I'd done with it. I must have put it up on the top shelf with the tins of steak and kidney puds. I'm so pleased I didn't lose it." He was relieved it had come to light. "I've been looking everywhere for it but never thought it would be up there, at all."

"That's a really strange place to keep it. Perhaps it was a good hiding place!" Ethan smiled at his Uncle.

"Well, this old man might be getting a little forgetful. That reminds me, I must queue up next Tuesday and get my rations otherwise my business will be swimming down the gutter."

Dylan used his own rations in the shop. He always said, "It's sharing me lot, that it is." Then he would finish off with, "Sharing is caring, and I care. I can't take it with me, now can I?" and then he would chuckle.

Rationing hadn't come to an end yet. Everyone queued up waiting for their meager items if they were available. Butter if one were lucky, margarine, cooking fat, bacon, some meats, tea, and some coffees. There were talks of ending the rationing totally. Sugar seemed plentiful. At least there was no longer a ration on that. It lifted early in 1953. The 50's in Wales was a time of spam fritters; salmon sandwiches if you could afford a tin of salmon, tinned fruit with evaporated milk, and fish and chips.

One of the necessities was olive oil. Very small bottles were sold in the chemist. A little warm olive oil was good for earache and to loosen the earwax.

"Uncle, when you get down from there tell me what you'd like me to help you with today."

"Catch this son, I'm not balancing all these tinned steak and kidney puds very well!" As soon as he mentioned it the tins slipped out of his hands and fell on to the stone-slab floor. "Well, look at that; none of them burst open. They must be using a thicker layer of aluminum these days. Just a little dented, that's all." It amazed Ethan how his Uncle found humor in almost everything.

"Well now, let's see." Dylan stood with the tins in his hand thinking and then realized Ethan was there waiting for his instructions.

"Could you open these for me? You know where the tin opener is. But you might need a bit of lard to put around the screw like you did the last time." Dylan thought, as it would be Saturday tomorrow, it would be a nice change to have steak and kidney pies cooked ready in case any of his customers fancied a change.

In no time at all Ethan shouted, "They're done, Uncle. Tins open and ready."

"That was quick! It must be those younger fingers; they move faster. I'll get that big pot down there, so let me pass you, son." Ethan was standing by the fish fryer.

"Which one, Uncle? I'll get it for you."

"Oh, the one with two handles." Ethan reached down and jumped back suddenly.

"What's the matter, son?"

"There's a spider in there. Oh my God."

"Oh that's one of John's kids. They only come and sleep when I haven't used the pots for a while. It's alright Ethan; they don't bite in this country. Just get a bit of newspaper and scoop him out."

Ethan reached for the paper and put it gingerly on the inside of the pot, so as not to disturb it and smushed it hard. Dylan laughed. "You haven't changed; you behaved exactly like that when you were a young boy."

"They look so big and creepy." He crumpled the paper and tossed it in the rubbish.

"Well, look at it this way. John has one less kid to follow around now!" Dylan gave Ethan a smile, although Ethan was still a little anxious.

"I'll wash the pot out for you now in the deep sink. Did you know it has a smaller pot inside?"

"Yes. That's what I put the steak and kidney pies in to steam 'em. Alright then. When you swill it out, can you fill the big pot with water about a third full and lift it up on the burner for me? Don't light the burner, I can do that tomorrow, but it will be there ready to use. Did you swill the smaller pot out as well?"

Ethan quickly washed it out and watched carefully as Dylan took a bit of lard and smeared it all over the inside of the smaller pot and placed the pies, still in their tin bottoms, one at a time on top of each other with greased wax paper between them. Then placed the smaller pot inside the bigger pot.

"Somewhere down there, there are two lids that go with these pots. It's that big lid there and probably the little one is under it. Can you swill them out for me please?"

Ethan stood just looking but not moving anything out of place. "Ethan I don't think anymore of John's kids are around. They've gone home by now with all the noise we made."

Ethan smiled, a little embarrassed but took it all in his stride. "So you put one pot inside the other pot, then and lids on the both of them?"

"They all steam together in the same time that way. This way I can do other things while they are cooking. The smaller pot keeps them dry and cooks them with steaming hot water all around the small pot. When they are cooked all the way through, which takes nearly two hours after the water has boiled, I can keep them hot on low heat.

"When I am ready, I lift out the small pot, take 'em out and lay 'em separately under the gas burner. They only take a few minutes to get crisp up on the tops. They look better with a crisp cap on 'em." He nodded his white head.

"There seems quite a bit to learn when you have your own business."

"That's only part of it, son. There's more to learn on the buying side. You know ordering supplies; hopefully make a profit. It's touch-and-go sometimes but it all works out in the end. People have to eat even if there is a slump. I'll show you next weekend. It's time to order supplies again and I have to make a list of what to order. It will save a bit of time if you can help me with that."

Ethan took it all in but looked a little concerned. "Of course, I will help, I'll be here."

"We must get busy now with the lunch, making the batter and cutting the spuds. Oh yes, and putting on the peas. We don't need any steak and kidney pies today as its Good Friday. We'll be eating only fish today."

Ethan knew where the peas were and got down three tins. He carefully opened them and put the contents in the saucepan on the spare burner, not forgetting to get the last bit of juice out of the tins. Then proceeded to help Dylan with the chips and batter.

"It's so good having you here, Ethan. It reminds me of old times when my Olga was here. God rest her soul." He made the sign of the cross and looked up at her picture on the wall. "She was a good woman, my Olga, that she was."

"How is Lina doing?" Dylan asked Ethan, changing the subject.

"She's busy at our house making a dress for Mary for Church."

"Is that so? She is a good woman."

"She really is. Lina has helped us so much and I can't imagine life without her being there for us."

"Lina is not looking after herself and I'm afraid the day will come when she won't be able to take care of herself let alone help anyone anymore, she will need our help, that she will." Dylan's head hung low as he continued, "*Ìe*, I am sure the cancer is back." He looked at Ethan at his side. "Gilberto needs to know, he does."

"Lina won't tell Gilberto, she says his job requires him to travel and she doesn't want to trouble him. Well, that's what she told Mary." Ethan shrugged.

"Trouble or not, he needs to know his mother is sick. I have Lina's sister's phone number; Mari lives in Erdington, Birmingham. Lina told me Mari has her own problems with her disabled husband, Arthur. She also lost Trevour, he was a Missionary in Africa just like his Uncle Treavour. She doesn't know how he died but she got a telegram. There was no address or anyone's name. Oh what a lot of sadness Mari's family had, too."

"Is there anyone else you know that could help Lina that we haven't considered to help get in touch with Gilberto?" Ethan was anxious.

"Her other son, Haro, I told you he had polio so he is crippled now. I certainly don't want to cause anxiety for him. There's just Angel, and she is too young to understand."

"I think Angel knows that her Nene is sick because she doesn't like to leave Lina alone. If she comes up to our house she is anxious about the time and says that she has to go home to Nene Lina. Mary has been asking Lina to come up a lot lately but she won't rest. Lina continually pushes herself to do things to help us. We would like her to just sit sometimes."

"Well, you know Lina can't just sit. She's on the go all the time." Dylan assured Ethan.

"We must get the fish on, then we can talk some more." Dylan moved to the fryers. "Don't let me forget to tell you I found something, too." He got busy for a minute. "I'll drop the fish in the basket and get some of the chips started."

The door opened in the shop, they turned to see their first customer. "Good morning Mrs. Rhys-Jones. Your usual today?" He wiped his hands and turned to face her.

"Did you hear about that film Richard Burton is doing?" She asked him.

"Oh I heard something about it from Mr. Thomas."

"Well, he probably didn't tell you about all the millions that Richard Burton will get for it."

Dylan listened carefully to her gossip and tried not to comment too much for fear of her insistence on giving her opinion to everyone that walked in the door. He did comment, "He is a worker, that's for sure."

"If you ask me, he just wants to be in the limelight again, showing off, you know." Mrs. Rhys-Jones was too vocal for Dylan's world. Dylan remained silent until her order was finished and handed it to Ethan to wrap up, raising his eyebrows.

"That's two and six today Mrs. Rhys-Jones."

"Has the fish gone up then, it's two and six?" She was a little assertive this time.

"Remember, I told you last week that the fish had come from Scotland, not our local supply so it's the shipping fees that made it go up."

"Well, I don't want fish from Scotland, I want our fish."

"There, there, Mrs. Rhys-Jones we don't have any control on where the fish comes from. I'm just glad we can have fish."

"Well, why didn't you get our Welsh fish? I don't want to pay an extra thrupence for old Scottish fish."

"It's alright Mrs. Rhys-Jones, it's very good fish from Scotland. Our fishermen had a bad season and some went down with flu so we buy whatever the wholesaler has in stock."

"Well, I don't like it. Do you hear me? I don't like it. Why should I have to pay more for fish I don't like?"

"I tell you what, let me give you back the thrupence, and you let me know how you like the fish next week, alright? Here's your thrupence." Anything to get the woman out of the shop!

"What fish are you going to get next week, then?"

"Actually, I don't know. It depends on what the wholesaler has for me, it could be Welsh, it could be Scottish, or it could even be Alaskan."

"Alaskan! Oh my God, what is the world coming to? Alaskan fish! Next you will be telling me it's from China."

"Mrs. Rhys-Jones, calm yourself. It's good cod. I had some myself yesterday."

"Well it could kill us, you know?"

"Uncle Dylan is trying to say he enjoyed it last night and he will probably have some more today. I need to take some home to Mary and the family."

"Huh! Listen hear now. I don't want to have any fish from Alaska or China. Definitely not from China, that's too far to bring fish. It could be off by the time it gets here!"

"It won't be off, they pack it in ice and it is kept frozen."

"Frozen! It's not fresh. I'm going home. Give me my fish and chips and I'm going to discuss this with my Tom." She flounced out of the chippie, a gust of wind, leaving behind a flavor of distaste.

Ethan stepped back into the store, "Has she gone yet, that Mrs. Rhys-Jones?"

"She's gone." Dylan sighed and nodded.

"Thank goodness. What possessed her? She was really upset about the fish from Scotland."

"Yes, she was that. At least it got her off the subject of Richard Burton. She can be hard to tolerate."

"How does her husband put up with her?"

"That's a thought, poor Tom. I expect he gives her his deaf ear and tries to ignore her comments."

"I wouldn't want to be married to her, that's for sure." Ethan lowered his voice.

"I'm thinking Tom probably wishes he wasn't sometimes." They both laughed at the thought.

"Alright then, Mrs. Rhys-Jones has gone and now we have Mrs. Thompson. Praise the Lord she is milder." Ethan listened intently.

"Good morning, Mrs. Thompson. How are you today?"

"Oh, fair to middling I'd say."

"Well, what has been happening up in the hall this week?"

"A lot of surveying going on. In fact, they even mentioned Cradoc's old farm."

"They did? Well how about that? What was said then, Mrs. Thompson?"

"They were trying to discuss where the end of Cradoc's property was and where the joining property is because Herbert's great grandson has laid claim to Herbert's land."

"Is that so? What did they determine then?"

"They are estimating at the moment. They really need to find Cradoc's heirs and see if any of them are alive." She stepped up to the counter. "That could also include you, Dylan. He was your brother, right?"

"*Ìe*. Yes, that's right but how could I help? They need his children or his children's children," Dylan told her.

"Well, yes and well no. Whoever is alive now in his lineage; children or grandchildren, that is."

"Right then. What do his children or his grandchildren need to do then?" Dylan enquired.

"They need to come to the town hall with evidence and their birth right."

"What do you mean by birth right, some document or something?"

"Of course Dylan, they would have to bring their birth certificate, marriage license and any plats to the property."

He kept asking questions, hoping as Ethan listened, he'd find an interest in his grandfather's property on the mountain. Maybe this was a way out of Ethan's depression.

"I know Cradoc's two sons died down the mine but they had children. I'm not sure how many survived. You know most of them went down the mines. It's hard to say if any are still around." She pulled her purse from her handbag. "What do you know then, Dylan?"

"Oh me, not a lot Mrs. Thompson but I do know one of the grandchildren is still alive."

Ethan stayed silent and listened to the conversation. He did not want Mrs. Thompson to be probing his family's existence, and it seemed that Dylan wasn't going to give much information away either.

"Hmm. If he is still alive he will have to come forward. Herbert's grandson seems to be in a hurry to get things done."

"Well, I do have a question. This grandson of Herbert? How much land did he inherit, exactly? Can you tell me that?" Dylan asked, leaning on the counter.

"Not as much as Cradoc's land but still a lot. We have to determine where Cradoc's land is exactly."

"Hmm. That would be a problem if Cradoc's heir, his grandson doesn't come forward."

"Not really, the surveyor could determine an estimate and the court would go from there."

"An estimate? What if the surveyor is wrong?"

"Well, that would be a great loss for Cradoc's grandson. He owned a great expanse of Perhiwgwynt. It is very fertile. Cradoc also had a lot of horses, wild horses he caught on the mountain, and started a stud farm. He bought Croatian horses to breed." She shook her head. "Let's put it like this, he had a lot of land, probably more than Herbert had."

"Is that so, hmmm? Well, let's hope that Cradoc's grandson comes forward. Otherwise this bloke might get more than his share."

"I agree with that. Herbert's grandson comes from England, you know. They do business different over the border." She leaned in, glancing at Ethan busy working.

"You said England, did you?" Dylan asked.

"Yes, that's right Dylan."

"Now what does an Englishmun want with Welsh land?"

"Oh Dylan. It's money. It's money. He could make a fortune. I didn't get the idea that he wanted the land for himself, but maybe to sell."

"Sell. Oh dear that would be a shame. Who would he be selling it to do you think?"

"Wales is a multi-cultural country so we do have a lot of immigrants, mostly from Pakistan, that settle in the South. The Pakistanis usually have large families; they do work hard. They do, even their young children all have duties in a business."

"No, I didn't know that. I thought they only had restaurants up in North Wales."

"Well, they do. We have some families just come into the Rhondda, too. Maybe they are looking for land. I'd better be off then, me fish and chips might go cold. I hope this Scottish fish of yours won't turn by the time I get home." She smiled and winked at him. She'd heard Mrs. Rhys-Jones.

Mrs. Thompson left and Dylan looked very relieved.

The day passed and they worked until everything was cleaned and put away. Ethan was getting ready to head home. The weather had changed and the rain stopped for the time being.

"Uncle, it's such a pleasure to help you. You always have a good attitude about things. Even when I am depressed and down in the dumps I can guarantee by the time I leave here I am happy again." He didn't mention anything about the conversation about him. Ethan knew Dylan was referring to him as Cradoc's grandson.

"Come on now son, don't get too emotional on me. I'm just telling you the true facts. Of course we all need to relax with a bit of humor, don't we? There's nothing better than something to laugh about. It cleanses our soul."

"I suppose so, Uncle."

"That reminds me. I said I had something to tell you. Let's finish up around here. All my usual customers have got their fish and chips. You said you wanted to take some home, right?"

"Yes please, I can pay, don't worry about that. How many fish have we got left? Will there be any left over, enough for Lina, Angel, Mary and the rest of us?"

"We have plenty. In fact, I have another tray full I didn't even start on. Let's see here? How many are there already cooked. Why, there's eleven pieces here."

"Really? I only need six pieces."

"Hhhmmm. If you take two each for you, Lina and Mary and one piece each for Angel, Ian, Dylan and David. Then that would leave one piece left and I could have that. Perfectly worked out today."

"Then I will buy the fish and chips for the family."

"No, you won't pay." Dylan frowned at him, flapping his hands. "Do you think I am going to make you pay when you come here and help me so much, and you are, after all, my great nephew?" He shooed Ethan toward the door.

"You better be going, Ethan. The fish and chips will get cold. They won't go off 'cause they're from Scotland." Dylan roared with laughter that he made Ethan laugh. It was a wonderful sight to see two men of different generations laughing together.

"I don't think we will be too busy tonight because it's Good Friday night and most likely everyone will be late out of Church. You're going with Mary to Church are you, Ethan?"

"I'm not really sure about that. I get so depressed at that late service. I'll see."

"Well, if you don't go you are welcome to come up and help a bit while Mary is in Church. We can talk some more. I still have to tell you something. Not now though, your fish will definitely be cold."

"Now what was it?" Dylan murmured to himself.

"That's alright, Uncle you can tell me tonight, when you remember. Oh before I forget something, do you have any Sloan's Liniment?"

"Of course, son. What's the matter?"

"I fell down the stairs this morning and landed on my backside on the rug, but my back hit the bottom step. I must have looked daft because the kids were laughing so hard that it brought Mary out of the kitchen to come and see."

"You must be more careful, Ethan. The stairs are dangerous in those houses. They are built steep to avoid using too much space so I'm not surprised you fell if you were hurrying down them."

"I was a bit, and making a lot of noise, too. I was trying to be funny telling the kids that the king of the elephants was coming."

"I expect that was funny to the kids, but you must be more careful. None of us are getting any younger. You being down that pit probably put a strain on your back and other parts of you."

"Where do I find the Sloan's Liniment, Uncle?"

It's up on the next shelf down from the steak and kidney puds. There are some other medical things there, too. It should be close to the Syrup of Figs and Beecham's Powders. Do you see it?"

"Yes, it's here. Also, there is something else here wrapped in dusty newspaper. A kind of ornament, it looks like a, well what is it? Oh, I see it now, it's a ram. Uncle, did you know you have a ram up here? I'll get it down."

"If I had a ram he'd eat me out of house and home! Well, look-e-here, the ram ornament. I wondered what had happened to it." Dylan gave it a shine with his apron and took it into the parlor and put it in his china cabinet. "I put it up high to stop the children from getting it when they were younger. They liked to go into the cabinet and play with those little spoons, the carved ones. Those kids were you and your brother. Your brother loved to find things. He used to say he found treasures."

"Did we really go into the cabinet and get your spoons?"

"Of course you did, it amused you both very much, kept you both quiet that's for sure. I didn't mind but your Mam was livid. She called it snooping. She slapped both of you on your backsides and made you sit in those parlor chairs until you stopped crying. You don't remember?"

"Not really. I do remember my brother pretending to cry about something and she got so mad about it. I can't remember what it was now. He made such a noise she got madder and madder and told him if he didn't stop crying she would give him something to cry about!"

"Your brother was a comic, that's for sure. He'd be screaming his head off one minute and then giggling the next and sometimes you did too, Ethan."

"Yes I did. I remember that, I'll never forget Evan when he was working at the post office. He left work when the sirens went off and ran to the pit to help those miners to safety but died himself, when the shaft collapsed.

"I remember too, one time we were in bed and he farted. He used to like to do the silent ones you know; those that creep up on you. Then he would waft the covers in my face and laugh his socks off. He knew that would make me move quickly. I think that was his intention, to get more of the bed."

"It's good you remember the good times besides the bad ones, Ethan."

"Did that ram have any significance, Uncle?"

"Not so much to me, son but to your grandfather. It was presented to him at a sheep auction. Funny thing, that was. To be given a ram at a sheep auction. I could understand if it was a ram auction. He was so pleased he won something and never would have thought he would win that ornament.

"It's Welsh biscuit porcelain you know, and made in Swansea. It's engraved on the bottom, underneath, Ethan. Can you see those initials? I. W. that's the modeler's initials, he was once famous in these parts; Isaac Wood was his name. There were only a few made in 1817 and Cradoc was presented with one of them. You should have seen him, a big mountain man holding a little thing like that with so much care."

"It's that old Uncle, over a hundred years?" Ethan was astonished, looking with new eyes at the small figurine.

"Yes it is, and I mustn't get it broken as it was Cradoc's. I just said that, didn't I? I was so proud of him winning first place at the sheep auction. He definitely knew how to breed the best Welsh sheep. That's why he got the ram.

"Alright then, I'll see you later, son. Bye now, your fish and chips will be cold." Dylan lost his humor. Ethan knew he was upset but tried not to show it. Memories of his brother must have been hard for him. He got out his handkerchief and blew his nose.

"Bye, Uncle. Thank you for the fish and chips. It doesn't matter if they are cold. We'll still eat them."

"Alright, son."

Ethan opened the door. "It's raining again, Uncle."

"That it is, I'll be worried on a day when it doesn't rain. It's Wales, we need the rain to keep our valleys green." He chuckled and then went on to hum the tune of *How Green was my Valley* that was sung by Harry Belefonte in 1941.

Dylan went upstairs to his bedroom as soon as Ethan left the shop. He knew somewhere in his trunk he had documents that once belonged to his brother, and of course he knew he had the death certificates for both Cradoc and Clarenda in there. These might help Ethan claim his inheritance, but the question would be when would he do that. That trunk originally belonged to Clarenda, she brought it from Croatia. It was made of wood with a thin layer of copper and lined with leather. It once had a large decorative latch and padlock made in brass, but over the years the original padlock was lost. Cradoc wasn't much of a person to keep papers orderly, or even keep important documents like birth certificates and their marriage license.

When Dylan and Olga moved in with Cradoc and Clarenda, Dylan gladly accepted keeping things in an orderly fashion. Dylan after all, had finished grammar school unlike Cradoc, and had a little background in setting up some form of bookkeeping showing their business transactions. Couldn't say they were profits, more like losses as Cradoc had a tendency of giving more than he received for his labors. Those days were long ago now and only the memories lingered in Dylan's mind. It was not an easy task for Dylan to open up the trunk again; old photographs of his dear Olga and Cradoc and his love, Clarenda were hidden in the trunk just like a few things that belonged to his Mam.

This time it seemed to be important, almost urgent, to fumble through piles of papers and memorabilia that once belonged to his family. Sure enough, he found a sketched drawing of the two valleys in the Rhondda drawn on a piece of cloth with arrows and signs that were unfamiliar to him.

There was a long leather pouch tied with ornate golden stitched ribbon. Clarenda embroidered the ribbon as the bundle contained Cradoc's and Clarenda's birth certificates and marriage license. Dylan dug deeper and found another piece of paper, more like parchment of rectangles and squares. Hours went by while he looked through his memories. It was too much to bear in one sitting. Dylan looked at his pocket watch to see it was almost time to get started on the evening opening. He put the papers inside the trunk. He carefully pulled the trunk lid down, covering all his memories and laid the sketch and pouch on the top. Perhaps next time he could find something more useful, like a document containing evidence of ownership of the land that once belonged to Cradoc. Of course the Town Hall had something. He remembered that Mary had told him she went on her search. All the same, it would be good for Ethan to have something positive in his hands if he was going to court.

Dylan needed to refresh himself and wipe away his tears. He rinsed his face and brushed his hair, taking a quick glance of himself in the mirror, making sure he looked respectable and not shabby to serve his customers. His hair was thick and almost white all over except for a few strands that were still grey. He looked much like his brother did years before, but Cradoc had darker hair and was stockier built.

It was odd for Dylan to stop and linger at his reflection, but the imagery was so real that it made him think more of Cradoc again. If he hadn't have died, Clarenda wouldn't have died from a broken heart and their boys would probably have been running the business. That could have meant Ethan may not have gone down the pit. He could have been with his family up on the mountain sharing a good life. Things would have definitely been different for Dylan and Olga, too.

They could have spent their lives in the fresh air and not down in the valley of black dust. He was saddened again that he covered his face and sobbed. It felt like he was reliving those memories.

Chapter 17

It was Saturday morning and was a little overcast, but the sun was trying to shine through. The day would be good. Dylan went outside and stood on his front doorstep with his hands on his hips breathing in the fresh air and looking up at the still Penrhiwgwynt with its foggy haze slowly lifting to the top.

"Here comes Milkman Rhys and his sheep."

"Good morning, there Mr. Dylan. How are you?"

"Very well, very well, thank you. Why, it's Jones. What happened to your father this morning?"

"Me old man, you mean? He's got a cold so Mam said he should stay at home."

"Son, it's not good to call your father old man, you know. Have respect for your elders. He has raised you from a little mite and put food in your mouth and clothes on your back." Dylan shook his finger at him.

"I'm sorry Mr. Dylan. I just didn't want to deliver the milk and watch them sheep. They run all over the place and I have people shouting at me that they tipped over their dustbins."

"I know son; you don't like doing that but it helps your family. Your mam and dad have always worked hard, you know, and I have never known them take a day off. It's good you help them."

"I suppose, but I still don't like it."

"Now what would you be doing at this time of the morning if you weren't out with the sheep?"

"I could be sleeping."

"You can have a nap later, son. Be thankful the Lord has given you two good parents. "

"Alright then. Hmmmmm. How much do you want this morning Mr. Dylan?"

"You can fill up my churn. It's Easter weekend so I will need extra for the blancmanges and trifles tomorrow."

"Alright then, the churn is full. I'll write it down and tell my dad."

"Thank you, Jones. Tell your mam and dad we'll expect them down for the street party Monday at around 3pm. It will be in John Street. You come, too and bring your sister. Alright."

"Alright then. I'm sure Olwyn will be there."

"That's good, maybe you'll be at Church tomorrow, too. It's a big event, you know?"

"I think I might be there. "

"David and Angel are singing, you know. Perhaps your mam and dad might come with you."

"I'll tell 'em. Come on, Arthur." Jones slapped the reins. "Get a move on, we haven't got all day." Poor Arthur, he must have been sore that morning after Jones kept slapping him.

Jones was impatient and a bit on the lazy side. Arthur was almost as old as the hills. He was a good working horse and had seen better days, but still swished his tail as he trotted off. The sheep trailed behind pooping currents as they went by.

"I must get a shovel and scoop up Arthur's puddings. That'll be good for my broad beans," Dylan thought to himself. Dylan had two broad bean plants planted in one-half of the beer barrel. The beer barrel had been cut into two halves. In the other half he planted two pea plants in the little alleyway at his back door near his outside toilet. To his amazement they were all about to be in bloom, new little shoots up their vines. Dylan didn't have to bother with them much as they were getting natural rainwater off the roof and were sheltered from the very cold weather by the walls of the little alleyway.

Dylan didn't have a garden lot anymore, just these beer barrels that he called his vegetable garden. He always said if you just try you can grow anything in anything. He would continue to say, the Welsh were good at trying to grow things with limited means. By this he meant there was not much earth left as it was all covered in black dust and slag in the Rhondda valleys.

The street woke up to a bicycle ring. It was Bobbie.

"Mr. Taff, I have some news for you," he shouted as he dismounted his bike and stood it up leaning on the curb.

"Come in, Bobbie and tell me what news you have."

Bobbie took out his little black pad from his pocket as they went into the parlor.

"Sit there. I'll make us a cup of tea. You look like you have some really good news to tell me."

"I have, actually. I think you will be pleased, too."

"Tell me Bobbie, what is it?"

"You remember those culprits that robbed you, well, they've got 'em."

"Is that so, Bobbie? How do you know these lads in custody are the ones?"

"The two they have in custody were up in Ystradgynlais, where this year's Eisteddfod is being held."

"You mean they were to be participants in the Eisteddfod?"

"No, Mr. Taff, no. They were already there. One claimed his Uncle was singing in the Eisteddfod."

"Alright then, so his Uncle was Welsh then?"

"Funny that is, he said he was from Birmingham and he was going to wait for him in Ystradgynlais."

"You are pulling my leg. Since when have they had an Englishmun participate in the Eisteddfod? They've only had Welsh singers and poets participating in this festival since it started in the 12th century."

"Exactly, Mr. Taff. They were in the jewelers in Ystradgynlais. The one in the suit said he wanted to look at pocket watches as a gift for his Uncle who was going to be in the Eisteddfod in a couple of weeks. It's March, the Eisteddfod is going to be in August. Mr. Jones there in Ystradgynlais was not taken by surprise when the Englishmun claimed his Uncle sang in last year's Eisteddfod and was competing in a couple of weeks for the 1954 Eisteddfod.

"What? Everyone in Wales knows the Eisteddfod is every four years, not every year."

"Exactly. That's why Mr. Jones sent his assistant to the station and asked Bobbie Thomas to come quickly. Oh yes, they got 'em, alright. Silly buggers, they must think the Welsh are daft. They got 'em, Mr. Taff."

"Alright then."

"They caught 'em red-handed with other items they had stolen on the way. It's taken a while but they definitely got 'em."

"So what will happen to these two now, then?"

"They have gone to Cardiff Station and will appear in court next week. It depends on the judge's decision if they serve time in Cardiff jail or go back to Birmingham. We'll find out soon enough."

"What happened to that young lad that gave himself up?"

"I believe that lad was sent back to Birmingham and is on probation. He wasn't a bad lad he just got mixed up with the wrong people. These two won't get away with it that easy. They will be in jail before long."

"Thank God for that, then."

"I agree, thank God. Maybe now our lives will get back to normal."

"It would be nice to go to bed and not worry about the doors needing to be locked."

"No, no, no. We must still lock our doors and windows. It was easy for these three to come here and steal from us. We don't know what will lie ahead."

"Lie ahead, Bobbie? What do you mean?"

"Mr. Taff. The Eisteddfod will bring many travelers. Those participating and many spectators will arrive for this event. We'll have people from London and all around, for such an event. We'll have antiques on display and I'm sure other Welsh items like our Welsh harps and love spoons, will be for sale."

"We'll all have to watch out, then?"

"Mr. Taff, it's a big event for Wales. We must take care."

Dylan knew that the Eisteddfods had the highest standard of Welsh competitors and brought a lot of revenue for Wales, but Bobbie needed to show he was delivering all the information so he just let him carry on.

"Alright then, Mr. Taff. I must get back to the station. Don't forget to keep everything secure and locked up."

"I will that, Bobbie. Thank you.

"Mary was delighted when Lina and Angel arrived in the morning. Lina had brought with her the ribbon and the shoes she'd mentioned.

"Lina, Lina come in. How are you this morning? Angel, I have something for you. I think you will like it."

Angel rushed in to see David and tell him of the conversation she had with her grandmother, "I asked Nene if I could go and see Buttercup tomorrow if it's not raining. Will you come with me?"

"What did Nene Lina say? Did she say you could go?"

"She said I could go if you can go with me, and of course Ian to protect us from the big bad wolf."

"Ha, ha, ha, that's funny, little red riding hood! Of course I want to see Buttercup, too. Let's ask Ian if he will come with us."

Both David and Angel ran to the front room where Ian was drawing. "Ian, will you come with us to Penrhiwgwynt, if it's not raining?" They kept their voices soft.

"What, today? I have things to do today."

"Tomorrow, Ian. It's Easter Sunday and my Nene said I can go if David and you will come with me."

"What do I need to go for?"

"My Nene said to keep the big bad wolf away!" Angel told him with a smile.

"There aren't any wolves up there. Hm. Oh, I get it." Ian started to laugh, "To babysit you both."

"Well, will you come with us, Ian?" David whined.

"I suppose so. Mam wouldn't want you up there by yourself."

"Oh goodie." David and Angel grinned at each other, excitement bringing a flush to their expressions.

"Nene, Ian said he will come with us to see Buttercup."

Lina and Mary were busy talking about the belt on the dress when Angel interrupted. "Nene, look there's flowers at the bottom of Auntie Mary's dress, and they look so pretty just like daisies. Are you going to cut around them?" Lina looked more carefully at the design of flowers rather than the sewing of the dress.

"Actually, they do look like daisies. Let me take a closer look. Angel, that was good you saw them." Lina turned to Mary and showed her the line of daisies that Angel had pointed out.

"What do you think if we cut around the bottom of the daisies like Angel suggested? It might look like a frayed edge but not really a frayed edge. We could start a fashion of our own right here in Porth. What do you say?"

"Well, if you think it will look good, alright." Mary was thinking hard about what Lina said concerning the frayed edges and the fashion trend in London. "Why not? Let's do it."

"If you don't like it we can just turn it up like a proper hem. Would you like to start cutting around the bottom of the daisies, Mary?"

"I'm not sure if I could do that good enough to make it look nice. Will you do it for me please, Lina?"

"Let's see. It just takes a little practice and a little confidence. I'll cut around the first couple of daisies to show you, and then you try, alright?" Lina pulled out her sharp scissors and started cutting off the excess fabric just halfway around the bottom of the first daisy, then the next daisy and stopped to look at it.

"I think it looks really pretty, just like the lace on the bottom of Angel's little dress."

"Now it's your turn." Lina let out a little laugh. "Try cutting around the next few daisies?"

Mary took the scissors and was very careful not to cut too much away. "Am I doing it alright?"

Lina took the hem in her hands and carefully looked at what Mary had done.

"Perfect, absolutely perfect actually. You are a quick learner, Mary. Would you like to do the rest of the daisies while I make the belt?"

"Yes, I can do it." Mary was eager to show her newly acquired skill and smiled at Lina.

Angel waited patiently to repeat what she said but not to interrupt Nene and Mary's conversation, "Nene, Ian said he would come with us to see Buttercup tomorrow."

"Well as long as he asks his mam, that's good then."

Angel ran off again to the front room where the boys were, "Ian you have to ask your mam if you can come with us tomorrow." Then she sat down beside David. "Is it my turn, David?" she wanted to continue to play dominoes.

"I'm still thinking where to put my piece."

Ian was getting frustrated. "Hurry up, will you, it will be bedtime by the time you make your next move. Well, as he's taking so long I'll go and ask Mam about tomorrow."

Turning around to look at Angel as he got up from the chair, "You could have asked her Angel, you were right there in the kitchen."

"I don't think my Nene would like me to ask for you."

Ian made haste to the kitchen. "Mam, can I go with these kids tomorrow to see that soppy horse? It's probably ran off to Tim-buck-too by now."

Mary was taken by surprise; her mind was elsewhere. She just finished cutting the daisies all around the hem and was admiring what she had accomplished.

Ian spoke a little louder this time, "I'm supposed to keep the big bad wolf away."

"What are you talking about, Ian?"

"Mam," then he went silent. "Mam, those kids want me to go with them up the mountain. To keep the big bad wolf away."

Lina and Mary looked at each other, and laughed. "Yes, Ian. Go with them to Penrhiwgwynt. Just don't let them get into too much trouble and definitely not break any legs!"

Mary turned to Lina. "What time do you think they should go? After lunch?"

"I think that will be a good time. They will have changed out of their Sunday best and into their play clothes by then."

"Alright, you can all go after lunch, tomorrow," Mary replied.

"I'll tell them." Ian ran off to join David and Angel.

"Haven't you moved yet? How long is it going to take you?" Ian asked them.

"Are you still thinking? You only have three dominoes left," Angel pointed out to David.

"I know, but I want to win for a change. Ian always wins," David told her absently.

"You could win if you hurry up." Ian was more impatient than before. "If you don't hurry up I won't be going with you tomorrow."

"Alright then, there." David placed his piece heavily on the board.

"Is it my turn now?" Angel enquired. It had been a while since her last play.

"No it's Ian's."

"Ha, I'm going to win again."

Mary stood at the door and shook her head as to say NO to Ian. Ian understood and screwed up his face. Ian said quickly, "I can't go."

Angel was about to play but there wasn't an end she could lay her dominoes. "Oh no, I can't go." She looked saddened. "It's your turn again, David."

David was happy to place his domino piece on the end of a line. "I have one piece left, ha, ha!"

"Well, now. It's my turn." Ian was eager to lay another domino but remembered what his Mam just indicated. "I can't go again. What's wrong with my pieces?" He turned to Angel. "That means it's your turn, then."

"Yes." Angel added her last domino and shouted, "I've won. I've won." And she got up and rushed into the kitchen to tell Lina. "Nene, I won dominoes."

"That's very good, Angel. I am so proud of you." Lina showed she was happy for Angel, hugging the excited girl.

"It's my first time, Nene. I won for the first time." Lina gave Angel another little hug.

David came out of the front room. "I lost, Angel won." He looked a little disappointed at first but soon got over it when he noticed Lina's smile and a pile of chocolate biscuits she had placed on the sideboard.

Ian showed his face at the kitchen door, "Yes, Angel won."

"Try it on with your petticoat and shoes and let's see. I've almost finished the belt." They returned to the dressmaking. "There are biscuits there for you three," Lina told them. David and Angel each chose one and nibbled them as they headed back to the front room.

Mary ran up the stairs, delighted at her accomplishment of finishing the hem. Soon she was back down with her dress and newly acquired shoes.

"Oh you look beautiful. Angel, come and see." Lina called her to the kitchen.

"Aunty Mary, you look like you're going to a wedding." Angel paused at the door, looking at the beautiful dress.

"Let me put the belt around you and tie it in the back." Lina was wondering if the belt might have been too long but it was just right with it tied in a loose bow at the back. "Now let me see you." Lina stood back and viewed the dress admiringly. "Beautiful." Lina looked down at the shoes. "How do the shoes feel?"

"The right one feels a little tight just there." Mary bent forward and showed Lina. "The left is good."

"Hmm, let me think. What size shoes does Ian take? Maybe he could put his foot in that one and stretch it a bit."

"Ian, come here please?" Mary called from the kitchen. He'd gone in to put away the dominos. The kids were helping him, talking about getting another biscuit.

"Mam, what is it?"

"Well it's me actually that wants you," Nene Lina explained. "I want to ask you to do something really special for your mam."

"Yes, Nene Lina. What is it?" He answered respectfully.

"I need you to put your foot in this shoe to stretch it so it doesn't hurt your mam's foot."

"What? I have to put on a lady's shoe? Everyone will laugh at me." Ian's face flushed with embarrassment.

"No one will laugh at you, Ian. There's no one here. It's too tight for your mam, and my feet are smaller than your mam's so I couldn't stretch them for her. She would like to wear them tomorrow with her new Easter dress."

Ian took the shoe and hid behind the door and took his sock off.

"You don't have to take your sock off, it's alright put it back on it will cushion your foot while you stretch the shoe and your foot will slide in easier then," Lina was directing.

"I can't get my foot into it." Ian was hopping around on one foot looking rather foolish.

"Have the shoe on the floor and just bend forward to put your foot in the top part of the shoe. It doesn't have to go all the way in. We just want you to stretch the top a little bit." Lina kept directing him, holding her laughter at his antics.

"How long do I have to have my foot stuck in this shoe? It will go dead."

"Just a few minutes, let me get you a chair and you can sit down." Lina showed her compassion.

"I'm tired, Nene Lina," Ian said, any excuse to get out of the shoe.

"If you fall asleep that's alright, you won't fall over." Lina winked at Angel as she approached to get another biscuit after hearing Ian complain.

"Go to sleep? It's alright."

Angel ran back to David. "David come here and see Ian." She put her finger to her mouth to motion a silence. "Hush, he mustn't see you." David followed Angel. "Shhhhhh. He'll hear you."

David came to the kitchen door. He could see Ian's hand holding the edge of the door trying to hide behind it. David peeped around the door and jumped back with his hand over his mouth to stop making a sound or even laugh.

"Alright, David go back into the front room and you and Angel play with the cards or the snakes and ladders, they're in the cabinet in there."

"But Mam," David protested trying not to say any more.

"No. Do as I say. Just go ahead or you can do something useful. The newspapers need to go up to Uncle Dylan's." Now David looked pleased, a chance to get out of the house.

"I'll take the newspapers." Turning towards Lina, David asked, "Can Angel come with me, Nene Lina?" At first Lina didn't answer, she was concentrating on Ian making faces behind the door.

"Nene, can Angel come with me to Uncle Dylan's?" This time David spoke a little louder.

"Oh yes, David. I'm sorry, I wasn't listening." Then turned to Angel and looked down at her shoes, "Angel, tie your shoes up properly so you don't fall over." Angel bent down and tied her shoes, then ran off in the direction of the front door with David.

"How much longer Mam?" Ian was still sitting with his foot propped in the front part of the shoe. "My foot's got a cramp," Ian complained.

"You can take your foot out now. Thank you, Ian." Ian took the shoe off and limped up the hallway with his other shoe in hand.

"That should do it." Lina turning to Mary said, "Try them both on again? This one should be good now. Poor Ian, I do feel sorry for him, I totally got carried away and wasn't paying any attention. You have a good boy there, Mary. You have done well with all your children."

Mary smiled, "It hasn't been easy, you know that."

"I do know that, and you have been an excellent mother, especially when Ethan was down the pit."

"Well, that's what I meant. Being alone with all the children screaming and yelling, not to mention the fights they had." Mary took a deep breath and was silent for a few moments. "But, I have to laugh, though. It wasn't too long ago when Ethan stopped working. Ian was having a pillow fight with David upstairs on the landing. The pillowcase split open and also the pillow cover inside. He was shouting and laughing at the time and had his mouth open. That was so funny the pillow broke open. He had a mouthful of feathers and was covered from head to foot with feathers." Mary turned towards Lina, "Were you here then? I think you were?"

"No, I came up just after it happened. I was at the door and I could hear all the screaming and laughter. I was glad I heard laughter, otherwise I would have been very worried. Wasn't that the day when Gerald came and left something for Ethan?"

"It was. Ethan needed a battery for something and Gerald said he had some at home he wasn't using."

"What a mess all those feathers made." Lina chuckled at the thought. "Let's see the dress and shoes on again."

Mary slipped her feet into both shoes. "That feels much better, thanks to Ian."

"I agree. Turn around again, so I can get a better look at you." Mary turned and stood with her feet together. "You look beautiful. Wait when Ethan sees you. I do like the daisies at the bottom of the hem."

"I'd like a better view but I don't have a long mirror." Reaching for the mirror off the wall Mary gave it to Lina, "Can you hold it for me, please?" Mary stood back and stared into the mirror. "It's beautiful, oh thank you so much Lina. It really is beautiful."

"I knew you would like it. It looks very, very chic, as they call it in France."

"Have you been to France, Lina?" Mary was curious, studying her reflection.

"No, but I saw a picture at the doctor's office of the Eiffel tower. There was a lady standing in front, it could have been his daughter or someone. She was dressed so well. I just closed my eyes and imagined I was there. It was very refreshing to think I was somewhere else."

"Does that help then Lina, to think you are somewhere else then?"

"Dr. Jones thinks so. He told me once when I was first diagnosed with cancer to imagine a beautiful place like the top of Penrhiwgwynt. To close my eyes and imagine I was there, surrounded by buttercups and birds singing in the air. I tried it a few times and actually it was very relaxing."

"Are you up to a walk tomorrow, Lina? We could all go together up Penrhiwgwynt," Mary asked her.

"That would be a lovely change. I haven't been up there for a while. Do you think Ethan might come, too? It would be good for him." Lina nodded, thinking she might feel better.

"Hmm. We could ask him. Dylan is closed on Easter Sunday. Do you think if you asked Dylan, Lina, he would like to come, too?" Mary took off the shoes. "He hasn't been up there for years but I think Ethan might go with us if Dylan went, too. What do you think?"

"I could ask him and see what he says. I have to go that way since I need to visit with Mrs. Catherine Hughes in the Mothers' Union." Lina waved her hand. "I'll stop at his chippie. I would like to buy some steak and kidney pie for us all, if he has any left."

"Oh that would be nice. Yes, please will you ask him?" Lina nodded.

"Now then, before I go, which style are you going to have your hair tomorrow for Church?"

Mary hadn't thought about her hair and started running her fingers through, brushing it towards her face. "I'm a bit old to have it falling all over my face and I don't want it stuck up in a bun; that will make me look really old. What about if I had a ponytail or just clipped it back on either side?"

Lina was thinking of the styles she saw in London when she used to go. "Can you get me a comb and let me see what I can do?"

"Yes, I have to go upstairs, so I will hang up my dress and petticoat so they don't get creased." Mary ran up the stairs and returned quickly with her brush and comb and her hand mirror.

"That will be a good idea." Lina took a biscuit and pulled a chair close.

"Here you are Lina, will this comb be alright?" As Mary came down the stairs, David and Angel returned from the paper delivery. They moved into the front room to join Ian after they waved at Lina.

"It is just the right type. Hmm, now let me see." Mary sat at one of the kitchen chairs while Lina brushed her long hair. She combed it so gently that Mary hardly felt it. "Would you like it partly up or in a down style, what would you prefer with your new Easter dress?"

"I don't know which way would look the best." She told Lina with a shrug of her shoulders.

Before Mary could even finish her answer, Lina had Mary's hair pulled off her face and looped through making a soft roll on either side and the rest of Mary's hair flowing below where the two rolls met. It had a natural wave towards the ends that made it stay together just like a waterfall. "What about this way?"

Mary held the hand mirror up but couldn't get a good look so bent forward and picked up the mirror off the table where she left it and looked at herself. Smiling she exclaimed, "Oho is that really me, it looks so much like …. I don't know …. it looks …. It looks so beautiful. It's long and looks so tidy. I like it. Yes, I like it. Thank you. Oh, thank you." Leaning forward a little she gave Lina a hug. "Thank you so much. What do you think Ethan will say? Do you think he will like it?"

"First of all, he will be shocked. He will think he is married to a princess, especially when you have your Easter dress on. Mary, I am so happy you like it. It's so easy to do, too. Let me show you how."

Lina helped Mary until she could do the twist easily. She gathered her jacket and was to leave.

"I'll be going in a few minutes. I'll stop and talk with Dylan on my way back." Lina was going to meet Catherine Hughes who lived in Birchgrove, one of the ladies from the Mothers' Union.

"You can leave Angel here to play if you like. She seems quite content playing in the front room with the boys."

"That will be nice. You are really kind, thank you. I appreciate you, Mary. I'll pick her up on the way back then?"

"Yes, that will be alright."

Lina looked around the front room door. "Angel, Aunty Mary said you can stay here while I go to Uncle Dylan's, alright?"

Angel ran towards her and hugged her with a big hug, looking up at Lina, "I love you Nene," and rubbed her face into Lina.

"And, I love you, my Angel." Lina left closing the front door behind her. Mary was busy ironing Ethan's shirt for Church that she didn't notice Angel. Angel walked into the kitchen and tapped Mary on the arm. Angel looked concerned.

"Aunty Mary, is something wrong with my Nene? Why is she going to see Uncle Dylan by herself? She always takes me with her."

"No, Angel. Nothing's wrong. She's going to see a lady from the Mothers' Union first. I think her name is Catherine. On her way back she's going to stop at Uncle Dylan's chippie and see if he has some steak and kidney pies left. Don't worry now, everything's alright."

Lina stopped at Dylan's on the way back from seeing Catherine. Dylan was pleased to see her. "Hello Lina, is everything alright, where's Angel?"

"I left Angel with Mary. I just wanted to ask you something about tomorrow. I know you're not usually open on Easter Sunday, and I think you said last week you would be going to Church."

Dylan was curious why Lina should come to visit him without Angel and to ask if he was going to Church on Easter Sunday. "*Ìe*, that's right, I like to go and hear all that beautiful Easter singing and I think David and Angel are singing, too. Tomorrow is a great opportunity. I'm not opening the shop."

"Angel and David will be singing." Lina nodded. "I also want to tell you that Ethan said he might come to Church, too. He doesn't know that Mary has made a brand new dress for Easter. It will be such a nice surprise for him. It's not often that we are all together. Maybe you could sit with us in the front pew?"

"Well, I can't refuse that offer, now can I? I'll be sitting with two lovely ladies and one beautiful little girl. Yes, I'd like that. Us sit together." Dylan noticed that Lina was thinking deeply about something. "Lina, I know something is wrong, what is it? Lina's face was showing signs of concern but she obviously didn't want to say anything of her thoughts. Dylan thought it best to offer a seat for Lina.

"Let's go in the parlor instead of standing in the shop, shall we?" Lina stepped into the parlor and Dylan motioned to her to sit in his big armchair. When she sat, he put his hand on Lina's shoulder, "What is troubling you, Lina. What is it? You know I will help you anyway I can."

"Oh, Dylan." Lina sobbed and put her head on the armrest.

Dylan bent forward and put his arm around Lina and gently eased her upright. "There, there, it can't be that bad. Come on now, tell me what is wrong."

It took Lina a while to wipe the tears from her face and blow her nose in her little embroidered handkerchief. After a deep breath she mumbled, "Oh Dylan, what am I going to do?"

"What is it, what are you going to do with what, Lina?"

"We're all going up to Penrhiwgwynt tomorrow after lunch. I'm hoping that Ethan will come, too."

"That's very good Lina, you can't be sad about that?" Dylan enquired.

"No, no. But I don't think I am going to make it." Lina breathed heavily and then sat back down in the armchair and put her head on the arm.

"Make what, what's the matter, what is it Lina? Tell me?" He was getting a little impatient.

"I just don't think I can get up there. Angel will be so disappointed and she will be worried about me but I'm so tired, Dylan."

"She will understand if you say you're tired and you don't want to walk up those steep pathways."

"No Dylan." Lina stood up but could not keep her balance and yet still continued to try and talk to Dylan, "I don't think she will understand, she watches me all the time. She won't let me out of her sight."

Dylan steered Lina to sit in the chair. "Sit back down Lina. You are pale. Why do you say she watches you?" After he got her seated, he joined her, the tea forgotten for the moment.

"I see her sitting outside my bedroom door with her bear."

"What, in the night? You see her sitting there?"

"Yes, Dylan." Lina wiped her cheeks and took a deep breath. She hadn't meant to breakdown in front of an old friend.

"She's not sleeping then? But what is she doing sitting outside your room in the middle of the night?" He kept her hand in his.

"She doesn't sleep. I see her there when I turn over. I ask her what's the matter? She says she wants to hear me breathing and wants to make sure I'm alright." She turned to

Dylan, "What can I say to her? I'm tired, I'm frightened, and I worry about her."

"*Ìe,* she knows you're not sleeping well. She's worried about you just like I am. So, what is it, Lina? You must tell me, otherwise I can't help you." He petted the hand he held, wishing there was more he could do for her.

"I don't really know, Dylan. I'm just so tired."

"Have you talked with the doctor?"

"Yes, and I have another appointment next week."

"Lina that's good, but you haven't said what it is. What are you worried about?" Dylan leaned back on the other chair.

"I don't know, Dylan. But, will you please come with us tomorrow. Please? Please, Dylan?"

"I haven't been up to see the old girl for years you know, not since my Olga passed away."

"I know Dylan, but please will you come with me?" Lina pleaded with Dylan.

"*Ìe, Ìe,* of course. I will come with you. You look so worried, maybe we can talk on the way tomorrow. Do you know if Ethan is going for definite, then?"

"No, I don't know for certain but I am hoping he will. Maybe you could encourage him."

After a few moments, Dylan said in a soft voice. "*Ìe* I could. *Ìe.*" There was a pause then Dylan spoke "*Ìe,* I will suggest that he comes with us, especially as we are all going to Church together. Maybe that way he won't feel we are forcing him to go. He hasn't showed any interest in going; maybe because he doesn't like heights." Dylan looked at Lina's face and he could see a look of sadness. "I will do my best, Lina. Leave it to me, alright?"

"Yes, I know you will do your best. It would be so nice for Mary to have Ethan there with the children. It's been so long that they were up there as a family."

Chapter 18

"Easter morning is here, Ethan." Mary turned to look at Ethan. He hadn't quite woken up. She was getting so excited about wearing her new dress and the new hairdo Lina had showed her that she closed her eyes to imagine her appearance. It took Ethan a few minutes to wake up but finally he opened his eyes to see Mary beside him with her eyes closed and her dark hair flowing all over the pillow.

Ethan rose up on to his elbow, admiring her. "You are so pretty, Mary," he said in a soft voice. She opened her eyes and surprised him; she wasn't sleeping.

"Now what are you looking at?" she grinned.

"I was just looking at you and thinking how lucky I am. You are so pretty, Mary even after all these years."

"Who me?" Mary teased Ethan.

"Yes, you. The love of my life, you haven't lost your beauty."

"Oh, Ethan." Mary leaned over and kissed his cheek. "Well, my love, we have to get up, our baby elephants are awake, and we must be ready for Church. Lina and Angel will be here soon and we haven't had breakfast yet." She kissed him again. "Don't you hear those elephants?" She whispered to him.

"Oh yes. I hear them. They couldn't make any more noise if they tried." Ethan's thoughts of romance quickly diminished.

After breakfast everyone was ready and standing at the door except Mary; Ethan started to worry.

"Mary, love, are you ready?" He called up the stairs; hand on the banister, ready to leap each step to find her.

"I'm coming. I'm coming. Just getting my shoes on."

Ethan turned to look at the children once more and started adjusting David's tie when Lina and Angel came to the door. Ethan realized it must be getting late at that point and was about to shout up the stairs again. He turned suddenly, and Mary's face was within close proximity. "Oh my God, oh my God." For a moment Ethan was stunned and not quite himself.

"Dad, what's wrong?" David asked, turning at the sound of his father's voice.

Ethan steadied himself enough to gabble out, "Oh God Mary, you startled me. You look so different."

Lina put her head around the door to see what was going on. "Is everyone alright in there?"

"Yes, yes, for a moment, I thought. I don't know what I thought." Ethan pulled the front door open more so the sunlight lit up the hallway and he took a long hard breath. Mary touched his arm.

"Are you alright, Ethan?" she showed concern.

"Yes, yes." Ethan gulped for more air. Everyone walked through the door and was standing on the porch, waiting for Ethan and Mary.

Mary asked again, "Ethan, are you alright?"

Ethan closed the door leaving everyone outside and Mary and himself on the inside in the hallway.

"Ethan, oh my God, what's the matter you look so pale, what is it?"

Ethan just looked at Mary until he finally was able to say something. "Mary, I thought I saw a.. I thought something had happened to you. It was you but it wasn't you."

"It's me, Ethan. Alright?"

"Oh my God, you looked like an Angel. I was scared something had happened to you."

"No, nothing happened." She lifted her hand to his cheek. He was flushed and beginning to sweat. "Ethan, are you sure you are alright?"

"I am now. Oh, you look so beautiful. Mary you look so beautiful. You really scared me. What did you do to your hair?" He turned her to look at the back. Then turned her into his arms. He held her close and breathed in her scent. So light and fresh, he'd been so scared his heart jumped, but she was here, in his arms.

"Lina helped me. Do you like my dress? "

"I love all of you." He kissed her deeply, expressing the love he couldn't say out loud.

There was a bang at the door, "Mam, Dad are you coming to Church?"

"Yes, yes we'll be right there. Is Nene Lina with you?" Ethan managed to shout.

"Yes Dad, she's waiting too."

"Walk with Nene Lina and Angel, and we'll catch you up. Alright?"

"Alright, Dad."

Nene Lina was a little concerned but didn't say anything. She just smiled to herself thinking that the dress and hairstyle had definitely caught Ethan's eye.

Mary was getting concerned herself. "This is wonderful, Ethan, but we need to go. They will think something is wrong."

"Mary, I got scared I thought, I thought you had left me and you were an Angel. It worried me as I didn't recognize you."

"You just said that, Ethan," and she held his hand. "This is the dress that Lina helped me make. Do you like it?"

He took her hand, holding it above her head and guided her slowly through a full turn.

"It's beautiful. I can't believe you both made it so quickly."

"We are going to be late, we have to go." Mary blushed, smiling softly at Ethan and busied herself adjusting his tie. "You look so handsome this morning, yourself," and touched his shoulder.

Ethan gently grabbed her and kissed her.

David yelled his words close to the door. "Dad what are you doing in there? We are going to be late."

"I'm giving my princess a hug and kissing her on the lips." It was actually difficult for him to release her.

"Can you do that later? We're going to be really late." David didn't quite hear what Ethan had said but his impatience sounded clear from the porch. Mary laughed at Ethan.

"Alright, let's go." Ethan turned to Mary and joined in her laughter.

"I expect he's heard it from us enough. Out of the mouths of babes we hear a reflection of what we say."

It wasn't too long that everyone arrived at the Church. Vicar Llewelyn was on the front steps as usual, shaking everyone's hand as they entered. There were three ladies on the side nattering together.

"Who's that, done up like a dog's dinner with Ethan this morning, and he has his children with him? I wonder where Mary is this morning."

Lina heard the comments and went over to them, "Good morning Mrs. Evans, how are you now that you have got over that terrible cold?"

Mrs. Evans didn't reply about her cold but without any hesitation repeated the words she had just said, "Lina, who is *that* with Ethan, done up like a dog's dinner there? And he has his children with him too. He ought to be ashamed of himself and coming to the Church with *that* as well."

Lina laughed, "*That*, as you put it, is Ethan's wife. Mary." Mrs. Evans looked shocked and disbelieving. "And you think she's done up like a dog's dinner. She would laugh at that."

"It can't be Mary Edwards. She never dresses like that, so classy."

"I can assure you, it is." Lina turned to Mary. "Mary dear, come and show Mrs. Evans the beautiful new dress you made."

Mrs. Evans snorted, more disbelieving. "She couldn't have made that. It looks like it's come from Paris or somewhere like that."

Mary stepped forward towards Mrs. Evans. "Hello, Mrs. Evans. Are you alright? You look …um."

Mrs. Jones, also disbelieving but gentle in nature said, "Shocked, if you ask me," and turned to Mary with a sweet smile. "I have never seen you dressed up so beautiful, and you really made this dress?"

Mary looked at Lina for a little help with the probing questions.

"Mary did, and look at the hemline, it's the latest fashion." Lina was so happy to share news of Mary's talent to the gossiping women. Plus, she hoped it taught them an important lesson. Their mean words could hurt others and they needed to keep their words to themselves.

Ethan came to the rescue and linked his arm in Mary's. "Come on, my beauty. It's time to go into Church. Ian and David have already gone in with Uncle Dylan." Ethan nodded to the ladies and escorted her away. Leaving the ladies with open mouths of disbelief.

Mary was happy to walk away from the old mother hens, and so was Lina. Angel took Lina's hand and looked up at Lina with a big smile.

Everyone was in Church and the music started. Mrs. Thomas thumped on the old organ and seemed to linger on one note. She suddenly disappeared out of view. A few minutes passed and people began whispering all around the Church. No one could see her. Suddenly her head reappeared behind her music stand and she was waving her shoe in the air. Apparently it got caught in the foot pedal. How embarrassing for her, but the Church was in an uproar, giggles, and laughter in every pew. It certainly gave a different atmosphere from the usual solemn Sunday service.

Vicar Llewelyn stood on the top step near the altar and shouted, "Well then, we seem to have a little problem with the organ this morning but that shouldn't stop us from enjoying our morning service." Giggles and laughter continued, slow to die down. Vicar Llewelyn himself wanted to join in with the hilarity but did his best to compose himself and motioned to David and Angel to open up the service with a hymn. It suddenly went quiet, not a sound could be heard.

David and Angel started singing the *Lord's Prayer* and Vicar Llewelyn joined in. When they had sung half way, he motioned for them to sit down on the steps, one on either side of him. The old mother hens sat mesmerized. His voice echoed as he sang with his mellow tenor. When the singing stopped it was so quiet one could have heard a pin.

Llewelyn then stood and continued with words that they had not heard in a Church service before.

"Maybe this is what's needed, a surprise at the beginning of the service to get everyone's attention, something different! We are in a different time and different things are happening all around us. Let's give thanks to our Lord for our differences and the differences we share with others as we experience them."

Uncle Dylan shared in a whisper to Lina hiding his mouth with his hand. "It's been years since I've heard Llewelyn sing. I had forgotten he had a good voice."

Lina agreed with Dylan. She remembered Llewelyn singing at the Christmas service.

At the end of the poignant Easter message, everyone filed out of the Church quite noisily. Vicar Llewelyn was at the door wishing everyone a very happy Easter. Dylan shook his hand and said, "How long will it take you to get ready? Come over to my chippie and ask your Mrs. to come when she's ready. I've made plenty of sandwiches for everyone. I thought it would be a nice change from fish and chips. It's Easter!"

He looked at Lina and motioned to Mary to come closer, "Will you help Lina make the tea? I know she won't sit still. She'll want to be busy serving everyone. We'll be there soon. Alright?"

Dylan winked at Lina, and quietly assured her, "I'll take care of everything." Meaning he was setting up his plan to have Ethan and Llewelyn up the mountain. He pressed the key to the shop into her hand. That way the women could open the shop and start lunch. He'd follow after with the men.

Dylan and Ethan were left standing in the street with Llewelyn, "There's a workingman's club here somewhere that serves beer on Sundays, as the Pubs are shut; but by the time I find it, the ladies will be restless. Now, how about both of you coming over to my chippie for a beer? How long will it take you, Llewelyn, to change? Unless you want to come in your dog collar?"

"I haven't been invited out for a very long time." Llewelyn thought to himself, "Dylan knows I wear my clerical collar so why did he mention that?"

Dylan broke the silence; "Our town is dry on Sundays, nowhere to drink. Many people want the ban on drink lifted but it looks like it will be a very long time and I'll be dead and buried by the time that happens."

Llewelyn muttered, "Me too, no doubt." Then he let out a bellowing laugh.

"I always keep a few beers for the weekend. Alright, what do you say? Come to my chippie and we'll have a beer together for a change."

"Alright, then. Let me run over to the vicarage to tell Pagua and I'll be back before you can say Jack Robinson." Ethan stood quite still. He hadn't heard his Uncle Dylan say he had beers before.

Dylan shouted, "Lina, you and Mary go ahead. We will see you in a few minutes. We're just waiting for Llewelyn. Alright?"

Dylan turned to Ethan, "Alright then, you know that means you too, Ethan. We can have some time with Llewelyn as well. He can be very interesting to listen to sometimes, you know?"

Ethan wondered what his Uncle Dylan was up to, but agreed anyway.

It took Llewelyn no time at all to be dressed and out of his vicarage. "I have some Easter eggs for the children. I was going to come over a bit later but I might as well give them the eggs now."

"Alright then," Dylan was eager to ask Ethan to join everyone on the walk up but had to wait for the right moment. So rather than put Ethan on the spot, he decided to ask Llewelyn first. "Llewelyn, how long has it been since you went up to see the old girl?" He gestured over his shoulder at the mountain.

"Let me think, to the top? It's been many years. A long time ago, but last year we picked blackberries just above milkman's farm. My wife, Pagua, likes to make jams and trifles almost immediately after we've picked them. You know they are plentiful around there. We don't have to go far and carry buckets. We'll be going again when the berries are ripe." They walked a couple steps. "That reminds me Ethan, she has some jams for Mary. I should have asked her before I came out."

"Thank you, I can get them when we come back." Ethan was thankful.

"She's busy now pickling onions in her kitchen and it stinks like hell in there."

"Really?" Ethan was surprised as Llewelyn's house was always spick and span.

"Of onions, mun." He chuckled at the thought. Once Llewelyn started talking it was really hard to stop him.

Perhaps that's why his Church services were so interesting, with pieces of news and his reflection on the town's interesting events.

It wouldn't take long to walk to Dylan's chippie so Dylan slowed the pace and mentioned to Llewelyn their walk up the mountain. Dylan forced a stop at the corner of his street, "Would you like to come with us, it looks like it will be a good day."

"I'm not sure," Llewelyn was a little shaken at first. "I haven't been up there since your brother Cradoc died, you know that." As Cradoc's friend and priest, he'd been the one who prayed over his cut up body. Llewelyn even took off his own shirt and covered my brother. Those memories surged at the thought of returning.

Dylan quickly replied and included a hint that Ethan might capture too, "I know. But we must face the ogre and live again. Come on, mun. It's Easter, we haven't had a family picnic for donkeys' years."

"Alright then, I hope I make it to the top." Llewelyn replied. He took a deep breath, his gaze straying to the shadow of the mountain.

"It's not that bad really, just steep. The pathways Cradoc built were a good way of getting up and getting down. He made them originally for our Mam so she could visit him."

"Hello little ladies, we are here. Now then, where did I put my key to my drinks cabinet?"

"Uncle, there's a bunch of keys on the wall by the side of your Welsh dresser," Ethan remembered.

"By jove! There they are!" Dylan was surprised, as he honestly didn't remember where he put them.

"Now then, what will you have? Let's see…." Dylan called out the names as he pulled out his selection of drinks for the men to see.

"I'll have a shandy," Llewelyn said a little nervously.

"A shandy? That's like drinking pop. Come on, mun. You used to drink lager or Guinness."

"Alright then," looking a little more embarrassed this time Llewelyn said, "A pint of Guinness, then."

"That's better, now we're talking." Dylan turned to Ethan "What will you have Ethan?"

"I'll have a half pint of lager, thank you Uncle."

"Alright, then." Dylan knew Ethan didn't drink too much but he did enjoy a lager now and again. Dylan grabbed his pint glasses from the hooks on his Welsh dresser and opened the bottles. Then he went back to get the half-pint glass from the other side of the dresser. Everyone's drink was ready and he sat down at the kitchen table where they were sitting. "It's not always I have the pleasure of sitting with two respectable men and having a drink on a Sunday." They all laughed heartily. The beer and lager were warm and smooth and Ethan knocked his back as if he was thirsty. "Another one, Ethan?"

"Well." He looked at Mary for her nod, "I don't mind if I do."

"What about you Llewelyn? You've finished your pint. What about another one?"

"Oh no, no thank you. One's enough for me."

"Don't be daft, mun, I know you like your Guinness. I'll pour you a half then, alright?" Dylan got to his feet, walking back to the dresser to get the last half-pint glass. "Alright then, a half it is for Llewelyn." Llewelyn finally looked comfortable. Perhaps a drink in his belly helped his nervousness.

"The children both sang beautifully again this morning, Llewelyn, didn't they?" Dylan was happy to announce.

"I think they would have sung more hymns if the service was longer but you know how it is, babies start crying and people get restless."

Dylan turned to Ethan. "I'm going to walk up to Penrhiwgwynt with Lina. Mary is taking the children. What about you joining us after we've all had our sandwiches?"

He turned to Llewelyn. "You're coming after your sandwiches, right?"

"Oh yes. After I've had some of that tea, too. I wouldn't miss a walk for all the tea in China."

"You found the cards, then did you?" Dylan looked at Ian. Ian was content playing patience.

"Yes, Uncle. David knew where they were," Ian replied politely.

"Right then, I haven't seen many of those sandwiches eaten. If we don't finish them here, then perhaps we should take them up Penrhiwgwynt. We can have a picnic." After everything was wrapped up, everyone moved from the chairs at the table. "I'm just going upstairs to change out of my Church suit. I want to be comfortable this afternoon."

Lina and Mary packed the sandwiches and pop, a treat for later, in the baskets ready for the picnic.

"Vicar Llewelyn, I didn't know you could sing like that." David smiled as he made his comment.

"Oh son, I used to sing when I was in school with Angel's father, Gilberto, except he was much better than me. I loved to sing. I had an offer you know, to join the Treorchy Male Voice Choir? My Mam was very proud and so happy."

Angel said politely, "That must have been really exciting to sing with a big choir. Did my dad sing with them as well?"

There was a pause before Llewelyn answered. "Well." He paused again, not sure how to tell Angel.

"He didn't like it?" David was very inquisitive because that was his dream to sing with the best choir in Wales.

"Oh no, Angel's father enjoyed it. We were practicing one night for a big singing contest against some other male voice choirs in the Rhondda." A man of many words, he fell silent again.

"That must have been exciting." Angel sensed something but didn't know why he stopped talking. Was he waiting for some more questions?

"It was only a short time that Gilberto and I were with them." Llewelyn rocked onto his toes, hands in his pockets.

"What happened?" Angel asked politely.

"Well, my uncle died in the pit accident. Eighty men, to be exact, died in that explosion. It was caused by a pocket of gas."

"Where was the gas, Uncle Llewelyn?"

"It's under the ground and coal mining disturbs the gas and it can explode."

David was thinking what it would be like if he couldn't see his father. Rarely serious, David's face reflected the sadness in that thought. "Did you see your uncle again?"

"No, I didn't, son. I didn't see him again, and I still think about him." Llewelyn was quiet for a few moments but broke the silence with thoughts that lingered in his memory. "My Uncle moved in with us when his wife died. He was alone and my mam asked him if he would like to live with us and be a family again, brother and sister. He was funny and tried to make us laugh." Llewelyn found a smile.

"I remember him leaving very early in the mornings. I wasn't supposed to be awake at that time but I'd watch him from the top of the stairs leaning on the banister. He'd kiss my mam on the cheek and say 'bless you'. He'd put on his helmet, then take his sandwich box from her, and put it over the handlebars of his bike." His hands came out of his pockets and the constant rocking from toe to heel paused. He lifted a hand in memory. "He'd turn on the light on his helmet and wheel his bike out of the front door as quietly as he could, not to disturb us. My mam would stand watching, say something and close the door."

The ladies and children finished their drinks while he spoke. Lina said she and Mary would go home and get the children changed so they could go for the walk but David continued asking his questions, and to be honest it was interesting for Lina and Mary, too. So everyone sat back down again.

"What did she say when William left in the morning?" David asked.

"I don't know. She whispered very quietly. I expect something like, 'take care of yourself William', or 'see you tonight'."

"What happened, then?" David wanted to know.

"Well, son. The streetlights were off then even though it was so dark in the mornings. It was difficult for anyone to see if they didn't have a torch or light on their helmet. I'd run up the stairs as fast as I could when the door closed and look through the front window, but if I didn't get there fast enough my Uncle might be out of sight. I pulled up the window sometimes and leaned out. I could get a better view and I would watch him go. I remember him tinkling his bell as he went down the street. I could see the other men in the street coming out of their houses and doing the same. By the time they got to the end of the street there was a crowd of moving black shadows with lights, tinkling their bells."

"All of them?"

"Yes, all of them. Black shadows on moving wheels."

"Wasn't that scary to see black shadows?" David was still a child and the image of shadows would scare him, early in the morning.

"No son, not really. I knew who they were. My Uncle was the first one out on the street and started tinkling his bell as soon as he got out of the front door. My mam said it was to let the others know it was time to go to work so they could all go together."

"How many of them went on bikes?" David couldn't imagine many men on bikes. He'd only seen a few around town his whole life.

"Every man or boy that lived on my street from age fifteen years and upwards worked down the pit and their bikes were the only transportation they had back then to go to work."

"From fifteen?" David was thinking why his brother, Ian, wasn't doing the same.

"Yes son, from fifteen. There was one boy, John Davies, he was only twelve. John lived in Ferndale. Even though he was young, he had to work to help his family as his father died."

"I'm not going down the mine, am I?" David was worried that his dream of singing wouldn't happen. He glanced around the room, looking at everyone with the question.

"No son, your father stopped all that. He remembers what it was like and he wouldn't let you go down. Not even your brothers." Llewelyn touched David on the shoulder to indicate it was alright. David still looked anxious about it all.

"I remember my mam looking very anxious every night until my Uncle was home. Life was hard for my Mam with all my brothers and sisters, but she was determined none of us boys would go down the pit for fear we would end up like my Uncle." Llewelyn smiled at him, back in the day he'd be training for the pit. He leaned down to be face to face with the youngster who hadn't shaken off the fear.

"Son, it's alright. Don't look so worried. I can promise you your father wouldn't let you go down the pit, or Ian for that matter." Llewelyn needed to think quickly of some good stories to lesson David's anxiety. "Those days are over; nearly everyone lost a lot of loved ones from their families. Then the mines shut down and we had to look for other work."

"I remember…. I got a job on the railway with Angel's father. I was a porter to start with just like him and we used to sing as we swept the platforms and helped people with their bags. People liked to hear us singing. Some of them said it made them feel happy." He smiled at David. "We made up things to sing. I hear you do the same, young man."

"People liked your singing when you were on the railway?" David was trying to understand all that Llewelyn was saying. "Oh, yes sir. I do make it up as I go along."

"He does, Uncle." Angel nodded and smiled.

"Oh yes, Angel's father and I would get the other porters singing, too. Sometimes we would make up songs but mostly we sang the songs we knew, and sometimes our Church hymns."

"What kind of songs did you make up?" David was interested because he did that too, up the mountain.

"Well, there was one that everyone seemed to like. It didn't really rhyme but we could sing fast or slow, high or low and the other men would come in with the chorus."

"Would you sing it for us?" David always wanted to learn another new song. One he could practice.

"Alright." Llewelyn smiled and took a breath. "Good morning, good morning."

"We get up with the birds, they make us go to work,
We sweep the platforms clean so you can start and dream
Your days to come, with happiness and love,
We wish you health, we wish you wealth,
We wish you dreams come true,
But most of all we wish, God….. be…… with……
you."

He grinned at the assembly in the kitchen. "I thought I'd forgotten that. The others would chime in when they remembered the words. We'd dance with the brooms, you see. Swinging around them, our hearts were so much lighter then."

"Do you still make up songs?" David was more curious.

"Sometimes when I'm by myself or out walking." His hands went back into his pockets, his body rocking up to his toes and back to his heels again.

"Can you sing another one now?" David was impressed.

"I know what will be better. I'll sing with you up Penrhiwgwynt this afternoon, alright?"

"Yes, yes, that will be alright. How did you get to be a Vicar then?"

"I'll tell you that later too, on our way, alright?"

The ladies and children finished their drinks. Lina said she and Mary would go home and get the children changed so they could go for the walk.

Lina, Mary, and Ethan left to change out of their Sunday best and take care of the children. Ian followed to get his sketchpad. Ian would have been happy wearing his Church clothes. He always had the thought he might meet a sweet young girl somewhere he could sketch. He always wanted to look good.

"We'll see you back here in a little bit, then." Dylan was anxious to get started on the walk but at the same time, while they were all gone, he wanted to talk with Llewelyn when no one would be around.

"Llewelyn, I'm worried about Lina. Have you noticed anything different about her when she's at Church or the Church Hall?"

"I have that, that I have, Dylan." Llewelyn was slow with his answers, almost as though he was thinking every word he muttered. "Lina is private. She wouldn't want me to know in case I tell my Mam. They are sisters you know, Mari and Lina. Sometimes I forget that because we have very different lives."

"Alright then, Llewelyn. She looks tired to me. I think something is wrong." Dylan expressed his concern.

Llewelyn confirmed, "I believe she is sick but she's never been one to express her sickness. Lina always says she's tired if you ask her anything."

"That I'm getting, but if she doesn't tell me, how can I help her?" Dylan put his hand on his cheek as he was in deep thought.

"I suggest you both stay on the first pathway and talk. She won't make it up, I don't think, from what I have seen at Church and on our Mothers' Union night. I could take Ethan with Mary and the children and go up if you think that is a good idea," Llewelyn suggested.

"Well, I hope Ethan will go. He needs to go up, get some fresh air, and clear his lungs and definitely his mind. Be careful, he is afraid of heights." Dylan nodded.

"He is? I never knew that. I thought he would be alright after being 400 ft. or more down in the dark pit all those years." The mineshaft lowered the workers on ropes and pulleys. Their only light was from their helmets. It was claustrophobic and smelly. Llewelyn had experienced that himself when someone got stuck under an avalanche of coal, he would risk his own life to go down and share prayers.

"Well, I think Ethan would rather that, it was what he got used to all those years. It was like a tube. The mountain is open air with no sides. He needs to leave the mines behind him and start to live again. If you could distract him by talking he might not realize how far up he has gone, but when he gets to the top you might have to steady him a bit. I would like to make the effort myself but I'm so worried about Lina, you know. I'll stay down a bit with Lina like you suggested."

"Yes, that would be better to stay down with her and talk a bit. Find out what's going on." Llewelyn hesitated a little. "Is Gilberto aware of his mam's condition?"

"Well, we don't know that," Dylan fretted. "But I suspect she hasn't told Gilberto. She would say why worry him he has a lot on his plate already. Lina sees the doctor again next week."

"I think somehow we should try to get Gilberto here; don't you think, Dylan?"

"*Ìe,* I do that, that I do, but she says he's busy working."

"His mam's health is far more important. After all, look what she's doing for him, taking care of his daughter. She's not getting any younger, you know, and she had a bad time looking after *that* Edwin when he got sick after his stroke."

"Now don't get all churned up about Lina. You get so upset before you know what's going on." He flapped his hands at Llewelyn. "Don't get so upset." Dylan was anxious not to alarm Gilberto about Lina but did agree he should know something.

"Dylan, I've been a man of the cloth for so many years. I have seen conditions worsen with the bat of an eyelid. I've spent enough hours sat at the bedside of some poor soul trying to hold on to their life for someone or other who doesn't even bother to visit them. It's time we got Gilberto to understand he has a mam who has done more than her fair share, and needs him right here." He paced the floor, stretching his legs as he thought. "I wonder if my mam knows. She lives in Erdington, near another of her and Lina's brothers."

"She won't have it you know. Lina is a very hard working lady who will not give up until her last dying breath," Dylan managed to squeeze in before Llewelyn's nostrils were flared up again.

"And that it might be if we don't do something about it, and do something quick." Llewelyn was very anxious to do the right thing for Lina and it didn't matter what it took. "Alright then, who else can tell us how to get in touch with Gilberto if my mam doesn't know? How does Lina get in touch with him? She must have an address or a phone number somewhere. I don't recall seeing mam here or Lina going over the border to see her. We must get in touch with Gilberto."

"Now, now LLewelyn, for God's sake, mun, don't get your trousers in a twist. Let's wait and see, alright?"

"Dylan, it's been a long time since someone close to you has needed help but I think this is the time Lina needs us. We must be prepared for whatever happens."

"I told you already, she said she's going to see the doctor again tomorrow. She said she should know something then."

"Well, we can't wait for that. What if the doctor admits her; then what are we going to do? We have to think of Angel, she's so young and getting Gilberto here will be another thing. We must be prepared."

"Mary and Ethan told Lina that they will take care of Angel as their own, but Lina doesn't believe that Gilberto will ever let her stay here."

"Well, where will she go? He can't look after the little girl. She is so happy here with her friends and in the Church."

"Llewelyn, we must be careful you know. If we rock the boat, he could take both of them now. One time, Lina shared with me that Gilberto was working to buy a house, he wanted to take Lina away from the Rhondda. He said to give her a better life. Gilberto is very sensitive about his mam. Perhaps he is thinking if he provides a home for her near your mam's he is helping her."

"Well does Lina want to go over the border?"

"I overheard her once in Church, you know. She was praying in a whisper; she didn't think anyone was listening. She wants to stay strong and not be so tired so she can stay here and take care of Angel. I know Lina doesn't want to leave here. This is her home, where she grew up as a child, and this is where her beloved Ernesto is buried." He quieted for a moment, cleared his throat. "It's Angel's home, too. This is the only place she knows. I told you what happened the last time she went to England when Lina was in hospital. That was a bad experience for Angel."

"Dylan, we can't stand in Gilberto's way if he wants to give his mam a better life."

"Llewelyn mun, Lina doesn't want to go, I'm telling you." Llewelyn gave Dylan a look of disgust.

"Now, what happens if Gilberto takes Lina and Angel to Birmingham and then Lina dies? God forbid. I don't want to think about it." Dylan made the sign of the cross upon his chest. "What will happen to Angel? Gilberto couldn't look after her, he can't leave her in his new house by herself while he works, and he couldn't take her to your mam's. Mari has enough problems; her youngest son, Cliff and his family are living with her, aren't they? The last time when she had to stay at Mari's it was a disaster for Angel."

"Surely, Gilberto will listen if his mam says she doesn't want to go and would honor her wishes," Llewelyn instantly replied.

"Llewelyn, you don't understand. When a stubborn man, especially like Gilberto, is prepared to work God knows where and how many hours to provide a better home and life for his mam, do you think he will listen to anyone or let her stay here?"

"Well, what do you suggest? We can't just wait around for something to happen before we do anything, Dylan." The men stared at each other across the warped flooring, wondering what next.

"That I know. I'll talk to Lina when we go up Penrhiwgwynt. Angel is worried about her, too. Lina said she sits outside her bedroom door listening to her breathe. That can't be fun for a little girl knowing something might be wrong with her Nene."

"I wish I had an answer, but I will pray. That I will do. In fact, I will mention her when I pray for the sick next Sunday too at our Sunday service."

"Oh my God. Don't mention her name or she'll know I've told you." Dylan showed his concern.

"No, I won't do that. I will have a special prayer in a broader sense. Not with too many details for all our sick friends and neighbors and not mention her name."

"Alright then. We must wait for Lina to go to her appointment and then we can see what needs to be done. I think you mentioned Lina this morning in prayer. I thought then you might have been thinking about Lina."

"I was, but I didn't know what was going on. I also wanted to include Mr. Hughes. He is bedridden now, you know. That reminds me, I must pay him a visit tomorrow."

"I didn't know about Mr. Hughes, but Mrs. Hughes has had it hard since her son died in that pit accident." Dylan shook his head. "And now her husband. Bless her. Does she have any family in these parts?"

"No, Dylan. They moved over the border years ago. They did occasionally visit when they went up the valley but haven't seen them for a while."

"Shame, that is. When young families leave for other parts they seem to forget their parents and definitely their grandparents. Such a shame."

"We must be getting ready. Mary and the children will be here soon and I hope Lina will walk here with them, so we won't have to be worried about her."

"Alright then Dylan. Let's see what happens?"

"We don't know what's going on yet and we don't want Lina and Angel to see you like this."

"I think I hear them," someone knocked on the door. "Come in, come in." Lina was with Mary. Dylan sighed in relief.

Chapter 19

"All right then everyone. We can leave the dishes. I'll have something to do when we get back." Dylan grabbed the sandwich bag and told the children to get some water or pop to carry for themselves.

It wasn't too long before David was questioning Llewelyn about his life before the Church.

"When did you become a Vicar, then?"

"I didn't exactly become a Vicar right away. When I was on the railway I was offered another job to do the books in the office."

"Did you sing then, when you were doing the books?"

"If I didn't, my colleagues would have thought there was something wrong with me so I'd have to come in every morning singing the songs I knew. Fortunately for me my boss also liked to sing. He would join in. It was a very happy office. When I left he sang for a while and soon encouraged the others to participate. Some of them did well but there was one who couldn't carry a tune, but that's alright, they all had a good time at work."

"How did you get to be a Vicar, then?" David was trying to figure out the transition from the railway to the Church.

"Well, son. I think I found something missing in my life. Going to Church was one thing for me but actually taking a part in it and trying to help people in the town was what I wanted so I went to seminary."

"Do you get paid in the Church, then?" David was eager to know where he got his money.

"Just a little. I probably would have earned more if I were mining or still working on the train tracks. Thank God I'm not down the pit."

"My dad was down the pit," David told him.

"I know son, and to be honest I'm glad he's not there now."

"Me too. I get to see my dad every day now."

"Yes you do. You do that."

Angel was skipping in delight when she turned to Lina, "I hope we find Buttercup, Nene."

"That would be nice, we'll all have to keep our eyes peeled for her." Angel beamed.

"Good afternoon," Llewelyn shouted across the milkman's farm. There was a reply from the barn where the milkman was spreading hay. He did finally come out and leaned on his fork to acknowledge the party.

"Well, where are you all going on this fine afternoon?"

"Were going up to walk on the old girl," Llewelyn shouted back.

Ethan started to look nervous until Llewelyn asked David to sing something as they walked. David and Angel were definitely a very nice distraction for Ethan. His face gradually relaxed into pride as he heard David singing with Angel.

Dylan realized how far they had gone and noticed Lina was walking slower and slower. "Shall we rest here for a while, Lina?" Lina was pleased and agreed. They sat on the nearby bench. It was very pretty looking down the hill.

"Did you know that this bench was made by my brother, Cradoc? He wanted our mam to have somewhere to sit on the way as she made it up to the top. He didn't want her to get tired. There are a few of these benches. I expect you have noticed them."

Angel turned around to look at her Nene and ran back, "Are you alright, Nene? What's the matter, Nene?" She looked so worried.

"Nothing's wrong, Angel. It's my back, I carried some coal in last night and I think the load was a bit too heavy. I've asked your Nene to sit with me for a while and we'll catch you up. Will that be alright?"

"Yes, yes. If my Nene is alright."

"She is. Your Nene is alright. She's going to take care of me. Tell Vicar Llewelyn will you? Tell him that we will catch up later."

Angel skipped off but turned a few times waving at Lina and Dylan.

"Angel does love you, Lina but I see her concern." Dylan paused to see if Lina would offer any explanation. It was silent for a while and that seemed to make Lina uncomfortable. "I have been meaning to tell you something and I suppose now is as good as anything."

"What is it Dylan? Do you need me to do some washing for you? I told you I can help you with that."

"There you go again, worried about other people."

"I've stopped doing Mrs. Thomas's washing. She said she's a lot better now."

"No nothing is wrong but as always Lina, you are always thinking somebody needs something done." He gazed over the field where they sat, the voices of the kids a soft echo from where they sang ahead.

"Lina, I have watched you over the years and I can tell something is deeply wrong. I can see that worry on your face again like last time three years ago, but this time it seems a little more intense. What is it?"

Lina sat quietly but did offer a comment on the bench. "Cradoc knew what he was doing when he made this bench. It's strong and sturdy."

"*Ìe,* it is that, that it is," Dylan replied.

Another silence made Dylan speak his thoughts finally. "Lina, I was about to say that all these years I have watched you struggle. I am an old man now but you have always been my friend and helped me with chores and washing and I've appreciated it very much. Since your Ernesto passed away," Dylan made the sign of the cross on his chest and continued, "I have been worried about you for years. I have watched you clean, cook, taking in neighbors' washing, help make clothes for our Mary, but your struggling never stopped. I wonder if that was my fault." He looked at her on the bench. Her hair was just beginning to show grey streaks, her cheeks worn and beautiful with time. Her eyes still almond shaped, the rich chestnut as bright as the day they changed after her birth.

"*Ìe*, I could have asked you to marry me and I should have long ago but I was conscious I wasn't a young man anymore and I really didn't have anything to offer you more than companionship. You deserved someone better, someone that would love you and take care of you and your boys. I knew there could be no-one on this earth that could take Ernesto's place." Lina started to cry. "There, there, I didn't mean to make you cry. Come on now, this old man doesn't like to think that he has made any lady cry, especially you." She wiped her eyes. "Now, if I had been a younger man, *Ìe*, I think I might have swept you off your feet, or at least tried. I could have brought that silver carriage to your door and dressed up like Prince Charming." Lina smiled a little, trying to fight back her tears. "I should have done something and somehow helped you. Please forgive me for not doing that." He took her hand in both of his. His eyes filling as she struggled for control.

"Dylan, you always helped me, and helped me a lot. I didn't have money and you fed us, me and my boys. You were there for a lot of my boys' lives. You helped build them into manhood. I could never have done it alone. You were there even if you think you weren't. They knew where to come if they needed anything or wished for more. I thank you for that. Oh Dylan." Lina blew her nose gently into her little lacy handkerchief.

"I was a bit younger then, but not young enough, I thought. Then *that Edwin* came along and broke you down to marry him. He never tamed down his temper. He realized he couldn't live with hopes and dreams that couldn't come true. There was one good thing about him, he was able to get a house with his job on the railway. Llewelyn and I never thought he was good enough for you, though."

"Oh Dylan, don't say that," Lina interrupted.

"We constantly prayed for you, that we did. We prayed for you to make the right decision or for *that Edwin* to disappear back wherever he came from. I couldn't interfere, could I really? It wouldn't have been right for me to tell him to bugger off and leave you alone." Lina tried to smile. "What could I have offered you? I felt I was too old and of course people around here would have gossiped forever about you marrying an older man. So, I backed down and didn't talk about my intentions and interest in you. You were definitely too good for that bugger. I don't think that your eldest son, Gilberto, was too keen on him either. He saw his mam working too hard, then being married and still having to take in washing to make ends meet!" Still nothing from Lina, she wouldn't speak a word, just looked around at the scenery. She couldn't argue with anything he was saying. She wasn't deaf and she'd heard what others said when they didn't think she could hear. She sighed; her life would have been so different with Dylan. Now she feared it was too late.

"It's beautiful when we get up here on Penrhiwgwynt, away from the grey slag of the Rhondda isn't it? What a contrast a beautiful deep green it is. All this fresh air and beautiful scenery and wild life that God has given us, free, we just need to look around us." He wasn't looking at the scenery. He was looking at her.

"Dylan," there was a silence and then Lina sighed. "I knew you were a very good man but I never thought you would have wanted to marry a woman with the burden of two young boys. I had to do something for my boys, quickly.

It was difficult and I didn't have two pennies to scratch together. I really didn't want to marry Edwin but there was no one else that showed any interest in me. God knows I didn't want to be alone." Lina sobbed quietly.

"It's all in the past now. We must think of the future." Dylan consoled Lina by holding her left hand and his right arm around her shoulders while she recovered from sobbing.

"What future Dylan? How will Angel grow up? I'm not going to last forever."

"None of us will last forever, Lina and that's no reason to be so upset. It has to be something else. What is it?" Dylan was determined to find out what was bothering Lina.

"I haven't seen the doctor yet but I know what it is." Lina's cheeks were wet with tears and her eyes wore a look of sadness.

"If you don't know yet try and trust in God. He has the power to overcome, as Llewelyn would say."

"I know, Dylan but it still makes me scared. What if…" Lina sniffled and sobbed more.

"Now there, there my dear; it will be alright. Let's continue to pray that it is not as bad as you are thinking. Llewelyn is also worried about you. I asked him to come on our walk so he could go up ahead with Mary and the children and encourage Ethan on the way. You know he doesn't like the thought of going up Penrhiwgwynt still. I can't understand that, after so long."

Lina confirmed her interest in getting Ethan to visit his grandfather's property. "It would be really nice for Mary and Ethan to go up, maybe this could lead to a good outcome for them."

"Yes, I agree with you," Dylan confirmed.

"It's a long way; how much further do we need to go, Vicar Llewelyn?" Ethan walked beside the older man, gaze flicking to the steep sides ahead and the long drop below.

"Don't worry about the distance, Ethan. Look at the children, they are so excited."

David and Angel ran ahead as soon as they saw the old tree and Mary strayed behind trying to catch up with their short energetic legs.

"Ethan, do you know much about your grandfather, Cradoc?"

"No, not really. I only knew the few things I overheard my mam say once and that he was killed. Uncle Dylan told me about the horses trampling all over him and my grandmother died from a broken heart."

"Yes, that's right, Ethan. Did you know your Uncle Dylan took care of your father and his brother when your grandmother died?"

"I didn't really know that until Uncle Dylan told me one day when I was helping him in the chippie."

"It wasn't long after your grandmother, Clarenda, died and was buried next to your grandfather that your Uncle Dylan and your Aunty Olga came down to Porth and brought your father and his brother with them. Dylan wasn't such a good horseman as Cradoc. He didn't have that terrific strength that Cradoc had. We never knew where Cradoc got that strength. He was definitely an outdoors man. He could survive in the bitter cold on the mountaintop and hunt for his food - maybe that's what cultivated his strength - and he would eat berries and whatever the land offered him.

"Your Uncle Dylan on the other hand, was good with numbers, money, and transactions. He was the only one that did well in school. I think Cradoc was happy that Dylan was good with the paperwork and bills, doing the books you might say. Don't misunderstand me now, your Uncle Dylan did more than his fair share. He helped out with feeding the horses and taking care of the sheep, goats, and chickens as well as the books. They worked well together. Clarenda and Olga were sisters, so you see, there was another blood bond there."

Ethan listened carefully to what Vicar Llewelyn had to say and agreed that he knew a little, but not all. "You know Mary tried to ask my mam a lot of times why we didn't go up the mountain to live. My mam was very ill then and said when my father died in the pit she lost interest in life. She had hoped one day my father would come home from the pit and say, "Let's go up to Penrhiwgwynt and start a new life." Ethan shook his head, gazing at the trail under their feet. "She talked sometimes about all the stuff they had from his parents that Uncle Dylan had kept for him and thought of what it would take to move our family up there. She shared with Mary that it would have been a struggle for them to start again, but it was just a dream because my father died in the pit."

"Have you ever dreamt about leaving the town and coming up here?"

"Not really. This is the first time I've really come since Mary and I were married." Ethan glanced around them. It was a beautiful place.

Llewelyn remembered what Dylan had said about Ethan not liking heights so was careful not to say anything about looking down over the valley, but more about the clean air and beauty of the mountain.

"Didn't you come a few times with Mary before you got married?"

"We did. In fact, that tree over there where the children are playing is where I proposed to Mary." He pointed, a relaxed smile finally curling his lips.

"You did? Then that is where we need to go, bring back some good memories and be with the children and Mary over there."

The children were enjoying the day. David was swinging on a branch and Angel was pushing him. David

was singing his old song about Angel's hair was like a
horse's mane. Angel would laugh and sing back at him. Then
David exaggerated his fall from the tree into the long grass to
see if Angel would run to his aid.

In the meantime, Mary walked over to the tree trunk and
placed her finger on the initials carved on either side of a
carved heart shape. Mary didn't notice that Ethan was close
to her and he slipped his arms around her. She jumped at first
but then rested on his chest. Ethan turned her around and
kissed her tenderly.

David made sounds. "Whooooooo, my dad is kissing my
mam!" Angel chuckled. It was so good for Llewelyn to see
them happy as a family.

There was a rumbling sound in the distance. David
immediately shouted, "There's horses coming."

"Buttercup, Buttercup?" Angel was so happy and ran
after David into the distance.

Mary was concerned. "Ethan come on quickly, we must
stop the children."

Ethan panicked. "Oh my God. Oh my God. Llewelyn
come on!"

Llewelyn wasn't used to rushing anywhere. He was a
man of the cloth. Life for him was devoted to scriptures and
services, marriages, baptisms and funerals, and visiting
people. Definitely, his life was the opposite of rushing
around, panic-stricken.

David and Angel stopped, watching the horses kick up
the dust as they leapt across the top of the mountainside. An
avalanche of color swept before their eyes, black, and brown,
white, brown with dusty patches of cream. The dust hovered
in the air behind them. Some trailed a distance away what
looked like mares with their foals - cream, grey, and brown -
in a hurry, but not at speed like the others. David and Angel
got a little closer as the stampede passed by to see the foals.

"David, there's Buttercup. Look, she has a baby with
her." Angel found her quickly and pointed her out.

"How do you know that's Buttercup?" David scoffed, leaning to see around the shifting bodies to look where she pointed.

"Look David, she's slowing down. She must have heard her name." Angel ran ahead of David. "Buttercup, Buttercup. It's you, Buttercup."

"Angel stop; it might not be. That could be another one that looks like her."

"It's Buttercup. Come on David. It's Buttercup." The excitement made Angel trip and fall. As Angel was regaining her steps, the horse slowed down and came to a halt. Angel got up, rubbed her knee, and charged towards the horse.

"Angel, be careful. It might not be Buttercup," David cautioned her again.

"It is, it is Buttercup. She heard me call her. Come on David, come on."

Angel didn't realize how fast she was running. She tripped again and lost her shoe. Got up and ran with one shoe. "Buttercup, Buttercup."

The horse moved slowly forward towards Angel. Angel got closer and stretched out her arms. In an instant Angel was clutching the horse's chest. "Buttercup, oh Buttercup I missed you. I missed you." Her cheek was pressed against the warm hide.

Mary was running as fast as she could but was soon overtaken by Ethan running through the long grass to catch up with the children. "Oh my God, Angel, what are you doing? David why did you let her go? That horse - that horse is - that horse is wild.... get ....!" Ethan slowed his words, as he looked at them in amazement. The horses head drooped forward and Angel stood underneath hugging its chest, it's foal standing by.

"It's Buttercup, Dad. It's Buttercup. Look, Dad. She recognizes Angel."

"Oh my God. I don't believe what I am seeing. Where's your brother? Why isn't he with you?"

"Oh, he's here somewhere. He came to see the horses running so he could draw them."

"Ian, where are you?" Ethan shouted.

"Hhuh?"

Ethan could hear something that resembled a hhuh, "Ian is that you, what are you doing lying down in that long grass?"

"Dad, I'm drawing. What a sight. It's that horse we saw last autumn and she has a foal now."

Mary came running up behind panting, "Where's Angel, I don't see Angel."

David was inching forward to see Buttercup. Ethan shouted, "David, stop! I'm not sure if that's wise. You never know, the horse could be spooked and then what?"

"It's alright, Dad. She remembers Angel and she'll remember me. I'll be alright." David waved his hand behind him to his dad.

As Mary came closer she shouted, "What is she doing, Ethan?"

"Angel's alright," Ethan answered quickly, "That horse must remember her."

"Is that her foal? It's grey." Mary quieted, standing close to Ethan.

"Yes, that's right. It must be one of those Lipizzaner horses. Their foals are born almost black and get lighter as they mature into full grown like its mother, unless They're mixed breed."

"How do you know that, Ethan?"

"When I was talking with Uncle Dylan he explained that my grandfather bought some horses from the Croatians and they were white, a breed called Lipizzaner."

"David, I said I didn't think that was a good idea if you get closer. Angel could get hurt if you spook the horse." Ethan kept an eye on the kids.

Before Ethan could say anymore David had his arm stretched out and he was singing, "Buttercup, Buttercup do you remember me, too?" The horse lifted its head and looked towards David. David was still inching forward with his arm stretched out.

"Ethan, do something." Mary watched growing more tense the closer David got to the huge animal. "It's wild."

"I don't know what to do, that horse doesn't know me and the kids could be in danger if I start walking towards it." Ethan kept his distance from the scene taking place just steps away from them.

By this time, David was standing close to Angel. Angel still had her arms around Buttercup's chest and looked up at her.

"David, she recognizes me." Angel turned slightly to look at David. "She recognizes me."

"Yeh." David wasn't hesitant about touching Buttercup. "Buttercup, you came back, you came back to see us."

Llewelyn was still walking as fast as he could towards them. "What's going on here?" He definitely looked a little disheveled, but still managed to stutter, "Good Lord, I've never seen such a beautiful horse, and with a foal. A grey foal at that." He waved his handkerchief around his face trying to waft some air around himself. "Where did it come from? It can't be wild; I don't think a wild horse would allow children to be that close." He stopped beside Ethan, joining them watching the children and the horse.

"I'm a little shocked myself. I don't think this horse can be wild, it must belong to someone, otherwise it wouldn't let anyone go near it." Ethan was curious.

"Well, no-one owns horses up here. In fact, no one owns anything up here other than Cradoc, your grandfather. How did it get here, did you see where it came from?"

Ian got up from the ground, and called, "It was at the back of the pack. Those wild horses galloped off and left it behind."

"How do you know that?"

"Last time we were up here we saw a white horse and its leg was bleeding. It must be the same one. David and Angel made such a fuss about the soppy thing. Maybe it remembers them." Ian shrugged. He'd quickly sketched the horses he wanted.

David and Angel were very happy talking and hugging Buttercup as she moved her head towards her foal. The foal inched as close as it could to Buttercup.

"Look, look her baby has different fur, it's grey! But she is so pretty." Angel was excited about Buttercup's baby, too. "We need to give her a name. What shall we call her, David?"

"Alright then. David and Angel, I think you had better leave the horse alone now." Ethan grew nervous watching the foal hide beside her mother.

"Awe, Dad. Buttercup remembers us. Can we stay with her a bit longer?" David glanced back.

Llewelyn tapped Ethan on the shoulder. He'd recovered from his fast walk over. "Ethan, let's walk a bit over there shall we, while we're up here." Llewelyn was determined to get Ethan a little further towards his grandfather's property. "You know, I haven't walked this far for so long. It's quite nice and so different from our town."

"I'm not happy about leaving the children here alone with the horse while we roam around the mountain." He didn't move his gaze from the kids.

"It's alright Ethan, I'll stay with them. You go ahead with Vicar Llewelyn. We'll catch you up." Mary would have done anything for Ethan to see his grandparents land. She didn't know what she could do if the horse attacked the children, but Ethan moved away.

"Are you sure you'll be alright?" Ethan was more than a little concerned at first but felt more at ease afterwards, as the horse seemed very passive with the children.

Ian was packing up his drawing supplies and was ready to go with Llewelyn and his father. Maybe he'd see some of the other horses. Ethan shook his head. "Ian stay here, will you, with your mam and the kids."

"Awe, Dad. Do I have to? I want to see the other horses, maybe I can sketch some more."

Ethan was about to turn and show his authority as a parent but Llewelyn touched his arm. "It's alright Ian, we'll be back soon. I want to talk with your dad a minute."

"I suppose so." Ian turned to his mam who was standing there in amazement at the horse and foal. "I wanted to go with them, Mam. I don't want to be babysitting all the time."

"Ian listen, Vicar Llewelyn wants to talk with your dad. Maybe they will find grandfather Cradoc's land. That would be nice."

"I know where it is, I could show them. We found it when we came up in the autumn and found all those things."

"It's alright, let them be. It would be more exciting for your Dad to find it. You can talk to me and still draw this beautiful scenery. I haven't seen this for so long. It's so refreshing." She pulled him into a hug. He resisted like any teen, but let her have her hug.

"To you? I suppose," Ian snarled back.

"Ian, come on now. This isn't like you. Don't be like this. Enjoy this view and the fresh air while you can."

Ian plonked himself back down on the ground and looked around. "I suppose it's not bad." He got out his sketchpad and pencils and started to draw.

Mary was standing near the horse just watching Llewelyn and Ethan disappear into the distance, then sat beside Ian. "That is good, Ian. Let me see." Ian handed his sketchpad to his mam. "My goodness, you are good. I didn't know we had such a good artist in the family. Can I look at the other drawings you did?" Ian nodded with a shy smile as Mary turned the pages. "Oh that is beautiful. It's Angel patting the horse and her foal beside her. Ian you are very good and quick. I wonder whom you could show these pictures to. Have you showed them to your teacher?"

"No, Mam. I'm not sure if Mr. Trotman is interested in drawing. He says we must leave school with a good sound education so we can find a good job. He's never mentioned art. It's not like infants' school. We drew pictures every single day."

"Well, next week after the Easter holidays, you will be back at school. See if you can show your drawings to Mr. Trotman. You must show your dad, too when we get home."

"Daisy. Shall we call Buttercup's baby, Daisy?" Angel said to David.

"You chose the name Buttercup. I think I should give her baby a name," he insisted.

"Yes, David." Angel was quiet for a while, but she would agree to almost anything that David said.

"Hhhmmm! I know, Dusty. What do you think?" He smiled down at her.

"I like Dusty," Angel replied.

"Those horses sent clouds of dust in the air as they galloped away." David was still thinking as he approached the foal. The foal stood closer now to Buttercup but wasn't too nervous. Just nuzzled its head into its mother. David was pleased Angel was happy with the name he chose.

"Hello, Dusty." David glanced at Buttercup for approval. Buttercup shook her head gently as though she was in agreement, David thought. "Hello, Dusty." David stretched out his hand towards the foal and the foal responded by wagging her tail. "Dusty, I like you. You are so pretty." David had a tender side, even being a boy and so young. "I think you like the name, Dusty."

Looking at Buttercup David said, "I think your baby likes me, too." Buttercup started scratching the ground with her hoof.

"What is the horse doing?" Mary looked towards Ian with concern.

"She probably wants to leave. She can't stay there all day with soppy kids."

"Do you want to go now?" Angel leaned her head into the horse's side, arms spread wide in a hug. "I love you Buttercup, will you come back? Please come back." Angel looked sad.

David stepped backwards one step at a time from the foal and caught Angel's left arm and motioned her towards Dusty. "Feel her fur, it's almost as soft as Buttercup's."

"I don't want Buttercup to go, David." Angel was almost pulling her hand back towards Buttercup. Buttercup turned her head towards her foal. Angel was between Buttercup and the foal. Buttercup shook her head towards Angel and then pushed her gently sideways to her foal.

"See, Buttercup wants you to feel Dusty's fur, too." He laughed with joy as though he was right and that Buttercup was introducing Angel to Dusty.

"Dusty, you have pretty eyes." Angel patted Dusty and then looked up at Buttercup. Buttercup moved her stance slowly and pushed her foal gently with her head. "Are you telling Dusty you want to leave now?" Angel was getting a little emotional and her voice quivered. Buttercup dropped her head in front of Angel and Angel could see her reflection in Buttercup's big brown eyes.

"I love you, Buttercup." Angel put her arms up around Buttercup's face. Buttercup was gentle and stayed a moment while Angel embraced her, then backed up a little very slowly and lifted her head and then leaned towards her foal. Dusty turned and they both walked away.

Angel started to cry, "Come back please, Buttercup?" She stood there a while and David stepped forward and held Angel's hand. "Do you think Buttercup will come back?" Angel sobbed.

"I don't know, but I think so. She knows we love her," David answered.

Mary commented, "I've never seen a wild horse this close before, and her actions so loving towards you is real love. Horses can never lie about their love. I believe she will look for you when she is here again." Angel, still with tears running down her face, watched until Buttercup and her foal were out of sight.

Mary was a little unsure of what just happened, herself. She realized that horses could be tamed if they were treated with love and compassion. It was indeed a lesson for Mary, and a lesson for Ian too but he was only interested in drawing and not had any real interest in anything else. David and Angel still held hands as they approached Mary.

Ian glanced up from his position on the ground only to say, "David's got a girlfriend. David loves Angel."

"Stop it at once, Ian," Mary shouted at Ian. "That's very mean, say you're sorry."

"What for?" Ian was still in his world.

"For being mean and teasing Angel and David."

Ian still couldn't understand what all the fuss was about. He interpreted holding hands as being in love.

"David was showing Angel comfort."

"Alright, alright." Ian looked disgusted as he turned towards David and Angel, "I'm sorry." Then muttered under his breath, "Soppy kids."

"Ian hush, no more mean comments."

Mary looked towards where Ethan and Llewelyn went. "I wonder how much longer they will be; they've been gone a long time. We could walk a bit further up the trail. We might meet them coming back."

Ian grabbed his stuff and walked ahead of the others. "Don't wander off too far, Ian. My legs aren't as quick as yours." She looked at Angel who was still looking a little sad. "Angel, would you like some water? We have some left."

It took a few moments for Angel to say anything, "Yes please." Her heart was sinking and her mind was filled with sadness about Buttercup and her foal. "Do you think Buttercup and Dusty will come back, Aunty Mary?"

"I think so. It's a mother's instinct to protect her young ones and I believe that Buttercup loves you because she trusted you enough to introduce you to her foal."

"They'll come back," David reassured Angel.

"I hope so."

"As I said before, horses never lie about their love and I do believe she loves you, too."

"Where do you think they live?" Angel was looking up at Mary.

"If I could guess, I think they just roam around enjoying this beautiful scenery."

"No one looks after them?" Angel showed her concern.

"They probably don't need looking after. They are used to being free to go wherever they want," Mary replied.

"Hhmm. Lucky. They can go wherever they want," Ian snarled back.

"Ian, what's wrong with you? You have a home, a roof over your head, and food in your stomach, and don't forget you have a mother and father, brothers and a sister. Now how would you manage if you didn't have all these people in your life to protect you and care for you?"

"I'd live like great grandfather, Cradoc. A mountain man."

"A mountain man, for goodness sake. Let's see what your father has to say about that."

Ian looked away as he realized what he had heard from his mother. It was true and he should be grateful.

Vicar Llewelyn and Ethan were well into the distance, like two dots on the horizon. They were deep in conversation, not aware of how far they'd walked away from the family.

"Ethan, have you thought of coming up here and finding your grandfather's land?"

"I've thought about it a couple of times."

"Well, where do you think it is?" Llewelyn enquired.

"Actually, I think it might be over there, where those trees are in the distance."

"How do you know that, Ethan?"

"I remember my mam brought us up here a few times and we had to walk a long way before we reached the trees. When we were in the middle of those big trees she cried out not to go near the well."

"There's a well, too? Why do you think it's those trees over there?"

"I don't know why, but I just have that feeling."

"Just a feeling, Ethan? It's good to remember even a few things and then you can piece all the few things together and you get a better picture. It's just like remembering verses from the Bible, when you piece them together you have a better understanding of its contents." Ethan nodded in agreement with Llewelyn.

"What else do you remember?"

"There was a circle of trees, big huge ones all spaced out, and a well somewhere in the middle or maybe on the side. I remember my mam was picking fruit from the apple and pear trees somewhere in between the bigger ones and shouting at me so many times to keep away from the well, and not be foolish climbing onto anything."

"That was good instruction from your mam, she didn't want you to have an accident or fall into the well. What were the trees like? Do you remember what kind of trees they were?"

"The fruit trees were apple and pear trees, I remember that. They were laden with fruit. The branches were bent down with the weight and of course, there were so many it was difficult to carry them home. I remember that she brought a sack with us and we had to try and carry it between us."

"Look, Ethan those trees over there." Vicar Llewelyn was determined to get Ethan talking and walking as far as he could without Ethan exactly suspecting his intention.

"I'm not sure, they could be. But, I remember they were somehow in a circle." Ethan started to walk so quickly that it made it difficult for Llewelyn to keep up with him, but he was determined to be with Ethan and encourage him as Dylan had suggested. They must have walked miles and miles before Ethan mentioned, "My mam loved to pick fruit in the harvest time somewhere around here I think." Then Ethan hurried on as if he was on fire.

Ethan shouted back at Llewelyn, "Look, Vicar. Look. The trees over there, they look like the fruit trees and they do look like they are in a circle in the middle of the big ones. I can hear my mam shouting at me."

Llewelyn answered quickly, "No son, it's your mind playing tricks on you, because you remember vividly your mam's words."

"I wonder if it could still be here?"

"Well, I don't know. It could be. Be careful now, I don't want to lose you somewhere down a well. I can't get you out by myself and we are miles away from Mary and the children."

"Vicar, I am going to walk in a straight line in front of you, come with me so we are together."

"I'm not sure if I want to walk and fall in a well," Llewelyn answered quickly.

"Vicar, don't be daft. There was a wall around it, I remember that."

"Well, there may not be one now and that's what's bothering me. Be sensible now, Ethan."

Ethan walked ahead of Llewelyn. He didn't hear very much of what he was saying until Llewelyn caught up with him. Llewelyn arrived huffing and puffing, it appeared as if it really took the wind out of him a bit, but he was happy to catch up with Ethan. Just as he approached the trees he saw Ethan on all fours eagerly trying to pull up some of the long grass that grew in what might be the middle area of the circle of the trees. "What are you doing? You think there's some buried treasure down there?"

Ethan looked up at Llewelyn. "I think the well might be here somewhere. I do remember it was somewhere in the middle but it's so overgrown it's difficult to know. I'd have to get all the grass and stinging nettles out of the way first."

"This is a very big area, Ethan. It's big as a field with trees around it. You need help to do it. You can't do it alone. All these years it's been covered up out of sight. It would be impossible to find it in a few minutes."

"I must try, then I know." Ethan kept looking, determined to find a sign.

"Alright then, what else do you remember, Ethan?" Llewelyn was trying to distract his efforts of pulling up the grass and weeds. He shoved his hands in his pockets and raised his heels up and down. This was his usual stance when he thought deeply or reined in his impatience. He also rocked as he put words together, and sometimes the rocking motion continued into a lengthy conversation until he felt comfortable again.

"Like what, Vicar?" Ethan was doing his best to pull and tug at the grass and weeds but it would take several people quite a long time to clear the area. "I wish I knew exactly where it was. I see some piles of old stones here and there that must mean something. Oh my goodness, look at that." Ethan sounded surprised and excited.

"What Ethan, what is it?" He turned to see what Ethan meant.

"Look, look, look at these old keys, look." He held up his rusty find. "And another. And another. Three keys! Look."

"Good Lord. Those are very big keys. I wonder what they open."

"Look over here too, there's a horse shoe. It looks like an old one, like the one I found down in our basement."

"I declare; I believe the Lord has brought you somewhere close to your grandfather's land, if not already on it."

"You really think so, Vicar?" Ethan got to his feet, dusting off his hands.

"Of course, the Lord moves in mysterious ways. You remember the trees and the well. You visited here with your mam. It must have been for a reason besides picking fruit."

"I must tell Mary. She has talked about finding my grandfather's land for years but I never had time to think about it working down the mine. Mary, oh oh, what time is it? I forgot about the children and Mary waiting back there."

"It's time to leave, it's past 5 o'clock. We must go. We can't keep them waiting back there. The children will get bored and Mary will be tired. We must leave now, Ethan. I hope Lina and Dylan are alright waiting down at the bottom."

Ethan and Llewelyn made their way back to where they left Mary and the children. The day had been successful. Llewelyn witnessed the excitement Ethan had displayed at finding something that belonged to his grandparents and the land that had been forgotten in time.

"I can see them. We can't be too far now," shouted Ethan.

"Yes, I can see them now. I think in the distance." Ethan hurried towards them and Llewelyn hurried behind as best as he could.

"Mary, Mary I found my grandfather's land. I saw the trees where my mam used to pick fruit."

"Yes, it was quite a sight. A nice looking area and it's peaceful up there," Llewelyn commented with a proud smile.

"Look, I found these old keys and an old horseshoe."
He was every bit as excited as the children when they
showed off their finds.

Mary displayed sincere interest. "It looks just like the
horseshoe you found in the basement in that old desk,
Ethan."

"Come on gang, it's getting late. I'm worried about Lina
and Dylan. We left them all the way down the bottom,"
Llewelyn shouted over his shoulder. He'd only paused and
continued walking. They would overtake him soon enough.

The journey down didn't seem as bad as the climb up.
They had tracks to follow. The view was beautiful high
above the grey looking rows of houses that made up the town
of Porth. They could see the Corona pop factory with its
huge chimneystack towering above, Hannah Street shops, the
railway lines next to Lina's house, and the river. In the
distance were the big wheels of the collieries, the mountain
ranges that surrounded Porth, and the only road winding
through the hills to nearby villages and towns up the valley.

The children picked wild daffodils, bluebells, and lilies-
of-the valley and Mary's arms were full of their labors. Soon
they were down at the bottom. Lina and Dylan were still
sitting there on the bench chatting like two elderly people
enjoying the wonderful fresh air and beauty of the green land
above the valley.

Angel ran towards Lina excitedly. "Nene, Nene we saw
Buttercup and she had a baby foal."

"You did, that's wonderful. Did she recognize you?"
There were no longer any traces of tears on her face.

"Yes, Nene. She did and her baby foal is so beautiful.
David named her Dusty."

"Did Buttercup let you pet her foal?"

"Oh yes, Nene. And she let me hug her, too." Angel's
face fell and she went from excited to sad. "I miss her, Nene.
Do you think she will come back again?"

"Well, she is a wild horse." Lina noticed Angel's facial expression as she was saying the words, so quickly reassured her with a more positive answer, "I think so. She obviously loves you. And she let you meet her foal. She will come back." Angel hugged Lina and turned facing Dylan, "Uncle Dylan, I saw Buttercup."

"I just heard what you said to your Nene. That I did. I am very pleased she came back and brought her foal to meet you. Tell me more, what else did you do up on the mountain?" Dylan was trying to get the children to tell about their adventures to brighten Lina up.

"Uncle, it was so much fun. David swung on the tree and sang to us. Then we saw all these horses gallop by and when they went, Buttercup and her foal stayed behind. She let me hug her and pet her foal. That was when David gave her foal the name Dusty."

Ethan intervened, "A wild horse, and these kids are hugging it, and they could have got killed."

Dylan ignored what Ethan said and turned again to the children, "So you had a good time?"

"Oh yes, Uncle. It was so good and we picked flowers. See, Aunty Mary has all the flowers I picked for Nene. You can have some, too if you want." Angel ran back to Mary and David.

"Lina, Angel really loves you. Please will you do as we discussed and get the answer from your doctor?" Dylan leaned close as the others were gathering around them.

"I will Dylan." Lina looked down at the ground so Dylan wouldn't see her tears. "You know how much I love Angel."

"I know. That's why you must take care of yourself and find out what's going on." He greeted the others with a smile, giving Lina a moment to regain control of her emotions.

When they got to the bottom and through the milkman's farm, Lina said goodbye to Dylan and walked home with

Angel at her side, carrying the flowers that Angel had picked for her. It had been a lovely day. The sun smiled on them and the air was fresh and Lina had enjoyed being in Dylan's company. She silently walked with Angel holding on to her skirt and thought about the conversation with Dylan.

How her life may have changed if Edwin hadn't persuaded her to marry him. Life would have been easier and Gilberto wouldn't have to worry about her or Angel. They would both have been safe and taken care of. Lina felt disappointed that she didn't have a life with Dylan. She found out finally that Dylan really cared about her. It was too late now. Time had passed away and a life she could have had was no longer.

Vicar Llewelyn offered to walk back with Dylan so Ethan and Mary and the boys could go on home as it was getting late.

Well, Llewelyn? What happened up there?" Dylan was anxious to know the details of what transpired.

"I think we came across some part of the land that Cradoc owned. I'm not sure if Ethan just has a curiosity about it or if he is actually interested in finding it. It was strange, he found the trees he said his mam used to pick fruit from, and he was trying to pull up the grass and weeds in the middle of the land saying there was a well there."

"That is odd. In the middle of the land is where Cradoc had his horse troughs and his stables. The well was more to the west of the land."

"It's possible in a child's mind it could be anywhere." Llewelyn reassured Dylan it didn't really matter where exactly the well was situated. "He found some old keys, Dylan."

"Keys you said? What kind of keys?"

"Some very large old keys on a ring, and also a horseshoe."

"Is that so, keys? I thought we had taken everything with us when we left. I don't remember leaving any keys or missing any. Come and have a cup of tea with me Llewelyn, before you go home to the Mrs."

"Well, I don't mind if I do. I'm sure my Mrs. is still in the kitchen cooking something or other for the party tomorrow."

Soon they were at Dylan's chippie. "Let me put the kettle on. Llewelyn you know where the cups are." Dylan busied himself in the kitchen warming the pot and preparing the tea.

Chapter 20

Ethan woke up with a smile and told Mary he would go up and help Dylan after breakfast. Mary was happy to learn that a day on the mountainside had helped Ethan relax and hopefully sparked a genuine interest in his grandparents' land.

Before leaving, Ethan mentioned, "I will help you get the tables and chairs in the street when I get back. Tell Ian to wait for me and not go and disappear somewhere as he normally does. Is that alright?" Ian was known to leave and wander off to draw in his sketchpad.

Dylan was preparing his daily chores as normal when Ethan arrived. "Good morning, Uncle."

"Good morning, son. How was your walk yesterday?" Dylan was very curious but did not want to show his enthusiasm to Ethan.

"Uncle, I think I might have found my grandfather's land up there. It was quite a sight. I saw some of the fruit trees I remember my mam used to pick her fruit from." Excitement laced his words as Ethan recalled his finds and the happy memories.

"Is that right, son? I'm sure there's more up there than just fruit trees. Will you go back up there, then?"

"I think I'd like to do that but will you come with me?"

"Well, it's been a while since I was up there and you know I didn't get there yesterday."

"Are you alright, Uncle? Will you be up to it? I know it's a long walk but I really would like you there."

"What do you want an old man with you for?" Dylan scoffed at the younger man but was pleased to hear Ethan's change of heart.

"Uncle Dylan, if I find my grandparents land I would like you there with me. You are, after all, my grandfather's brother and it was your home as well."

"*Ìe,* I am that, that I am Cradoc's brother. I would like to see the old place again. I think I could make it up the mountain." Dylan was blindsided by Ethan's thoughts. He'd put the family first and Dylan was the last one in Porth. Of course he wanted Dylan to see the old homestead.

"What about next weekend, Uncle? Do you think it would be possible for us to go together then?"

"Let's hope the weather will be good for such a visit to the old girl." Dylan laughed with excitement. "Today would have been a good time to go up as its Bank Holiday Monday, but the street party will be this afternoon. We don't want to miss that now, do we?" Dylan paused in his labors, nodding. "If I can get a few things prepared for tomorrow, I could join everyone at the party this afternoon. What do you think Ethan?" He turned to the youngster.

"That would be just like old times. Can I help you get some of the things done, Uncle? It will be quicker with two of us."

"*Ìe.* That it will. Now let me think what I need to get done. Can you do the spuds as you did before? Then cut them up into daps and chips and we'll put them in the bucket and cover them with water. They will be ready for me to cook tomorrow."

"I'll get the batter done, as well." Ethan knew the ropes. "That won't take long. Let me get started." Ethan started washing the spuds and then cutting them as Dylan taught him for daps. "What about the papers, I'll cut them as you normally do them and set the counter up for you."

"You are so quick, Ethan. I'm wondering if you have business in your blood, too."

"I don't know what's in my blood, actually. I've only recently learned that my grandmother was Croatian and my grandfather was a mountain man and a horse catcher." The men shared a smile.

"You have quite a variety of skills in your blood. It is said that some lives are linked in time, Ethan. You just never know what God has in store for your future."

"Now then, it looks like we are almost finished. Is there anything else you need doing before I go home? I have to get the tables and chairs out in the street." Ethan changed the subject, not knowing what to say to Dylan. He'd grown up in the pit with a wife and family he'd rarely spent time with. His skills were strength and the ability to work in almost complete darkness.

"I think we're done. I'll get some coal in for tonight and then I can get ready." Dylan rubbed his hands together, looking around at the finished chippie.

"No Uncle, I'll get the coal. In fact, I'll get enough for a couple of nights. Alright?" Ethan was so happy to help Dylan.

"Thank you, Ethan. You're a real blessing to me. Now what was it we were going to talk about? We've been busy and I overlooked it."

"It was going up the mountain next week."

"*Ìe,* it was, was indeed. I think Sunday would be good. Chippie is closed on Sundays after Church and lunch." Dylan was finalizing details in his mind. He snapped his fingers. "I remember, hang on a bit." He hurried from the room, leaving Ethan a bit confused. Dylan soon appeared, papers in his hand.

"Perhaps, if that's alright, I could take the children. It would give Lina and Mary a break."

"That sounds good." Dylan nodded absently, focused on the papers he brought to show Ethan. "Alright then. Ethan, I was going to tell you. I found some maps and things that belonged to Cradoc in Olga's old trunk. These things might help you find the actual location of your grandfather's land. It's always helpful to go armed with something that can determine the actual borders."

"Thank you. Then we had better take them up with us when we go. What do you think, Uncle?"

"I think that will be a good idea, a very good idea. Do you want to take them home with you or leave them here?"

"Well, can I leave them here and we can look together tomorrow when I come to help in the morning. I don't want Mary getting all excited about it until we know for definite where the land is."

"I think that is a very good idea. Our woman folk do tend to carry on a bit about things. I remember my Olga when she had a bee in her bonnet, she just wouldn't stop until it was turned upside down or thrashed out."

"Yes, Uncle. Mary is a bit like that. Alright then, I better go now. See you this afternoon."

"*Ìe,* you will do that, that you will. I will see you this afternoon about 2:30 and I'll put the rolls on in a little while when I'm ready. They only take a few minutes."

"Bye, Uncle. Come lock the door behind me."

Ethan found Mary busy as normal preparing things for the afternoon tea party in the street. Lina was also there with her pinny on, and her hands covered in flour, rolling out dough. "What are you making, Nene Lina?" Ethan was always interested in food.

"I'm helping Mary make current buns for this afternoon's tea party," she told him with a smile. Ethan reached out to pull a bit of it away to taste. "Now stop that. You'll have worms eating raw pastry." David came into the kitchen just as Lina tapped Ethan's hand in the bowl of left over pastry.

"Ha, Ha, Dad got caught…"

"Well, I'm surprised you and Ian haven't been here already," Ethan told him, popping the stolen pastry into his mouth where Lina couldn't see him.

Mary quickly replied, "Ian's been here, love, already. I was making a chocolate cake and his fingers were all in the bowl. Then he was licking his fingers and trying to stick them back in the bowl again. I had to banish him to the basement to find more chairs." She pointed towards the door, a puzzled look on her face. "That reminds me, is he still down there? He's been gone a long time."

Ethan shouted down the stairs, "Ian where are you, your mam said you've been down there a long time. What are you doing?" Ian didn't answer. "Ian, did you hear me? What are you doing?" Ethan moved to the top of the stairs. He listened for his son. A faint response came from the basement.

"Er. I found something."

"Now what? What have you found? I hope it's the chairs your mam asked you to find."

"No, not exactly."

"Stop playing around, your mam asked you to find the chairs and bring them up. We'll need them in the street soon."

"Dad, can you come down here?" Ian didn't sound his usual self.

"Oh my God. What is it now? I need to get the tables down the street, too." Ethan went down the stairs to the basement. "You know sometimes it's beyond me. When your mam asks you to do something, you just dilly-dally around and it takes you forever. Where are you down here, anyway?" Ethan was by now impatient and getting irritated.

"Over here."

"What are you doing on the floor? I don't see any chairs ready to take up." Ethan looked around the room.

"Dad, I found this box. I was picking up one of the old chairs and this box was underneath it."

"It's just an old box, some rubbish no doubt, we stuffed down here."

"Dad, maybe you need to see what's inside." He held up the box for Ethan to look at.

"Ian, for God's sake, we don't have all day. Put it down. Your mam wants to get things ready so people can bring their shawls and cardigans and lay them on the chairs."

Ian didn't pay much attention to what Ethan said but opened the box and pulled out a bunch of old papers. Almost all were stuck together, probably from the dampness. "Look Dad."

"Now what did I say to you?" Ethan was looking around for the rest of the chairs and swung around to look at Ian as he spoke. "Good God, what is it?"

"It looks pretty important, maybe a treasure."

"Alright, alright, put that stuff back in the box and bring it up with the chair. We better get cracking your mam will be worried we haven't got things together. She doesn't want the neighbors talking about us."

They climbed up the stairs carrying the old wooden chairs that were stored in the basement. "I wouldn't be surprised if they haven't got woodworm by now, being down here so long," he told Ian as they carried the chairs upstairs. At the door, he looked over at Mary, busy with Lina, happiness about her.

"I really must spend time going through all that and get rid of the rubbish," Ethan said to Mary at the top of the stairs.

Ethan went to get some more chairs from the basement. "Ian come on now, and let's get the job done."

"Mam, I found this tin box downstairs. Dad doesn't seem to be interested." He put the old box on the table beside her, turning as his father yelled from below.

"Ian, did you hear me? Come on now, it will be quicker if two of us are getting the chairs." Ethan had finally lost his patience.

"Oh, he's shouting again, I'd better go downstairs." Ian remained concerned about what was in the tin.

"You are a good boy, Ian." Lina smiled in his direction. "Better hurry along."

"I wonder what could be in this tin box." Mary was anxious, trying to pry the lid
off. She looked inside and gasped. "Oh my goodness, there's some old photographs in here but they look like they've got stuck together."

"They do when they get damp and left a long time." Lina moved to her side, looking into the box with Mary. "Don't worry, there's a trick how to separate them, I learned many years ago," Lina was happy to announce.

"Really!" Mary looked up at Lina. "There's a way of getting them apart?"

"I watched my mam do it. She always saved the stamps on the envelopes if they weren't franked at the post office. Can you boil some water please, in the kettle?

"Yes, I have some water in the kettle already. I'll just put it back on the oven, shouldn't take too long."

"In the meantime I'll get on with the cakes, then they'll be ready." Lina wanted to be helpful.

"Lina, how would I manage without you?" Mary gave Lina a hug. Lina smiled a bit and patted Mary's back. She was embarrassed if anyone other than Angel showed her affection.

"The kettle's boiled, I'll bring it over. I have a pad so it won't burn the table. "Mary carefully picked up the kettle off the oven with a rag and brought it to the table.

"Alright then, this is what I saw my mam do. She held what she was separating very carefully, with a tweezers, I don't have one." She looked at Mary, "Do you have a tweezers, Mary?"

"Yes, I do. I kept it in the bandages and stuff from when I had to take out Ethan's stitches. I'll get it."

It didn't take Mary long, as it was kept close by, and placed it on the table. "I'll hold the edges with the tweezers over the steam from the kettle. It takes a little while for the steam to get up through the layers. When it becomes a little dampish and limp like it is now, carefully separate the layers.

If they are still stuck fairly tight then we can put it over the steam again. It's probably easier to ease the first one off first so we can lay it down to dry. Then do the next layer, and so on."

"I never knew you could do that." Mary was definitely interested. "Some of the pages in my old cook book are stuck, this will be good to separate them."

"Yes, here you are. Oh, there's not much steam now. Could you put the kettle on again please, so I can finish this for you?"

"Yes, and let's have a cuppa, too."

"Good idea. It's getting close to the time we should be taking things down to the party, but I want to finish this first." She worked quickly and carefully, placing each layer on the table to dry. "I did it, all of the pictures are separated. We don't need any more steam now." She stood back with Mary and looked at every picture and paper she left to dry. "They look very old so we must not touch them until they are completely dry." Standing in silence for a moment, Mary smiled at what Lina showed her another trick to preserve the past.

"I'll make the tea then." Mary was happy to make a cup of tea for Lina. When she finished and brought the cups to the table she was surprised. "Look at those hairstyles. Look at him, he has a huge scruffy beard."

Ethan was back to the top of the basement stairs when he heard Mary talk about one of the pictures. "A huge scruffy beard?"

Mary saw Ethan in the corner of her eye, "Come and see. Look, Lina separated those old pictures that Ian found in the tin box, but we must let them dry before we touch them."

"When this one has dried I'd like to show it to Dylan. I think that might be my grandfather. If it is, all those stories about him being a mountain man are absolutely true. His beard is almost all over his face." Ethan studied the picture, wondering if Dylan could tell him.

"Did you bring up all the chairs?" Mary enquired.

"Almost all of them, there's another couple down there. I could get those if you think we'll need them."

"Let's see if we have enough in the street first, we can always come back up and get some more." Mary was pleased that Ethan and Ian had taken the chairs and put them in place.

"I've finished the cakes, Mary." They will be ready in time for the start of the party.

"Oh, thank you, Lina. How would I manage without you?"

"One day…" Lina couldn't finish what she was thinking. She felt tears coming and had to compose herself for another time. Angel came rushing in the kitchen.

"Nene, I won. I won at dominoes. I beat David." She was excited.

David stood by the door and looked at Mary. Mary knew that David had let Angel win again, and smiled back at him.

"Come here, David." David thought he was in trouble so he started to drag his feet. "It's alright David, you're not in trouble." When he approached Mary, Mary smiled and put her arms around him and whispered in his ear, "You're such a good boy, I could squeeze you." Mary leaned forward and kissed him. "I know that you let Angel win again." David was happy. He was assured he did the right thing, even if it was more than once.

Uncle Dylan knocked on the door. "Thought I would come down and see if you need me to do something to help. I've just been down the street, what a display!"

"Here, Dylan. You could carry the pastries out. We have a few more to add to them."

There was so much on the tables - already laden with many different sandwiches, cakes, trifles and biscuits and lots of pop in the crates. The children were entertaining themselves playing hide and seek.

After everyone was there, Vicar Llewelyn stood up, as he was about to give the blessing so the children were directed to sit quietly. "Let us give thanks. Please everyone bow your heads." Not a pin could be heard, even the blackbirds high up on the chimney pots were perched silently. "Lord we are grateful for you for rising on the third day. We give you thanks, not only for this wonderful spread of food but also for allowing us to share in the festivities of your rising this Easter Monday. Thank you Lord for this food that we are about to receive and for everyone that prepared it for the nourishment of our bodies. May we continue to do your will in our daily lives, Amen." Everyone said, "Amen."

Amanda, being the oldest child in the street, and a couple of the other girls and boys handed out the pop bottles to everyone. Cakes were cut and trifles dropped into bowls.

"Here comes the jester," someone shouted. Everyone applauded. Children sat in amazement as one of the neighbors performed card tricks and juggled balls. Next, the children's' display of costumes – some were representing chickens, rabbits, fairies, princesses and princes and those who didn't have real costumes made their own out of cardboard boxes.

Ian, although he initially complained it was soppy, stepped forward in a cardboard box in the shape of a television with an Antenna made from wire. Herbert from number 11 made a cardboard ship with a big Welsh flag protruding from the top and he wore a captain's hat. Christopher from number 32 made a cardboard castle. It was hard for the judges to choose the best one of the cardboard cutouts because they were all good. So everyone received a surprise gift.

Ethan finally had a chance to talk with Dylan. "Ian was helping me get out some chairs from the basement and came across an old tin box."

"Is that so?" Dylan suspected what it contained but didn't want to take the excitement from Ethan to tell him. "What was in it, did you look?"

"I was very surprised. There were some old pictures of people, and even more surprised how Lina separated the pictures without damaging them."

"Lina knows many helpful things. Did you recognize any of the people then," Dylan again never imparted any information.

"Not really. I wouldn't have even bothered to look until I heard Lina and Mary talk about a scruffy beard someone had in one of the pictures."

"Is that so?" Dylan nodded his head, leading Ethan along as Ethan displayed his inquisitiveness.

"What did my grandfather really look like? I remember you saying your mam said he looked like a tramp and a real mess."

"Well now. Let me see how best to describe Cradoc."

Ethan held on to his patience. He knew by now Dylan took a while to answer. "Did he look just like Mam described him, a mountain man? He was only interested in the land and what he could do with it." Ethan sat patiently waiting for more information.

"*Ie*, that is right. He had a beard, a big beard. He wasn't much of a dresser. His clothes looked like they were handed down from people, that they were, and seemed always too big for him. Most likely dirty. Tied together with a rope, the times I saw him. Always a rope around his waist to keep his trousers up." Dylan grinned with pride. His brother was different from any other man. "He had no interest in cleaning himself up, he enjoyed life on the mountain too much and didn't care about all the material things life had to offer him."

"Could it be him in the pictures then, my grandfather?"

"It could be. I'd have to see them to be sure. He was the only man in these parts that I knew had a scruffy beard. God rest his soul, he was a good man." Dylan made the sign of the cross on his chest and began to look sad.

"Uncle, I'm sorry. I didn't mean to make you sad."

"No, no I'm not sad. Not really. I just miss him. He was a good man and taught me so much about wild life, horses, the land, and business, even though he was limited on knowing the business side. Thinking about it, if it wasn't for him, I would definitely not have my chippie."

"You had the fish and chip shop back then?"

"No, son. After Cradoc and Clarenda died. It was sometime after. When we came back down I thought of having a small business. He had already taught me how to handle a business, keeping records, ordering, and selling. Things like that."

"But you said you had my father and his brother then, too?"

"*Ìe*, that is right. My Olga was a good mam to all the kids. We all came here and back then my chippie was a house."

"A house?" Ethan was thinking hard. "I can't imagine it being a house."

"In those days the chippie was once the front room. Just like you and Mary have a front room."

At the sound of Mary's name Ethan looked for her in the crowd of people. She was sitting close to Lina. "Uncle, you and Lina stayed behind while Vicar Llewelyn and me and the kids went up yesterday." There was a silence.

"*Ìe*, that's right, son." Dylan was waiting for Ethan to say more about the conversation he had with Llewelyn but as Ethan didn't continue, Dylan needed to enquire. "Yes, son, but you had a good conversation with Llewelyn didn't you?" Dylan didn't want to say anything about his conversation with Lina at that time.

"I did, Uncle. Llewelyn is very interesting. But what about the conversation you had with Lina?" Ethan was more interested in their conversation.

"*Ìe*. I sat with Lina. An old man sat with a stunning younger lady." He laughed a little.

"Well, I thought you were going to ask Lina what was wrong. Did you find out anything? Did she tell you?" Ethan was definitely concerned.

"I must be careful no one hears," Dylan started to whisper after looking around them. "Lina is sick, that she is. She said she is always tired but she didn't come out with what was wrong exactly. She goes to see the cancer specialist next week."

"She has cancer?" Ethan's voice rose. "Oh my God."

"Shhhhh, she might hear you." Dylan was worried and was anxious to change the subject, and quickly.

But Llewelyn heard the name of God and approached during the conversation. "Now, what is causing man to shout the name of our Lord?" He kept his voice lowered, believing he knew the subject discussed by the men.

Dylan didn't wait for Ethan to reply before he probed the question, "Llewelyn are you busy next Sunday afternoon?" Dylan stopped.

Ethan was just standing there looking worried, but obviously in shock, he couldn't say anything.

"Not in the afternoon. My Mrs. will be in the kitchen as always, preparing something or other and experimenting with her herbs. She likes to show off with her cooking at the Mothers' Union, you know. Why, what have you got in mind, Dylan? I can see your mind working." He put on a good face, jovial as he covered for Ethan's outburst.

"Is that so," Dylan replied. "Ethan asked me to go up the top of the old girl again. Thought you might like to come with us this time. Just us men and the kids."

Ethan was still in his moment of thoughts about Lina.

"Yes, I'll tell the Mrs." Llewelyn wanted to get back to the table where his wife was sitting.

Dylan touched Ethan's shoulder, "Come on son, and pull yourself together. We must join everyone and not show any concern at the moment."

When Llewelyn got back to sitting next to his wife, Llewelyn told Pagua, "Dylan and Ethan are going up Penrhiwgwynt next Sunday and asked me to go with them."

"Well, what did you say? You know I'll be busy in my kitchen. But that will be good for you to get out of the Vicarage and get a bit of that fresh air with your men folk." Pagua resented not being with her family except for every couple of years when they made their visit back to Greece.

Llewelyn was looking at Dylan and Ethan walking to the tables as Pagua was talking. "You can pick some fresh dandelion leaves while you're up there. Then I can make some dandelion soup. Alright, Llew?" Llewelyn wasn't listening, he was still concentrating on Dylan and Ethan, he felt something was wrong.

"Are you listening to me, Llewelyn?" Pagua nudged his arm.

"I'd like that very much, that I will." Llewelyn with half a mind on the conversation was delighted that his Mrs. said she didn't mind him going for a walk with Dylan and Ethan next weekend. "Of course, I won't forget the dandelion leaves." He turned to Pagua, "What makes you think that?"

"I noticed you weren't giving me your full attention, Llewelyn," Pagua insisted.

"Now dear, you know I listen to every word you say." Llewelyn had to reassure her, otherwise she might have one of her Greek tantrums. He had to listen carefully, he didn't dare mishear her.

"Humph, I hope you are listening. The dandelion leaves, Llewelyn," Pagua insisted.

"That will be alright. There should be plenty of them up there. Ethan didn't pull them all up."

"What are you talking about, Llewelyn?" Pagua's conversation was getting heated again.

"Nothing really. It's a joke, only a joke. When we were up there, Ethan started weeding. Just a joke." He turned to Pagua, put his arm around her and squeezed her gently. "I've got to talk with Dylan, alright?" Pagua gave him the eye, rolled more like it, and Llewelyn walked back to Dylan and Ethan.

"Right then, what time are you going next Sunday? I can't go until after Church and of course our Sunday lunch, otherwise I'll never hear the rest of it."

"Ha. More like you wouldn't see the rest of your life!" Dylan joked. "That's alright, we all need to eat before we go up, including the children. Perhaps I'll make a couple of sandwiches to take for a picnic. You can bring some pop if you like." Dylan was already preparing in his mind what they should take for a quick snack, not that he was interested in any picnic. It was to get Ethan up there.

"Mary love, I forgot to ask you about next weekend, Sunday to be exact. Uncle Dylan said he would come with me up the mountain. We thought it would be good to take the children, what do you think? And Angel if you think Lina will be alright with it?"

"Ethan you know I don't mind you taking the children anywhere. It would be good for them to have some time with you. I'll ask Lina for you. It would certainly give her a few hours to herself."

Ethan rejoined the other men, continuing their talk. Mary tapped him on the back, interrupting. "Ethan, Lina said yes for Angel to come along."

He leaned down and kissed her quickly, smiling at her blush as she moved away, her fingertips to her lips.

"Well, then that's settled then. That it is. We will all go up to see the old girl next Sunday afternoon, children as well, now then, let's pray for good weather." Dylan turned to

Llewelyn, "That, I will ask you to do. Pray for some good weather, Llewelyn."

Llewelyn sounded somewhat irritated but more exasperated. "Dylan, you have the strangest way of asking for things. Do you think I do a sunshine dance in the Church, like the Indians do a rain dance for rain? You know, we can all pray for the weather to be good. We don't have to have someone specific to pray for our desires or needs. We all need to pray for God's glory in all this." At that Llewelyn walked away shaking his head and then laughed that he had got their attention.

The afternoon went splendidly with all the grownups as well as the children wearing different costumes. Everyone had a good time and while Mr. Jenkins was still dressed in a bunny outfit, he was convinced to play hopscotch with the children. He'd taken Mr. Probert's place after the accident.

Mrs. Probert frowned at first but laughed when he was suddenly twisted and not sure which way he should hop. It brought the others happiness to see the widow find a smile.

Mary sat opposite Lina, "Lina, Dylan and Vicar Llewelyn are going up the mountain with Ethan next weekend to see if they can find the well." She leaned close, excited to tell her friend.

"Oh, that will be good. I have been praying for Ethan to be interested in something connected with his property." Lina showed her happiness and was convinced he would fight for his property now.

"I'm really pleased because lately he has had some nightmares. I hear him shouting in his sleep. "Mam, I'm falling, I'm falling!' I'm not sure what is on his mind."

"Oh dear, that does sound like a nightmare. He didn't like heights, I know that."

"It really has been going on a few weeks, but not as bad as last night," Mary explained to Lina.

"Maybe it was yesterday's walk that did that." She pondered for a moment then smiled at Mary. "He'll be alright."

Mary agreed, "But it's been a long struggle to get Ethan interested in anything since he was laid off. Since he's been having these nightmares, I am wondering if that has anything to do with him not wanting to go alone, so having Dylan and Vicar Llewelyn there, he might be alright."

"Oh, poor Ethan. That puts a strain on his mind and that is disturbing for you. You are not getting your rest either."

"I've been worried for a while but I think it might be anxiety. His fear of heights, and as you say, not wanting to go alone and feeling worthless sometimes."

"That it is. I think you have knocked the nail on its head. I do believe it is anxiety." Lina knew more of anxiety than anyone.

"Ethan said they could take the children and it would get the children out from under our feet for a few hours and give them some fresh air and a place to romp around. What do you think?"

"That would be good for the children. I know Angel will be happy."

"It would be good for you, too. It will give you some free time to rest a little. You have been looking tired lately."

"I know. I am tired these days but I feel I could do with some company and help out at the same time. I miss Angel when she's not around me."

"Oh Lina. You do help me and I've started to feel you are doing too much. I am so very grateful for your help but why didn't you tell me you wanted company as well?" Mary felt bad she had not picked up on Lina's loneliness.

"Well, I feel I might be in the way, but I like helping you because I am doing what the Lord wants me to do, and that is helping your family get back on its feet. I get your company while I'm helping you."

"Oh Lina, I am always happy to have you around me. I have often thought you would be far too tired to go down Hannah Street or even sit here with me a couple of afternoons. I don't mind admitting it. I'm very lonely and still want adult company. When Ethan was working down the mine, you probably noticed when you came up, I was almost going nuts with depression."

Lina agreed, "Yes, the burden was far greater than I had wished for you but I wasn't sure what it was and I could not really interfere. I thought the best way was just try and give you support and help with the chores and the children. I never thought you would like to just talk." Both had missed the signs of loneliness.

"If you are not too tired, would you like to come up on Sunday or I'll come down to your house when they go up the mountain? I would love to have your company even if we just sit. You have always been my best friend and you know Angel is David's best friend."

"Yes, I would like to share the afternoon with you. I'll bake a cake or a pie."

"No, Lina. I want to make you something and we can share a cuppa together. You are always helping me. I'd like to do something for you this time. What would be better for you? To come up here or would you like me to come down to your house?"

"Mary, I would love to have tea with you. Thank you and I'll come up. I always feel more relaxed at your house anyway. I don't like looking at the same four walls day in day out, all the time."

"That will be lovely, we will spend Sunday afternoon together."

"I'll like that, very much, thank you Mary."

"Also, anytime you would like to go to Hannah Street we can go together. I don't get the opportunity to get out much myself, you know that."

Hannah Street was the main shopping street in Porth with a lot to occupy anyone's eye, the butcher's shop, fish shop, chemist, ironmongers, teashop, picture house, clothing shop, tailors, market vegetable and fruits, newsagent, coffee shop that served home made ice cream, and the second hand furniture shop. At the top of Hannah Street once a week there was the street market with items from Birmingham, Manchester, and London. Particularly fabrics, handbags, stockings, and suspender belts for ladies; trousers, shirts, jackets, and socks for men; and lots of aluminum pots and pans, toys and balloons. Much of the items were cheaper and of substandard quality that didn't take much wear and tear.

It was always an exciting day having street visitors with their wares to add color to the grey streets.

"It's getting late, perhaps we should get up and let the men put the chairs away. Would you like to come up and have a fresh cuppa with me, Lina?

"That will be nice, yes. Just let me take the bowls back to the house and I'll be up in a short while, alright?"

"Shall I take Angel with me while you get ready?"

"Well, I'd like to take Angel home with me first so she can get changed and hang her princess dress up, and then we'll come to your house soon."

"I agree; Angel's dress is so pretty it would be a shame to get it dirty. Are you sure you aren't too tired? It's been a very hectic afternoon."

"I'd love to have a cuppa before bed. It will give Angel a little time to use up all her energy and have a good night's sleep, too."

"Take your time Lina, come when you're ready, alright?"

Chapter 21

"It's me, Ethan," Mary called down the hall toward the kitchen as she hung up her shawl. "Sorry I didn't get a chance to help you bring things up, I was having a good conversation with Lina."

There was no answer but Mary could hear a lot of noise in the basement. She walked to the head of the stairs. "Ethan, are you down there? What are you doing?"

"Just putting things away, Ian's gone up to bed but David is down here with me. Come on son, it's getting late. What are you doing?"

"Dad, what's this?"

"What's what? What are you doing? We need to go upstairs."

"I don't know, but it's locked."

"Now what could be locked down here? There's so much and no room to move."

"It's this, it looks a bit like the other box you found. The metal one."

"Alright then, give it to me and let's get upstairs."

Mary smiled as the fairy elephants came up the stairs to the kitchen. She moved to fill the kettle and put it on to heat. Ethan closed the door and carried the box to the table where the pictures dried, only a couple edges curling. "I invited Lina and Angel up after they change clothes."

"That's alright." He held the box, forgotten by David.

"Alright, Angel is coming up! I'll get the dominoes." David skipped into the front room.

"That sounds good to me. It's been a long day but a good one; I think everyone had a good time." Ethan put the box on the table and got some screwdrivers. A knock on the door interrupted him.

"That's Lina and Angel." Mary smiled.

David let them in, taking their jackets. Now the sun slipped over the mountain, the valley cooled off. As Lina walked into the kitchen Ethan gasped. He'd wedged the box open and looked inside, eyes wide with shock.

"What is it Ethan?" Mary and Lina stood waiting to find out what it was that caused Ethan's sudden emotion of shock.

"Oh my goodness." Ethan sat down at the table just staring, his mind racing at what he saw in the box. David had found a treasure for sure. There were two gold wedding rings, one very large and worn and the other smaller, and a cross amongst some papers and an odd key.

"Let me see, let me see, Dad." The sudden silence in the kitchen drew David and Angel. Mary and Lina came to observe and looked at each other.

"I wonder what else is down in that basement?" Mary was a little surprised at David's find.

"My guess is they belonged to your grandparents, Cradoc and Clarenda. How exciting," Lina told them. "Perhaps Dylan might know. He and Olga were their only relatives and lived with your grandparents up on Penrhiwgwynt."

"Tomorrow I'll take them to Uncle Dylan with the other tin. He told me he would like to see the picture I found."

"The kettle is boiling, let's have a cuppa shall we?" Mary announced. "We have some cakes and pies left if anyone fancies a bite with their tea." The evening was exciting with the find and Angel and David were scheming at the thought there might be more treasure down in the basement besides up on the mountain.

"Angel, I forgot to tell you that I said you could go with David and his dad and Uncle Dylan next Sunday up the mountain."

"Yes, when Nene?"

"After Church if you would like to go with them. You could have a picnic or go after lunch."

"Oh, goodie, goodie gum drops." Angel was more than excited and skipped into the front room to tell David. David was on the floor with his cowboys and Indians and horses. "My Nene said I can go with you up the mountain next Sunday. Maybe we will see Buttercup again and her baby foal. Nene said we could have a picnic or go after lunch."

At the mention of the foal, David was excited. "Dusty, oh that would be good. I really want to see Dusty again."

Ian chimed in, "A soppy horse named Buttercup and now a soppy foal named Dusty. Not to mention two snotty kids. What next?"

"Ian, what did I just hear you say?" Mary yelled from the kitchen.

"Nothing, Mam."

"If I hear you say mean things to your brother and Angel again, you won't be going anywhere next week. You'll be on restriction."

Ian put his head round the doorway, "Mam, I didn't say anything mean." His head bobbed back into the room.

"Ian, I haven't finished with you. Come here."

Ian came to the door with his head bent low, "Yes, Mam."

"I will not allow you to talk like that to your brother, and definitely not to Angel. Do you hear me? If you continue to talk like that, you will not be going. Do you hear me?"

"Yes, Mam," Ian replied hastily and turned to walk away.

"Ian, that's another thing. Do not walk away from me until I've finished talking to you, do you hear me, Ian?"

"Yes, Mam. Sorry, Mam. Can I go now?"

Mary shook her head in frustration and replied to Ian, "You can go now, but be polite next time."

"Yes, Mam."

David was peering at the door and ran back to Angel as if he had a secret. "Ian got into trouble," he whispered.

"Oh dear, I hope your dad doesn't find out or he'll be on restriction."

The following week was exciting for the children. School was closed for the second week of Easter break. They enjoyed having fun together, playing rounders' in the street.Taking it in turns to ride the three-wheeler down the hill. Lina and Mary enjoyed passing time and shopping together.

Lina went for her appointment at Cardiff Hospital with Mary at her side and was told the result of their findings. It was not what she was hoping for but was told to wait and see how things developed in a week or two, then return to see her doctor. Thanks to Mary, Lina was able to lean on her for companionship and support. At times Lina cried and expressed her concerns, not for herself but for Angel and Gilberto.

Gilberto was visiting that week and Lina promised the specialist to share her concerns with Gilberto. Lina could not bear the thought of worrying him anymore than he was already. What could he do anyway? He had a job and was trying to make ends meet, besides building a house for her and Angel. Houses weren't built quickly in a country that had its fair share of wet weather and cold temperatures. The ground had to be leveled then the foundation laid before waiting approximately six months for the ground to settle before proceeding with the walls or repairing the foundation. A long procedure governed by building regulation.

Lina avoided the subject when Gilberto visited. It was his time to be with Angel especially as they were such short visits. Why cause him anxiety and concern? It was supposed to be a joyous occasion. Gilberto left without knowing her medical concerns but reassured his mother as he was leaving that the home he was buying was being built in Four Oaks, Sutton Coldfield. A quiet residential area away from heavy industry, and he was immensely excited to tell her it would have an indoor bathroom with toilet, electricity, and running water.

The day was bright and sunny. Church was good that Sunday. Vicar Llewelyn's sermon was highlighting God's blessings on His people. Blessings they have already received and blessings to come and to always wait patiently on Him.

After a quick lunch and change Lina took Angel up to Mary's house so that Angel could join them for the walk up the mountain. Excitement was high for Angel and David. The thoughts of having fun ran rampantly through their minds and maybe finding treasures.

"Everyone ready yet?" Ethan shouted. Ian was already in the hallway adjusting his shirt and scarf. "Hhmm! My oh my, what a lot of fuss you are going to just to go up the mountain. Are you expecting to see someone up there, Ian?" Ian smirked at that question but in his mind it was always better to be prepared.

"Alright then, I told Uncle Dylan that as we were going that way we will stop at his chippie. He's probably waiting for us by now. Then we'll all stop at the Vicarage and meet Vicar Llewelyn as we are all ready to go."

Angel ran to Lina and hugged her, "I love you, Nene." She then turned to Mary, "Ta ta, Aunty Mary."

David repeated, "Ta ta, Mam."

Ethan kissed Mary on the cheek and everyone left through the front door.

"It has suddenly got very quiet, don't you think? Let's have a cuppa shall we."

Lina nodded a yes. "I'll put the kettle on and lay the table." Mary was anxious to have everything ready and not let Lina get up and start helping. "I'll just go in the pantry a minute," Mary explained as she disappeared out of sight.

"Now look what I found." Mary was holding a plate full of small chocolate eclairs she had made especially for Lina.

"Mary, oh my goodness. Where did you get those from? I haven't seen them for years."

"Actually, you probably don't remember but I was watching you make the choux pastry one day, a long time ago and I remembered you said you liked them, they were your favorite."

"You remember that? That was so long ago."

"I remembered because I had the best teacher. You told me once if you learn something you'll never forget. I didn't forget and I was waiting for the right time to make them for you. Today I felt was the right time."

Dylan and Vicar Llewelyn were on the doorstep of the chippie, waiting. "Beautiful day today, sun is shining to bless our way," Vicar Llewelyn announced.

"*Ìe* it is that, that it is," Dylan replied.

"Well now, let's be off then." Llewelyn was anxious to get started on his walk.

Angel and David skipped ahead, happy as could be, while Ian was still adjusting his clothing as they walked towards the milkman's farm.

"Now then, let us stop a moment and say a prayer to our Lord." Everyone halted at the thought of a prayer and being obedient to the Vicar. "Heavenly Father, it is a good day and we thank you for that. We are about to embark on a journey that I hope will freshen our souls as we become closer to thee in the beauty of the land and sky that you have created for us to enjoy. Let your Will be done and may we receive your blessings. Amen."

"Hello there, milkman Rhys! It's a beautiful afternoon. Would you like to join us for a walk this afternoon up to the top of the old girl?" Vicar Llewelyn was an extreme organizer.

"*Dim diolch*, I have a lot of barn work to do."

"*Iawn wedyn*," replied Llewelyn.

"You haven't forgotten your Welsh then?" Dylan teased Llewelyn. Rhys joined the banter.

"*Sut Cradoc gallwn i anghofio fy iaith hun. Mae llawer o bobl wedi anghofio ond mae fy Mrs yn dod o Ogledd Cymru ac mae hi'n hoffi i sgwrsio yn Gymraeg.*" Llewlyn replied.

Ian was more than interested, "What are you saying, or is it a secret?"

"No son. Your Uncle Dylan was challenging me to speak Welsh. He thought I had forgotten as I don't preach in Welsh anymore," Llewelyn replied with a smile.

"What did you say then?"

"I said, how could I forget my own language?"

"You said all that in Welsh?" Ian was surprised.

"Many people have forgotten but my Mrs. is from North Wales and she likes to converse in Welsh," Rhys told them. "Well son, they are teaching more English at school nowadays so you must learn from your family to keep our language alive. Welsh will become popular again very soon, mark my words."

They started up the mountain after waving bye to Rhys, the milkman heading to work.

"Actually, it has a ring to it. Highs and lows it's much like David's singing," Ian trumped in and then chuckled.

"Look there's a post Cradoc stuck in the ground to mark how far up we were," Dylan pointed out. "It's weathered all the storms of time and still here." Dylan was happy to see memories of his brother on the mountainside.

"Cradoc did a lot for us and our mountain," Llewelyn was happy to include another comment into the conversation. "Do you remember that time when he caught his first wild horse? We all celebrated. What an event that was. He wanted his horse baptized."

"I remember that well and he was so serious. We all looked at him dumb founded, baptize a horse? He was a comedian, but he was dead serious," Dylan replied with a smile.

"You baptized a horse?" Ethan was surprised at the very thought.

"*Ìe*, we did," Dylan replied. "Well, he baptized it." Tipping his head to Llewelyn and laughing.

"What do mean he baptized it?" Ethan watched the older men.

"We were having a little celebration. Cradoc was so happy catching his first horse, and that horse was his pride and joy. It was the start to his horse farm, you know."

"What happened Uncle, how did he baptize the horse?" Ethan was getting a little impatient trying to find out all the information.

"We were celebrating, *Ìe*, we, were. Celebrating…"

"Go on Dylan, get to the point, young Ethan is waiting." Llewelyn was also a little short on patience these days.

"Well, we were celebrating. Ha ha ha,ha."

"Go on mun, get to the point," Llewelyn postured another comment.

"*Ìe*, I we were celebrating, ha ha ha. We were drinking Guinness. The horse's head turned towards Cradoc. Ha ha ha."

"Go on for God's sake, Dylan." Llewelyn's patience had totally run out.

"Where was I? Oh yes. Cradoc loosened the reins on the horse so he could get a swig of Guinness. Low and behold the horse grabbed his mug in its teeth. Cradoc was speechless, we were too. We thought the horse was going to swallow the mug whole or crush it with its teeth and there would be glass everywhere. Instead, it maneuvered its head and the Guinness squirted out and sprayed all over its face and up on his mane. Ha aha ah." Dylan continued to laugh, holding his sides.

"What?" Ethan wasn't quite sure if he heard correctly what his Uncle was explaining.

"The horse christened himself. Ha ha ha." Dylan was almost doubled over with laughter.

"Oh what a sight it was, if I was a betting man, I think the horse liked the taste of Guinness. It followed Cradoc everywhere that night," Llewelyn said and then burst into laughter.

"You were there too, Vicar Llewelyn?" Ethan was curious for a man of the cloth to be involved with all this.

"I was there with my Mrs. She was not amused, allowing a horse to drink Guinness. 'Whatever next?' she said." Llewelyn definitely found it funny.

"Cradoc had to be careful, his stock of Guinness was kept out in the barn. He used to buy it by the barrel. The horses would turn over anything they could find if they thought there was food around. In this case drink, Ha ha ha." Dylan was almost hysterical. "Can you imagine a drunk wild horse that christened himself, and with Guinness?"

"Oh my God, it was too funny for words." Llewelyn was almost hysterical himself.

By this time, they were at the top. David was already swinging on the tree and Angel was amusing herself picking wild flowers. It was a glorious afternoon. Blue sky, puffy white clouds, a gently breeze and everyone was enjoying their conversation.

"My brother, Cradoc was definitely a tender hearted man even though he appeared a tough mountain man on the outside. He slept with that horse that night. Clarenda wasn't too pleased but as they were both drunk, Cradoc and the horse I mean, it was better they both stayed out in the barn."

"The horse was drunk you said, Uncle?" Ethan was amused by the tale. He'd not noticed he'd made it up the mountain.

"*Ìe*, it was. Drunk as a skunk both of them; Cradoc and the horse, and he named this horse Guinness. Cradoc found it easy to train this horse, as he was eager to drink his Guinness, the horse I mean. The more Cradoc drank the more the horse drank." Dylan had a hard time getting the words out for laughing. "Cradoc shared his drinks with his horse. He was a very funny man with a great sense of humor. I will never forget him.

"Cradoc sometimes drank syrup of figs too, and so did the horse. Oh my God, you had to get out of the way, that's for sure." Even though Dylan was laughing, he got out his torn handkerchief and blew his nose, then turned away so he could wipe his eyes. Dylan's memories were locked in time; even humorous memories were still a wound that had not healed. He missed his brother even all these years later.

"What happened to Guinness?" Ethan asked.

"I can't say it was alcoholism but even a horse has its limits. He was a good friend to Cradoc and good company. He was the only horse that Cradoc could train just like his sheepdog. Maybe because he was his first horse. Clarenda wasn't so keen on a drunken husband and a drunken horse around the place but she put up with it so long as they both didn't drink syrup of figs too often. Otherwise, they would both have to get out into the barn, and quickly."

"You mean she let the horse in the house, too?"

"*Ie*, she did, she wanted a happy husband and Clarenda didn't drink, so she put up with the horse. She sat with them in the kitchen conversing but as soon as it was time for her to go to bed, off she went and left him with his friend. Cradoc had a lean-to attached to the kitchen with a straw area and a half door so the horse could lean over the door and enjoy a drink with Cradoc."

"What? You're pulling my leg," Ethan scoffed.

"No son, Cradoc loved his horse like he loved everything else. A life, whether it was animal or human, it didn't matter. He cared for it. Mam always said you take the good with the bad if you love a man that much."

"Ian, where are you?" Ethan called.

"Dad, I'm right here by the fence with these two soppy kids."

"Ian, that's enough. Your mam told me you have been talking like that a lot lately. What is wrong with you? You know that's not right."

"Sorry."

"Alright then, let's keep going while the weather is good." Dylan was anxious to keep walking.

"Are you ready for another walk, Llewelyn?" Dylan asked as Llewelyn steadied himself on his walking stick, a stick that had most likely been packed away. It had an intricate design made from mother-of-pearl all the way up its leg and into its arm, and had a leather strap that could be looped around the wrist to carry when not in use.

"Oh my goodness, look over there." He pointed to the circle of trees Ethan found a week ago. "Those trees look familiar even from here and after all this time."

"Where, Dylan? What trees are you talking about?" Llewelyn was asking.

"Over there, put your specs on and look over there." Dylan grinned.

Llewelyn fumbled in his pocket for his spectacle case and then attached his specs to his ears, carefully returning the case to his pocket. He adjusted his waistcoat and looked to the direction that Dylan was pointing. "Oh my goodness, are those what I am thinking they are, Dylan?"

"*Ìe*, they are, that they are." Dylan turned to Ethan, "Come on son, we are going to investigate your family's land, let's make haste." Off he marched at a speed no one had encountered for years, almost as though he had taken a tonic.

"Now lookie here Dylan, I can't keep up with you mun. What got into you?" Llewelyn was in a turmoil adjusting his waistcoat and gathering his limbs that hadn't had this kind of exercise for years.

"Don't dilly dally Llewelyn, we haven't got all day you know!"

"I didn't know you could walk this fast, Uncle." Ethan was used to Dylan ambling around his chippie at a slow pace, not at a marching speed. It was quite refreshing to see his Uncle with such enthusiasm to go across the mountaintop.

"The closer we get the better view we will have of things." Dylan was excited to say the least.

"Is that a person or a horse over there, Uncle?" Ethan pointed way beyond.

"Let me focus a minute." Dylan stopped and squinted, "I do declare. It's a person. That's not a horse. What is someone doing here in these parts anyway?" Curiosity took over Dylan's mind. "Come on, we must see what's happening over there."

Llewelyn was struggling to keep up the pace but was not far behind. On the other hand, Ethan was right there at Dylan's side. "What could be there that's got someone's attention, I wonder?"

"We'll find out very soon, come on now."

It wasn't too long before the individual was in view, stooping down.

"What is he doing? Is he hurt?" Ethan asked.

"We'll soon find out." Dylan was getting short winded as he struggled to talk and walk at a fast pace. "Hey you, are you alright?" Dylan was wondering why this person was bent over.

"I am," the voice replied.

"What's wrong then?" Dylan shouted back.

"I found a wounded foal. That's the second I found," the man said.

"Where's the other one, then," Dylan enquired.

"I just let it go."

"Go where?"

"I left it, had to get back down."

Dylan's heart sank when he heard that. Ethan was shocked and bent down to the foal that was staggering to get back up on its legs

"I think his leg is broken. Help me, Uncle." Ethan took off his shirt and started tearing off the sleeves. "Can you tear this up for me? I must find some strong branches so I can make a splint."

Dylan did just that and shook his head at the person who obviously had no feelings for wild animals. "What are you doing in these parts?" Dylan asked, trying not to show his disgust.

"I'm plotting out my grandfather's land."

"Oh, you are? Where would that be then?"

"It's here."

"Here, are you sure, this can't be it. This it can't be," Dylan replied quickly.

"Oh I can assure you, this is it. I have deeds to state this was my grandfather's land."

"Where are you from, son?" Dylan was now more than interested in what this young grandson had in mind.

"I live over the border."

"That would be England, then?" Dylan was still tearing Ethan's shirt for the foal but tearing it with more force than before.

"Yes. Manchester to be exact."

"Is that so?" Dylan was careful with his words now. He did not want to be treading on thin ice with a young Englishman. "Now what would you do with the land up here on the mountain?"

"Sell it of course, it's no use to me. I like city life."

Dylan swallowed hard but did not want to have any more conversation about the land.

Chapter 22

Soon Ethan came with some branches for the foal's leg and started breaking them off into sizes that could be used as splints.

"Uncle, can you hold him steady while I put some splints on his leg?"

"Let me first assure the foal we are not intending to harm him, let me massage him a bit."

"What, massage a foal?" the young Englishman was on the verge of laughing.

Even Ethan wasn't sure of what Dylan was going to do, but would not laugh. His Uncle was older and far wiser. Dylan started massaging the foal's head, behind his ears, under his head around his neck, and down his back towards his tail but did not touch his tail, then under his belly and then thighs and the other legs, not the broken leg until last.

"He's almost asleep. Where did you learn that, Uncle?" Ethan spoke softly so as not to startle the foal.

"From my brother Cradoc, actually. He used massaging as a method to relax the horses. In fact, it worked wonders when there was a new life to be born in the barn.

"Son, did I tell you about the day that my Olga and Cradoc delivered Guinness's foal?"

Ethan turned and looked down at Dylan, "What? I thought Guinness was a stallion, not a mare!"

"Of course son, Guinness was a stallion, but he knew which mare was having his foal, alright."

"Really? What happened?" Ethan crossed his arms over his chest, settling in to listen to another long story from Dylan.

"Well, his mare was definitely showing signs of her delivery. I say his mare because he was always with her other than the times he was with Cradoc, drinking."

"You mean he actually was going to sire a foal?"

"Oh yes son, otherwise I wouldn't be telling you. We called her Sherry."

"His mare had a name, too. Sherry? Why Sherry?"

"Well son, she was a sweet mare and was always friendly to my Olga, unlike some of the other wild mares. So my Olga named her Sherry because that was the drink that my Olga enjoyed, when she drank of course."

"So Sherry was Guinness's mare?"

"You could say that, son."

"Did you name all the horses, then?"

"Not really, son. Only the horses that stayed around willingly and were close to us, like Guinness, Sherry, Petticoat, and Sweet Pea."

"Petticoat and Sweet Pea?" snorted Ethan.

"Yes, Petticoat and Sweet Pea. But I'll tell you about them later." Dylan waved his hand around while they talked.

"As I was saying, signs of birthing were obvious for Sherry. She was restless. She paced around the barn sometimes banging her head at the walls and then backing up. You could tell she was in some pain, bless her."

"What, a horse was in pain?"

"Of course, she was in pain just like your Mary when she was about to deliver the babies."

"I wouldn't know that, Uncle. I was down the mine for every birth. It was the midwife who delivered the babies, or Lina. Lina delivered David."

"*Ie*, she did and a wonderful midwife she made, too. I remember Ian came running up to my chippie with his elder brother, to tell me that Lina helped his mam when she delivered another baby boy. Oh, Ian was so excited he had a baby brother."

"I don't think we could have managed without our Lina all these years." Ethan was in great thought.

"I honestly don't think that any of us would be as well off as we are without our Lina helping us one way or another," Dylan told him, nodding, keeping his hands on the sleeping foal. The other man stood to the side, listening as well.

"Uncle, you were going to tell me. What happened to Sherry?"

"*Ìe*. That I was, going to tell you about Sherry, that I was." Dylan thought for a few minutes. He didn't want to give too much away about the old life while they were talking because he wanted Ethan to enjoy the view, the scenery. "*Ìe*, Sherry she was in pain alright and was prancing around the barn then lifting her front hooves up and banging the barn walls and finally she stopped and let out a loud squeal."

"What happened then, a loud squeal you said?"

"*Ìe*, son. A squeal. Not the usual kind, it was a horrible loud squeal."

"Was something wrong?"

"Terribly wrong, poor Sherry she was in pain, that she was. She flopped down on the ground. Cradoc came running out of the barn shouting, 'Get Clarenda and Olga quick, and bring my bag.' Dylan was clearly reliving the day.

"Guinness was outside the barn and banging the walls. He could have easily knocked down the barn door but he was up against the wall closest to Sherry. Almost as if she would know he was close by. Between Guinness outside and Sherry kicking the stall down, it was a really unsafe place to be. The barn could have fallen down easily."

"What happened?"

"I was getting to that." There was another silence as Dylan gathered his thoughts.

"Uncle, what happened? Was Sherry alright?"

"Not exactly, son. I raced back to the house and was shouting, shouting, shouting no one was coming. I nearly banged the door down before I saw Olga coming round the corner. They were in the vegetable garden picking beans or hoeing or something like that." He paused, scratching the foal behind the ears. "I remember Sweet Pea was with them."

"Uncle, what did Olga say?" Ethan was getting a little impatient like he always did, but Dylan had to collect his thoughts.

"Well?"

"Olga could tell something was wrong. She picked up her skirt and raced inside the house and got Cradoc's bag while shouting to Clarenda to hurry up and come with her."

"What was in the bag uncle?"

"I'm getting to that. Give me a chance to breathe, will you?"

"Alright, Uncle. Sorry for being so impatient." Ethan noticed he'd been twisting the branches. He'd have to get more at this rate. At his feet was torn bark and shreds of wood.

"You were telling me about Sherry, Uncle."

Ìe that I was. Now where was I? Oh yes, I remember."

"Thank God," Ethan secretly thought to himself. "Uncle Dylan takes so long to tell me something. It takes absolutely forever but I must remember he is elderly and he is all I have left of my older generation, bless his whiskers!"

"When Olga came with the bag. Cradoc took it from her and threw it on the ground, the contents spilled out. He grabbed the cord and tied Sherry's tail up so it wouldn't get in the way. Then he fumbled to get his old stethoscope. He shouted to Clarenda to fill the lamps with oil, as he didn't want to be without light and it was getting darker. He tried to listen to Sherry's stomach with the stethoscope but Guinness was making such a racket outside it was hard to hear. Then he got out the Sloan's liniment and started massaging her belly to try and calm her down."

"What? Where was Sherry when he tied her tail up?"

"She flopped on the ground and she was groaning, oh poor thing, groaning up a storm. Rubbing her head on the ground backwards and forwards, and her mouth was so dry."

"What did you do, Uncle, while all this was going on?"

"Well, I knew it was better for a female to have clean everything around her when she gives birth even if she was a horse. Alright then, I thought to myself, let me get her new hay so she could lie on a clean bed of hay. We had lots of fresh hay in the loft above the barn, so I dropped a few rolls down. Olga and Clarenda were sweeping the barn and brought water in a couple of buckets."

"Did it take long? For the birth, I mean."

"I don't know son. We weren't worried about time; we were concerned about getting that foal out alive."

"What, a foal could be born dead?"

"*Ìe* it can, just like a baby. You remember son, don't you? You lost two babies at birth."

"Yes, we did. I couldn't be there to be with Mary. I had to work." Ethan was getting depressed and Dylan could see that so he had to say something quick to bring him back to the present.

"Well son, we had to act quickly. There's only so much time with a horse birthing its foal. Clarenda poured a bit of water over Sherry's mouth hoping she would drink a bit as her mouth was so dry. Olga was on her knees with Cradoc. Olga got a clean rag and dipped it into one of the buckets and washed under Sherry's tail as she was bleeding."

"She was bleeding and making noises. Oh my God.

"Oh terrible noises, when a horse has contractions during birth it's almost like they scream so loud it's deafening. The foal is about seventy-to-ninety pounds, you know. I'm sure it must hurt and they have to push it out. Cradoc and Olga knew Sherry was having trouble. Although the sac of water had come out, there was only one leg hanging through the birthing canal. Normally, the front hooves and legs come out first, one leg in front of the other, and then the head. Cradoc was worried. He pulled Sherry up to make her stand."

"So, she was standing to deliver the foal?"

"No son, Cradoc got her to stand to reposition the foal. She was breathing heavily and making such awful noises and she pulled the leg back in. Then she flopped back down on the ground. Sherry was a heavy horse, and Cradoc knew that. He had to be careful that the horse didn't break a leg or fall on him."

Ethan was silent while Dylan explained, but was eager to know all the details.

"Cradoc knew he had to act quickly. He washed his hands and arms in one of the buckets. Sherry was pushing alright, and another sac of fluid came out and burst that time. That meant the foal should be coming. Well, the foal didn't appear and Sherry was making terrible, terrible noises and trying to get up again, thrashing her head on the ground and her legs flying around."

"Uncle, didn't the vet come?"

"What vet, son? There's no vet up here. Cradoc said to his vet friend, if he would ever come up the mountain he would give him a horse to ride."

"So why didn't he come?"

"Son, he didn't and we couldn't go all the way down the mountain to get him. Cradoc had to help Sherry, otherwise, like I said, the foal would die and possibly Sherry, too. She was pushing as best she could. Anyway, Cradoc lubricated his right hand and arm with a bit of Vaseline and then pushed his hand and arm gently into her birthing canal."

"What? Inside the horse? Inside Sherry?" Ethan studied the sleeping foal, the other man forgotten.

"Of course, son. How else would the foal come out if the mare can't deliver it? It's just like that drain you had stopped up, you put your hand in, and all the way up to your elbow to clean it out, didn't you?"

"I know about cleaning out the drain but, oh my God. I didn't know that about a foal."

"Son, there's lots of stuff you learn about when you're up the mountain. Good common sense stuff that city people know nothing about."

"Was the foal able to come out then, Uncle?"

"Well, he had to feel for the two legs, then the chest, the nose and the head. When he said he found its chest and head he could help Sherry by pulling out the foal."

"He had to pull out the foal?"

"Yes, son. That was how Armour was born." Dylan could tell that Ethan was in deep thought.

"Armour. You named her foal Armour?"

"*Ìe. Ìe* we did. Armour was born with the help of Cradoc's hand and arm."

"How many others did you name?"

"Oh not too many after Armour."

"Why not, Uncle?"

"Well, we didn't have any new horses then that were pregnant and we had a number of other animals to take care of. Goats, cows, bulls, sheep and of course our sheep dog, Taffy."

"I remember that, Dylan. I was there when Cradoc delivered that foal. It was legs first in position, it was upside down, and the mare was in serious pain. He massaged the mare's belly and her thighs and then her hindquarter. She was so relaxed when he put his hand up to turn the foal. That amazed me so much that I preached on it for about a month." Llewelyn joined the conversation. Not worried so much about waking the foal.

"*Ìe*, you did that, that you did. I thought you were going to get down from the pulpit and shout you were coming to live with us. You were so enthused to tell all the vivid details, too. It's funny that, because Cradoc said many times a Vicar on the farm would be a blessing! I wasn't quite sure exactly what he meant, but in time I learned that he was a very spiritual man. He enjoyed it when you came up with your Mrs. and had dinner with us. He loved that Bible game you both played. You even calmed the storm many times when those Croatians came over."

"Those definitely were the good old days. We had a lot of fun."

"I always thought you and grandfather Cradoc were serious horse farmers and didn't have time to waste having fun." Ethan was definitely learning about life on the mountainside without experiencing it.

"Son, I just wish you could have been there. He worked hard but it wasn't all work, you know. We had good times, too. Those were the best years I ever had with my brother, and my Olga was with me, too."

"This little foal is not only tired, he's exhausted and most likely hungry. We don't know how long he's been left here." Llewelyn touched his head and prayed that he would soon be healed.

Ethan wrapped his shirt pieces around the sticks that Dylan held firm on the foal's leg and stood back. He was wondering what could he do, he couldn't leave the foal there.

"Uncle, will you and Vicar Llewelyn stay here while I run back to the farm and see if Farmer Rhys has a board or a plank and some rope and maybe we could get him down to the farm. He'll die if we leave him here."

"Well, son. I hadn't planned on sitting with a foal but I agree we can't leave him here to die. I will stay."

"I will stay, too," Llewelyn chimed in.

"Oh my God, are you Welsh people crazy? Going to take the foal down the mountain."

"Well, let me ask you something young Englishman," Llewelyn asked. He put his hands in his pockets and rocked back and forth on his heals thinking how he should say something without intimidating this young man. Before he could say anything the young man was anxious to say what he would do.

"I wouldn't bother, I'd leave it here, like the other one," the young Englishman blurted.

"Oh God, help us and bless us with the wonders of your love." Llewelyn was dead serious as he prayed. He turned to the Englishman and questioned him, "What happened to the other foal? When did you find him?"

"Last week. I left it there. It was almost dead anyway." He shrugged glancing between the three Welshmen.

"Oh God," Llewelyn rocked even faster and shook his head while he murmured as quietly as he could the rest of his prayers.

Ethan ran back to where they left the children. "Kids, I must go to the farm, we found a foal and he is hurt. I need some planks to get him back. Do you want to come with me or stay here?" He waited while Angel and David exchanged a look. "I'd rather you come with me down to the farm."

David nodded, "We'll come back with you, won't we Angel?"

"I'm coming with you," Angel replied eagerly.

"Ian are you coming, too or are you staying here?"

"I'll come back with you." He nodded but dragged his feet. It was a wasted day for him.

"Alright then, let's go quickly. I need to get that foal back down the mountain before it gets too late."

"What happened to the foal, Dad?"

"How did it get hurt?" Angel asked as tears filled her eyes.

"It will be alright if we can get it down to the farm. It has a broken leg and he can't stand up."

"It's not Dusty, is it?" David worried.

"Oh no, it's not Dusty is it, Uncle Ethan?" Angel started to sob.

"No, it's not Dusty. It's a patchy brown looking foal but it needs our help and quickly. He is most likely hungry as well as in pain."

Chapter 23

Angel and David ran ahead, Angel almost tripped in her haste. "Hold my hand, Angel, so you don't fall," David clasped her hand in his and both hurried down the hill. Ian and Ethan followed a bit slower.

"Ian, I'd like you to come back up with me and help get the foal down. We can let David and Angel wait at the farm for us. I know milkman Rhys won't mind. In fact, his wife will most likely give them dinner if we are a long time and it gets late. They're very caring." He slipped a bit and caught his balance. "I'd like to see the foal safely down in the valley than be left up there by itself," Ethan stated with no thought of the heights he traveled this day.

Ian thought of the work ahead. But he was older now and his dad asked him for help. Pride uncurled in his stomach. "It's alright, Dad. I'll come back with you."

"Thank you, Ian. That's a good decision to make."

"There's milkman Rhys, outside by his barn."

"Hello there. Are you alone? I thought you went up the mountain with Dylan and Llewelyn. Where are they? You haven't left them up there have you?" Rhys asked the fast moving party.

"Yes actually. We found a foal that's hurt. They are looking after it while I came down to get some supplies that would help me get him down here. Can you help with some rope and planks, or anything like that I can use?" Ethan had to catch his breath.

"I can do that. Come over the fence, you are welcome to get them. I have rope in the barn; let me get it for you." The milkman went into the barn and came out with the rope and an old blanket. Ethan held a wide plank he'd found leaned against the side of the barn. "Take this blanket with you. Wrap the foal up in the blanket and then tie the rope around it. The blanket will help prevent the rope from cutting into its skin."

"That's a good idea, I didn't think of that. Alright then. Come on Ian, let's get back before it gets too late."

Back up on the mountain Dylan and Llewelyn were in deep conversation after the young Englishman left.

"That's young people today. Don't think about wild life and probably don't care much."

"No, I don't believe that totally. I believe that this one is just plain selfish, wants to sell his grandfather's land because he likes city life! Oh my God. I think his grandfather would curl in his grave if he did just that." Llewelyn shook his head in disgust. "Thank God he's gone Dylan; I don't know what I might have said."

"Think about it a moment, what do you think you might have said?" Dylan asked.

"I am absolutely disgusted. I wouldn't want to help him, so I have no idea what I would have said," Llewelyn uttered. "But, I do feel really sorry for his grandfather. This grandson has no respect for the dead, especially his grandfather. He worked hard just like your brother, Cradoc. This young English bloke is just a money hungry bugger. He is letting his grandfather down with his youth and big city life."

"*Ìe*, he is that, that he is and he doesn't seem to care either, shame that."

"Here's Ethan coming, maybe now we can get this poor animal down the mountain."

"How is he, Uncle?" Ethan and Ian were a little out of breath.

"He's relaxed but he has been flinching a bit, I think he is in pain."

"Let's wrap this blanket around him and then wrap the rope around him and the plank. I'll pull the plank. We must take care not to move that leg though."

"He's light as a feather. He can't have much flesh on him. Bless him," Llewelyn said with empathy. "I wonder how long this poor animal has been lying there?"

"Alright then, let's get this plank up and I'll hold the ropes over my shoulders. Ian, you check back there and make sure he doesn't slip, it could hurt him."

"Dad, I'm not sure if he's alright. His eyes are closed."

"Let me see, lower him carefully will you?" Ethan requested.

"I'll massage him again." Dylan gently massaged the foal's head and behind his ears. The foal slowly opened his eyes but his eyes then closed.

"He needs sustenance, bless him." Llewelyn was concerned.

"Alright then, let's get going," Dylan told Ethan. "We must get down there quickly and give this poor animal some sustenance, otherwise he is not going to make it."

Ethan lifted the plank again and grabbed the rope over his shoulder and pulled it down the lane. The lane had many potholes from the rain that ran down the mountainside. "Please watch him, Ian. We can't let him down now."

"I'll hold on to the plank as well to steady him over the bumps," Dylan told them.

Ethan looked at Llewelyn. Llewelyn prayed as he tried to keep up with them.

The group was on the way down to the farm. "Ethan, stop. It's a bit too bumpy for the foal. Let's just carry him like he's on a stretcher. It's not too far now," Llewelyn told them.

"*Ie*, it is bumpy, that it is bumpy. Good idea Llewelyn." Dylan nodded agreement.

They noticed Mrs. Rhys on her way up. When she got "closer to them she held up a bottle.

"Hello there, I have a bottle for the little foal."

"Well, that is very kind of you Mrs. Rhys," Llewelyn stuttered. He was already out of puff from the experience and excitement of helping care for the foal.

Ethan was anxious to take the foal to safety but realized it would help revive the foal with some milk. He lowered the rope, letting the plank rest on the ground, the rope holding the foal secure.

"This is fresh goat milk. It will have more nutrition than poor Bessy's milk. She is already tired from being milked this morning. I am sure he won't care as long as he gets something. I made a teet from one of the fingers off my rubber glove and tied it around with string and then cut a tiny hole at the top for the poor little thing. Let's see if he will suck."

Llewelyn crouched down by Mrs. Rhys. She put the bottle near the foal's mouth. "By Jove, he's sucking. He's alright. Praise the Lord for his great mercies." Llewelyn turned around and looked up at Ethan and Dylan. He was happy as a lark and started singing, "Joyful, joyful we adore thee...."

"Thank you, Mrs. Rhys, for bringing the milk. For a moment I was worried that he may not have the energy to even suck at the bottle, but he made it," Dylan exclaimed.

"Oh I'm certain he will make it down to our farm now. You showed love and caring for this poor soul and you have the Vicar with you to pray, also."

"*Ie,* we do have him, have him here we do," Dylan chimed in happily.

"Let's try again. Let's pick him up now, so we don't drag him."

"Alright then, one, two, three," Llewelyn chimed in. "Ian, have you got him firm? We don't want him falling off now we are so close."

"He's alright, he just winked at me." Ian was chuckling. Mrs. Rhys picked up her skirt and pinny and ran back down to her farm.

"She's a tough lady and has an abundance of energy."

"Look at her go down the path. It must be all that fresh milk and fresh air she gets. She hasn't lost her energy, that's for sure." Dylan was astonished.

About thirty minutes had passed and they were down on the farmland. David and Angel ran to greet them. "Is the foal alright, Dad?" David shouted as they ran up.

"Did he drink the milk?" Angel echoed behind him.

"He seems in good spirits," Llewelyn was happy to report. "He did drink the milk. We just have to get his leg to heal now and he will be happy to bounce back up the mountain."

The milkman came out of the barn. "I laid some fresh hay for him to lie on and water and oats. He will be well taken care of, don't worry."

"Can I stay with him, Dad?" David pleaded.

"Me too," Angel butted in.

"I don't know if your Nene would like you to stay in a barn with a wounded wild foal, Angel," Ethan told her, still walking to the barn with the foal.

"Can I stay, Dad? Please?" David continued to ask.

"Let me think about it. I wish your mam was here to make these decisions."

"That means I can stay, then?" David was more than excited but Ethan still didn't answer.

Ethan wasn't paying much attention to David at that point, "Let's get him in the barn." Everyone carefully carried him into the barn and laid the make-do stretcher down on the ground. "Now be careful, I wonder how the best way would be to get him off the stretcher on to the straw?"

"Ethan, I have a suggestion." Dylan stood back with his hands on his hips.

"Alright then," said Ethan turning to look at Dylan.

"We could do it the same way they did in the hospital with my Olga. Take off all the rope and we'll pull the blanket on one side off the board and lay him as close as we can on the straw."

"How do we get the blanket off without rolling him over?" Ethan asked.

"We just leave it under him. It's warm and it will have his smell now, so he will be comfortable and he won't be scared. I'll massage him again." Dylan took charge of the situation, massaging the foal on his side and belly then around his shoulder and head.

David asked Angel, "I wonder what we should call him? He isn't the same color as Dusty." The children stood in the aisle, watching the men and the foal.

"What names are like a brown color?" Angel asked. Her chin propped on the stall door, eyes bright as she watched them move the foal gently onto the straw.

David ticked off names finger by finger. "Well there's, Brownie, Cocoa, Chocolate, Coffee, Chestnut…" David was interrupted by the Vicar jumping away from the foal.

Llewelyn sprung to his feet, "Oh God, I forgot my Mrs.' dandelion leaves. I'll be in the dog house when I get back."

"Llewelyn, I have a patch of dandelions growing behind the barn, I use them for my soup, too. You can pick what you need."

Llewelyn left the stall and raced as quickly as he could out of the barn in search of the dandelions. Before Mrs. Rhys had chance to say anymore, Llewelyn yelled. Much louder than he'd ever sounded from the pulpit.

"Aahhhhhhh…" Then they heard Llewelyn mutter, "Bloody. Hell. Fires." Everything went still and silent in the barn. Mrs. Rhys looked up with a smile. "I guess he found the horse manure pile. I don't have to tell him to look out for it now," Mrs. Rhys announced. Everyone burst into laughter at her solemn comment. Even the foal whinnied as if joining in the humor.

Llewelyn walked much more slowly back to Dylan and the rest of the group. "Oh my God, you certainly stink and you look like you rolled in it," Dylan sputtered, choking back laughter.

"Well, you found the poo pile alright. Now, what are you going to tell your Mrs.?" Dylan and Ethan still chuckled.

"I'll have to tell her the truth, won't I?" Llewelyn pulled up his trousers and put his hands in his pants, looked straight ahead, and continued confidently, "I slipped and fell."

"*Ìe*, you did that, that you did, slipped and fell in horse poo. Behind the barn where you were supposed to be picking Mrs. Rhys's dandelions because you forgot them up the mountain. Ha, ha ha." Dylan laughed so much his sides hurt. "You will definitely be sleeping in the dog house tonight unless you can get some of that poo off your backside."

"I doubt if I could get rid of the smell, it's even turning my stomach," Llewelyn replied with a wince.

"That will be a good introduction for your next sermon," Mrs. Rhys commented. "You do like to take situations in life to make your point. Here's a good one of you falling in the poo." She laughed heartily as she had never done before.

"And not to go in haste without waiting for instructions." Mrs. Rhys said looking at Dylan. They both chuckled.

"It says just that in the Bible. That is a very good idea. Maybe you would like to help me with the sermon when you come to Mothers' Union Thursday night?"

"I could do that and I'll try not to laugh, Llewelyn."

Llewelyn started to look embarrassed at the very thought.

"We better go home. Come on kids, it will be dark soon." Ethan was trying to gain his composure, as he enjoyed hearing the older folk making their humorous comments.

"Dad, I thought you said I could stay with the foal?" David fell into step with his father.

"Actually, David, if you were listening carefully you would have noticed I didn't say anything. I think your mam might want to hear about the foal first, so let's make haste. You can come back tomorrow after school."

David ran back to the barn with Angel to say goodnight to the foal.

"He looks so sad; I hope he's not in pain," Angel said.

Dylan was right behind them. "Well, let's see if he needs some more of Cradoc's magic massage - you only have to ask me." Dylan was pleased he was there to help. "It's a good thing he's not shoed yet, I wouldn't be able to do it."

"What do you mean shoed, Uncle?" David asked.

"Well, let's see how best to describe this. When horses are ready to work or race, and that is when they are about two years old, they need shoes on the bottom of their hooves, like the horseshoe your dad found in the basement."

"Like that? That is heavy and I think it's made from iron, isn't it?" David answered.

"That's right, they have to be made from iron so they last a long time."

Angel was interested and asked, "But why do they have to wear shoes?"

Dylan was good at explaining. "Like you when you go out, you put shoes on your feet to take care of your feet and not to get them dirty or cut from the ground."

"Where do they get the shoes and how do they put them on their feet, Uncle?" David, as always, was full of questions.

"The blacksmith, you know we have one here on the edge of Tonypandy. He makes the shoes over a very hot fire and bangs them into the shape of the horse's hooves, and then he puts it in very cold water to cool off. Finally, they are cool enough to be nailed on the underside of their hooves."

"Not all over his hooves like our shoes?" Angel asked, her dark eyes wide with surprise.

"No Angel. He only needs shoes under his hooves."

"On all four of his feet? Nails as well? Doesn't that hurt him?" She twisted her hands together, worrying.

"No, Angel. If the horse is ready for shoes then his hooves will be strong enough to have nails and it won't hurt. In fact, the horses seem pleased because they have shoes to walk on over rough paths, roads and up the mountains if they live on farms."

"How do you know the horses are pleased?" Angel wanted to know the details of the horses.

"Well, most times, they shake their head and make a nay sound and then woosh their tail. Those are the happy signs horses give us." Dylan smiled at the little girl.

"David where are you, is Angel with you? Come on, its time to go." Ethan returned to the barn, looking for the kids.

"You had better go now, and I'll finish off the massage. Then this foal will be sleeping contentedly, like a baby again." Dylan was a good instructor.

"Come on now, mam and Angel's Nene will be wondering where we got to."

"Dad, Uncle Dylan told us that horses wear shoes, I didn't know that." David walked beside his father, sharing what he'd just learned.

"Yes they do, to protect their hooves. The milkman has shoes on his horse. We can hear his horse a long way away, before we actually see the horse and the milkman in our street."

"So it's a warning signal? Like the train when it goes choo-choo before it comes into the station?" Angel asked.

"Yes, you could put it that way. The horse's shoes tell our street that the milkman is coming with our milk so we can have our churns and buckets filled up."

"The horse goes clipity-clop, clipity-clop." David was eager to give his interpretation.

Ethan turned to Angel. "Most times you will see our neighbors outside, ready. Like your Nene." Then he looked at David. "And your mam. As soon as they hear the noise from the horse's shoes they are outside waiting for the milkman." The children began talking to each other, leaving Ethan to walk in silence.

"We're almost home. Nene will be waiting for you, Angel. You can go with David tomorrow to see the foal, if it's alright with your Nene. I'm sure it will be alright with Mrs. Rhys."

Angel and David ran into the house.

"Nene, they found a foal and it's hurt. Can I go tomorrow and see it with David after school?" Angel was out of breath from skipping, then racing David into the house to ask for permission. "It's at the milkman's house. Please? Please? Nene. Can I go?"

"Oh my goodness, a foal." Nene was surprised as the milkman only had his old work horse.

"Mam, there's a foal at the milkman's house, can we go and see it tomorrow?" David spared his Mam all the details to make sure she heard him and he received her permission.

Mary and Lina looked at Ethan for some kind of explanation. "It's a long story, but we carried it down and he's now resting in the barn at the milk-farm."

"How did you find it?" Mary was as eager as David now, trying to get his answer.

"Go and wash your hands as Nene and Angel have to leave to go home." Both of them rushed out into the kitchen. When they were busy, Ethan continued. "There was a bloke up there crouched over. We could see him from a distance, and we rushed to see if he was alright. He was alright but there was an injured foal. This bloke said he had come across it but he was going to leave it like the other one. That made us all mad, very mad."

"How did you get it down?" Mary asked, careful to speak softly.

"We made a stretcher and carried him down." The children ran back into the room so Ethan cut the details short.

"See you tomorrow, Mary," Lina said, and Angel waved to everyone. Angel was tired. She could hardly find the words to say goodbye.

"David, you've had an exciting day. Please go and get ready for bed, you have school in the morning," Mary instructed.

David ran upstairs shouting, "Alright Mam."

"Alright then, what were you trying to tell me, Ethan?"

"I wanted to tell you there was a young English city bloke up there. He said he was measuring out his grandfather's land, as he wants to sell it. I was very upset. He said he found another foal and he just left it there. I had to do something. I couldn't leave this foal and let him die."

David came back into the room, "Mam, can I have some milk, please?"

"Yes, and you can take it up to bed with you, as it's getting late."

"Yippy." David was happy and poured his milk into a night mug and went upstairs to bed.

"Ian, are you still in the front room?"

"Yes Mam," he replied grudgingly. He believed he was too old for a bed time.

"Come on then, go to bed too, it's getting late. Don't forget to turn off the television."

"Alright Mam," Ian went upstairs. "Good night, Dad, good night, Mam."

"Goodnight, son." Ethan hadn't referred to Ian as his son for a while. It felt good.

Ethan continued to tell Mary about the English bloke. He was pacing around the room, still angry. "How can a person do that? He didn't seem to care either."

Chapter 24

"Good morning, Uncle," Ethan was eager to get started on the chores for the daily opening.

"Good morning, son. What an unusual day we had yesterday. I didn't sleep too well last night thinking about everything."

"I didn't either, Uncle. I cannot believe that someone would intentionally want to let an animal suffer like that."

"That attitude really was too much to bear hearing that bloke's comments about the foal he left behind and the one we brought down. And, then to top it all off, what he said about his grandfather's land. I got up several times in the night thinking about it all." Dylan was still upset.

"Uncle don't worry, I'm here to help you." Ethan immediately started with the batter, cutting the spuds, turning on the fat, and laying out the papers.

"I appreciate your help, son and I hope you know that. I see you are getting everything in order already. What a blessing you are to me," Dylan continued. "You know, I finally got out of bed about 4 o'clock. I just couldn't sleep after that."

"Uncle, don't worry so much. I'm getting it done for you. Just let me know if there is anything else I can help you with."

"You know, I should have bought his grandfather's land when I had the chance. He offered it to me, you know? When my brother Cradoc died, and then poor Clarenda, I didn't want to go on. I just wanted to bring my Olga and the babies down here. I was afraid. I didn't feel I had enough experience and knowledge about breeding horses and keeping the farm going. I learned a lot from my brother but I still felt I hadn't learned enough. I helped out and did his books but I wasn't the one that did all the hard work. He was. It broke my heart losing Cradoc and then Clarenda."

This was the first time Dylan actually admitted he was brokenhearted when Cradoc and Clarenda died. "Having to let those beautiful animals go, Oh my God. How could I take on more land without Cradoc? I had the money to buy it, that wasn't the problem. And I felt in my heart that Herbert would have almost given it to me. He said his sons weren't interested. It was getting too much for him so he moved down here with his youngest son and wife for a while and then his son went over the border when he died. God bless him. Oh God, he was a good man."

"His grandson wants to sell his land, what do you think? Would you buy it now?" Ethan wiped up after cutting the potatoes.

"Ethan my son, I am too old to work the land now. I just wish I hadn't been so eager to come down here. If I was younger, your age Ethan, I could get that fresh air and see the beauty that God created. To watch the sunrise and the sunset, hear the birds, watch the rabbits hop around and horses gallop past. That really would make me feel I was in heaven. It was so peaceful up there." He absently stirred the batter, his thoughts on the mountain.

"I could hear the wind rustling the leaves on the trees." A woodpecker pecked out his home in the tall fir tree that stood at the side of the house. He was a noisy bloke; busy taking care of his family.

"Oh, those were happy times, I miss them so much and my Olga and Clarenda would be singing softly in the rocking chairs on the porch. Even when I closed my eyes, I could see God's glory all around me."

"Uncle, you sound as though you really miss it."

"*Ìe*, I do that. It was the time I was so happy being alive even though it was tough. It was so endearing to me." Dylan was still, his eyes were closed, and tears fell gently down his cheeks. He turned to the picture of Olga on the wall and touched it gently, muttered something quietly and slipped away into his kitchen parlor. Ethan caught him crossing himself as he left the chippie. He looked around to see what chores were left to do. Finding nothing he looked toward the parlor.

Ethan followed slowly, waiting for his Uncle to gain his composure and asked, "Uncle, if somebody else bought the land what do you think they would do with it?"

"Well, that would have to be seen really. They could keep it just to own land, and not do anything with it. Some people do that, you know? But, if they were really smart they would start up a small farm even if it was a very small one raising chickens, cows, sheep, and get a horse or two and then branch out with those beautiful horses, wild horses and train them."

"Oh God. Not for the pits, Uncle?" Ethan straightened in alarm.

"No mun. Never. Those poor animals had a terrible life! Maybe train them for pleasure riding, horse riding schools or competition, something like that. Anyway, coal is coming to an end and the pits will all be closed eventually."

"Why didn't you sell grandfather's land?"

"I was hoping one day that one of you would want it and bring it back to life again. It's family land and you wouldn't have to buy it. You just take it. Start it up again where Cradoc left off."

"That would be difficult for some who didn't know the ropes."

"No it wouldn't be, Ethan. Don't be daft, mun. Those who have a sincere heart for animals and have the ability to work the land will be successful. Otherwise, they might as well not bother."

"Hm. Well, I wonder who he will sell his grandfather's land to." Ethan leaned against the doorway, crossing his arms.

"Maybe we should go and see the lady in the records department at the town hall. Now, what's her name? Oh my goodness, what is her name? If you like, we could do that Thursday if you are not busy, Ethan."

"Uncle. Since when have I been busy? I don't work down the pit anymore so life is so different.

It's slowed down. I am able to smell the daffodils, so to speak. But we have to open up, Uncle. Lunchtime and evening, we won't have time to go to the Town Hall."

"I've never thought of doing this, but I was told that Jim at the Cardiff Fish and Chips does it occasionally when they have to be away."

"Do what Uncle?"

"I was getting to that, son. Tomorrow I could cellotape a note to the door to say, 'Thursday only - closed for lunch and open for dinner.' Then our customers will know we are closed only in the morning but they can come and get their dinner."

"That sounds a good idea." Ethan was excited at the thought of putting a note on the door. "Are you sure, you don't mind closing in the morning to go to the Records Department?"

"Why not?" His good humor restored, Dylan was ready to start his day. "I could do with something else to keep me excited. Edith will let us know all the details." A sudden grin split his wrinkled face. "I remembered her name, Edith, that's right. Edith Matthews.

"That English bloke will have probably spilt his beans mentioning how eager he was to get rid of the land. We might even find out when he is thinking of putting his grandfather's land on the chopping block. In fact, we could check on the deeds for your grandfather's land, too." Dylan held up a finger.

Ethan didn't say anything but was far away in thought. Dylan studied him, happy knowing Ethan was coming along. It was in his straight shoulders, his half smiling face.

"Alright then, let's get the fish on, it's getting time."

"Oh it is; I was far away then," Ethan admitted.

"*Ìe*, you were son and I believe you were having good thoughts. You were smiling to yourself." Ethan let his lips curl into a full smile. There was much work to be done, time they got on with their daily routine.

On the way home from school Angel and David visited the milkman's farm to see if the foal was any better, but he wasn't in the barn. They ran to Mrs. Rhys almost in tears.

"What happened to the little foal? Where is he?" Angel pleaded.

"Oh, he's resting behind the barn with Kip." Kip was her Welsh sheep dog. Hard working, at that.

Angel and David rushed behind the barn to find the foal was lying in a pile of Mrs. Rhys's dandelion leaves. "Oh no," David gasped.

"Oh no, is he dead?" Angel twisted her hands, afraid to move closer to the foal. David elbowed her.

"Stop whining," he told her.

Mrs. Rhys came around the corner. "He was playing with Kip, and then started eating dandelion leaves. I expect with all the excitement he had today he was so tired he fell asleep eating his leaves. Kip seems to be equally as tired."

Oh what a sight, the foal, and the dog fast asleep in the dandelion patch behind the milkman's barn. Angel and David sat down beside them, relieved that they were alright.

"Angel, did you think of a name for him?" David asked as they settled into the grass.

"I've been thinking but I'm not sure. He is covered in patches of different colors so it would be difficult to call him Brownie, Chocolate or Coffee."

"I know. Let's call him Patch shall we?" David replied.

"I like that name, Patch. Yes, Patch." Angel clapped her hands together softly not to wake the sleeping animals.

"I think it will take a few days for Patch's leg to be completely healed. Sometimes it could take longer, maybe a couple of weeks," Mrs. Rhys told the children.

"How can he run on it with Kip, if it's not healed then?" David's curiosity knew no bounds.

"It truly amazed me, too but wild animals are resilient, they have to be. They take care of themselves, because there is no one that can take care of them other than their parents. But if they are left on their own, there is no one.

"Your great grandfather, Cradoc, he had a special way of taking care of his wild animals with love and kindness. Foals have an inward knowledge of knowing they must take care of themselves but they are very loyal to those humans who do take care of them. In this case it was good your dad found him, otherwise he could have died. He was really hurt and couldn't stand up. He was in bad shape but when he gets his strength back he can run and romp around again.

"If your dad hadn't found him it would have been disastrous. I think he would have eventually died." Mrs. Rhys saw their faces turn sad so she quickly said, "This is a smart foal, and I think the name Patch will fit him really well. Patch is not only a name given to a pattern on something like his fur, it also means other things. We put patches on our clothes because they have got torn or old and to last longer. I think because he was hurt your dad put another kind of patch on him, the splint." She wiped her hands on her pinny, nodding at them with a warm smile.

"Now I must get back to cooking my potato soup ready for my husband. He will be hungry."

"It's alright if Patch stays in the dandelion patch?" David asked.

"It's a soft bed for him to lay on and it won't hurt him. Kip is there and she will take care of him, too. If he wakes up his food is lying all around him!" She took a step, then she heard Angel.

"Kip will take care of the little foal?" Angel questioned.

"Oh yes, they're already friends. They have been prancing around that field as if nothing was wrong with Patch's leg. They saw a wild rabbit, that's what did it. It amazed me how well they got along; both of them chasing that poor rabbit. It got away just in time, I think.

"Come again tomorrow if you would like to visit, but make sure your parents know where you both are so your Nene won't be worried and neither will your mam. Alright?"

"Tatty bye, Mrs. Rhys. Thank you for taking care of Patch." Even in her young years Angel didn't want Mrs. Rhys to think they were ungrateful.

They were soon at David's house and dinner was already on the table. Angel was happy that her Nene was there so she could tell her about the foal and Mrs. Rhys's Welsh collie. It was a good evening. The two families had a lot to talk about. While the children were in the front room, Ethan shared with Mary and Lina what he had discussed at Dylan's.

"Uncle Dylan thinks we should go down to the Town Hall and check on the land papers."

"That will be a good idea. I was thinking just that when you were telling me about that English city bloke yesterday," Mary commented.

"I asked Uncle Dylan if he would buy the land next to grandfather's but he said he is too old now."

"Oh dear. He didn't say that, did he?" Lina gave a small snort. She'd fallen asleep in the rocking chair close to the warmth of the fire. Mary lowered her voice. "I hope he's alright. That reminds me, I was talking with Lina today. She said Gilberto might be coming again to see Angel around her birthday."

"When is Angel's birthday?"

"It's 4th of July, the same as American Independence Day."

"Oh yes. That's right, but they have big celebrations over there in America, it's in the newspapers. It's just another day here for us."

Angel came out of the front room and said, "Patch, the foal I mean, and Kip were chasing a wild rabbit." As soon as she saw her Nene dozing she lowered her voice.

"They were? Even with a broken leg?" Mary smiled assurance at her, asking a question to show all was well.

"Yes, Mrs. Rhys said that Patch was getting better because wild animals have a hidden instinct to take care of themselves sometimes."

"That's right, Angel. Did you know that there was once a king, that tried to kill all the wild rabbits in Wales because he said there were too many of them and they spread diseases?"

"How could he kill a little bunny rabbit?" Angel moved to the side of the table where Mary and Ethan sat.

"Sometimes people don't care about the little bunny rabbits, like they don't care about little foals, but it's the power they want to have over other people." Ethan noticed behind Angel, David looking very concerned. "It was a long time ago, in the Middle Ages actually."

"Oh, we were learning about the Middle Ages at school. The thatched rooves on some houses were from the Middle Ages but they can catch on fire," said David.

"Yes, that's true David," Mary replied. "They have some of those houses in Stratford-upon-Avon where Shakespeare lived. My goodness you are learning a lot at school these days. I don't think I learned anything like that until I was in high school."

Lina woke, listening to the conversation. She didn't move at first, soaking in the pleasant picture and the love in the house. They couldn't stay and that was a knife in her heart. She cleared her throat.

"Angel, it's time. We must go home before it gets too late; you have school tomorrow." She moved out of the chair and wrapped her shawl closer around her. Picking up Angel's little jacket, she walked to the door. "Good night everyone. Ethan it's so nice to hear that you will be going to the Town Hall soon." She helped Angel into her jacket and made sure she had her satchel.

"Yes, I'm actually looking forward to it now." Ethan nodded, he'd wondered if Lina overheard their soft conversation.

Angel ran back to see David. "Can I come with you tomorrow to see Patch?"

"Every day you can come with me," David answered with his eyes beaming and a broad smile. Even at a young age hearing David say those words warmed her heart. David had been her friend from far back as she could remember and she felt safe with him.

The next couple of days passed by quickly. Each day, the foal was getting stronger and enjoyed playing with Kip the collie. Mrs. Rhys was pleased because they didn't have but a few sheep left and a couple of cows for Kip to herd. It seemed that hard times had hit their pocket, too. But watching Patch and Kip have so much fun it was reassuring that a domestic dog and a wild foal could play happily together. To her and Mr. Rhys, the two new friends made them laugh a few times. Kip rolled over on to her back and rubbed her back into the dirt. Low and behold, Patch did the same. Almost as though he was copying her and scratching his back on the dirt. It was fun to watch them both.

Thursday came. Ethan met Dylan at his chippie and went down to the Town Hall together early as the doors opened. Dylan was dressed up as if he was going to Church and Mrs. Edith noticed. "What a striking man you are, Dylan, when you're all dressed up."

"Oh my goodness, now don't tell everyone that, they might be jealous. You admiring an old man." He smiled and brushed his hair behind his ears with his right hand. Perhaps he was a little embarrassed. Edith smiled at Ethan.

"Well now, how can I help you this morning, Dylan?"

"We saw a young whippersnapper from over the border up Penrhiwgwynt last weekend and he was going on about his grandfather's land, but he was on Cradoc's side. I'm a bit skeptical about him already and I don't even know him."

"I know who you are talking about. It's Herbert's great grandson, the city boy. He definitely isn't interested in the land, that's for sure. He's only interested in getting money. His grandfather would turn over in his grave if he knew." She shook her head and tsked.

"Well, he might now." Dylan nodded. Edith looked strange at Dylan's statement. "And yes, yes I believe he is turning over in his grave."

"For a minute I was wondering what you meant." Ethan was paying more attention now.

"Well, Edith. Perhaps you can help us. You know the land my brother Cradoc had? Do you have any records, plans, or pictures on it?"

"Funny you should ask that. That city boy asked me that too, but I had a good answer for him."

"What was that then?" Dylan enquired.

"Oh, I told him Cradoc's family were still alive so he had no business looking at anything to do with that land. He did look a bit surprised. Thought he could pull the wool over my eyes, he did," Edith went on.

"I'm glad he now knows that he can't shove his way through things." Dylan was pleased to hear her comments but he was still worried. If Herbert's grandson brought one of those city solicitor's with him, then her comments would be in vain.

"Well now, I found these when Mary came in some months ago," Edith continued, rustling papers behind the counter.

"When Mary came in?" Ethan was more than surprised. Mary hadn't told him anything about a visit to the property records department.

"Yes, she came in. Just enquired if we had any records on your grandfather's property. That's all."

"I don't know why she would. She didn't say anything to me."

"That's alright, Ethan. I did a quick search after she left and I found some other things that might be interesting to Dylan."

"What would that be Edith?" Dylan kept touching his neck but it looked like he was scratching it.

"Sit down, both of you, while I go back into the archives again. I put things in the corner for you. I knew eventually you would come in." She smiled with a wink and turned to find the items for them.

Dylan and Ethan sat for a while and then Dylan loosened his collar, leaving his tie hanging but still tied.

"Uncle, are you alright? You look like you might be in pain there?"

"Not pain exactly but my collar is rubbing on that blasted boil."

"Let's go to the chemist on the way back and see what the chemist might have for boils," Ethan suggested.

"It's a mustard poultice. That's all I need, but I might need to get some more mustard now I think about it. Remind me, will you, to go by the Co-op for some mustard."

Edith came back into the room with rolls of paper under her arm. "Alright then, this is what I found, Dylan."

"All that?" Ethan was surprised as Edith dropped the rolls of paper on the table.

"You might say your brother Cradoc took care of everything. Amazing, that may seem, as he didn't have time for the business side of things." Edith started laying them in order.

"Cradoc, you never forgot a thing. My God, you were a hard working good man."
Dylan again muttered, "You have no idea how much I miss you." Then blew his nose with his ragged handkerchief.

"Uncle, are you alright there?" Ethan was a little concerned.

"Ethan, when we older folk talk about our deceased family members we get a little emotional. We are truly Welsh, you could say. The Welsh are known for remembering, our memories are passed down through generations if the family members were indeed loved ones," Edith did her best to explain without causing too much anguish for Dylan.

Dylan composed himself. Folding his handkerchief, he put it back into his pocket and took his jacket off, folded it and placed it on the back of the old chair in the room. He rolled up his sleeves and adjusted his armbands to hold them in place. He took out his spectacles and put them on. He was a true gentleman, gentle in nature and a distinguished looking man when he was dressed up.

Dylan leaned over the table, opening up a few of the old rolled papers. Suddenly he sat back down crouching over his knees holding his head.

"Are you alright, Uncle?" Ethan asked.

"*Ìe, Ìe*, son. I am just staggered to think that we worked all those years up there on that land once," Dylan slowly got up from the chair. "Look, Ethan. The land ran all the way back over there. I had forgotten how much there was beyond the woods. What a sight on paper."

It was almost too much for that large sheet of parchment paper. To think that it had been scrolled up all those years. It was a lot for Dylan to comprehend. How wonderful it was being there in person with his brother, his thoughts lingered in the past.

"Where's Herbert's land, then?" Ethan asked. Studying the page and the marks. Dylan stood up straight.

"It's there, that part there." Dylan pointed to the rectangular shape of land.

"That was it?"

"Yes, that was it. And, now it looks so small compared to Cradoc's." Dylan had to sit down again, not only from leaning over the table, but because of the amount of land Cradoc owned. Dylan turned around towards the chair. "I must sit awhile and think."

Edith came back into the room. "Well now Dylan, you finally get to see for yourself all that land up there that's going to waste. Or should I say gone to waste?" She didn't mince words and didn't hesitate to put her few bob in the conversation.

Dylan sat motionless just as if he was in a trance.

"I'm going to make some tea, would anyone like a cuppa?" Edith obviously knew something was needed to bring Dylan back to the present. There was no response from either man. Edith repeated, "I'm going to make a cuppa, anyone want some?"

Ethan answered that he would like a cuppa and Dylan finally replied, "*Ìe* Edith, *Ìe*. A spot of tea, tea might be what I need right now." Dylan stuttered the words.

Ethan walked closer to Dylan and sat down on the next chair. Neither said anything until Edith came back into the room.

"Dylan." Dylan didn't move or look up. "Dylan *bach*, here's your cuppa." It was a few seconds before Dylan raised his head. His cheeks were wet and his eyes were bloodshot as though he had cried rivers of tears.

"Come on now, Dylan. It's alright to be sad but you can't go on like this. Cradoc is resting with his Clarenda up there on Penrhiwgwynt, enjoying the changes of the seasons as we speak. He knows how much you loved him." Edith handed Dylan his cup of tea and patted him on the shoulder. "I put two sugar lumps on the saucer for you. If you want more, I have plenty." Then Edith handed Ethan his cup with sugar lumps on the saucer, also.

Edith went out of the room and then appeared with her cup of tea and digestive biscuits and sat down on a nearby chair. "Ethan love, hand the tin to your Uncle. I think he could do with a biscuit and help yourself, Ethan."

Ethan took the tin from Edith and handed it to Dylan without making any conversation. Ethan knew his Uncle was clearly lost in time. Dylan slowly took a biscuit and dipped it in his tea and then held it to his mouth. "Edith, what do we have to do to claim Cradoc's land?"

"Nothing really, it's yours. You were his only brother, and if I'm not mistaken you are also mentioned in the register under ownership. Let me finish my cuppa and I will look and see." Edith drank the remainder of her tea, patted her lips with a serviette, and went into the document chamber.

Edith found the set of old leather books and took the one marked "E" from the shelf, blowing the dust off it as she returned to the room. "Here it is, now we can see. I am sure Evan told me your name was in this register on the land, besides your fish and chip chippie." Edith opened the leather book on the table and turned the pages until she found the right one. "Now look-e-here, he was right, Dylan. Your name is here next to Cradoc's." She pointed her wrinkled finger towards his name.

Dylan stood up, his slender body slightly bent in sadness. He wiped his face with his handkerchief and carefully folded it back up and put it back into his pocket. He leaned forward to the book but had to control his trembling by steadying himself with his two knuckles on the table.

"Uncle, are you alright? Let me get the chair up closer so you can sit down." Ethan watched him closely.

"No, no. I'm alright, that I am, alright. I need to stand. I'm not used to sitting you know. I don't sit. No I don't sit, until my work is done in the chippie." Dylan seemed a little flustered but took a deep breath and composed himself. "Now where did you say you saw my name?"

Dylan tried to pull himself together but Edith saw that he was still very emotional. Trying not to bring too many memories to the forefront.

"It's right up there, Dylan. I see your name. Can you see it?" He looked through his spectacles, following her pointed finger.

"Oh yes." She shut the book quickly. "Now Dylan, there's some more papers I want to show you."

"More papers for what?" Dylan was now more perplexed at the very thought.

"Well, Herbert apparently started transferring his land to you when he came down here. The land was listed as Cradoc Brothers annexed land. You remember when he went to live with his son here in Porth? His son wasn't interested and he didn't move over the border until your dear friend Herbert died."

"He did? Herbert annexed land to us? I didn't know that."

"Well, he did. In those last few years when Herbert was living, he annexed more and more of his land to you and Cradoc. That left the rectangle you saw and pointed out to

Ethan as Herbert's land. That rectangle was what was left. He knew his son wasn't a farmer or a countryman but thought his son would eventually take it and build a house up there and a small holding, perhaps for his growing family to visit. Instead, his son forgot all about it and he passed away after a few years over the border."

"This English bloke must be Herbert's great grandson?" Ethan asked.

"Yes, he must be. The memory of some land was handed down from family to family but nothing was ever done about it and no one enquired about it either." Edith shrugged her shoulders, explaining it to Ethan.

"Does he know it's such a small portion of land?" Ethan interrupted.

"No, I doubt it. He didn't have any documentation with him and I didn't let him see anything either. He was only interested in your Uncles' land. That struck me as very odd, very odd indeed."

"Oh my goodness, this is really too much to comprehend." Dylan was flabbergasted at the vast amount of land. "Edith, so was the land beyond the woods once Herbert's land? Is that the annexed land? I don't really remember it jutting beyond the woods."

"Let me get the other plans, maybe you can see it better. It has a different type of legend on it." She left the room.

"Uncle, how much land is up there then? I thought when we saw that English bloke that was basically the border of the land."

"No, it wasn't the border of land and I didn't want to talk to him about where our land ended and Herbert's was. Obviously, I hadn't got an idea either. Oh my goodness, it's going to take a very good solicitor to sort this out."

"Now what do you need a solicitor for?" Edith had heard Dylan talk as she came back into the room. "The land is fair and square yours. There's no doubt about it. Look at this."

She unrolled a much bigger scroll of parchment on to the table and said to Dylan, "See, look here then, Dylan." She pointed. "See the markings and the dates and those numbers?"

"*Ìe,* I do see them," Dylan replied. "But, what does all that mean?"

"Dylan, come on now." She didn't believe that Dylan did not understand and she was right as she pointed.

"Yes. E 6.7p17. 'E' for Edwards, 6.7 for 6th July, p17 for page 17," Dylan identified.

"That's right, Dylan. Let me go and get Register E." She returned with a longer book, leather bound with metal corners. "Register E. Let's turn to 6 July then." She flipped through pages. "Here it is. Now we go to page 17. Here Dylan, what does that say?"

Dylan read aloud, "Land marked by Herbert Griffiths this 6th day of July and annexed to Cradoc and Dylan Edwards value "0". What?" He looked to Edith for clarification. The deed showed the land had no value. "No value. How could that be?"

Edith explained, "Herbert gave you the land for free."

"What?" That was as much as Dylan could say at the time.

"Dylan, read the next portion marked on the parchment, will you?" Edith asked.

Dylan looked at the parchment, at the next portion identified, reading that aloud again. "E 15.1p37. for Edwards, 15 January page 37." He translated the code for a puzzled Ethan.

Edith turned to the pages carefully not to cause damage. "Here it is. That was easy to find."

"How many annexations did he make, Edith?"

"Actually Dylan, he divided the land up for his seven children, but not one of them showed any interest in claiming it. So, as he found out their intentions he annexed each part over a period of time to you, but kept one part for the son who lived here in Porth." She placed her palm over the book, flat out. "*That's* the land, Herbert's great grandson that you met, is entitled to."

"But, that's not a lot of land left for Herbert's great grandson, is it?" Dylan asked.

"That's not your concern, Dylan. That's what Herbert wanted so that is how it was done, legal and binding. There's nothing you can do unless you want to give up the land that Herbert gave you and Cradoc all those years ago. You know Herbert's great grandson doesn't want it and is eager to sell it." Edith glanced between them, their heads bent over the book, the information sinking in slowly.

"Uncle, I think you should keep it. Herbert must have cared a lot about you and grandfather Cradoc."

"Son, what am I going to do with all that land? I'm too old to start tilling the land and rearing horses. Oh my God."

"Uncle, it's getting late we must get back to the chippie."

"Oh my goodness. Yes, time is going by." Dylan turned to Edith. "Thank you Edith, but now I have more worries than I wanted to think about."

Edith walked them to the door and quietly said to Dylan, "Take care of that boil, will you? They get very, very painful if it gets infected."

"*Ìe,* I remember, I will do that. We're going past the Co-op on the way back, so I will get more mustard."

Dylan and Ethan walked quietly towards the Co-op shop. Neither felt they wanted to talk about Cradoc's land, let alone Herbert's annexation.

"Good day to you Dylan, and to you Ethan. It's a surprise to see you today. Your chippie not opening today?" Gwyneth said.

"For dinner we will be open," Dylan replied.

"Oh that so, you must have been busy this morning then?" Gwyneth was a busy body minding everyone's business except for her own.

"Let's see. I need a large box of mustard and a large vinegar please, malt vinegar," Dylan asked.

"You putting mustard out for everyone now, are you?" she asked with raised brows.

"No, I just like a spot of mustard myself sometimes."

"Well, you won't want a big one then, will you?" She was nosy and Dylan had no time for busy bodies.

"I'll take a large one this time, I won't have to worry; it will last me a long time then."

"Oh no, Dylan you won't want a big one, I'll get you a small one," she insisted.

"Gwyneth, I would like a large box of mustard, please." Dylan spoke slowly and clearly so she would not mistake his order.

"Dylan, you won't want that much surely? I'll get two small boxes so one won't go off if you have it a long time."

"Gwyneth, I want one large box and the large vinegar. We must go. No time for chit chat this morning."

Dylan was determined not to say he needed a large box of mustard for his boil. He was in pain already and didn't need to be dilly-daddling around while she continued to argue about the size of the mustard box in the hopes he would tell her what he really needed it for.

"Oh, Dylan. I was only trying to help you. Don't get your knickers in a twist, mun." She realized she'd been abrupt.

Dylan thought, "it's time to take matters into my own hands. She is always trying to push me around or correct me on my purchases."

"Gwyneth, my dear lady. If I say I want a large box, I want a large box. So be kind enough to put my order of the large box of mustard and the large bottle of vinegar in a bag and then tell me how much I owe you. And, by the way, it is you who wear the knickers, not me. So be a good lady and don't get yours in a twist until I leave the shop." Dylan came right out with what he was thinking.

"Alright then, if you put it like that. The vinegar is one and six and the mustard is one and three, making a total of two and nine. Two shillings and nine pence to be exact." She put out her hand without another word.

Dylan was now exasperated. He took a deep sigh and gave her the money without a comment, one half crown and thrupence. As he clasped the bag in his hand he said, "Thank you, Gwyneth, my good lady."

From his demeanor she understood very well he had had enough of her nosiness and her comments.

Outside the air was fresh and the sun was making an effort to hold its head high for the rest of the day. Bobbie rode his bike tinkling his bell to announce he was there and waved as he went past. "I will see you this evening, Mr. Taff, for my usual."

"*Ìe* Bobbie, *Ìe*," Dylan shouted. That eased the tension that Dylan was feeling enough to utter some comments to Ethan. "Oh my God, that woman. She is enough to drive me up the wall."

"She was a bit nosy. I wonder if she is like that with Mary?"

"No doubt," Dylan answered. "In fact, she is so nosy that she would ask the most personal questions in a way you wouldn't realize they were personal to you by the comments she makes."

"Then I will avoid her as much as possible," Ethan confirmed.

"*Ìe*, it would be better that way, *le* it would." They chuckled, putting the confrontation behind them.

There was still a little way more to walk and Ethan kept silent until Dylan wanted to talk.

"Well, we're almost there. I'll go home and change. Will that be alright, Uncle? I'll come as soon as I've changed to get the dinner started."

"*Ìe*. That will be a good idea. By then, I should be calmed down from that busy body, Gwyneth."

"Oh Uncle, don't let her upset you like this. Sometimes when I was down the pit all those years, I would have wished for someone to flutter their feathers just to bring a different atmosphere down there. All we could do in between coughing and spitting was to sing. We certainly had a good pit choir. We had those poor horses as our audience."

"Those poor buggers! What a life they had. Up and down, up and down those tracks. No sunshine or fresh air to inhale. May God forgive us what we have done to the creatures He created."

"Uncle, I'll see you in a bit, alright."

"Alright son. I'll be there."

Dylan walked back to his shop and Ethan went back home to change.

Lina was coming up the street. "Hello, Nene Lina, coming up to wait for Angel?"

"Actually, yes and no. Ethan, you look mighty fine in those trousers."

"Thank you. I think you were with Mary when she bought them from the Tailor shop. Mary said they had a big sale going on. They were selling off items that weren't picked up."

"Yes, that's right. I certainly enjoyed myself with Mary finding bargains. I always do."

"Well, I'm glad you both found these trousers. They fit just right, and they don't need any alterations. In fact, Mary said they are in fashion with the turn ups."

"They certainly are in fashion."

Ethan held the door open for Lina and they both walked into the hallway. "I'm home love, I'm just going up to change. Nene Lina is here." Up the stairs he ran to change into his work clothes to help Dylan.

"Hello, Lina. You look a little more rested today. Are you feeling a bit better?"

"I am a bit. I never feel like I have any energy though."

"Come and sit down. I have something to tell you, Lina." Mary put the kettle on and got out the pretty cups and saucers, spoons, and matching plates and then brought out the tin of biscuits Mary made that morning.

"Mary, are we celebrating something important? You have the best china out. What is it? I can't wait."

"Alright then, kettle will be boiled in a minute. Look, I made some digestive biscuits from the recipe you gave me. I'll get some chocolate when the Co-op has a sale and I can make chocolate digestives then. Just a minute, sorry Lina, I must run upstairs and ask Ethan something before he goes."

Lina sat quietly and patently, although she was anxious to hear Mary's news.

"Ethan, well, what news do you have? I want to tell Lina, she has been waiting for this day when you and Dylan go and see about your grandfather's land."

"Oh, what a shock. There's more land than Uncle Dylan even thought of. Herbert annexed most of his land to my grandfather and Uncle Dylan.

"I'm sorry. I don't understand. What does annexed mean?" Mary needed clarification of something she had never heard about before.

"I must be quick, love." Ethan was tucking his shirt into his old trousers and doing up his belt. "Uncle is waiting so I can help him with dinner time." Ethan put on his shoes without untying the shoelaces. Mary noticed he squeezed his feet into them.

So this is where Ian gets it from, she thought to herself. All these years she'd been telling Ian he was lazy for not untying his shoes before taking them off, so when he puts them back on they are still done up and sometimes are in knots.

"I've got to be quick, Herbert added his land to Cradoc and Uncle Dylan's land, free. That's what annexation means. I'll tell you the rest when I get back."

"What?"

"Exactly, it's a shock that Uncle Dylan is having difficulty with. You can tell Lina; she might know what that means better than me. Also, he has one bit left. Herbert I mean, or rather his great-grandson that English bloke we saw up on Penrhiwgwynt. Got to go now." Ethan kissed Mary on the lips quickly and rushed down the stairs and out the door. Mary followed, but at a slower pace and back to the kitchen.

"Mary dear, is everything alright? I saw Ethan run out the door?" Lina showed concern.

"Oh, yes. Everything is alright. At least I think so. Let me make the tea now, the kettle is boiled." Mary filled the teapot and placed it on the tablemat on the table.

"I don't know exactly what this means, but Ethan said I could tell you and you might know what it means." There was a short silence and Mary caught her breath before repeating what Ethan had said.

"Herbert annexed his land to Cradoc's and Uncle Dylan's land before he died. Uncle Dylan didn't know and Herbert has one small piece of land left."

Lina thought for a moment and then repeated, "You are saying that Herbert gave most of his land to Cradoc and Dylan without them knowing?"

"Yes, I think that's what it means. Annexing I mean. Does it mean giving away?"

"As far as I understand that is right. Herbert added his land to Cradoc's and Dylan's."

There was a quietness before Mary spoke. "Lina, please help yourself to the biscuits and tell me did I hear things. Is that right?"

"If Ethan said that Herbert annexed his land to Cradoc and Dylan's land, then that definitely means adding it to their land, giving it to them, and if they didn't know it means the land was free." She shook her head, chose a biscuit to nibble. She wasn't hungry but needed something to help her think.

"What a man Herbert was. He loved to the bitter end. He loved his wife and his children and his friends, Cradoc and Dylan. Herbert's children had no interest in any land up there. They went to live in cities in England. They deserted him here, after all the things he did without for his family."

"Did Herbert live in England, then?"

"No, he lived here in Porth with one of his sons. Herbert's youngest son lived here in Porth until Herbert died. He didn't put Herbert into a nursing home, although his wife wanted him to. His wife was from over the border, she wasn't Welsh."

"I didn't know we had any English living here."

"There's just a few, not very many in South Wales."

"Why not, they don't like Wales?" Mary humphed, taking affront at the very thought of not liking Wales.

"They probably don't like the weather." Both Lina and Mary laughed. "It's always wet." They laughed some more.

"They don't like the Welsh really, although if you asked them they would say different. It's because the Welsh are not rich people but they work hard. The Welsh are mostly miners or farmers and of course singers."

"So Herbert was able to spend the rest of his days with his son?" Mary asked.

Lina definitely wanted to make a point, although she was always soft spoken. "That's how it should be. Spend the rest of your life with your family or your dear friends, not be uprooted and taken away if you are old or sick. That's the true Welsh culture, to care for your loved ones just like they do in the Mediterranean."

"Have you ever been to the Mediterranean, Lina?" Mary was interested.

"I don't think so, but I have seen it in my dreams. My mam used to tell me about it. It is so beautiful. She told me that Italians made wine from the grapes that grew over their door and down the pathway. Made brandy out of apricots. Olives and figs grew on trees in the fields and the fish was so fresh it had just been caught from the sea.

"You could see the sea beyond the green fields. It sounded so beautiful, just like Penrhiwgwynt. When I was young I always wanted to go and see for myself but of course my father wouldn't have let me go anywhere."

"He didn't? Why not." Mary looked so sad.

"He had his perfect person in mind and I wasn't it, neither was my sister, Mari. Mari lives in Erdington, Birmingham. She always said if she didn't marry Arthur, she would run away."

"Who was Arthur?"

"We used to call him Arthur the Great. Because he came along just in time to rescue Mari. Mari always said that. Arthur was Ernesto's brother.

"Ernesto was my knight in shining armor. He came along when my father was in one of his bad moods. My father was a tailor but business wasn't very good then. Ernesto was so handsome, tall, slender, same color skin like me, and dark eyes."

"Really? I never met Ernesto, did I?" Mary sipped her tea.

"No, love. He died a very long time ago. Gilberto and his brother were very young then. It's funny, you know, when I think about it. Gilberto has darkish skin and blue eyes and so does one of Mari's sons. My father would turn over in his grave if he knew that." Lina shook her head as she remembered.

"Knew what, Lina?

"That Gilberto had olive skin and blue eyes. I think my father hated me because I had that same color skin, too. He always said I wasn't his daughter and my Mam would cry all night and be so sad."

"Angel has your color of skin, a nice deep rich olive, much like Ethan's. Except I always used to tease Ethan about it, and say he still had coal on his face and needed to wash his face again."

"Ethan is so handsome, those dark rich ringlets and his skin tone and when he smiles he reminds me so much of my Ernesto. I miss him so much." Tears rolled down Lina's face.

"Oh Lina, please don't be sad. You have Gilberto, his son, and Angel she loves you so much."

"I know, I know and that's what I worry about."

The door swung open. "Mary, love, I've come back for those things David and Ian found in the basement. I must show them to Dylan now." He ran down the stairs to the basement. On his way up he said, "Did you tell Lina about Herbert's land?" and through the front door he went as fast as he could.

Mary was trying to cheer Lina up a bit. "Was that Ethan, or did I imagine his handsome chops running through the house?" Lina did laugh.

"Oh my goodness. I used to say something like that to Gilberto when he was young, now wash that biscuit off your handsome chops. How memories come back."

"It's getting a bit late Mary, do you think Angel and David are alright? I know Angel said they would be walking past the milkman's farm."

"Do you fancy a bit of a walk Lina, and we can talk while we walk there?"

"I think that might be good. I'd rather be walking towards the farm than sitting here worrying about them."

"Alright then, I'll take me pinny off and put me shoes on. Ready?" Mary dropped her y's sometimes and referred to e's instead when she tried to make others happy.

Both ladies left the house and walked towards the milkman's farm. On the way, they passed Dylan's chippie. Mary tapped the window as they walked past.

Ethan ran quickly to the door and called, "Hhmm! Now. Who's that pretty little thing going down the road?" Mary turned and gave him a smile and Ethan blew her a kiss. It was good to see the romance still left inside of them both after such a hard life.

"Lina, I don't think I finished telling you about Herbert's land. Ethan said that Dylan got very upset."

"But why would he get so upset?"

"I think he realized how much Herbert cared about them, grandfather Cradoc and Uncle Dylan I mean. Uncle Dylan and grandfather Cradoc were Herbert's best friends, and also Vicar Llewelyn. They got along really well."

Chapter 25

Soon they were at the farm. There were David and Angel, sitting on the fence, watching Patch and Kip playing. Every time Kip rolled over, so Patch tried it. It was a bit more difficult for a foal, especially one with a broken leg. Then, when Kip stood up on her back paws, Patch tried to do the same. Then they would chase each other around the field, then flop down and roll over again.

Mrs. Rhys came out of the farmhouse when she saw Lina and Mary. "Look at those two. You wouldn't think that they would be such good friends and Patch's leg has healed so quickly. I am going to miss Patch when it's time for him to leave us."

David shouted, "Can Patch stay? Please?"

Then Angel chimed in, "Oh please? Can Patch stay with Kip?"

"Kip will be so lonely again," David piped in.

"Well, I thought about that myself but I'll have to talk with my husband, Mr. Rhys first. He may say it will be too much work for us as we are getting on a bit."

"We can help," shouted Angel.

David shouted, "Promise Mrs. Rhys, we can help!"

"Well now, I will have to talk with my husband, like I said."

Mrs. Rhys reassured Lina, "They will always be safe if they stop here. What about us all having a spot of tea together? I'll have the kettle on in no time. Come on now?"

Mrs. Rhys ran into the house kicking up her heels as though someone had put a match to her underneath! Most probably to alarm Mr. Rhys that two women would be coming into the house so he should do up his trouser buttons and pull up his bracers.

Mr. Rhys always used to slouch in his armchair with his bracers down and his trouser buttons undone so he could digest his food better, or so he said.

Lina knew that, so she tapped the window in the kitchen door and patiently waited until she heard, "Come in," before they entered the farmhouse.

Mr. Rhys was making an effort to flatten down his hair and not look such a mess as he normally did when he took a nap. It was funny really, almost hysterical. In his own house he felt he needed to jump up and also pat the cushions he had been slouching on. It made everything more noticeable. Lina fought her smile at his antics. He wasn't fooling anyone.

"Here we are, gather round my kitchen table. Here's some lardy cakes and custard pies. Mr. Rhys loves his custard pies. I have plenty, so please help yourselves."

David and Angel came running in behind the ladies. "Oooh, is that lardy cake and oooh, custard pies?"

"Yes, you can both have some. Go and wash your hands first then come and sit down at the table," Mrs. Rhys told the children with a smile.

David ran to the sink almost knocking over Angel. "Come on, wash your hands and we can have some of that lardy cake," David nudged Angel to get a move on.

"Alright," Angel said slowly. And followed David to the kitchen sink.

A few minutes later, "Right then, everyone at the table?" Mrs. Rhys asked, glancing around at her full table. "Well, let's say a prayer of thanksgiving for the beautiful day, and the tea and cake, shall we?" Mrs. Rhys announced.

"Oh, can I say the prayer please?" David interrupted.

"Why of course, David. That is kind of you." Mary looked inquisitively at David, as he stood and Mrs. Rhys nodded.

David started, "Thank you, Lord for this lovely day, bless this food we are about to eat and may the Lord make us truly thankful."

Mrs. Rhys was about to say her Amen, just like everyone else but David continued, "And Lord, can Patch stay with Kip please? Amen." Mrs. Rhys started laughing and so did Lina and Mary. Mr. Rhys was oblivious to anything more that David had said and was in his own little world enjoying his cup of tea and his cake. Mrs. Rhys winked at David and Angel. David nudged Angel and they both smiled at her and each other.

"Now then, anyone interested in another cup, as I'm going to fill the kettle up and boil the water again."

"Oh yes, please," said Lina. "What tea leaves are you using Mrs. Rhys? Are they PG tips or the new one they have in the Co-op this week; Lipton's Ceylon Tea leaves? It's very nice."

Mr. Rhys chimed in, "Very nice. Very nice indeed. Yes, nice indeed. I'll have another cuppa as well if I may, please," in a posh uppity voice.

"If you may, for goodness sake. Who are you trying to impress today?" Mrs. Rhys flicked her cloth at his shoulder as she reached for his cup. "Putting on your airs and graces in front of the ladies. It's Lina and Mary, not Mrs. Evans." All the ladies laughed, including Mrs. Rhys.

Mr. Rhys continued, "I was only kidding. It's good to have a joke now and again. It is you know." Everyone agreed by nodding their heads. They were all too eager in eating those delicious pies and cake that Mrs. Rhys had made.

"Oh my goodness, just look at the time. I forgot. I must go to Dylan's and get fish and chips." Mrs. Rhys suddenly realized it was almost 6 o'clock. "Anyone want fish and chips? It's my special treat?" she asked and everyone acknowledged they would like fish and chips, too.

"Looks like everyone is going to leave me," Mr. Rhys said. He waited for the last person to go thru the door and was ready to settle back down on his chair, but first undoing his top button on his trousers and pulling down his braces. This time he undid his shirt collar and took it off by undoing the button at the neckline at the back of his shirt and laid the detachable collar on the table next to his chair. Pulling out his shirt, he picked up the South Wales Echo newspaper and sat down on his chair, reaching over for his spectacles, lying on the table.

"Peace at last!"

Ethan was pleased to see Mary at Dylan's chippie. "What brings you here at this time, my love?" Ethan looked at everyone.

"Mr. Rhys and I are happy to announce we are having another member of the family."

There was silence. What? Mr. and Mrs. Rhys were having a baby? The silence thickened. 'No this can't be' was repeated in everyone's mind.

Everyone sighed, Mr. and Mrs. Rhys were in their senior years and the small group of neighbors couldn't imagine that Mrs. Rhys might be pregnant like Sarah in the Bible. Mrs. Rhys quickly let out, "Patch is going to stay with us, unless he wants to go back up the mountain, but I have a feeling he likes it too much on our farm with Kip."

"You really mean it; Patch can stay?" David shouted.

"Patch can stay?" Angel followed.

Ethan was delighted and so was Dylan, even in the middle of being busy with serving fish and chips there was a sudden lightheartedness in the shop. The children had been so much happier in recent days since Patch came. Everyone, was happy and chattering loudly.

"I think we are having a party so let's be comfortable. Go in? Go into the parlor? Everyone go in, eat your fish and chips at the table."

"That's a good idea. I'll get one of Dylan's plastic table cloths, then we don't need to dirty plates, we can eat out of the newspaper wrapping." Lina was ready to get the kettle on to boil.

"Let me do it, Lina. You look a little tired, sit down a while."

"Thank you, Mary. Thank you."

Mary had the kettle on and cups ready.

Dylan and Ethan were discussing the land while they were cleaning up and finally got to sit down and enjoy some conversation.

Dylan was still in shock with the amount of land that Herbert had annexed to him. His main concern now was what was he going to do with it, in addition to his own land. He certainly didn't want it to sit there with no real purpose like it had over the years. There were reasons why Dylan and Olga didn't stay up there after Cradoc and Clarenda died.

Dylan wasn't really a mountain man. He couldn't do what Cradoc did, but he loved Cradoc and supported him the best way he could. Cradoc was considered as fierce as a lion and yet gentle as a lamb, whereas Dylan was more placid all the time.

The best course of action would be to encourage Ethan to at least give it some thought about moving to a farm life rather than just ambling around in Porth and living from day to day.

Dylan thought about his own life. Where was it going? He too lived from day to day keeping busy so he wouldn't be depressed and think about his old life with his dear wife, Olga. He missed his family life with her up on the mountaintop and with Cradoc and Clarenda. Now that was just a memory. He thought that he would probably pass away from old age sooner than later. After all he was near 90 years of age.

His sons had gone and had no thoughts of coming back to South Wales and what would become of Taff's Fish and Chip Shop? His little 'chippie' would be boarded up and possibly auctioned off for pennies to some interested bidder.

He could not see young people having a real interest in a Fish and Chip shop as a business. City life, sports, travel, and stardom were more on their mind. Most young people were leaving because they considered South Wales was dying from lack of industry, coal mines closed, the Corona Pop factory was being considered to be bought out by an unannounced interested party, and houses were left empty as the older generation passed on. He had drifted into depressing thoughts more than once in the last couple of days.

Dylan didn't want the farmland he shared and worked hard with Cradoc to be abandoned any longer and now with extra land it seemed a double burden on his shoulders. He had a real love once for the wilderness and wild life. The hard work he and Cradoc invested would be wasted.

He was sure under the surface of the land, even though it was covered with overgrown brambles and grass, there laid fertile soil ready for harvesting any crop and enough extra land for stables and breeding livestock.

The old homes they once shared could be rebuilt, the foundations and the well were still there and would stay till eternity.

But Dylan needed help to interest Ethan enough to look at the whole property and interest him in possibly moving his family up the mountain, away from the town, to the countryside and enjoy the land of his grandparents.

There was much to gain for Ethan, if he would search his heart. He had three sons at home. The others were out of the house and faring well, considering other people's standards.

Ethan needed to visit the mountaintop and be acquainted with the land, but quickly. Time was passing for all of them. Maybe if he could suggest a visit over the next weekend would help Ethan. Sunday would be good for Dylan as his chippie is closed and after Church would be the best time for Llewelyn if he would like to join them. Dylan needed to talk with Llewelyn and find out if he would like to go, too. His wife would be busy cooking and puttering around as she did most Sundays. His wife, Pagua was Greek from Athens and had a fiery temper, she loved to play her music loud and Llewelyn would rather be out of the house than be in the house with her.

Dylan brought himself back to the present when a loud knock was heard at the door.

"Hello Dylan, I have news for you. One of our Bobbies was taking a stroll with his Mrs. across the mountain and he saw some young bloke banging stakes into the ground. I was wondering if you knew who he was. I thought for a moment you might have sold your land up there and he was the new owner."

Everyone in the parlor stopped to listen at the conversation. "No I haven't sold any land. Where was he exactly?" Dylan was more than curious now.

"Our Bobbie said he was close to the woods. I am not sure exactly, but I can get him to come and tell you, when he's next on duty."

"*Ìe*. that might be a good idea. We saw some English bloke up there last weekend but we didn't see any stakes with him. He was leaning over a foal that had injured his leg and I didn't particularly like his attitude. He didn't care if the foal was injured and needed help. Thank God Ethan was there."

"Is that so, was he near the woods or somewhere else?"

"Actually, we saw him on Cradoc's land. He said he was Herbert's great grandson."

"Oh yes, I've heard about him. It's funny that you should mention him. People are saying he's some young city bloke wanting to sell his great grandfather's land for a quick bob."

"*Ìe*, that's him."

"Well let me know if there's anything we need to know about up there. Anything that's not in order, anything you think might be against the rules. You know, anything that's against the law."

Why didn't he say 'might be against the law' in the first place instead of mincing around like a little mouse, Dylan thought to himself. "I might need your assistance if I find him on Cradoc's land," Dylan assured him.

Ethan returned from the parlor into the shop. "What was all that about, Uncle?"

"Bobbie just confirmed that Herbert's great grandson might be marking off land for his revenue."

"Well, he can't do that if it doesn't belong to him." Ethan's hair was starting to stand up on end.

"We must go up there again, Ethan, and find out what's going on. We can take the kids and Llewelyn. I think Llewelyn would like a break away again."

"Doesn't his wife complain?"

"He was telling me that his Mrs. and her loud music were getting on his nerves."

"I never thought Vicar Llewelyn ever complained about his wife."

"He doesn't, but lately she's been really fiery again. She's never held anything back, you know. His own words were, if he keeps his mouth shut he learns much and the only way he can keep his mouth shut is by reassuring himself God is there in the midst of all her anger. He thinks another trip to Greece is imminent."

"I didn't know that Vicar Llewelyn liked to fly."

"No, he won't go by plane but he will drive his little car across to Greece like he did a few years ago. He tells me all the time that His divine mercies blessed his car for many more journeys to come." Dylan was a little amused but then he himself believed there were miracles performed to those that God sees fit.

"Do you want me to get Llewelyn, he's sitting talking with Lina. The kids are playing with your dominoes."

"No, no don't interrupt him if he's talking with Lina, I hope he is giving her a blessing. She certainly does need a blessing, better still a miracle."

"Has she heard anything from the doctor yet?"

"If she has she isn't letting me know. I need to sit down and talk with her again. She is looking very worried all the time, but she says she's only tired. I don't believe that of course."

"Maybe Vicar Llewelyn can ask her. He is a man of the cloth."

"Talking about Llewelyn, did I tell you he was a Chaplin in the Army? That's how he met his wife, he was in Athens at the time. Then when he retired from the Army he came here with his family, by then they had a little boy. But now Llewelyn is talking about going to Cambridge. He's been offered a professor's position in the Chemistry and Mathematics Departments of the University."

"Oh my goodness he has those type of degrees, too?" Ethan was very surprised.

"Oh yes, a couple of them actually. You know he's already a retired Army Chaplin," Dylan repeated himself. "He worked hard since he was a boy, just like Gilberto. It will be really sad if he goes. Porth won't be the same without him and you know St. Paul's will have to find another Vicar."

"I didn't think of that. Will he go before they find another Vicar?"

"That depends on the Archbishop. Llewelyn wants to be closer to his mam, Mari. That's Lina's sister, you know? She's not been in good health either. Personally, I think she has worked too hard just like Lina. She looked after her children and her grandchildren too when her husband died. Her husband was Ernesto's brother."

"You mean Lina and her sister, Mari married Ernesto and his brother, Arthur?"

"*Ìe* , that's right."

"Oh my goodness, what a coincidence. Did any of Mari's children have olive skin and blue eyes like Gilberto?"

"Funny that you should ask."

"Mari had three boys and one girl, Trevour, Llewelyn, Selina and Clifford. Trevour was the oldest and a missionary in Africa but he never came home. Mari was told he died there but no body was sent back and his mam never knew what really happened. Strange that is. Llewelyn is here, the Vicar, as you know. Selina married a pilot in the Air Force and had one child, Sandra, about Angel's age. Now Clifford, the youngest son, still lives with his mam. He has olive skin and blue eyes, and he's roughly the same age as Gilberto. Clifford was Mari's youngest boy. She spoiled him really."

"What do you mean by that?"

"Well. Lina had two sons, Gilberto and Haro. She worked hard to encourage both of them to do something with their lives. They were brilliant mathematicians but Gilberto was interested in music. Besides singing in the choir, he loved the sound of the guitar, so he learned classical guitar. It's very surprising from a poor family in these parts. Then when Gilberto's marriage broke up with Angel's mother, it destroyed him. He had no interest in anything much but always wanted to help his mother and brother. Haro, his brother had polio, you know."

Ethan was comfortable in asking a lot more questions about people and Dylan didn't mind answering them, as he hoped Ethan would eventually want to know more about the land. For now, Dylan was happy.

"How did Haro get polio, Uncle?"

"Well when Haro was young, like most boys his age, he was extremely adventurous and liked swimming in the reservoir. It's the reservoir at the bottom of our mountain on the northern side. There were always dead sheep in it. That was before they put the guardrail up to prevent the sheep from falling into the reservoir in bad weather. The doctors told Lina there must have been a lot of bacteria in the reservoir and as he was so young his body couldn't fight it. It was inevitable for him to get the polio disease and be paralyzed from the waist down."

"Did he get over the polio?"

"No son. There is no cure for polio. He has been crippled since he was eight years old and missed the opportunity of going to University because he was crippled. Hopefully in the future, medicine will make a breakthrough and there will be no more polio because everyone will have inoculations, like chickenpox and mumps." Dylan glanced around the chippie. "Well Ethan, lets clean up and call it a night, shall we? Nearly everyone has gone home except for Llewelyn. I think Llewelyn is still here."

Dylan shouted towards the parlor, "Llewelyn, are you still here?"

"I am still here, Dylan."

"I need to ask you something before you go."

"Alright, what is it?"

"I was thinking about making another trip up. What are you doing next Sunday after Church and lunch?"

"Nothing other than listening to Pagua yelling, and her loud music."

"Just wondered if you would like to come up Penrhiwgwynt with us in the afternoon? I want to check on Cradoc's land. Bobbie came a bit ago and told me that Herbert's great grandson was seen up there with stakes plotting out his great grandfather's land. Bobbie was suspicious. That's why he came to see me. Now that I've found out that Herbert annexed most of his land to me and Cradoc, I'm afraid there's not much left for his great grandson to claim."

"How's that Dylan? I thought there was a lot of land?"

"*Ìe,* there was that. We went to see Edith at the property records department and she said that Herbert had been annexing land for a long time over the years before he died. Now, if Herbert wanted his grandchildren to have the land, why didn't he leave it directly to them? I don't quite understand why he would want to give it away like that. We already had a good amount of land."

"Well, Dylan if he annexed however much land it was to you, then it's yours no question asked."

"It's still making me think something is not quite right and I certainly don't want to cheat the young bloke out of anything."

"Don't worry about it right now, it will all sort itself out in the wash."

"I do need to worry about it right now, Llewelyn. I'm eighty-nine, mun. How long do you think I'm going to last?"

"You're in good health, Dylan and of sound mind. God forbid mun. It's not like you are going senile."

"Well, I want to take care of things before that happens."

"Are you sure there's nothing else troubling you, Dylan? You sound too anxious and worried. It has to be something else besides land. What is it?"

"No. It's nothing else exactly. I just want to make sure that Ethan gets what he needs before that time. Problem is, I have to get him interested and that is a tall order at the moment."

"Alright then, I'll be glad to join you both. Pagua will be better off if I'm out of the house. She'll be on her own. She shouts at me as though I've gone deaf. She thinks I understand every word she says! I don't know Greek like a native. I wonder sometimes what I did to make her so angry at times." Llewelyn seemed relieved to get his thoughts off his chest.

"Before we go I'll go in my trunk again and see where I put those drawings. I'll take them to Edith and see if they match what's in the archives. I'll know if they are accurate then before we go."

"Well, I'd better go now, Dylan."

"Llewelyn. Before you go did you notice anything about Lina? Is she alright?"

"I'm not quite certain, Dylan. She starts to tell me something then she stops and goes quiet. I'm not sure at all if Lina is alright or not."

"Something is bothering her. Maybe she will tell Mary. They are close, you know." Dylan nodded.

"I think that would be a good idea to talk with Mary, another woman. Alright then, I'm off."

"Alright Llewelyn."

"We've almost finished, Ethan. Then, I think we should turn in for the night."

It wasn't too long that Dylan was alone and decided to look in his trunk before he went to bed. Thinking to himself, he knew he had some other papers in that trunk that he didn't take much notice of. He piled all the papers on the floor at the foot of the bed for the morning, as it was getting late and he needed to get up early to start the day off well.

Chapter 26

Bright and early in the morning, Dylan stirred. He could hear the birds high up on the trees that grew in pots close to his coalhouse. This particular morning, the birds chirping reminded him so much of the time when he was with Cradoc. He laid there for a few extra minutes while his mind wandered.

He had overslept and Olga was already in the kitchen with Clarenda making breakfast while Cradoc was out in the barn feeding the horses. Guinness was close behind as always, waiting for any break in his routine to get some attention.

Olga shouted, "So you made it finally, from your slumber?" With her beautiful Croatian accent. Then Clarenda would repeat, "You finally made it, from your slumber." Both would laugh and Olga would come and rest her head on Dylan's shoulder until he made his excuse why he was late rising. It was not very often that Dylan would sleep in, but to him it was a real treat to sometimes just lie there and dream. When he finally appeared in the morning, Olga gave him a little bit of extra attention and he loved it.

Olga had long brown hair with streaks of light she twisted into a long braid that fell down to her waist, with wisps of fine curls around her face. She was a natural beauty with no extra modern day makeup. When she let her hair fall without a braid it was thick and wavy and fell gently over her face. He could feel his heart beating as it did the first time he saw her.

She had a smallish frame with a tiny waist. Whatever she wore did not detract from her natural beauty. It was a pleasure to just sit in his rocking chair and admire her when they were all taking a break in the summer evenings. The warm breeze and the fragrance from the flowers that they planted around the porch, gave an enchanted memory that lingered in time.

Dylan got up and dressed when Ethan came to help. "Good morning, son. Did you sleep well last night?"

"Yes, actually, I was surprised because I was thinking about the conversation you had with Llewelyn about your land," Ethan explained. "I've been thinking. Er um, I would like to know more. I only know the little bit my mam told me."

"That's my boy. You should, because it's your land, too you know."

"Uncle, how can it be mine? I didn't know anything about it really, only what I've overheard you talk about."

"Of course son, it was your grandfather's and mine and you are a direct heir of the property."

"But, what about Thomas and Garreth? It's theirs too isn't it?" Those were Dylan's sons.

"I understand what you are saying, but quite honestly my sons aren't interested at all. I've approached both of them about it many times and the last time I saw them, they told me they are financially well situated and don't want the burden of any land that's here when they are way up in North Wales." He flung up a hand, gesturing in the direction his family lived.

"What will you do with it, then?"

"Give it to you, of course." Dylan nodded wisely, his plan all along.

"To me?" Ethan paled at the suddenness of the news.

"*Ìe*, Ethan, to you. You are the rightful heir of Cradoc's property, whether it be land or anything else."

"But, what about you? It's yours, too."

"It's like this Ethan, I am not going to last forever." Dylan's voice dropped and he shook his head.

Ethan interrupted Dylan, "Please don't talk like that, Uncle."

"Son, I don't have the energy to start a farm at this late stage in my life and anyway, I still have the chippie. I think my Olga would agree that I should make sure you are secure, too. My Olga loved the babies and raised them like our own children but both are gone now and you are the last one I must provide for while I can. I should have done something before now but I was waiting for you to heal from the pit. What a life you led down there, but now all that is behind you and life is starting to change for you."

"But Uncle, I honestly don't know what to do. I feel like a ship out of water these days."

"I know and that's alright son, I'm here to guide you and help you as long as I can." He patted Ethan's shoulder. Suddenly remembering the pages, he held up his fist, one finger unfurled. "That reminds me, I found some old papers in my trunk. I need to take them to Edith at the Town Hall so she can verify they are good and legal. Maybe this afternoon we can do that together."

"Will we have enough time, as we must open again for the evening?"

"*Ìe*, it will be alright, nothing to worry about, son."

It was another busy morning but both Ethan and Dylan worked concentrating on the morning's chores and preparation for the evening. The potatoes were peeled and cut and the batter made in the bucket all ready. As soon as they had finished, Ethan said he would go home and change into something that didn't smell like fish and chips, and then laughed!

Dylan was soon changed and looking through the papers he had laid on the floor of his little bedroom while he was waiting for Ethan to return. In the bundle, there were small pieces of sketched papers marked with small symbols that could represent each part of the property. Cradoc was careful to make sure he had everything outlined. This would make it easier for Edith.

When Ethan returned they walked to the Town Hall.

"Edith, I would like you to check on these bits and bobs of documents for us please. We can leave them with you if you like, so you won't have to stop what you're doing and we'll come back in the morning, alright Edith?

"That will be good, that way it gives me a little more time to take a good look at them."

After the evening rush Ethan was anxious to get home and talk with Mary, while Dylan said he would see if there was anything else in the trunk before he went to bed.

Lina and Angel were just leaving as he arrived at the door. "Ethan, you look worn out. Has it been a busy night for you and Dylan? You will probably want to go to bed early tonight."

Ethan replied, "*Ie*, I am that, that I am."

"You sound very much like Dylan."

"*Ìe*, I expect some of Dylan has rubbed off on me, that it has." Both Lina and Ethan laughed amusingly.

"Dylan and Llewelyn asked if I would like to go up the mountain on Sunday. Are you interested in joining us with Mary and the children? It would be nice to all be together again."

"That would be nice, I'll see if I can make it up to the top this time."

"Alright then, I'll tell Mary."

"Is that you Ethan?" Mary shouted from the kitchen. "You just missed Lina."

"I just saw her, love."

"She says she's feeling somewhat better today, I think spending a little time with us helped her a bit. I think having adult company makes a difference for her."

"It might have done just that because I asked her if she would like to come up Penrhiwgwynt next Sunday afternoon and she said yes."

"That's good. I think she needs a break and to get some fresh air, but I doubt if she'll make it to the top like last year." Mary was thinking out loud about it.

"That's a shame. I was hoping she would be there too as Uncle Dylan is anxious to show me the land."

"Well that's good, love." Mary was waiting for some reassurance that Ethan finally might be more than interested.

"I have been thinking for a while that it might not be a bad idea if I did see it after all. Uncle Dylan is eager for me to know all the details; that's why we went to see Edith at the Town Hall."

"Well, I agree with him. You really should. Like you should see to the basement, too." Mary gave Ethan a smile, teasing him about not finishing the cleaning.

"Alright, I promise to clean up the basement, too." Ethan gave Mary a grin. "There's so much stuff down there, I don't know what to chuck out."

"Before you start chucking out stuff, have a good look at it, love. Like Lina proved to me, things can be used for something other than what it was originally for. You remember that lace tablecloth and the sheet she brought up here?"

"I remember Lina did make a beautiful dress for you, and David's shirt and a dress for Angel. You're right love, I will make sure that I take a good look."

"Alright then, when?"

"That wasn't fair, you led me up to that. I hope you're not meaning tonight."

"No, love, but soon, alright?"

"Alright then. Maybe Ian and David can help, too."

The following day Dylan was ready when Ethan came to help. "I'm going to the Town Hall to see Edith. Would you like to come now, Ethan?"

"Yes, don't mind if I do. We'll have to get things prepared for the lunch right?"

"Well don't worry too much about that; I've already started. See over there in the corner, I've already pealed a bucket full of spuds, and almost finished cutting them up into chips. If we just make double the amount of batter, we will have enough for the evening as well. Alright?"

"You must have got up really early this morning?" Ethan teased him, seeing all the work done.

"*Ìe*, I did that, that I did. I couldn't sleep. I just laid there thinking."

"I was doing the same. Just thinking."

"Well son, what were you thinking about? Anything in particular?"

"It might seem daft but I was thinking about Penrhiwgwynt. Going out on the land and seeing the horses, like the kids."

"Well that's good. Now we're getting it."

"Getting what?"

"Oh son. If only you knew. It took me a long time to realize maybe I was too anxious to have a life down here, and now without my Olga it doesn't seem worth it anymore."

"What are you saying Uncle? You wish you weren't down in Porth anymore?" Ethan looked at Dylan but Dylan had his head down and looked as if he was wiping his eyes. "I'm not quite sure if I understand, Uncle."

"All that land up there, gone to waste really, and we're down here cooking fish and chips."

Ethan wasn't sure what to say at that point other than to encourage Dylan that they would be seeing Edith about the land.

The batter didn't take long and the rest of the chores passed quickly and they tidied up the shop. "I'll go home and change and see you back here in a bit, alright Uncle?"

"*Ìe*, I'll be cleaned up by then and look presentable to go to the Town Hall again."

Ethan left and closed the door. Dylan went upstairs to his room and picked up the final few things that were on the floor of his bedroom, changed his clothes, and came back downstairs.

Bobbie was standing his bike against the shop window when Dylan noticed him. "What are you doing here at this time? I'm shut, mun."

"I know that, you silly bugger, I haven't lost it yet! I was coming to tell you that Herbert's great grandson is on the rampage. He went to see Mr. Evans, the solicitor."

"What about?"

"Oh he has a bee in his bonnet about the land his great grandfather gave you and Cradoc."

"How do you know that?"

"The first place he went was the police station. He said you needed to be arrested for stealing his great grandfather's land."

"He did? Why did he think I stole his land when Herbert annexed it to my land?"

"I don't know, Dylan. He seems to have gone nuts with anger. He was at the pub last night and you know Gareth, he can't keep his mouth shut. He was talking about the great news that Herbert didn't have much land left after you had got most of it and there wouldn't be any foreigners coming here to live."

"What do you mean I got most of it? Is Gareth back on the drink? Is that why he's spewing up stuff again?"

"I think so. Word certainly got around mighty fast for Gareth to be shouting about land in his pub. He really got that young city bloke all upset last night."

"My God, he needs to know the true facts before he opens his big mouth again."

"Now Dylan, calm down. Don't worry, I told him. I suggested that he go to see Mr. Evans so he could be told the truth of the matter."

"Oh my God, that's all I need. A hot head around the place and a drunken big mouth to set things off again in Porth." Dylan was frustrated.

"What's going on? Is everything alright here?" Ethan asked as he stepped into the shop. "Uncle? What's got you so upset?"

"I was telling Dylan, that Herbert's great grandson found out last night at the pub that your Uncle owns most of the land. That young city bloke is not pleased, not pleased at all."

"Oh my God, oh my God. And I suppose Gareth had something to do with it?" Ethan didn't know what else to say, other than he already knew about Gerald.

"I told your Uncle that it's going to be alright. In fact, you know Gareth's been in trouble before for his disorderly conduct and slander. He might get banned again from the pub if Bryn Williams gets to hear about it."

"We'd better go while the shop is closed. Nice of you to come and tell me, at least I know what to expect if I run into either of them." Dylan was relieved to be able to shut the door and be outside.

Edith was anxiously waiting for Dylan and Ethan. "I was worried I was going to miss you both if you didn't come soon, as I'm shutting the office early today."

"Did you manage to understand any of the sketches and drawings, Edith?"

"I did, Dylan. They are legal parcels of land that Herbert annexed to you and Cradoc. Truly amazing, they were. Herbert knew what he was doing to have identified the parcels exactly. Good thing you kept them, Dylan. No one can deny that you are the legal land owner."

"So these are all the parts of the land, eight of them? What a lot of land. No wonder Herbert's grandson got upset."

"He has one part, Dylan. Don't worry. He should be grateful for that. Coming here and wanting to sell it off. His great grandfather must have known what he was going to do.”

"Well, I don't like making people upset." Dylan felt a little disturbed about it.

"Uncle, like Edith said, it was Herbert's choice to give you the land. You can't change that. And to think you didn't know about it."

"How is that boil on your neck?" Edith inquired.

Dylan quickly replied, "Oh, much better thanks to Lina. She put a hot mustard poultice on it."

The rest of the week passed by but the gossip heightened when the neighbors saw Dylan during market day. Soon the young bloke decided to auction it off, obviously to the highest bidder. Rumor had it, what would anyone want with a small piece of land they couldn't do much with up on Penrhiwgwynt?

Sunday came after a busy week and everyone was ready for Church. The sun was shining so brightly that it made the morning glow. Lina and Angel joined David and his family and walked to Church. Vicar Llewelyn was on the doorstep cheerfully welcoming his congregation.

Llewelyn's service was about helping each other in times of need. He was focused on people who lived alone. The congregation's journey in life was to humble themselves, and show compassion to those less fortunate.

After Church and a quick lunch, everyone was ready to walk up Penrhiwgwynt. Even Lina seemed to have pep in her steps.

David and Angel ran ahead and through the farm towards the barn. "Patch," cried Angel.

Then David shouted, "Where are you, Patch?"

Kip was running from behind the barn followed by Patch. What a sight. Both seemed to be having the time of their life. Mrs. Rhys came out and shouted, "Come and have some of my biscuits." Both of them ran to Mrs. Rhys and waited eagerly at the kitchen door. "Did you see Patch and Kip? They are really having a good time, just like best friends," she asked the children as they stood patiently.

"Patch won't leave will he?" Angel asked.

"I don't think so; I think he's enjoying himself with Kip. He wouldn't have so much fun up on the mountain, now would he? He'd be all alone."

David and Angel agreed that it would be very lonely for him.

"David, Angel, where are you?" Ethan was anxiously waiting for them to appear so they could all walk together.

"We're coming," shouted David.

"Tatty bye, Mrs. Rhys," Angel shouted. "Thank you for the biscuits." They soon joined the rest of the group.

Lina did very well walking up to the second pathway.

"Let's rest a while here," said Dylan, noticing that Lina had slowed down a little. "Cradoc put a bench here, too somewhere. Let me see now," and he walked a little off the pathway in the direction of Llewelyn.

Llewelyn shouted, "Here it is! It was just covered up with some brambles."

"Thank you, Llewelyn, I really want to see the top and look over the valley again, but I feel giddy. Perhaps you could stay a while with me?"

"Of course, I will be happy to," Llewelyn confirmed and turned to Dylan. "You go on up with Ethan and everyone, and I'll stay with Lina a while, alright?"

"That will be alright." Dylan turned around and told the others to continue their journey up. David and Angel were happy to go on at a speed the others couldn't walk, but the rest ambled along behind them.

"Have they gone yet, Llewelyn?" Lina asked with shortness of breath.

"Yes, they have and now out of sight on the next trail up. Dylan seems to be in full gear today, I often wonder where he gets his energy. He must be taking a lot more cod liver oil and malt than I am." Llewelyn chuckled.

"Llewelyn I need your advice, alright?" Lina placed her hand on his arm.

"Of course, what is it that's troubling you?" He covered her hand, patting her with full attention.

"The cancer is back," Lina said with her handkerchief over her eyes.

"Oh no, I am so sorry. I must pray for you and with you."

"Llewelyn, I don't know what to do," Lina sobbed. "Oh God, I have prayed for his mercy. I want to see Angel grow up, or at least get her through school." Lina continued to sob uncontrollably.

Llewelyn puts his arms around Lina while she cried. "There, there, now. God is in control of every situation. There, there."

"I know, but Gilberto needs my help and I want to do my best for him. Gilberto doesn't know how to look after a little girl who needs a mother, but I want to spend my last days here where my Ernesto is buried and take care of Angel. I don't want to burden your mother. She has enough to do with your brother and his wife living with her."

"You don't know if Gilberto wants you to go to England, do you?

"Yes, Llewelyn I know. He wants me to go. He told me." She sobbed more, and offered a broken prayer. "Oh God, please allow me to live a little longer."

Llewelyn was not able to comfort Lina, she just sobbed and sobbed. After a while she couldn't sob anymore. She was tired out, so Llewelyn just held her hand until she was able to speak again.

"Gilberto is working so hard; he is buying a house. It will be finished next year because they can't build in the winter. Llewelyn, I won't be there to live in it. Gilberto can't take care of a little girl by himself. He'll have to put her in a home, an orphanage or with people who don't care. They won't look after her like her own people."

"I believe he is going out with a lady, you never know, they might get married."

"No, Llewelyn not anymore, Dorothy died. She died in Gilberto's arms. Oh God, that's another tragedy he had. Dorothy had cancer and kidney complications, besides she was pregnant."

"Oh my goodness, I didn't know that," Llewelyn intervened.

"Gilberto loved Dorothy. He brought Dorothy and Sandra, her little girl from her previous marriage, to see Angel and me. He wanted to get married last year but Dorothy told me she didn't want to get married again. Gilberto was heartbroken when Dorothy died. He wanted to keep Sandra as his own, as he had hoped that Sandra and Angel would live together as sisters, but Dorothy's mother said the little girl was all she had left when Dorothy died. How could Gilberto insist on it? He felt very sorry for Dorothy's mother. Dorothy was her only child."

"I didn't know that. That is very sad."

"Llewelyn. Who is going to marry Gilberto now, knowing he has Angel from his previous marriage to take care of? Not many women would start a marriage with someone else's child in the same house at all times. It would be different if Angel lived somewhere else, and just visited from time to time, then the woman wouldn't be inconvenienced."

"Yes, yes, I understand what you are saying, Lina. You don't know for sure if it's cancer yet. Has the doctor done his tests?"

"I know, Llewelyn. I am tired, so tired and dizzy all the time, and it's worse than the last time." Time passed and Lina wanted to try and walk again, even if it was for a short distance. "I want to see Penrhiwgwynt again before it's too late."

"Don't talk like that, please. You don't know yet."

"I know, Llewelyn. Help me up please?"

Llewelyn told Lina she could lean on him if she had any difficulty. It took Lina a long time to reach the top but Lina was anxious, "I had to see my Penrhiwgwynt again even if it's for the last time. My favorite green mountain in Wales, God has blessed her with such beauty, words cannot express. Thank you, Lord for letting me visit her one last time."

"Sit, sit, Lina. There is a bench under this tree. Sit and get your strength back. You have walked all the way up. That's a long way when you are not feeling too good."

Far in the distance, Ethan and Dylan were walking along the very edge of the land that was drawn out in Cradoc's sketches.

"This is a lot of land, Uncle. What are you going to do with it?"

"I'm not going to do anything, you are." Dylan pointed his finger at Ethan.

"What, me? I don't know anything about land."

"Well, it's like this, son. You don't need to know much about the land itself. You see out there, as far as your eye can see? It's all yours and all you need to do is think what you can do with it. Alright?"

"Uncle." Ethan was speechless. He could not mutter another word.

"It's alright, son."

"I've had no experience. All I know about is the coal mine."

"Well you learned how to prepare and cook fish and chips. It's just like that, a learning process."

"Uncle…" Ethan then went silent again.

"Cradoc started from scratch. He had no idea what he was doing at first and there was no one to advise him, but he had determination and willpower. He made a successful business until his death."

"Grandfather Cradoc was a mountain man you said, he must have had some experience at least about mountain life."

"Not exactly, son. He chose that way of life because he wanted his freedom and didn't want to go down the mines like his friends." Dylan was trying to make Ethan understand that Cradoc was stubborn and was prepared to do anything to get his freedom by doing things his way. "Well son, see those muscles you are hiding under that shirt of yours? You got those from hard labor down the mine and you are wasting them cooking fish and chips."

"But, I'm trying to help you, Uncle."

"I know that, son and I appreciate that but you can't go on wasting your life cooking fish and chips for me. Who knows how long I'm going to last, what if I kick the bucket? Then what are you going to do? Mope around because I'm gone? No, son. That's ridiculous, I must give you the opportunity to make something of your life before it's too late. Put your life to some good use. If not for yourself, for Mary and your children."

"But Uncle, I know nothing about mountain life."

"Son, you can learn and you are a fast learner. I can see that."

Ethan started muttering to himself.

"Son, it's time to act. I could leave you my chippie instead but then you would have to wait until I kick the bucket. Of course, you can have it if that's what you want but you would spend a fortune doing repairs, and for what?

"The Welsh tiles on the roof must be removed and the rafters all need to be repaired or replaced because they are rotten from rain before you could put new Welsh tiles up there. The back small bedroom door I keep locked, I do, deliberately because the ceiling is coming down.

"Not forgetting the coalhouse outside, the asbestos roof is falling down that needs replacing, too. Then there's the toilet. Ha, that's a laugh, a toilet. You've seen what it's like. It has a wooden seat from one wall to the other with a hole in the middle. It doesn't flush like normal toilets. I have to keep a bucket filled with water to throw down the hole when I use it so everything goes through the pipe and into the sewage line. There's a coat hanger on a nail on the wall where I stick the cut up newspaper to use instead of buying a city toilet roll.

"Then the burners on the stove in the shop need replacing. There's no electricity except for the one light in the chippie itself that hangs over the counter. The place needs electricity all over. There's too much to be repaired to make it more modern for today's use and you would be wasting a small fortune to try. It would be best to auction it off and use the money for whatever your children need." He took a breath, looking around the mountain.

"I have a small insurance policy I bought when I came. That should pay for my coffin and burial."

"Uncle, please don't say these things. They're very depressing. Please don't talk like this." Ethan pulled upright, crossing his arms over his chest as if that would stop the words.

"Son, you've got to get a grip on your life."

"Yes, but Uncle I don't know anything and definitely nothing about the basics of land ownership."

"Neither did Cradoc and he was a puny little thing when he first went up there. He had no ideas, but he was determined when he first left. It was years before he had any muscles like you have. I am sure he slept under the stars many nights praying for energy to do what he did. It didn't come easy for him, you know, but he was determined. You are half way there.

"Built like an ox man, you can cut trees down, chop wood, dig holes for fences, and build a home. Poor Cradoc slept hidden under branches and on grass for his bed. He collected old stone to build walls, stone on top of stone. He knew what he wanted to do and did it. Now all we have to do is get your mind focused on what you could accomplish for yourself and your family."

"But, I'm not even sure if I am capable of doing that."

Dylan interrupted, "Well, son. Do you see all this land?" He turned around, holding his hand out to show Ethan the mountain. "It's going to waste. My God, Cradoc would turn over in his grave if he thought you didn't want it." Dylan turned to look behind him where they had walked.

"You've got to get your arse moving, son, before it's too late." Dylan had never said that to anyone unless he was frustrated and meant every word he said.

"Let's go back to the children and Mary now. Time is flying by again and it will soon start to get dark. Also, I must see where Lina and Llewelyn are."

"Mary and the kids will think we have forgotten them."

"Ethan, when we get back, talk with Mary and get a feel of what she thinks about it all. Also Ian. He is coming of age where he needs some kind of future that's meaningful. He can draw all he wants to if he helps you and he's up here permanently."

"I see the children, where is Mary?" Ethan started to be worried.

"I see her, she's standing by the tree, looking at the tree actually. I wonder why she's that close?" Ethan was curious and strode off to join her.

"Where's Ian, love?" Ethan could see David and Angel but not Ian.

"Oh, he's up near the next tree, he said he could get a better view."

"Ian, we need to go. Where are you?"

"I'm here, Dad." Ian jumped down off the tree and walked towards the rest of the family. "What a view, Dad. I could see you all the way over there and I saw the other mountains. In fact, I saw a few horses, too."

"Did you see Buttercup and Dusty?" Angel questioned emotionally.

"No I didn't see your horse, but I saw some other white ones and a couple of patchy ones way over there in a group." Ian pointed to the left of the land.

"You could see all the way over there?" Llewelyn was kicking up interest in the conversation.

"Yes, I could. In fact, I could see almost to the other mountain over there. There's another town over there, too."

"Yes, that's Tylorstown actually. That is a long way to see from that tree."

"It was quite interesting really. Look at my pictures." Ian showed his pictures to everyone. He never did that before; he didn't like to show what he'd done. Ethan looked at them, at the skill and talent he showed. On a small slate there was even one sketch Ian had of two tiny people in the distance in a circle of trees.

"You could see all the way over there. That is interesting." Llewelyn had his hands in his pockets again, and was swaying up and down on his heels. "Interesting that is."

"Everyone ready?" Ethan looked around at the assembly. "Where is Lina? Wasn't she with you?" He looked at Llewelyn.

"Look over there," Ian shouted.

"Well, look there, it's Lina," Dylan was happy. "Lina made it up. I'm so pleased. I really didn't think she would be able to get up this far." He hurried to where she was sitting.

"Praise the Lord, we made it," Llewelyn told them. "It wasn't bad really, we walked slow and we made it. Lina wanted to see Penrhiwgynte one –," Llewelyn stopped and changed the subject, quickly turning to Ian. "What else have you got there, son?" Ian showed Llewelyn his sketches. "Look, I saw these horses over there and then when I turned I saw Dad and Uncle Dylan in the distance."

"Oh my goodness you are quite an artist, Ian. How would you like to be up here all the time and sketch more?"

"That would be alright, but where would I sleep?"

"Under the stars, son." Llewelyn was trying to be humorous as best as he could in his own way.

"Well, now we are all here. We had better go down." Dylan turned to Ethan and Mary. "You both go down with the children and I'll walk with Lina and Llewelyn, alright?" Dylan looked over towards Lina and Llewelyn.

"Nene, is it alright if I walk with David down the mountain?"

Mary interrupted and said, "I'll take care of Angel, we'll have supper ready for everyone by the time you get back home, alright?"

"Oh yes, thank you Mary. I love you Angel."

"I love you." Angel ran towards Lina and hugged her before going back to David and his family.

Dylan told Lina, "Now we can take our own time. Those young people can go ahead of us."

"Thank you Dylan, I appreciate that. I have so longed to be up here. Can I sit a while and just take in the air a minute?"

"Of course, Lina. Take all the time you want. We have the evening. As long as we can see where we're walking we'll be alright. Otherwise we two old Welshman will have to carry you down."

"No, no, no, that won't be necessary," Lina replied.

"It's been quite a while since I had a girl in my arms." Dylan smiled at Lina.

Lina felt the rush of warmth in her face and just smiled at Dylan and thought as she was viewing around her, "Why didn't I take more notice of Dylan? He is a good man. I know I wouldn't be worried about what's going to happen."

"You were a long time, Ethan. What were you two talking about?" Mary walked hand in hand with him, the children walking ahead with Ian. The older boy showing signs of the man he would become.

"Well." There was silence for a few minutes. "Dylan offered me his land if I would go up and make a home for us all. There's so much land. I had no idea that my they owned so much."

"He did? What did you say?"

"I didn't really say anything, love. He did most of the talking," Ethan told her with a smile.

"Well, tell me what did your Uncle Dylan say?"

"He wants me to talk with you about the land but when we are alone, together, alright?"

"Of course, love. That would be better. I can't really watch the children and pay attention to what you are saying properly." They walked a bit in silence. "Well, for now are you thinking of going up?"

"Not without you." Ethan lowered his hand from around Mary's waist and gave Mary a little squeeze on her backside

"Hhmm. That will sure get you everywhere, Ethan Edwards."

"That's what I'm hoping, Mary Edwards." Ethan smiled a big smile at Mary and Mary flushed with embarrassment in front of the children.

"Good evening, all," shouted Mr. Rhys. "It's been good weather for a walk today."

Ethan shouted back, "It has that. Uncle Dylan and Vicar Llewelyn are still up there with Nene Lina."

"Really, Lina made it too." A surprised answer came from Mr. Rhys. "I will wait for them and maybe they'd like to taste my Mrs. cake on the way home."

"Cake?" Ian shouted.

"*Ìe*, we have cake. Would you like some, Ian?"

"Yes please." Ian looked towards Mary, "Is that alright, Mam?

"Yes, go but don't be late alright, Ian."

"Alright, Mam," Ian shouted and in no time he was over the fence and running towards the Rhys's back porch.

"I'll send some cake home with him, alright Mary?" Mr. Rhys shouted back.

"That's alright then. I don't want Lina to feel guilty she didn't make a cake today." Mary said in a low voice and then shouted eagerly, "Thank you. Thank your Mrs., too."

Ethan and Mary and the younger children were almost at their front door. "Look at that, we must have had a visitor." Mary pointed down to the bird poo on the doorstep.

"No, Mam," shouted David. "That's the bird that lives up in Mrs. Probert's roof. It must be hungry, poor thing."

"You mean Mrs. Probert has a bird living in her roof. Does she know?"

"I doubt it, Dad. She would shoo it away."

"Well, perhaps you had better tell her. Sometimes birds make a nest in the roof and make a mess. Not to mention have lots of baby birds."

"Baby birds?" asked Angel interested.

"Oh yes, baby birds. The mother makes a nest for her eggs and then when they hatch there's baby birds," Mary answered.

"You know, that's quite a way from the mountain. It's not normal that birds nest in the town," Ethan stated.

"Maybe it lost its way or is hurt." David showed concern. "Well, we must feed the bird and the babies."

"Alright then, kids. You can take your shoes off and play in the front room," Mary said to David and Angel. It wasn't long before Ian joined them. He carried a paper wrapped parcel. He put it on the table and turned to leave.

"Ian, I want to talk with you," Ethan told him, pouring a cup of milk.

"Now what have I supposed to have done?" Ian asked sarcastically.

"This time, nothing. I just want to talk with you and your Mam." Ethan wanted to get Ian away from the others so he could have an adult conversation with Mary.

"I'll put the kettle on and start dinner," Mary announced.

"Wait a bit, love, or rather just put the kettle on and come and sit down," Ethan chanted.

"Is everything alright, Ethan?" Mary was concerned now.

"Everything is alright. Just come and sit down, but I would welcome a cuppa."

Mary put the kettle on over the little oven by the side of the fire. It would take a good few minutes to boil. Then she got down the cups, sugar, and milk and came to the table.

"What is it, love? I can see concern in those eyes," Mary was questioning Ethan.

"Well, not concern really but…" he fumbled for words. "Just curious," Ethan replied. "Ian, how far did you see from that tree?"

"Why Dad, am I in trouble?" Ian took a seat wondering what he'd done.

"No, son. I just want to know how far you could see, that's all."

"Oh a long way, Dad. I could see like a forest or woods and I could see beyond it on that side, and then on the other side I could see the next town and the mountain."

"All that way from that tree?"

"Yes, Dad. It was beautiful and so quiet. So quiet and so beautiful," Ian repeated himself. "And, I could hear birds singing from the tree, too. They could have been annoyed with me because I was in their tree sketching on my pad and slate." Then he chuckled.

"Oh, let me see your drawings, Ian," Mary asked inquisitively.

"Look, Mam. See how far it was." Ethan leaned closer.

"Oh my goodness, that is a long way away. I didn't see that."

"If you were up the tree you would have, Mam."

"I expect I would. They are beautiful drawings, Ian." Mary looked towards Ethan. "Look at these, they are really good."

"Yes they are, really good, son." Ethan was quiet for a while then sighed.

"Alright then, Mary. How would you like to start a new life on the mountain?"

"Up on the mountain?" Mary was more than surprised and fortunately for Ethan, Ian wasn't taking much notice at that moment. "I hadn't thought about it really. I was hoping you would think about the land and the basement. I've been waiting for you to make a decision, but that was taking forever. So really, I've tried not to think about it." Mary was honest as she answered Ethan's question.

"Well, I'm thinking about it now. Uncle Dylan has asked me to think about it. He showed me all the land. Oh my goodness, there's so much. There's enough for four farms and families up there."

"There's that much?"

"Yes, Herbert annexed land to it years before he died. He knew his boys didn't want it."

"Oh my goodness, so that's why his city great grandson is here?"

"I expect so, but I don't think he knows about the annexation."

"Well, what have you decided, Ethan?" Mary was more insistent this time.

"It's really up to you and the kids. Would you like to live up there?"

"Yes," shouted Ian.

"I'm trying to have a serious conversation with your Mam." Ethan was already losing his patience.

"It's alright, Ethan. Ian needs to know too and it would be good for all of us to have the conversation."

"Alright then, Ian. You will help with a farm, then? Help with cows, chickens, and maybe horses?" Ethan looked over to Ian who sat at the other side of the table.

"Um. You said horses, Dad?"

"I did, but that would be in the future. Uncle Dylan said to start slowly and then see what happens."

"What about housing, love? We'll have to live somewhere, especially when the weather gets bad."

"I think another few trips up there will help me to see where exactly. I hope Uncle Dylan can come up too." Ethan then went into deep thought.

There was a knock on the door. Angel shouted, "It's my Nene," and she rushed to open the door.

"Hello Lina, you just came in time. Come on in. Have a cuppa with us," Ethan shouted up the hallway happily.

"Alright then, I can't say no to Ethan's invitation. I mustn't stay too long. Angel needs to go to bed so she won't oversleep in the morning."

"Look Lina, Ian brought some of Mrs. Rhys's cake. Would you like a slice?"

"That would be so nice, thank you." She looked more tired than Mary and Ethan had ever seen her.

"Angel love, get David for me will you please? There's plenty of cake enough here for everyone."

"Well, that is good cake. I must ask her if she added allspice or just a bit of cloves; it makes a beautiful flavor." Lina was happy to taste someone else's cooking for a change.

When Lina and Angel left Ian and David were getting ready for bed and Ethan and Mary remained in the kitchen. "Love, you know I am a bit excited, but worried at the same time."

"I know, love. It will take a bit of getting used to but it will give you a purpose for the future."

"I've been thinking about it but I'm scared I won't succeed like my grandparents and Uncle Dylan. Maybe I could find their graves. Uncle Dylan said he buried them up there before he came down here with his Olga."

"I think you will. Ask Uncle Dylan where they are buried. In fact, take time to talk with Lina, too. She might be able to shed some light on a few things for you that you hadn't thought about."

"Uncle Dylan, I've been thinking."

"*Ìe*, son. What is it?"

"I was talking with Mary last night and I'm wondering, can you tell me where exactly are my grandparents graves."

"*Ìe*, I can do that. It will be easy for you to find them. David and Angel found things near the ruins of their farm, their graves are not too far beyond where the sun sets."

"Beyond where the sun sets, how will I know if I have the right place?" Ethan questioned with a perplexed grin.

"When you are up there, take your time, Ethan, don't rush. Think about what is important. I know there's so much to think about right now. It's not just Cradoc and Clarenda's graves you need to find, it's your goals. Tell Mary, so she understands what's going on. If you rush up there just to find the graves, then what? What are you going to do when you find them?

"Well, that will show…." Ethan had to shrug. "I don't know, Uncle. I don't know."

"Alright then, let's see then." Dylan was thinking seriously of something that might interest Ethan in getting on with business without just looking for graves. "Lets go up this weekend another way. There is a small path that Cradoc made. It might be an arduous climb for you but I think it might be what you need right now. I'll do my best to keep up with you, alright?"

"Uncle, what will that do?"

"I'm not sure, but let's try it, alright?"

It was difficult to find the path that Dylan wanted to show Ethan as it was underneath layers and layers of weeds and debris the rain had washed down the gullies from the mountaintop. Ethan decided to climb just to show his Uncle that he was trying to understand the overall plan.

There was a sign, "Rocks Falling, No Climbing." His adrenaline was so high that he climbed and climbed. Admittedly, it didn't seem safe at first when small rocks fell over his shoulders and it did take him quite a while. Dylan tried his best to keep up with Ethan but it was really useless. He was much younger and his energy level was way above Dylan's.

Finally, Ethan came to a plateau, as he looked down over the valley his mind raced with the thoughts of being a boy again, even though he didn't like heights. The fresh air was so refreshing that he raised his arms and twirled as he did when he was a boy. He used to love adventure, just like his children did now, and he once had thoughts of travelling to other lands, making his fame and fortune. But in those days he had no means, he barely got through high school.

He looked into the distance at the other mountain ranges, but his mind raced backwards when his mam often said to him, "Dreaming again, Ethan? Nothing good will come out of dreaming unless your dreams come true."

She was right, of course. She wanted the best for Ethan but in those days it was hard work to be a single parent and encourage her young family. Her intentions were good and positive, but maybe her misfortune poured hardship on her boys.

Ethan walked a little further to the tree where he remembered carving letters – E and M. He traced them with his finger as more memories flooded and tears came to his eyes. The E was Ethan and the M was Mary. This is where he first stole a kiss from Mary; he remembered every detail.

Mary and the children walked up the pathway to meet Ethan and Dylan. It definitely wasn't as dangerous as the pathway Ethan and Dylan had taken. The children ran ahead and instantly David was up the tree swinging from branch to branch imagining he was Tarzan, while Angel sat on the fence watching him.

Mary reached the tree, where she met Ethan's eyes staring at her. Ethan's eyes were almond shaped, the pupils as midnight black as his hair. His brows were bushy and as he reached for Mary's hand his brow creased waiting for her approval; then smiled and bent forward to smell the lavender fragrance in her hair. He kissed her brow, her nose and then slowly and gently kissed her lips. He reached for her other hand in his. Sweet sunlight filled him at the touch of her arms around him. He felt the warmth of her chest close to him. His body pressed closer to hers and she could hear him breath heavier. It startled her at first, but soon she relished his kisses and his gentle grip around her shoulders. Her eyes closed and she melted in his soft embrace. They were once young and inexperienced when he carved their initials in the tree trunk, and now years later, it was if it had been yesterday.

A bird singing above brought them back to reality as they stood motionless under the tree. This is where the love he felt for Mary filled his heart and soul.

They were so young and such good friends. Yes, they fell in love and this is where they came to sit under the tree and think of how they were going to tell their parents they wanted to marry. They were young, so young, but in those days they could leave school and get married if they weren't fortunate enough to go to college. Ethan's family was poor.

His mother was a single parent with a family and Mary's parents were older than most. She was the last child at home; how would her mother take it if Mary left home? But then where would they live to begin a life together?

Ethan's mind had wandered back in time.

It would be a good place to begin his new adventurous career. Much work had to be done but it would be an exciting challenge for him.

He stood there inhaling the fresh air of the mountains and started to look down over the valley. His heart was filled again with adventure. This time with Mary by his side.

He saw old stonewalls that were used as boundaries and property markers, he heard the whinny of wild horses in the distance.

Tormented memories filled his head, of the horses that worked so hard in the mines. Once they became part of the mine it seemed that they were swallowed up as they gave their lives to their work and never saw daylight again. He saw the horses and remembered how he wished he could have set free the mine horses. His heart was heavy in those days and he had no ability to do anything but dig for coal in the mines.

Now suddenly his boyhood dreams could become reality. This was it! The motivation he needed, a challenge that would boost his ability to work again. As a boy, he had thoughts of owning his own farm, but this time his thoughts revealed more, possibly a horse farm. He could catch, ride, and train these beautiful wild horses. His dream could come true. And he would make his mam proud of him, as she looked down from heaven.

When surveying the old property and the surrounding fields he could see magnificent horses romping around the fields. A few cries of joy could be heard and he felt a sense of peace.

Ethan was spending another day on the mountaintop. He'd wandered the acreage, letting the peace sink into him.

Alone, he roamed the land thinking it could be done. He would live here; he'd bring the family.

Dark clouds suddenly formed over the sky. It was getting late, but most of all the weather was changing and was brewing up to a storm. The rumblings made the horses uneasy that they huddled together, then ran boldly. As the first crack of lightening came the horses stampeded towards the cliff edge. Ethan ran with all his might to reach them, as he thought they would gallop over the edge in fear. To his amazement there was yet another field, and a little less elevation that wasn't seen earlier and was lined with apple and pear trees.

For some reason these beautiful beasts ran into the field and huddled together in the distance. They knew where they were going. As Ethan got closer he saw the foundations of what remained of an old barn, it could have been a large barn. Admittedly, it was in such disrepair and was hardly a shelter for any animal. There they huddled together in piles of old degraded hay and broken wood pieces everywhere, even what remained of a milking stool, once had three legs but now scattered. It seemed as though they knew where they were going and obviously had sought refuge there before.

More memories flooded Ethan's mind. Is this where he came with his mam as a boy? Is this where he had thought his dreams? His grandfather tended to the horses while his grandmother milked the goats. He looked around and remembered picking up apples and pears that had fallen from the trees and dropping them into an old sack. Dreams and hopes came flooding back to his mind. An old shack that once was his grandparents' home, fields for crops, livestock, orchard and wild horses that roamed the mountaintops.

Could he change his destiny, is it really possible at this stage in his life?

Behind him was the old life he once knew of, working as a coal miner and of horses being led down into the mineshaft 400 feet below. Those horses pulled the mine carts and finally died beneath the ground. There was a saying, "Once down, never to return alive again."

Ethan could do it, move his family up where the sky met the green grass of the Welsh mountains, rebuild his grandparents' home, and enter into a life he had only dreamed of long ago when he was a lad. Ride the wild Welsh horses and train them and send them across the world to riding schools. These wild Welsh horses were derived from Croatian Lipizzaner, Egyptian, Celtic, Mustangs, and Apache breeds beside the Welsh ponies and other mixed breeds that galloped across the horizon.

He was anxious to go back down the mountain and talk with Mary, but he was a little afraid that he would give her false hopes and dreams he couldn't fulfill. It would take some money to start over. He could build a new house with running water, toilet, and lights. His mind wandered more as he was thinking of how he would initiate the conversation with Mary.

He wouldn't need planning permission to build his family's home. The land had lain barren all these years. Any local government authority probably had forgot it, so there would not be any back taxes. He just had to lay claim with the appropriate proof to show he owned the property. He was the only heir according to Uncle Dylan.

He had his father's desk and the head and foot rails from his old brass bed, some wooden chairs that his grandfather, Cradoc, had made. A rocking horse that belonged to his father. A treasure could be found in his own basement. Most of the family had moved on, found their next home, whether on earth or in heaven.

Could it work? Only time would tell.

Ethan and Dylan met with Edith and Mr. Evans the solicitor and claimed the land from Dylan with his signature and approval. Edith and Mr. Evans helped in documenting the land and arranging the stamp duty as the seal of approval.

Epilogue

Just as Lina had foretold, Lina and Angel moved with Gilberto. Not from choice, but with hearts broken as they left the Rhondda Valley, Wales. Lina passed away from cancer shortly after moving into Gilberto's new home, only to leave Gilberto with Angel. Angel was under age to live alone in his house so she was put into foster homes and later an orphanage.

Angel could never forget her best friend David, and could not forget his friendship and caring from her childhood. His olive skin, dark hair that glistened in the sunlight as he swayed from branch to branch, and dark brown eyes that held so much joy. The boy that stole her heart with his smile and kindness and with a voice that would one day be an inspiration to others.

She was too young to know how their lives would be dealt. In those days, the children lived day to day, and were grateful for the small mercies of friendship that life offered them; sugar sandwiches or a chip buttie was a treat for them.

Ethan cut down trees for the walls of the house and the thin timbers were used for the roof. He cleared the area of debris and made barns to house their goats, cows, and horses. Beside him, Ian worked hard. He took time to make a chicken coop for his mam.

Ian helped with the drawings of the property, carried wood that Ethan cut, and hauled household goods from their old home in Porth. Ian continued his drawings and signed a contract with the Welsh offices of National Geographic Magazine for his contributions of drawings for stories on the

Welsh hills and wild horses. He soon learned the farming business and handled the ledgers for his father as Dylan had done many years before for Cradoc.

On weekends, Ethan still went to help his Uncle Dylan with his chippie and then everyone would come up the mountain for Sunday afternoon after Church almost every weekend.

Dylan continued with his chippie but privately mourned the loss of Lina when she left. It was the last time he saw her. Dylan had spent many a night writing notes for Ethan on horse behavior, training, healthy feeding, and breeding until his death. Dylan passed away in his sleep with pen still in hand.

Vicar Llewelyn moved his family on over the border to Cambridge University to be closer to his mam in Birmingham. In later years, when he retired from the University, he and his wife moved to Weare Giffard in Devon.

Ethan's family was now settling up the mountain and worked hard on rebuilding the ancestral home with eagerness and enthusiasm. It was the only way Ethan could recover from his depression and have new beginnings with his family.

David, their youngest son, loved to sing and he practiced his talent by singing to the horses. His singing seemed to settle the horses that his father had captured and housed in the barn. Some were not trained then but they seemed to be comforted by his laments. They swayed in delight and soon they were asleep with one back hoof hipshot and the other three hooves flat on the ground, balancing their bodies. The winds carried his songs in the air across the valleys as they had carried it when he played and sang to Angel from his favorite tree.

When it was time to graduate from his high school he received the offer to attend Cardiff University to study music on a scholarship.

Not much of a school worker, David decided that was not for him, but applied for the position of junior tenor in the Rhondda Male Voice Choir, closer to his new home. He was accepted and as the youngest tenor singer he was urged to participate in the National Eisteddfod Contest. That year, the National Eisteddfod Contest was to be held in Cardiff, only about 15 miles away.

Cardiff was the capital city of Wales and was popular with the Royal Family. The Prince of Wales visited frequently and rumor spread that the Prince of Wales would be the guest of honor at the contest. If David was accepted to sing in the contest, he would have the opportunity of meeting His Royal Highness.

David's handsome face and talent brought many attractive young ladies into his life. He was definitely a charmer. During the weekends his performance as a singer of love songs and dancer at the local hall brought in many patrons.

David also helped his father with the farm. Ethan taught him how to lasso the wild breeds that came into view and harness the ropes to guide them to their field. It seemed that not only did he help Ethan with adding to his herd, he also assisted him with taming them. His soft dulcet tones, not the words, did most of the work. He was soon recognized in the valley as the horse singer.

It's true, just like Cradoc often said, "When you slip down that mountain and look back up you never realize until then, where you have been and how blessed you were. Because a heart that loved once, will love again, for the green hills of Wales."

Mountain Welsh pony

Local Life

1951 Merthyr-Tydfil Festival Street Party

Porth Square

Islwyn Terrace,Porth, Coronation Day 1953

Street Party

Porth Station

Taffs Fish & Chips, Porth

Corona Welsh Hills Works

Ynyshir United Football, 1950's

Porth Infants School

Porth Infants School, 150th birthday

Porth, Mary Street Junior School Photo

St Paul's Church, Porth

Local Choirs

1954 Treorchy Male & Glasgow Police Choirs

1956 Parc Colliery Men's Choir

1956 Winners Eisteddfod Aberdare

1959 National Eisteddfod Members

1959 Treorchy Male Voice Choir

Miners

John Davies, 12yrs

David Davies (Miner) & family

Glamorganshire, Rhondda, Young Miners

Miners going home

Miners cleaned up for picture

Rhondda Firemen

Pit Miners

Emrys Jones - Rhondda Miner & National Operatic Tenor

Collieries (Coal Mines) & stations

Cymmer Colliery, Porth south view

Cymmer Colliery, Porth

Lewis-Merthy Colliery, Porth

Lewis-Merthyr Colliery, Porth

Lllwynpia Collieries

Llwynpia Colliery

Mairdy Colliery, Tom Pentre

Tylorstown Colliery Pits

Tylorstown Colliery and Railway

Local Steam Engine with passenger cars

Pit Ponies

Pit Ponies

Coal Miners and Pit Pony

Pit Pony and Miner

Pit Pony and Miners

Pit Pony going down

Pit Pony

Swansea Porcelain Ram, 1817-1818

Dylan's Till

Welsh Recipes

Welsh Cakes Recipe

Bara Brith Recipe

Other Information on Wales

Welsh Red Dragon on Welsh Flag

Y Ddraig Goch

The Red Dragon

The origin of the Welsh Dragon is uncertain but its earliest mention dates to around 800 AD when it was linked with Wales in the writings of Nennius. In Welsh mediaeval poetry the dragon became the symbol of Wales.

It was used as a crest by the early Welsh Kings, Arthur, Cadwallon and Cadwaladr, and at The Battle of Bosworth Henry Tudor unfurled his standard bearing a red dragon on a green and white background.

In 1901 The Red Dragon was recognised as the Badge of Wales and was added to the Arms of The Prince of Wales.

In 1953 the Dragon was made the official Royal Badge of Wales and after this it became the authorised Welsh National flag.

Welsh Red Dragon & origin

Merlin - Legend of Wales

Welsh Lovespoons & meanings

Welsh Emblems/Symbols

To be born Welsh

Hen Wlad Fy Nhadau
The Land of My Fathers
Mae hen wlad fy nha-dau yn an-nwyl i - mi, Gwlad
beirdd a chan-tor-ion, en-wog-ion o fri; Ei gw-rol ry-
-fel-wyr, gwlad-gar-wyr tra-mad, Tros rydd-id - coll-as-ant eu
gwaed. Gwlad, gwlad, pleid-iol wyf-i'm gwlad, Tra môr yn-
fur i'r bur hoff - bau, O bydd-ed i'r hen - iaith bar - hau.

Welsh Patron Saint - Saint David

Welsh costume

Coracle boats & lady with Welsh hat

KEEP
CALM
AND
CYMRU
AM BYTH